Voices of Summer

Also by Diane Pearson

BRIDE OF TANCRED
CSARDAS
THE MARIGOLD FIELD
SARAH WHITMAN
THE SUMMER OF THE BARSHINSKEYS

Voices of Summer

A NOVEL

DIANE PEARSON

Crown Publishers, Inc.   New York

Published by Crown Publishers, Inc., 201 East 50th Street New York, New York 10022. Member of the Crown Publishing Group. Originally published in Great Britain by Bantam Press in 1992.

Crown is a trademark of Crown Publishers, Inc.

Manufactured in the United States of America

Library of Congress Cataloging-in-Publication Data

Pearson, Diane.
    Voices of summer / Diane Pearson.
       p.   cm.
    I. Title.
    PR6066.E18V6   1993
    823′.914 — dc20   92-17427
                                            CIP

ISBN 0-517-59192-8

10 9 8 7 6 5 4 3 2 1

First American Edition

To
Freddie Bartman
A very dear friend

AUTHOR'S NOTE

Voices of Summer was originally written as a serial – under the title *Operetta* – for a magazine, but the disciplines of a serial are confining: everything has to be as brief as possible and one cannot introduce too many characters. I always regretted the loss and development of those extra characters that I'd had in my mind and couldn't include.

The idea for *Voices of Summer* sprang from my very first visit to Vienna. I was only passing through on my way to research a book in Hungary, but the city so bewitched me that I stayed an extra day and have returned many times since. It is difficult to explain the importance of opera, operetta, and music in the life of the average Viennese citizen. Opera singers occupy the same national status as football stars in the West, and Viennese taxi drivers will discuss the politics of the State Opera House in the same way that we chat of politicians, the Royals, and the latest television stars. The Opera House is undoubtedly the centre of Viennese life and is – emotionally – a sort of combination of the National Theatre, Buckingham Palace, Wembley Stadium, and the Houses of Parliament.

So against that background I set my story, although mine is not a tale of glory at the *Staatsoper*, for while in Austria I saw a very tiny company performing a Lehar operetta and the tenor, a tall, handsome man who was obviously immensely popular with the audience, made a great impression on me. When the curtain came down an abundance of flowers and gift-wrapped packages went up on stage – for him, not the leading lady who stood in the line-up behind with a brave smile on her face, trying to look as though she didn't mind. And at that moment *Operetta* was born.

7

I should add that, although the idea for my novel came from watching a real performance, every single character and situation in this book is totally imaginary. All the names have been invented by me, other than those of real people such as Callas or Domingo. If, inadvertently, I have stumbled on a real name, it is entirely accidental.

I'd like to thank everyone who helped me with this book, especially Freddie Bartman, who once lived in Vienna, and if I've made any Austrian, theatrical, or musical mistakes, then apologies to Freddie and to my theatrical family and the profession generally. The one thing I have learned after being married to an actor for many years is that, in the theatre, anything can happen.

Diane Pearson
June 1991

CHAPTER ONE

Three months before the opening of the new Hochhauser Season, Direktor Franz Busacher – sad, craggy old giant who had once dominated the stages of the world's leading opera houses – realized that amongst the many pressing problems facing him, the most terrifying, the most urgent, was that of finding a soprano who would be prepared to suffer the humiliations and indignities of singing opposite Karl Gesner, the nastiest and most unpleasant tenor in the business. It was a measure of Gesner's growing awful reputation, reflected Busacher wearily, that in a profession as full of unemployment as the theatre, he could not find one reasonably competent, reasonably young, reasonably attractive soprano to accept an engagement of five months' work in one of Austria's most pleasant mountain holiday resorts.

He had pursued all the normal avenues of trying to find a singer who, although not exactly of top quality – Hochhauser didn't pay enough to attract performers in that league – would be good enough to provide a foil for Gesner. He had contacted all the agents, written and telephoned himself to singers he knew, or knew of, who might be prepared to come, and finally, in some desperation, he had tried to persuade last year's soprano, Hanna Brunner, to return for just one more season. In a prolonged and very expensive telephone call to Vienna, he had cajoled, pleaded, and finally begged Hanna to return. He had promised that he would be stricter with Gesner; that in any case, after last year's dreadful affair with the dancer, Gesner was more subdued, was behaving much better. He promised her solos would not be cut, her curtain calls upstaged, and that he would personally ensure that this time Gesner did not stand in the wings passing audible comments on her performance and appearance. In final desperation, he had even offered her an increase in salary. And the more he pleaded the more vehement Hanna became, until her vehemence eventually disintegrated into hysteria.

'I have told you no, Herr Direktor,' she screamed. 'No, and no, and no. I would sooner *clean* the theatre than sing in it with Gesner – sooner clean the theatre with my *bare* hands and a *scrubbing brush!*' Hanna was given to exaggeration and high dramatics. It was extremely unlikely she had ever handled a scrubbing brush in her life.

'And I tell you, Herr Busacher,' – normally she called him Franz – 'I have made no secret, no secret at all of that, that *Schweinehund*'s behaviour. I have told everyone in Vienna, everyone in Salzburg, everyone in Munich, just what kind of person he is. And, Herr Direktor, most of them already *knew*. I tell you – you will find no-one, no-one in the entire operatic world who will even *stand* on the same stage with him. Haa!' Her voice broke on a derisory laugh. 'You will have to perform operettas that do not require a heroine. Gesner would like that!'

'But, Hanna, my dear . . .'

'No. Never, I tell you. Never again!' Busacher held the telephone away from his ear just in time to diminish the noise of the receiver being slammed down. Hanna had all the makings of a full operatic prima donna, he reflected gloomily, but unfortunately everything she said was true. The world of operetta was a small one and Gesner's reputation, never good, had become the main delicious topic of theatre gossip in Viennese cafés over the last couple of years. Stories were repeated, exaggerated, and ultimately invented about his outrageous behaviour to the extent that if all the crimes attributed to him were actually true, he would have had very little time to stand on the stage of Hochhauser's theatre and sing.

But the curious and somewhat distressing phenomenon about Gesner was that the more unpopular he became backstage, the more adored he was by the Hochhauser audiences. His charm, which was undoubtedly there when he needed it, reached out over the footlights in a warm, all-embracing effusion that enchanted the summer visitors. The Hochhauser Company needed Gesner. They had very little else.

The Hochhauser Operetta Company was not a good one. It possessed a certain faded elegance, a sort of nostalgia, a *fin de siècle* sadness which owed its quality to the fact that many of the older performers had, in their time, been first-class singers and actors. But the versatility and range of the company was definitely limited and their programme – until recently – had had to be selected very carefully with the capabilities of the performers in mind. They had Gesner, the star, the one people came to see, but for the rest, the best that could be said of them was that they had courage. The lead baritone had, once upon a time, sung solo roles in all the great opera houses of Europe, but Alfred was an old man now. Like me, thought Busacher wryly, old, and terrified of leaving the theatre because, for people like us, people who have lived all our lives in this artificial world of tinsel and song, there is nothing outside except loneliness. Alfred still had considerable style but all his solos had to be adapted, cut, and repitched to fit his diminishing range.

Luiza's voice had remained remarkably good, but Luiza herself had deteriorated at a faster pace than her voice. Considerably overweight – which didn't matter too much as the contralto roles were more often than not the older parts – she had an arthritic hip which prohibited virtually all movement round the stage. It took considerable ingenuity to plot some of the operettas so that Luiza was always sitting down on a rustic log or a gilded ballroom chair (specially reinforced), or propped up against a more solid piece of scenery.

Freddi was good in the comic leads – he had been playing them for over fifty years and was still very spirited and agile; indeed it sometimes amazed Busacher just how well Freddi managed his little dances and shuffles around the stage. His pitch, however, had totally gone. Freddi's comic songs were now spoken against a strongly reinforced orchestral background.

The younger members of the company were really younger than they should be. Most of them came to Hochhauser for their very first professional engagement and many of them had been trained none too well. They had voices they didn't really know how to use and no acting ability or stage technique at all. Ingrid, the soubrette, the most experienced young singer they had, was in her third season with the company and while she was pretty and young, her singing and dancing had a rough, untrained quality about them. The best thing Ingrid had going for her was a great thick mass of naturally red, naturally curly hair and she had enough sense to use it whenever she could, flinging it around in wild gypsy dances and bending practically in half in stage embraces so that it swept the floor. Busacher, who had had years of spotting the young and talented, knew quite well that Ingrid was never going to make it in the theatre. Her voice just wasn't good enough and once her prettiness had faded she would be lucky to find work in the chorus. He would have liked to advise her to seize whichever was the wealthiest of her current boyfriends and settle for marriage and early retirement, but a natural kindness made him hesitate to demoralize her with such advice. And indeed he couldn't really afford to lose her at the present time. Where else would he find a soubrette at that price?

Together, somehow, with careful direction and the melodic scores of Strauss, Lehar, Offenbach, and Kalman (all suitably adapted) they managed to create the time-old illusion of stage magic. Somehow, every season, the miracle happened again and charming romantic nostalgia filled the Hochhauser theatre. But not one of them would have survived without Gesner.

Busacher rose from his desk and walked to the window of his study. It looked out over the valley and across to the snow-covered slopes of the mountains. It was a high blue day and the sun sparkled on the tops. Down in the valley patches of green showed where the snow was melting. Hochhauser was rather pleasant in the winter, quiet and dignified, and the few tourists who came were quiet and dignified too. The mountains in this part of Austria weren't dramatic enough for a winter resort, so the *jeunesse dorée* never came to ski. It was summer when Hochhauser came into its own.

'Problems . . . problems . . .' he muttered to himself. 'Why do I concern myself with such stupidities when I could pass the year happily, peacefully, with my music, my friends, my garden?'

He had enough money to live, if not extravagantly, then at least with some degree of elegance. He had his charming villa on the slopes of the mountain. He was not that far from Vienna – little trips to the theatre, concerts, were still feasible. Why did he bother with all the complexities of Gesner and the Hochhauser Operetta Season?

Because, old man, he said to himself, you are just like Alfred, and Luiza, and Freddi. You cannot bear to leave the theatre because you have nothing else. You have given up everything for music. You have no wife, no family – not as other people think of families. You have nothing but the theatre and you cannot bear to say, now it is finished, now I am done, now I will sit down with my memories and live in the past. Without the theatre you are nothing and no-one.

The theatre was his life. He knew no other and in some ways, although he had had a great and glorious career, this shabby, pathetic little company had come to mean more to him than any of his brilliant international productions. Partly it was because the Hochhauser Company was his own creation. It was also – if he was honest – because he had total control over everything, from choice of performers and repertoire, to how much they charged for the tickets. The only challenge to his absolute dictatorship was Gesner, mean, arrogant, and with a star-shaped temperament that defied control. And where, oh where, would he find a soprano prepared to put up with Gesner for a whole season?

He walked slowly back to his desk, sat down, took a deep breath and dialled a Viennese number.

'Hans!' he said, smiling joyously into the telephone just in case Hans could tell from his voice that he was worried. 'Hans, old friend, how are you?'

'Moderate, my dear fellow. Moderate. And you? We hear interesting things about the Hochhauser Season – apparently you are beginning to make money? The *Staatsoper* must look to its laurels, eh?' Hans finished on a whinnying bray of laughter that Franz Busacher found particularly irritating but decided to ignore. Hans had always had a slightly waspish tendency, but it was wise not to sting back. He was, after all, the most successful agent in Vienna.

'Hans . . .' He lowered his voice confidingly. 'Hans, we are having a slight problem with our new season and I am wondering if you would be able to help me.'

'Of course.' Hans's voice sharpened at once. The Direktor envisaged him drawing percentage signs on his blotter.

'I am having a little difficulty in trying to replace Hanna,' he said. 'She has decided to take a little rest from Hochhauser this summer.'

'So I have heard,' said Hans dryly.

'Which means we are temporarily without a lead singer.'

'Dancer too?' queried Hans with a note of glee in his voice. Franz ignored him.

'A pleasant place to work for the summer months, Hans. Away from the heat and dust of Vienna. Four roles to sing, no more, and the sunshine, the mountains, clean air . . .'

'And Karl Gesner,' interjected Hans quickly. Franz forced himself to laugh.

'Oh come, Hans. Gesner is not so bad. His reputation has been greatly exaggerated. He is . . . highly strung, what singer worth his fee is not highly strung? A little thoughtless perhaps at times, but really . . .'

13

'I'm sorry, Franz,' the agent interjected bluntly. 'The truth is that no-one wants to work with him and we both know it. It wasn't just the affair of the dancer – although don't I remember another dancer four years ago who also tried to commit suicide? – but no, that's not the real reason and we both know it. No soprano can sing opposite a man who constantly ridicules and demoralizes her. We know about singers, my friend. As you say, they are highly strung creatures and are usually only as good as their self-confidence. I can get you no singer of merit. I have no-one at all on my books of any experience who would be prepared to risk her reputation and her confidence on working with Gesner. Most of them would sooner be unemployed than sing with him.'

'Hans, I am desperate,' said the Direktor, dropping all pretence. 'I have three months to the opening of my season. I have a new production of *Luxembourg* and I must have a singer. Surely there is *someone*. I'm prepared,' he gulped a little, 'to raise the salary slightly. I must have *someone*.'

There was a pause from the other end, then came a sound which the Direktor finally recognized as the flicking over of cards in an index file.

'Ophelia Jones – an English singer. She wouldn't know too much about Gesner.'

'Does she sing in German?'

'She could learn, I suppose. She can probably sing but not speak it. She is on my books only because she came out once to sing some early English songs at a folk festival. I don't remember very much about her, I don't even know if she is free.'

'Is there no-one else?'

There was another pause, and then Hans said in a rather strange voice, 'There is someone . . . but I don't know what you would feel about her. I think she would come, in spite of Gesner. God knows if it would work, but I think she would come, even be glad to come, if you would have her.'

'I'm desperate, Hans.'

'Therese Aschmann.'

There was a moment when his mind didn't even register the name. Then his first reaction was to say no, of course not, because it was a name they had all rejected many years ago, many times. His second reaction was one of total astonishment.

'Aschmann? I'm surprised that she's still . . . I mean no-one has heard or seen anything of her for years. I don't even know where she lives any more.'

'Here. In Vienna.'

14

'And she can still sing?'

'She is only forty-four, Franz. You are speaking of her as though she were ancient. You know very well that a great many sopranos are only coming to their peak at that age.'

'Yes . . . but Aschmann . . . her voice went, her confidence went after that . . . that affair. She tried, we tried, several times to get her singing again and it always proved disastrous. I mean, Hans, have you heard if she can sing now?'

'She was on the radio the other day. She has been trying gradually to get back her old technique, her old gift. Mostly, since she left, she has been teaching, but about three years ago she began to do some religious singing, small engagements on radio, some supporting and dubbing in recording studios.'

'And the husband?'

'She finally divorced him. He has been in a clinic for nine years now.'

'She left it too late.'

'It was something that she did it at last. It took me years to persuade her to do it at all and she still sends money and has named herself his next of kin. But she *is* divorced from him. I finally made the doctors explain to her that he would never be cured – he'd gone too far for that – and that if she wanted to try and regain her voice she must cut herself free. I prevailed upon her never to go and see him again. Once she stopped seeing him she began to regain her composure.'

Beneath the Direktor's bemusement at the news that Therese Aschmann was not only alive, but trying to sing again, was another faint surprise. Hans was waspish, venal, a tough and occasionally unscrupulous businessman. Yet, from what he was saying, it appeared he had been in touch with Therese all these years, befriending her when she had run away from everyone else, urging her to make a clean start, encouraging her, and – the greatest surprise of all – keeping her on his agency books. Franz felt thoroughly disconcerted.

'You are very silent, Franz my friend. Have you nothing to say?'

'How much money have you made out of Aschmann over the last – what – it must be eighteen years? What commission has she earned you?'

Hans cleared his throat.

'I feel strangely betrayed, Hans. I thought I could always rely on you to be totally ruthless where business was concerned. I feel I shall never be able to trust you again. I am used to frogs turning into princes but when a shark or an alligator turns into a public

15

benefactor I feel the world has tilted under my feet. How many other deserving cases have you been secretly helping over the years?'

'I thought you wanted a lead soprano,' snarled the agent.

'I do. I do.'

'Well, do you want Aschmann or don't you?'

Unbidden, to Busacher's mind, came the memory of a golden girl, nineteen years old – too young really to be accepting professional singing roles – coming to him and auditioning at the rehearsal rooms at the *Volksoper*. A slim, laughing girl with a great thick mane of tawny hair. A girl whose voice rippled up and down the register, a girl who sang with such exuberance, such abounding life and vitality, that even when she stepped on to the stage in a minor role every eye in the audience turned to her. He remembered the excitement he had felt when he first heard her, realizing that he had found something special, perhaps a new Schwarzkopf or even a Callas, although her voice was different again from those great instruments. Every voice was different – there were the big voices, those that sent out a huge volume of sound that filled an opera house, whatever its size. And there were the heavy golden voices, the rich ones that thundered their way through Wagner. Aschmann had sung . . . effortlessly was the word that came to mind. She rippled up and down, seemingly without any strain, hitting the high registers with the same apparent ease as the low. It was a rich voice, but fluting and agile, a happy voice, he had once heard a critic describe it. Once, only once in a lifetime could an impresario hope to discover such a voice, and when the gift came with a young, radiant exterior and a superabundance of energy it seemed as though the gods had been too generous, too kind. As indeed they had, he thought sadly, remembering how it had all ended.

He had coached her carefully, anxious not to strain the voice before it was ready, but it was difficult to keep Therese Aschmann in check. She was careless with her voice, often singing just for fun, or joining in with the chorus, or singing at parties and in restaurants merely because she wanted to. Her teacher had confided to Busacher that he thought it would be all right. She had a natural voice that was there almost without training or breath control, or any of the things that were usually so necessary to groom the intrustment into a great and lasting sound. 'It happens every so often,' he had said to Busacher. 'She's been given a golden voice and it will probably stay with her for most of her life, no matter what she does with it. But we won't tell her that, eh? It's best not to take chances.'

16

But as well as all that Therese had had something else – a kind of radiance that bubbled out of her, a warmth, a love of life, a gracefulness of spirit that enhanced everything she did, everyone she came into contact with. They had all been in love with her. He had been well into his forties when he met her but he had fallen in love just as everyone else had, a harmless, joyful sort of love that made no demands. It had looked as though she was going to be the new discovery of her generation, the new diva, starting exception- ally young, singing leading roles whilst still in her early twenties. He had directed her himself in *Die Fledermaus*, then in *Bohème* and *Manon Lescaut*. She had been the most adorable, heartbreak- ing Manon he had ever seen. She had come back to him for an operetta season, already a little tense from the strain that she was under but still basically the same radiant glorious girl. And it was there, in that final season, that the glittering career, hardly begun, had ended. They had attempted, several of them, to help her, had encouraged her to try again, given her small roles, but it had been no good and after several embarrassing fiascos she had drifted away from them all. No. Not quite all. Hans had remained faithful, had obviously kept in touch with her all these years.

'Why did you do it, Hans? We all tried, but she didn't want us to help her any more. She told us to leave her alone, said she wanted to go away and never see any of us again. Why did you hold on to her when no-one else did?'

'The voice,' Hans said tersely. 'I believed in the voice. I believed it would come back.'

'What does she look like now? Would I recognize her?'

'Probably not. No-one goes through that kind of experience and remains the same.'

'You think I should see her, then?'

'It's up to you. You want a soprano. I have no-one else.' He sounded cross. Busacher couldn't define if it was because he had been caught out in an uncharacteristic good deed, or if it was because he cared too much that Therese might not get the job. Hans had been in love with her too, all those years ago.

'All right. I'll come up to Vienna. Can you arrange an audition room? Next Friday?'

'You can use the rooms here. I'll telephone her now and make the appointment at, say, two o'clock.'

'And, Hans, don't raise her hopes. No need to tell her I want her for a season. Just say I'm looking ahead and vaguely trying out some possible voices. I don't want her to be hurt again.'

'Neither do I. Goodbye.'

The Direktor replaced the receiver and stared out of the window again. A hawk hung high over the valley, swooping and gliding in the mountain wind. Suddenly Franz Busacher felt more cheerful. Perhaps he still hadn't got a lead soprano, or a replacement dancer, perhaps he still had a tiny budget, and the nastiest tenor in the business, but as he remembered Therese Aschmann, the golden girl, his spirits began to rise.

CHAPTER TWO

Therese dressed with great care for her audition. She cancelled her Friday pupil, which wasn't really necessary, nor could she afford it, but she felt she would need the whole morning, not just to dress but to think herself into the right frame of mind. She went to the hairdresser, something she hadn't done for years, and when she came back and stared at the rigid arrangement of 'casual' curls she wished she hadn't wasted the money. She was too nervous to eat any lunch but forced herself to heat some soup, professional enough to know she would sing better if she had eaten.

Her suit was old and the skirt was shiny across the seat but she had spent the previous evening steaming and pressing it, so that now most of the shine was removed. It would come back very quickly once she sat down but that didn't matter, just so long as it looked all right for her initial appearance. First impressions were so important. The suit was dark blue and well cut, even though it was old, and it made her look much slimmer than she really was. It was what fashion described as a 'classic' that would never date. For that, she thought to herself ironically, read boring, dull, and so tasteful as to be instantly forgettable. When she was young she'd had a natural inclination towards bright colours and outrageous styles. She still liked brilliant and unusual clothes, but now she lacked the confidence to wear them. The boring blue nebulous suit, she felt, made her blend into the background, provided her with bland anonymity. It was also suitable for her oratorio and church music.

Her shoes were well polished. She wore a new blouse with a silk tie bow at the neck. She had read somewhere that silk bows under the chin were flattering to older women. They softened the face and hid neck lines and a sagging chin. She applied her make-up with care, not too much, but enough to hide some of the ravages of time and give a little colour and glow to a pale face. When she had finished she gazed at herself in the mirror. It was – how long? – since Franz Busacher had last seen her. What would he think? Had the intervening years made a big difference?

She stared and the woman in the mirror stared back, a woman with a heavy body and faded short hair, no longer golden and tawny, but a pale mousy mixture of brown and grey. There were heavy lines around her eyes and forehead – a legacy from the terrible years with Friedrich – and her mouth had a pinched look, even under the carefully applied lipstick. The pinched look came from worrying about money and about the future, and economizing on good food. It was the cheap, filling food that had ruined her figure. A wave of fear swept over her and she felt her legs begin to shake. How on earth could she go and meet Busacher again, looking like this? She was mad even to try, mad to have listened to Hans, who had coaxed her back into singing and told her she was now ready to try another step forward, returning to a world she had left in disgrace. She suddenly realized how undignified she was, tarting herself up like a matron at a wedding in order to hawk her voice round the audition rooms again. She didn't need to do that! She could and did earn herself a living without stooping to this. She had provided herself with a home, rebuilt her self-respect, and was mad to risk it all on an unnecessary test of endurance.

She sat down on a chair to still her shaking knees and a small voice in her head said, a home? You call this a home? A one-room apartment over a stationer's shop off the Wiedner Gürtel? Other women of your age have proper homes, with husbands and children and gardens. And if they don't have those things then they have successful careers and cars and apartments with a telephone. They don't have to run downstairs to the stationer's shop to take a call every time there's another chance of a job.

'Don't be a craven coward, Therese Aschmann,' she said aloud. This is the best chance you've had in the last three years. If you get the job it will be, just as Hans has said, the next step back into a normal life. If you don't get the job you're still better off than you were nine years ago, even five years ago. You're singing again, you're earning money, even saving a little. You have friends again – that nice woman in the cathedral – you're having lunch with her on Sunday, remember. She knows nothing of the past. She likes you. She's a friend. She'll be thrilled if you go to her and say you auditioned for the great Franz Busacher. Even if you don't get the job it will be tremendous fun to talk about the audition with Elisabet.

She decided it would be better to leave at once and walk to Hans's office. It would stop her getting nervous and it would save the seat of her suit getting creased and shiny from sitting in the tram. It was cold when she stepped outside – she should really have worn her coat but it was far too shabby – so she marched briskly along, which served the double purpose of preventing her legs from shaking, and generating a faint feeling of warmth.

Hans's office was just off the Ring. She crossed over Schwarzenberg Platz and looked across at the palace. She had sung there once, years ago, at a gala charity ball. She could even remember what she had worn, a jade green silk dress with a huge skirt and long sleeves. She tried to remember what had happened to it. Had she sold it or was it one of the dresses that Friedrich had destroyed? With a faint inward shudder she pushed that thought away and concentrated on the happier memory. She had worn her hair high on her head and had borrowed a fake emerald necklace from the wardrobe department. She had sung the Waltz Song from *La Traviata*. She began to hum it to herself as she walked up towards the *Staatsoper*. It always cheered her to walk past the Opera House – she felt she was back in the living world that she knew, the only world in which she was really happy. She began to sing the words of the song softly under her breath and an old man with a stick looked at her and smiled. She raised her hand slightly and gave him a little wave, thinking that perhaps his smile was a good omen.

She was still early when she arrived, in spite of walking, but Hans came down the stairs and ushered her up into his office, offering her coffee, a seat by the fire.

'Or would you prefer to go upstairs to the studio and run through your music?'

'No. I shall grow nervous if I do that.' She laughed a little tremulously. 'I will sit here quietly, that is if your secretary does not mind. Dear Hans, please continue with your work. I'm sure you have much to do.'

He gave her a sharp look, then touched her gently on the shoulder and went back into his own office. The outer room had a pleasant green fitted carpet and orange and tan walls. She looked at the walls, the posters of concerts and operas and operettas. She felt a sudden wave of joyful nostalgia at the reminders of a world in which she had once been so happy. But I must not be ungrateful, she thought to herself. So much of my life has been happy. The first twenty-five years were marvellously happy. I should be so grateful for that, and I am. I must never, never forget how lucky I was. How secure my childhood was compared with others of that time.

Most of her own generation, born in the latter years of the war, had had a miserable childhood, hungry, bombed, existing in a doomed city and then, even worse, living in a country riven by guilt, occupied by the four great Allied armies and held up to international shame. She had only one bad memory and it must have been when she was very young indeed, no more than two or three. She remembered a dark cold room, a mattress on a stone floor, and Mutti crying softly in a corner. She remembered it because it was the only time in her life she could recall Mutti wearing drab clothes. The next memory was of dear Uncle Dimitri, lifting her high in the air and, in his execrable German, calling her his little rabbit, his little sparrow, his little crumb.

Of all her 'uncles', Uncle Dimitri had been the most colourful, the jolliest, the most fun. Mutti had told her, much later, that it had been Uncle Dimitri who had moved them to the apartment inside the Ring. Most of the inner city had been flattened by the Allied bombings, but some buildings remained and it was in one of these that Frau Aschmann and her little daughter had taken up sybaritic residence. Uncle Dimitri had been a colonel in the Red Army and had the conqueror's right to requisition anything he wanted.

It was a lovely apartment, and over the years it grew lovelier. Even after Uncle Dimitri had gone (recalled to Moscow because of his liaison with a capitalist whore) Mutti and she had remained there. They were only a few minutes from the river and very close to Rudolfsplatz. Mutti used to take her to play in the gardens every day.

She had been six when Uncle Dimitri left, tears rolling down his flat cheeks, embracing them both, vowing to return if ever he was able. She had wept too. Uncle Dimitri was like her father. She knew no other man and he had adored her as much as he adored her mother.

Mutti had been very worried after Uncle Dimitri's departure. She had talked to Theresa very honestly about their circumstances.

'You see, my darling, your foolish Mutti is not really very good at earning a living. I was married so young – I never really learned to *do* anything. So, my precious bonbon, I do not know if we can

22

afford to keep this nice apartment. Uncle Dimitri,' her eyes had filled with tears at the mention of his name, 'Uncle Dimitri arranged what he could. We can remain here for three more months, but even so your poor Mutti must try and find a job — otherwise we shall starve, my lambkin.'

Theresa knew about being poor. Vienna was full of poor people, sick children, wandering refugees. Sometimes she had wondered why she and Mutti never had to stand in the food queues like everyone else, or why they both had such pretty clothes.

Years later, when a member of a company she was working in referred to her growing up in 'Harry Lime's Vienna', she had vehemently denied it. She did not remember that time as a period of dark wet streets, of subterfuges and weird people. She did not even remember the Kursaal as Mutti would never allow her to go there. But then she realized that she was indeed a true child of Harry Lime's Vienna. Her poor little mother would never have survived without a man to look after her, and there were very few respectable Austrian men available. There were a quarter of a million widows in Austria after the war, and nearly as many again whose husbands were somewhere in Russia. Theresa had survived because her mother had indulged in a kind of mild and genteel prostitution and because everything they ate or wore was obtained on the black market. Neither she nor Mutti would have pulled through on their own.

Poor little Mutti, with her bright golden hair and huge blue eyes, had gone off to work behind the counter of a confectioner's shop, and fate had smiled yet again. Major Hugh Lennox (a British officer this time) had gone into the shop and Mutti had looked at him from beneath her long lashes, and three weeks later had come home with all her worries removed.

'Resi, my *kindchen*, I think it is all going to be all right! I think soon you will have another uncle. Such a kind man. Older than our dear Dimitri and not so . . . well, not so dashing or such fun as darling Dimitri, but he will do, my precious, he will do!'

Uncle Hugh had done very nicely. He was forty and attached to General Staff HQ in the British Sector of the city. He was quiet and rather thin with a small toothbrush moustache, but he did have the most wonderful smile. And he was, as Mutti had said, so very kind. It was to Uncle Hugh that Theresa owed her early education. He had been appalled when, after a few weeks of long visits to the apartment, he had discovered that Theresa was going to the city school with all the other children of her district.

'No, no, my dear Lisa,' he had said sternly to Mutti. 'We cannot have that! Don't you realize how much disease, how many epi-demics run regularly through the city? You don't see the statistics. I do. She could easily catch TB or dysentery at that school and she's a delicate child. No, we must make other arrangements.'

And so Theresa had gone to a select little school run by the nuns, first as a day girl, then later as a weekly boarder. Her classmates were the children of public officials, hoteliers, and anyone who had enough money to educate their daughters privately. There were quite a few, like herself, who variously referred to Uncle Pierre, Uncle Dwight, or Uncle Edward, according to which sector of the city they lived in (the Russians had become somewhat more circumspect under the stern eye of Moscow and did not enter so lightly into regular liaisons). The nuns, who were having as hard a time as everyone else in the city, didn't enquire too closely into the backgrounds of their pupils but set about giving them the best education they could. It was the nuns who, realizing that Theresa could play the piano by ear alone, taught her to read music and play properly and well. And when she was nine and they discovered her near-perfect child's voice, they began to give her careful coaching in that too. She sang in the convent choir both at services and in performances of sacred music. Uncle Hugh was terribly proud of her in his reserved and distant way.

'Not bad, Resi!' he said gruffly, after a particularly heartrending performance of children's songs in the school chapel. 'Your mother is very pleased, and so am I. So am I!'

They had both become very fond of Uncle Hugh although they never quite got used to his British sense of humour, and it was difficult sometimes to know when he was laughing at them. And it was typical of Uncle Hugh that, after giving them a wonderful holiday in the Swiss mountains, getting them exit papers and everything, he then broke the news that he had been recalled to England.

'Afraid I've had my last waltz in Vienna,' he said glumly. 'It's back to an Aldershot posting and life with Matilda.'

That was the first time he had ever mentioned his wife by name. They knew he was married and had a son who was nearly grown up, but he never talked about either his wife or son. He obviously thought it would be ill-mannered to do so.

The parting from Uncle Hugh was even worse than that of Uncle Dimitri, although the long-term effects weren't nearly so bad. Later – after Uncle Hugh had returned to Vienna – Theresa had realized he loved her mother very deeply, more than Uncle Dimitri and more than Uncle Abe who came later. He didn't cry like Uncle Dimitri, he just gripped Theresa hard by the shoulders, looked into her face, said, 'That's my girl,' and hugged her. Then he put his cap on and said to Lisa, 'Goodbye, my dear. I've done what I could for you, as much as I could manage,' and then he'd left. Next day they discovered he had arranged to have a monthly allowance paid to them. Mutti had sat down and cried, then with true Viennese practicality had dried her eyes and assessed their situation.

'Well, my darling, it won't be enough of course, not if we want you to stay at the convent – and Hugh *did* want you to do that – but it will be enough to give us time to decide what to do next. I shan't go and work in the confectioner's again. I shall just see what happens.'

There had been a few short-term uncles after that, all of them very nice and all of whom had been enchanted by Lisa's pretty little girl with the enchanting voice. Uncle Gaston had nearly become permanent, but then Mutti decided that after the *kindness*, the courtesy and consideration of Uncle Hugh, she didn't think she could live with a Frenchman, and finally Uncle Abe had moved in.

Abe loved Vienna, parties, Lisa and Theresa, but above all he loved music.

'The luckiest thing that ever happened to me, being posted to Vienna,' he would say gleefully. 'No other city like it in the world for real music.'

He was a curious mixture of boisterous American naïvety and skilled, almost intuitive expertise on anything musical. He couldn't sing, or play an instrument, but he knew nearly everything there was to know about opera, operetta, and the world of music. What would have happened to Theresa if he hadn't come along she often wondered. Perhaps she would have been happier. She would have remained Theresa – Resi – instead of becoming Therese Aschmann. She would never have become a professional singer – probably she would have taught music and languages at a school and married someone safe and orderly and nice. She would never have met and married Friedrich.

But Uncle Abe had recognized at once that Theresa's 'instrument' – though young and unformed – was going to be something special. He had gone along to the nuns who, serenely tactful, had ignored the fact that the man looking after Theresa's education seemed to have changed, and talked to them about a programme of voice development and special teachers. Abe was very rich – or so it seemed to Lisa and Theresa – and he set up a fund which couldn't be touched for anything except Theresa's musical training.

Abe was with them for three years, and when he went, so did everyone else, for it was 1955 and Vienna was a free city at last. Abe managed to stay long enough to enjoy the festivities of that wonderful year, the concerts, the opera, all the special performances, and then he said his cheerful farewell, happily returning home to his wife and children of whom he had always spoken with great affection. His last words were, 'Now, if anything goes wrong with Resi's training, you contact me at once. You hear now? The slightest thing and you let me know. It's important, that, Lisa. It's really important.'

Mutti had promised, and off Uncle Abe had gone, along with all the other uncles of the Occupation. Vienna belonged to the Viennese once more.

'And of course, it is wonderful, Resi my love, of course it is. To have rebuilt our lovely city and be independent again, but . . . oh dear, it is just a little bit *dull* without them. They were all such nice men, weren't they?'

And Theresa had to agree that they were, for not one of them had ever resented her or been embarrassed by her presence, and every one of them, even the short-lived ones, had been generous, and kind, and reassuring.

After Uncle Abe had left, Mutti had gone into a mild depression. She had passed her thirtieth birthday and, she said, she felt tired.

'Men are such darling creatures,' she said wistfully, 'and they have all been so good to me, so very very generous, but, darling child, I just don't feel I have the *energy* to find another uncle that we both like.'

It was then that Theresa had found the courage to ask about her own papa. She hadn't thought about it at all when she was younger. For a long time she had presumed that Uncle Dimitri was her real papa, then later, when she realized he couldn't be, it hadn't seemed important. But Uncle Abe's departure had made them both melancholy and from time to time, she did wonder who her real papa was. Sometimes she dreaded that he might have been a Nazi, in which case it would be better not to know, but now she decided she had to ask, just this one time.

'Your papa?' said Mutti, surprised. 'Why – he was Bernhardt Aschmann. You know that. It is on your birth certificate.'

'Yes, Mutti, but who *was* he?' she persisted. 'Was he Austrian, or German? Was he a soldier or,' she swallowed hard, 'was he a Nazi?'

Mutti stared at her.

'A Nazi? Are you mad? He was just a boy, eighteen years old, like I was. A soldier, of course. Everyone was a soldier, then. We met when he was on leave from the Russian Front, and we got married on his next leave.'

'Did I ever see him?'

Mutti smiled and placed a hand on her shoulder. 'No, my darling. You never saw each other. We married, he went back to Russia, and I never saw him again. I don't know quite when he was killed. They never told you exactly. So many died then. I wrote and told him when you were born but whether he got the letter . . .' she shrugged.

'Do you have a photograph of him?'

Mutti, roused from her glum lethargy, went into her bedroom and rummaged for several moments. When she came back she held a broken-cornered photograph in her hand. Theresa looked at it. A young and very thin Mutti in a dark suit and a hat tilted forward over one eye, holding a bunch of flowers and with her other hand tucked through the arm of a boy in an ill-fitting uniform, his face pale, no particular strong characteristics at all. She felt sorry for him, but that was all.

'Did he have any family? Do I have any grandparents? Any uncles and aunts?'

'I'm not sure,' said Mutti vaguely. 'I had an address in the Tyrol and I wrote for a while after we were married. One letter back – very badly written – I think they were farming people. I wrote when you were born but they never answered.' She shrugged again. 'Who knows what happened to them? It was the war. They're probably dead by now.'

'Do you have the address still?'

Mutti looked sad. 'No, my darling. Should I have kept it? I never thought about it then. Twice my room was bombed and many things were gone. I was so miserable and hungry and cold and I had no-one to help me. All I could think about was how we were going to survive, and then,' her face lit up, happy again, 'then Uncle Dimitri came along.'

They were both silent, Theresa thinking of the sad boy soldier whom she would never be able to trace now, and Lisa thinking about Dimitri, which only served to cast her back into gloom.

There was about four months when Mutti didn't do anything but go out and have lunch with a girlfriend, then come back and clean the apartment and listen to the radio. She seemed to have declined into an early, staid middle age, and then one day they heard a key

in the door and there, miraculously, was dear, darling, Uncle
Hugh, dressed in a civilian suit but otherwise looking exactly the
same. There was a moment's stunned silence, then Lisa threw
herself across the room and into his arms.

'It's Hugh! My darling, it's Uncle Hugh – our dear, dear Uncle
Hugh. I don't believe it – come in, come in! Some wine – no, we
don't have any. Theresa, my purse, run to Schmidt's and get wine.
I can't believe it! I . . .' She began to cry and dear Uncle Hugh just
held her in his arms with his eyes tightly closed.

He had been given a diplomatic posting to Vienna. It was told in
fragments throughout the evening. He had been trying to transfer
ever since he'd gone back to England. It had taken him three
years.

'But Hugh – your wife? Will she be coming too? The wives can
come, can't they? The diplomats' wives always come.'

Hugh's face had closed.

'Matilda does not wish to come,' he said. 'And my son is at
university finishing his doctorate. I am alone.'

Those were the best years of all, Mutti was happy, so was Hugh.
They became almost like an old married couple and Theresa, as
she got older, often wondered why Hugh didn't divorce the distant
Matilda and marry Mutti. Hugh was a Catholic of course, but
Catholics *did* sometimes divorce and he had once said that Matilda
wasn't a Catholic. Years later, when Therese was older and coping
with a terrible marriage of her own, she began to understand. It
was to do with commitment. You had made a promise, a vow that
somehow you couldn't bring yourself to break.

She decided she thought about it more than Mutti did. Lisa, that
enchanting daughter of joyous immorality, was just happy that
Uncle Hugh was back and she didn't have to look for a new
protector.

At sixteen Theresa left the nuns and began full-time musical
training. Abe's money had been well invested and every so often a
cheque from America would arrive with a small business card
attached – 'To Top up the Fund' on the back in Abe's handwriting.

When she was nineteen she had her first début concert which
Uncle Abe flew over from America to attend. It was all beautifully
civilized and Uncle Abe and Uncle Hugh both bought her
bouquets, talked to each other about her training and which
auditions she should attend, and then took her and Mutti out to
dinner where Uncle Abe showed them pictures of his family.

That début concert – shared with three other singers – had, she
often thought, been the happiest evening of her life. She had had a

special dressing room which looked like that of a real star, with a tapestry screen and lights all round the mirror. It was just like the theatrical dressing rooms you saw in American films. There were flowers from Mutti, from her professor of music, from her old friends at the convent, and even one from the nuns. The uncles' bouquets had been handed up on stage at the end of her performance.

She and her teacher had spent hours deciding on her début songs and, later, she had come to realize that her professor knew best. Theresa had wanted to sing German Lieder. She insisted that with only a piano to accompany the student singers, Lieder sounded best. Operatic pieces needed an orchestral backing. But Professor Hersch had forced her to sing only opera, Mozart, Verdi, Puccini, and he had been right. Lieder would never have done justice to that pure, lilting, golden voice.

It wasn't only the dressing room that was like an American film, so too was what happened after the concert. She had only just returned to her room, flushed, relieved, suffering the tearful embraces of Mutti and Uncle Abe and the quiet shining approval of Uncle Hugh, when there had been a knock at the door, and there stood a youngish man, slightly plump and with his hair already thinning, holding out his card.

'Hans Kramer,' he said. 'Agent. I should very much like to discuss matters with you and your . . .'

'These are my uncles,' she said, unfazed. 'Major Hugh Lennox from England, and Abe Bloom from America. And this is my mama.'

Hans had just left the biggest musical agency in Vienna and was trying to start on his own. He knew he couldn't hope to entice any of the big names to him, and so he was going to anything and everything where he might pick up some young and unagented talent. Theresa's voice had sent him scurrying backstage, terrified in case another agent got there first.

It was Hans who had changed her name from Theresa to Therese, Hans who had, incredibly, got the solo role of Micaëla for her almost at once in a four-week tour of *Carmen*. Her career had very nearly ended at that point. No-one, least of all the director of the production, or the fading star playing Carmen, could have foreseen what would happen.

Micaëla's tiny role, with just the one lovely song, had always been considered a fairly insipid part. It was necessary to have a clear, pure voice of course, but the dutiful village maiden nearly always came over as drearily unexciting compared with sexy,

29

naughty, trollopy Carmen. No man in the world would have chosen Micaëla over Carmen. Therese, quite unconsciously, changed all that.

She *was* young, she *was* innocent, but her Micaëla had such charm and also such a delightfully latent *promise* of sexuality, that the audience on the first night were totally confused. *Why* did Don Jose prefer the overripe tarty Carmen to the deliciously nubile Micaëla? As one cruel provincial critic put it, it was like choosing an ageing Mata Hari instead of Lolita. The opera made no sense at all, and a furious director, backed by an even more furious Carmen, had removed Therese after the first night, put on her understudy, and pushed Therese back into the chorus. It could have been the end of her had not Franz Busacher's scout been in the audience on her one solo night.

She had had such incredible luck all through those early years. First Hans, then Busacher rolling her career along at almost too fast a pace. And Uncle Hugh and Uncle Abe, standing firmly behind her, two fathers instead of one to protect her from professional predators.

Her upbringing, she supposed, had been scandalous, but it had never seemed so at the time. Whatever gift it was that her mother possessed – the gift of always picking the right man and then of making him so happy he never forgot her – it had resulted in a unique and privileged childhood and a specialized musical education. Mutti was special. All the things Therese had ever heard about women who lived off men, never seemed to apply to Mutti. She had never been ill-used or cast-off because they had tired of her, and they never forgot her. There had even been the curious occasion when a package had arrived from the Russian Embassy, a heavy package that contained a sable hat and muff wrapped round a kilo jar of Beluga caviar, and a set of wooden painted dolls. With them was a picture postcard of the Kremlin and, written on the back, 'All my love, to Lisa and little Resi'. Theresa had been sixteen at the time – dear Uncle Dimitri had always been forgetful – but they had both been deeply relieved to know that he had survived his disgraced recall to Moscow, and deeply moved by his faithfulness. Even Uncle Gaston sent postcards of Paris and, once, a small bottle of Chanel No. 5.

After the Carmen débâcle her career had never stopped. She auditioned for the great Franz Busacher and had immediately been taken into one of his productions. He had been wonderful to her, supportive, and seeing her through the difficult world of stage music. She had never really had the setbacks and struggles that other singers and actresses had. There had been sadness, yes. Darling Uncle Hugh had had a massive heart attack and died in the early sixties. She had been working in Vienna and had been able to 'see Mutti through'. And dear Hugh, faithful to the end, had made financial provision not only for the absent Matilda, but also for his shallow Viennese butterfly. But nothing cruel or savage or deliberately destructive had come into her life until she met Friedrich. Until that time she had known nothing but love and generosity. Perhaps that was why she had been unable to cope with the reality of Friedrich. She had been so spoilt until then, pampered and indulged by all the dear and varied uncles.

She was smiling faintly to herself as she remembered them, and she realized suddenly that Hans's secretary, a kindly, middle-aged woman, was smiling back at her.

'Are you sure you wouldn't like some coffee?'

'Thank you. No.'

'It shouldn't be long before the Direktor arrives. It is always the worst part of an audition, isn't it, having to wait?'

'Yes, I suppose it is.' And suddenly she was terrified again. She stopped pretending it didn't matter. It mattered terribly and not just because she wanted a home or an apartment with a telephone. Those things were not really important, except as tangible proof that she had pulled herself back into the world. That was what she wanted, to believe in herself again, to know that she still had worth and could do something really well. She wanted to have some reason to get out of bed in the morning – some days she felt so hopeless it hardly seemed worthwhile. She tried never to surrender to such self-pity, but some days it was harder than others. She wanted to sing again, to sing on a stage and become, once more, part of the easy camaraderie of the theatre world, the friends who thought and worked as she did, the jokes, the generosity of theatre people. And there was another, deeper reason it was so important to get this job. If she could sing with the Hochhauser Company, however far ahead the engagement was, then people would once more begin to think of her as just a singer, not as poor Therese Aschmann, whose husband had created that terrible scandal and finally drank his brains away. She wanted this job. She wanted it badly. She hunched into her chair, shrivelling with fear, feeling cold in spite of the electric fire. She heard slow footsteps coming up the stairs from the street. It was Busacher.

He opened the door and stepped in, immediately dwarfing everything in the room. His hair was quite white now but still stood out in a great shock round his large craggy face. He was thinner, too, which made his huge square shoulders even more prominent under his cloak. As he stepped into the room the door of Hans's office opened and Busacher strode towards him.

Franz Busacher had not seen Hans for about eighteen months but he looked just the same, stocky, sharp-faced with penetrating eyes.

'Hans – so – you're fatter. Too many lunches and dinners at your clients' expense.'

'Thank you, Franz.'

'Now. Where is she? Shall we go straight up and wait for her in the studio?' He observed a shuttered look drop over the agent's face, saw Hans's eyes turn to the corner of the room where one of his middle-aged secretaries was sitting by the electric fire. The other secretary stopped typing and there was a strange atmosphere in the office.

'Is something wrong?' he asked. 'Is she not coming? Have I travelled all this way and she's not coming?'

He saw the middle-aged secretary by the fire get up and walk towards him. Her eyes were very bright, her face red. An awful sense of social disaster began to creep over him.

'Herr Busacher,' the secretary said, holding out her hand. 'You do not remember me. Aschmann, Therese Aschmann. Of course it was many years ago. We have both changed, though I would have recognized you. It must be eighteen years, I think.'

Appalled, he took the proffered hand in his, noticing in the brief instant he held it that the hand was shaking. He was disgusted with himself, at his lack of tact, at the hurt he had unwittingly inflicted, but even more than that he was horrified at the change in her. People grow old, he himself had grown old, but they did not, should not, change as drastically as she had. A profound pity overwhelmed him, filled his heart, to be replaced almost at once with anger at the man who had done this to her – and anger also with her, Therese, who had *allowed* a man to do this to her.

'Therese! My dear!' He clasped her hand again with both of his, pulled her forward and kissed her on both cheeks. As he did so he caught an elusive scent that swept him back many years, a clean, floral scent, a mixture of the soap she used and possibly perfume, but also the essence of her skin and hair. How very strange that she should have changed so much but that the slight primrose tang should have remained the same.

'Forgive me. I am such an old fool these days, blundering everywhere without looking at the world about me. My eyes too – I can no longer read the scores without spectacles. You must forgive

32

me. And how could you say I do not remember you! We worked together on so many wonderful productions. How could I possibly forget you? Just that I am such an old fool these days. They were quite right to kick me out from the Opera House.'

She was not deceived for one instant. Her eyes remained very bright, not the brightness of the girl she had once been, but the brightness of unshed tears combined with a little anger perhaps. Oh God! He hoped she wasn't going to cry. There was no way he could cope with a sad, crying, middle-aged woman. Still holding her hands, he stretched her arms out to the side, as though she were taking a curtain call.

'Ah! Now I see what it is. You have cut your hair! It is always so difficult to recognize people when they change their hair. It used to be long, and you wore it loose, down your back.' And you were slim and lovely and full of hope and enthusiasm and gaiety. He saw her throat move as she swallowed.

'That's correct, Herr Direktor,' she said quietly. 'I had it cut some years ago. Long hair does not suit as one grows older.'

He cast a quick frantic glance at Hans, who had got him into this mess. Already he was planning how to reject her with the minimum of hurt, but he was furious with Hans. How could he have been so ridiculous as to suggest this poor, totally demoralized creature for an operatic season – and opposite Gesner of all people. He would destroy her before she even walked on the stage. But he had to find a way of rejecting her convincingly. Life had treated her badly enough without him adding to her other humiliations. Perhaps it would be best to take her to tea some-where, explain over pastries in as gentle a way as possible. And in a café there would be less chance of an embarrassing scene.

'Now,' he said heartily. 'Shall we go upstairs? I cannot tell you, my dear Therese, how very much I am looking forward to hearing you sing once more.'

With a final glare at Hans he strode across to the door and opened it with a courtly bow, leaving Hans to push her gently in the small of the back towards the stairs. As he followed them he began to talk, inventiveness coming swiftly to his tongue.

'I expect Hans has told you of our little problem, Therese?'

They entered the studio and she crossed and stood by the piano.

'No, Herr Direktor.' In his face she had seen everything he was thinking, pity, embarrassment, disgust. She wanted to get out of the room, out of the whole situation as quickly as he did. She felt humiliated and her stomach was churning, but they both knew they

33

had to go through this awful charade before they could extricate themselves with dignity.

'It is Gesner,' he said, thankfully deciding to land the entire problem on Gesner's shoulders. 'As you must have heard, Therese, Gesner is . . . difficult. He has casting approval and the entire choice of company and, I have to admit, he is extremely selective when it comes to his lead soprano. He has selected a list of about five or six singers he wishes me to hear.' He ignored the smothered cough he heard from Hans behind his back. 'Therese, my dear, you can think yourself honoured you have even been selected as one of the six! If you knew Gesner you would realize you could have no higher accolade. Of course, the final decision is Gesner's.'

'Of course, Herr Busacher.'

'And after you have sung, perhaps some tea or coffee. And we must talk about the old days – so much to talk of. Remember *Traviata*? You were the best Violetta I ever had – far too young of course – but the best I ever had. You remember?'

'I remember, Herr Direktor.'

'And *Die Fledermaus* – you remember the opening of *Die Fledermaus* when they gave you bigger calls than the leading lady? How angry she was! You remember?'

'Yes, Herr Direktor.' He was making it worse, reminding her of what she had once been. How could she sing now? When it was plain he didn't want her. Hans said her voice was still good, kept reassuring her, but she didn't know any more. She had never been able to judge her own voice and, in the bad years, with Friedrich, she hadn't been able to sing at all.

Busacher sat at the piano and strummed a few chords.

'So. What shall it be? How about the Grisette's song from the *Widow*?' he said.

A small thread of control suddenly snapped in her head, and was replaced by an explosion of sheer rage that swamped everything else, the churning stomach, the incipient tears, the humiliation and misery. *How dare he!* How dare he suggest that the best she could do would be the Grisette's song! Who did he think he was, the patronizing old fool? It was a chorus, a comedy item that hardly needed a voice at all. She had seen good comediennes 'put it over' virtually out of tune. At a pinch, if desperate, one could *speak* the Grisette's song and get away with it, providing one had nerve and a sense of timing. Did she look so hopeless that she would turn up for an audition if that was the best she could do? Did he think that her professionalism had gone, along with her long hair and her figure? She suddenly decided the last thing in the world she wanted was to work for this contemptible, insulting old hypocrite. She knew she wasn't going to get the job, had known from the moment he'd walked in, but she'd give him a good run for his money.

'With your permission, Herr Direktor,' she said, stony-faced, 'I would like to sing "*Einer Wird Kommen*" from *Der Zarewitsch*, and then the Jewel Song from *Faust*.' Her face was white as she glared at him with open hostility.

'Oh dear!' Busacher faltered. 'I do not think I can play those two accompaniments, Therese.'

The *Zarewitsch* number was hopeless for her, nearly the full operatic range demanded as well as a fine legato. Perfectly sung it was moving, passionate, and had undertones, like all Lehar's music, of poignant drama. Sung by any but the most versatile and agile voice it was a trap that frequently degenerated into off-key harshness. As for the Jewel Song, well, he doubted they would get to that, but he shuddered at the thought of what could happen.

Therese moved sharply towards the piano. 'In that case I can accompany myself, Herr Direktor,' she said icily.

The atmosphere in the studio was charged. Hans slunk into a corner, hunched his shoulders and tried, in best agent fashion, to ignore the tensions crackling all around him. He wondered what had possessed him. At best, ten per cent of a Hochhauser Season wasn't worth all this.

'Well . . . if you're sure . . . I will try.' Unhappily he began to play the opening bars and then she began to sing, and Busacher was suddenly riveted to his piano stool.

As a role she couldn't have chosen anything more unsuitable. It was the song of Sonja, a young ballet dancer smuggled into the Zarewitsch's palace disguised as a boy soldier. That boy's costume had been the downfall of even quite slim and pretty sopranos. The mind boggled at what it would do to Therese Aschmann. But the voice . . . At the first note he caught his breath, wondering if it were a fluke. It was not. Effortless, sustained, lyrical, the voice flowed, the golden quality still there, the way it had been eighteen years ago. The E major came, she reached it easily, almost rippling into it, held it and blazed into pure delight. The bright golden tones dropped, softened, picked up the gentle phrasing at the lower range, rose again and burst into a crescendo of absolute perfection. Almost before the echo in the room had died away he automatically went into the duet from the same operetta, and without having to be told she followed him, faltering once or twice on the words but never on the melody.

He finished, began the Jewel Song from *Faust* and again heard the trilling notes, the purity at the top end of the range, the richness at the bottom. She was word perfect, note perfect. He realized she had prepared this song very carefully for the audition. The *Zarewitsch* number she knew but had chosen on the spur of the moment. Her technique was more exact, more polished than it had been – had Hans said she'd been doing a lot of church music? That would account for it. The Jewel Song ended. Remembering *Fledermaus* he began the introduction, once more she picked up the melody, sang as long as he played, then skilfully led *him* into *Der Rosenkavalier*. The voice seemed tireless. He saw, in his mind's eye, pages of music with Therese's voice rippling through folio after folio, turning paper and notes into sheer magic. As the final notes died away he left his hands on the keyboard, feeling simultaneously exhilarated and exhausted. He turned to look at her and experienced a second minor shock. The voice had played tricks with him. He had expected to see the girl with the waist-length hair. For a moment they stared at one another, not knowing what to say. Then, more moved than he wanted her to know, he said reproachfully, 'Oh, Therese! Why did you leave us for so many years?'

'You know why,' she answered roughly. 'I had no choice. I had no voice, no confidence.'

'You should never have let everyone forget you, forget that voice.'

'I wanted everyone to forget! You know the scandal, the embarrassment. I didn't want people to remember me like that. And after, when he'd gone to the hospital, I had so little energy. You have no idea how tired, how demoralized I was. And it is so hard to make a comeback, Franz. You know that. How many of us have tried to come back and failed.'

Suddenly he took her hand in both of his. He had great big raw-boned hands, the two fingers on the left deformed by old frostbite injuries from the war. 'Therese,' he said earnestly. 'We must all do everything we can. You must work, you must lose weight. You know how much harder it is now. The days when the voice was enough have gone. The audience demand everything, voice, appearance, the actor's blood!' He laughed a little sardonically. 'They even believe that singers should be able to act. And in many ways operetta has always been more difficult than opera in its demands on singers. All that dancing and prettiness and speed.'

'Are you offering her the Hochhauser Season?' asked a voice dryly from the corner of the room. They both turned. Busacher was still so much under the spell of her voice that he forgot to be cautious.

'Just think, Hans,' he said gloatingly. 'Think of those two voices together, Gesner and Aschmann. Think what one could do with them.'

'He won't like it.'

Busacher thought ahead, foresaw the shocks, the tantrums, the rudeness, wondered if he could manage, remembered Therese's voice, and decided he would try. But what about Therese?

'You've heard about Gesner, Therese?'

'Even in the world of choral church music a few rumours have come my way,' she said dryly.

'He likes to destroy his partners if they are any good. Once he hears you sing you can expect the worst. Do you think you can cope with that?'

For the first time a huge smile broke over her face, an extraordinary young smile in the tired, ageing face. 'At the moment I can cope with anything, Herr Direktor.' She could feel a tremendous surge of triumph inside her. She was having to beat it down so that she didn't begin to whirl round the studio singing at the top of her voice. Later all the doubts would come back, about whether she was too old, had been away too long. Later she would begin to think about the sheer terror of walking on to a stage again after all these years. But at the moment she was exultant. Her voice had overwhelmed Busacher, she'd seen that in his face just as earlier she'd been able to see he didn't want her. She didn't care too much about her looks – at least she did, but not with people like Busacher and Hans, who judged her not for her appearance, but for her talent. She'd do something about the way she looked, lose weight, have her hair tinted, use some of her small savings to spruce up a bit, now she knew she'd have a salary coming in for the whole of the summer. But she could still sing . . . she still had her voice. No-one could take that away.

Busacher looked at Hans. Hans looked at Therese.

'There'll be problems,' said Hans.

'I want her.'

'You're playing at being Svengali, Franz. You're toying with the idea of creating a star.'

'Re-creating.'

'She can't dance.'

'We'll get round that.'

'I always used to,' Therese intervened. 'I can learn to do enough.'

37

'All right,' said Hans. 'Done. Now, how are we going to handle Gesner? He has approval.'

'We'll set up a meeting, here in Vienna, next week, in a restaurant, where he'll have to behave himself. He always behaves better when he has an audience. If he doesn't hear her voice, just sees her, he won't envisage any competition.'

They were talking about her as though she wasn't there and suddenly they realized it. Busacher smiled at her, rose from the piano, took her hand in his once more.

'Therese,' he said. 'Welcome to the Hochhauser Season.'

It wasn't until he was in the train, on his way back to Hochhauser, that he remembered with a sense of dread that their first brand new production to be launched this season was *The Count of Luxembourg*. And it was in Act Two of *Luxembourg*, eighteen years ago, that Therese's husband had hurled himself screaming on to the stage with a knife and tried to kill her.

CHAPTER THREE

When Willi Zimmermann, Burgermeister of Hochhauser, heard there was a chance that Therese Aschmann might be coming for the Season, he went into a state of trance-like shock, which was most unusual for Willi.

'And so,' the Direktor said, 'we agreed to meet at Sachers next week, Hans and Therese, Gesner and myself. About the other matter, the matter of *Luxembourg*, I asked Hans to speak to her, and I myself wrote a letter explaining that we were already committed to the production, that I hoped she would still want to come in spite of . . . everything. I don't know what her reaction will be. It will open many old wounds, I suppose, but at the same time it is obvious she is dying to get back into the theatre. I had the feeling she would put up with much, make a great many efforts, both practical and emotional, to be given this chance.'

'Aschmann,' said Willi, gazing into the air.

'Of course, with that voice, she should really be thinking about an operatic début, but one can see the problem. The confidence, the stage presence has gone and she needs a small arena to begin with. Also, even if the *Staatsoper* heard her, they would only put her into the chorus, and at her age it might be difficult to lift herself out of it. And here, in Hochhauser, we can nurse her carefully along. I myself shall give her extra private tuition. There'll be Gesner, of course, but she knows that and can only be on her guard. Here, she will be a tiny, re-emerging star in our very small sky. In Vienna, especially at the *Staatsoper*, she wouldn't survive.'

He stared at his friend. Willi hadn't said anything but 'Aschmann' for ten minutes. Usually Willi chattered, interrupted, interfered, laughed, drank too much, and sometimes became rather irritating. Franz loved Willi, couldn't have managed without him, but occasionally found his exuberance too much. He wondered if Willi was sulking because he hadn't been consulted on the question of a lead soprano before Franz had gone up to Vienna.

Although the Direktor thought of the Hochhauser Company as his, it really belonged to both of them. In fact it had all been Willi's idea in the first place and sometimes, when Franz found that his friend was irritating him beyond endurance, he would stop and remind himself just how much he owed to Willi. Willi had not only been his partner in operatic venture, he had also saved his sanity. He knew that without Willi he would, by this time, either have been dead or have turned into a self-centred and slightly mad recluse.

That first winter, after he had retired, driven out from Vienna by the ambitions of younger rivals, finding that he no longer had the stomach for the political intriguing necessary to survive in the strife of Vienna's musical circles, he had nearly succumbed to despair. He was sixty years old and had spent all his life in the theatre. He didn't know how to live without it.

He had been born in 1914. His mother had been the soubrette of a Hungarian touring company. His father, the second violinist in a Viennese orchestra, had been speedily mobilized into the Austro-Hungarian army just after his son was born. His mother had done well in the war – young officers on leave in Vienna wanted just the sort of entertainment she was prepared to give, not only on stage, but afterwards at Sachers and in her tarnished little apartment behind the Sud Bahnhof. Mostly, so he had been told, he had been looked after by the women in the wardrobe department and by his mother's dresser.

When his father was invalided out with tuberculosis in 1916, Franz was just old enough to remember – remember being carried home from the theatre in his father's arms each night and the shouting and screaming fights which used to wake him from sleep. The sounds he remembered most from his childhood were his mother shouting and his father coughing, but stronger than these were the wonderful noises of the theatre, the sweeping melodies that used to drown everything else, the full wonder of an orchestra playing Strauss waltzes, and voices, voices that were themselves like instruments. Even his mother's shrieking spiteful voice changed in the theatre, became a single part of a great complex sound.

When he was five years old she had run away with a German black marketeer. Vienna, in 1919, was a bleak miserable city and Germany, so he had been told, was worse, but somehow his feckless, pretty mother had managed to find one of the few men in post-war central Europe who still had enough money to provide her with a life of trivial luxuries. She had died soon after in the great influenza epidemic that swept Europe. He hardly remembered her.

But his father he never forgot. Every single day he thought of his father in some way, sometimes with humour, sometimes with sadness, sometimes even now with guilt, but more often he thought of him with some practical allusion to everyday work in the theatre. He would never, ever, forget his father.

By rights they should both have died in that terrible post-war Vienna. His father was just one of half a million consumptives in the new Austria, and there was little to eat other than black bread and potatoes. The city was a teaming mess of crippled war veterans, grey-faced widows, and children with rickets and lice. Every day his father, still dressed in his old army greatcoat, the only warm garment he had, would drag him round the city to wherever he was playing or rehearsing – sometimes in a theatre, sometimes only a cabaret or café orchestra. And in the middle of the day he would take him to the children's soup kitchen near the Währinger Gürtel. There he would leave Franz to collect his soup, bread, and cocoa and find his own way back to his place of work.

He had so many pictures of his father in his memory – hurrying away from the soup kitchen, his shoulders shaking as he coughed, sitting in the orchestra pit in his shabby dress suit salvaged from before the war. He had refused to die, leading Franz from theatre to theatre, from café to café, feeding and clothing him as best he could and teaching him always the craft of music, of the theatre.

At ten he was callboy, stagehand and bit player whenever they needed a child on stage – illegal, but who was to know or care when the city was in turmoil. By the time he was fourteen he could fill in for any violinist who was sick, could play the piano for the soloists at rehearsal, and adapt scores for most of the instruments in the orchestra. He was frequently used as prompt and would most probably have helped out in the chorus, too, if his voice hadn't broken and left him with a deep foghorn that he was professional enough to know would never improve.

They lived frugally. Even when conditions in the city grew a little better he and his father continued to share a room in the Hernals district, which was poor but close enough to the theatres

41

and cafés for them to be able to walk home late at night. Franz's father had impressed upon him very early the necessity of saving tram fares whenever possible. It was a habit he had never lost and, even at the height of his wealth and success, he could be seen striding the streets of Vienna, from theatre to rehearsal rooms, from café to concert hall. It was one of the reasons he was still so fit.

At night Franz and his father had cooked unappetizing meals on a portable oil stove that served both to heat and cook and also impregnated their clothes and none-too-frequently washed bodies with the smell of oil smoke.

Because he had been born in a war, and grown up in a vanquished and starving city, Franz took for granted the violence, hysteria, and poverty of those years. When the 1927 riots broke out they meant no more than the inconvenience of avoiding police bullets on the way home from the theatre. The strikes, the political street battles as faction fought faction, were important only inasmuch as the theatre or café or cabaret where they were working might be closed and a day's pay lost. He was too busy keeping alive and learning his trade to become conscious of political changes.

When he was seventeen he auditioned for a place in the second violins at the *Volksoper*. That was one of his good times, one of the good memories of his father whose thin, sallow face had flushed into triumphant excitement when he got the job. Franz had bought a bottle of wine to celebrate and he watched with a strange ache in his stomach as his father's hand shook when he raised his glass. The only time his father's hands were steady was when he played his violin. For the first time Franz began to question why they lived the way they did, why they had no money when now there were two incomes and life was easier in the city anyway. He began to wish he had money for himself instead of passing most of his salary to his father every week. Gratitude and an overwhelming protective love for the man who had raised him single-handed in spite of everything began to battle with adolescent resentment and the need for independence. He found he was ashamed of the way his father looked. The army greatcoat had been replaced by one equally frayed and threadbare. He got his shoes second-hand from the flea market and his appearance was seedy and pathetic. Franz was frequently embarrassed when the staff of the *Volksoper* saw them together. He began to hate his father. One week he spent all his salary on new, stylish clothes for himself. He refused to go home and eat with his father but spent his time in the cafés with his friends.

His father said nothing – he was a tired, quiet man anyway – and that was wrong too. When Franz tried to argue with him, berate him for his shabbiness, his meanness, he never answered and that made the seventeen-year-old boy even angrier. He wanted his father to fight back, shout at him so that he felt justified in hating the old man. For years afterwards the memories of the hurts he must have inflicted made him close his eyes and hunch up against the pain of his youthful cruelty.

At a morning rehearsal at the *Volksoper* he received an urgent message to go to the *Allgemeines Krankenhaus*, the hospital where his father had been taken after collapsing in a street near the Währinger Gürtel. He had run all the way, his violin case under his arm, breathing a silent prayer to God. Don't let my father die. I didn't mean all those things I said. He's the only person in the whole world I've got. Don't let him die. Please, God, don't let him die, not yet.

His father was in a public ward, skeletally thin with two ravaged patches of colour high on his cheeks. His brown hair had been tidied back by a nurse. It made him look strange and pathetic. Usually his hair hung forward, blew about as he played.

'Franz . . . good boy . . .' he breathed, the faded blue eyes staring tiredly out past him.

'You're going to be all right, Papa. You are, aren't you?'

His father didn't answer and that frightened him even more.

'You've got to get better, Papa. I can't manage without you.' Then his father had smiled a little.

'Oh yes, Franz. You can manage without me now. You've grown up. You're strong and you have talent and you can manage now.'

'Please get well, Papa! It's my turn to look after you. We'll get a better apartment – out in the suburbs where the air is cleaner. You can just rest, Papa. You don't need to work any more. I earn enough to look after us both. I . . .' he choked a little. 'I didn't mean those things, Papa. I don't want to keep my money. I want to use it to make you better. But please, please, Papa, try and get better!'

He took his father's hand in his and suddenly wanted to cry because the hand was so thin, so frail. Why hadn't he noticed before and tried to do something about it instead of criticizing the way the old man looked?

'Listen, Franz. I want you to listen to what I say. I've saved the money – all the money we both earned. I've saved it and now you are to go to the *Konservatorium*.'

'What?'

'I've been saving for years – for this. For you to go to the *Konservatorium*.'

It took a stunned moment for the words to break through his grief and anxiety and make sense. When the meaning finally did impinge on his consciousness, all it did was make the churning in his stomach worse.

'Papa! If we have money saved we shall spend it to get you well again. You can go away, to a proper hospital in the mountains, a sanitorium. You need to rest, Papa. You must rest.' He was trying desperately not to cry because he was grown-up and because he didn't want to upset his father. He wanted to hold him in his arms and beg him not to die but he knew he couldn't do that, not in the public ward with everyone watching.

'Franz . . . Franz . . .' His father had smiled, his face suddenly younger. God! How old was his father – not old – not yet fifty. That wasn't old. It wasn't old enough to die.

'Franz . . . I've saved the money, all we had, because I knew that someday you'd be ready. I want you to go to the *Konservatorium* . . . learn music the proper way.'

'I've learnt music from you, Papa. You're the best violinist in Vienna.' Tears were streaming down his face, and they both knew it wasn't true. His father had never been a great musician.

'No, Franz, but you could be. I knew, when you were a little boy and began to play . . . I knew that the time would come when you would have to have a proper teacher. Franz . . . you can be . . . someone in our world. You could be a concert performer, even a conductor – perhaps one day at the *Staatsoper*.' Animation briefly lifted the disease from his face, then passed. 'But things are more difficult now. You have to learn the proper way, you have to have teachers who will recommend you, you have to learn what to say to important people. You need technique, polish. This is why I saved. If you can earn a little to help with your food and rent, there should be enough for three years.'

'No, Papa.' He had put his hand up to shield his eyes. He wasn't a handsome youth, never had been attractive, even as a child. His face was too big-boned and raw and looked ugly when he cried.

His father had gripped his hand as hard as he could, a feeble clutch from the emaciated fingers.

'The money is saved – in gold. I knew it was no good any other way. This world,' his mouth twisted wryly. 'This world takes your money one day, and the next it is worthless. Every time I had

44

something saved I bought gold. Thank God I didn't put it in the *Creditanstalt*. You will sell the gold, a little at a time, just as you need it, no more. Do you understand? The banks could still fail. Only gold will keep its value. Do you understand?'

He had been unable to answer, thinking of the shabby coat, the second-hand shoes. He stared down at his violin case which was on the bed, and suddenly his father smiled. Very gently he began to stroke the case. 'You and I, Franz. We've had some good times.'

'Yes, Papa.'

'Music . . . the theatre . . . it's a dream world, Franz. The serious ones, the politicians, the bankers and businessmen, governments, they dismiss us as nothing. We are slices of *sachertorte*, butterflies who entertain for a while and have no place in a serious world. But I've seen the other world, the real world, the war, men dying, people being cruel, savage to one another. Such nightmares in the real world, Franz. Such hideous things. It is only the dreams that keep men sane.'

'You've made dreams, Papa. You've made people happy.'

'Perhaps . . . a little.' He smiled his gentle tired smile again. 'There will be more wars, more barbarism.' He sighed and closed his eyes for a second. 'Who makes the evil? I do not know. But God makes music and gives us our dreams. You will use the money for the *Konservatorium*, Franz.' Even sick and frail, the voice held the authority he had obeyed all these years. The voice that had made him practise his violin every day, made him go to the soup kitchen, walk instead of take a tram, hand his money over every week to be allocated as his father thought best. He realized, suddenly, with an understanding beyond his years, that this dream of his father, of sending him to the *Konservatorium* had been what kept him alive, working, hoping, all these years. Without that dream his father would have coughed himself to death when his wife had left him.

'You promise, Franz? You promise me you will go to the *Konservatorium*?'

Unable to speak the boy had nodded, then sat silently while his father closed his eyes and slept a little. They'd sent him away then, even though he had protested, afraid that his father would die when he wasn't there. But next day they had sat together again, the violin case on the bed, Franz holding his father's hand. He had died the following week, quietly, in the night, without giving any trouble to anyone, just the way he had lived.

His father had been right. He did need the *Konservatorium* to lift him out from the ranks of the professional home-grown theatre musicians into the flights of the super-professionals. He was way ahead of most of his fellow students but he had acquired bad habits in the orchestra pit. He came out from the *Konservatorium* with a polish that only added to his ingrained musicianship. Almost at once he was offered a year's scholarship in Paris. He was suddenly the golden boy of Vienna, the one they were all watching, the one who was going to do great and exciting things.

He could have remained in Paris, could have set off from there to conquer the world's concert platforms. His life would have been very different if he had been in Paris, or London, or New York when the war broke out, the second war. But he was Viennese and he was a theatre musician and so, when the *Staatsoper* approached him, he could think of nothing else but returning to his beloved Vienna. There was no other place in the world where music, operetta, theatre, was such an integral part of everyday life.

He had two years before the Anschluss blew his life apart. Two years before the Nazis marched through the streets of his city with more than half the Viennese cheering them, the new barbarians. Within a year he was in the army, and by the winter of 1941 he was on the Russian Front, not commissioned, not put into any kind of military band as were many of his colleagues. He was suspected of helping Jewish refugees to escape and was conscripted into an infantry battalion as punishment. He came back from Russia, his facilities as a concert violinist gone for ever. Frostbite in his left hand had rendered his violin-playing useless for professional purposes.

Sometimes he looked back and wondered if he ever would have been good enough for the concert platform. He suspected not. In any case his path was now clearly drawn for him, back to the world he had known from childhood: theatre, operetta, the world of singers, dancers, costume-makers, conductors. He knew more about that world than anything else.

He produced and directed opera and operetta in Vienna, Budapest, Berlin, Paris and London. He achieved a degree of fame that he probably would not have reached as a concert violinist. And as he grew older he turned more and more to operetta, the music of his youth. It was his first love and when forced to defend it against attack from the élitism of grand opera he could only say that it was 'happier' than opera. In his time he had worked with all the great ones, the temperamental ones, the talented. He had coped with screaming sopranos and bad-tempered conductors, with jealous tenors and obstinate designers.

46

He had retired at sixty after a severe bout of pneumonia had left him exhausted and aware that he no longer had the energy to mount his next production. Further medical tests had revealed that his father's old disease, tuberculosis, dormant for more than forty years, had established itself in his lungs. Now, of course, it could be treated instantly. He rested, took the drugs, thought of his father, and realized that somehow the fire had gone out of his belly. Sensitive to a lifetime of picking up café gossip with his own particular musical antennae, he became aware that the long knives were out . . . 'Busacher's slipping, don't you think?' . . . 'Did you hear he couldn't complete his last production? They had to get someone to take over. Poor health, of course.' . . . 'Time he moved out and made way for the young ones.' If he hadn't felt so ill, so tired, he might have fought back but he found he no longer cared enough. Vienna had ever been a centre of political strife as far as the musical world was concerned, with plots and counter-plots and factions always trying to seize power in the plum positions. At one time he had enjoyed it. Born and bred in Vienna he knew how to plot with the best of them but now, suddenly, he couldn't get excited about defending himself and saving his career. A bitter stiff pride made him announce his retirement before the vendetta had really got under way and he had the satisfaction of seeing his rivals – girded for a long and enjoyable pack fight – deprived of their victim.

He had indulged himself, slightly maliciously, in being charming to the most virulent of his enemies . . . 'My dear Leo! How right you were. I am, of course, slipping and indeed I couldn't complete my last production . . . poor health, as you said. Max reported your conversation to me, told me of your comments. I hope you will forgive me but I mentioned your words to the management when I handed in my resignation. I thought they would like to know how perceptive you are.' He had fired off one last delicious volley in the press, writing a long and extremely well-informed article on the deterioration of the structure of Viennese opera and who had done what to whom. He had managed to pull quite a few of his rivals down with him. He was still Viennese enough to have enjoyed doing that, but the truth was that the fight had gone out of him.

He had left with all honours. A benefit performance, several farewell concerts which he himself had conducted, a scholarship awarded in his name, and numerous rounds of parties, dinners, and formal lunches. There had been tears, flowers, gifts and promises from all his old friends that they would be visting him in

Hochhauser. And then, with a slight sense of disorientation, he had settled permanently into what had been his weekend villa, tired, dispirited, and, at first, not at all sorry to have left.

Those first two years in Hochhauser had been the loneliest of his life. His friends had visited once, then no more. He didn't blame them. There was too much to do when one was still in the full flight of a musical career. At first he travelled up to Vienna once a month to go to the theatre, lunch with former colleagues, listen to the latest gossip. But finally he stopped going because it made him feel too sad, too out of touch with things. The first summer, when he had still been ill and tired, it had not been too bad. He had rested and reorganized the villa into a comfortable year-round residence instead of just a holiday home. He had designed a garden, walked in the mountains, written a few articles for some music magazines and had felt himself growing stronger again. And then the winter had closed in.

He had sat in the big carved chair, looking out at the mountains as the snow line came lower and lower, as grey cloud blocked out the view, as the hours of daylight grew fewer. He, who had always said he didn't have enough time to listen to music and read, found himself descending into melancholy, constantly brooding on the past, thinking of his father who had loved him so much, and of his own son who did not love him at all. There were days when he saw no-one except Frau Schmidt who came up from the town to clean and cook for him, days when he found he could not even lift the telephone and try to make contact with the outside world.

It was during the second winter, when he began to realize that his melancholy isolation was sliding into agoraphobia, that he made the effort, every evening, to walk down to the Franz Joseph Hotel, take a seat at one of the terrace tables, and order a glass of wine. He would watch the good citizens of Hochhauser drinking and eating and occasionally casting curious glances in his direction. He did not realize that they held him in awe. He was internationally famous, an impresario, and they mistook his lonely depression for the deliberate forbidding grandeur of the famous. Everyone in Hochhauser was aware of him, the huge craggy elderly man with the shock of white hair who strode about the mountains in the summer months.

It was towards the end of that second winter that, one evening, he was astonished to look up from his table and find a fat, bald little man standing before him.

'Herr Busacher – I wonder if I might intrude on your privacy for a few moments?'

He had been so surprised that he, urbane charmer of Vienna's most sophisticated circles, had sat staring bemused at the little man.

'I am Willi Zimmermann, the Burgermeister of Hochhauser. Perhaps you may remember me? We met four years ago, when we asked you to open the new Concert Rooms in the town.'

Vaguely he recalled a platform of local dignitaries and a not very good concert that he had been forced to sit through as guest of honour. Social graces suddenly reasserted themselves. He stood and held out his hand.

'Of course, Herr Burgermeister. I remember you well. Please sit. Some wine?' He beckoned to the waiter for an extra glass while the little man eased himself into the chair on the other side of the table.

'I have a proposition, Herr Busacher. An outrageous proposition. My colleagues on the *Gemeinderat* and on the committee have informed me that I am impertinent even to suggest it to you.'

'You wish me to chair some local charity?'

'No – or perhaps yes, you could look at it in that light. A charity to help Hochhauser become a more popular holiday resort.'

The Direktor had smiled, distantly, frostily. 'I think your town is perfect as it is, Herr Burgermeister. It is quiet, dignified, and the only holiday visitors who come are the Viennese, like myself, who want to escape the hordes of foreign tourists who flood the Tyrol every summer and winter. What are you suggesting? A ski lift? A discotheque? A hamburger restaurant, perhaps?'

Beads of perspiration suddenly appeared on the round red face opposite him, and Busacher felt ashamed of himself. Two fat hands on the other side of the table nervously encircled the stem of his wine glass.

'You know the economy of our town, Herr Busacher. Farming, and the bicycle factory and a small tourist income in the summer months. Many of our young people are leaving because there is not enough work – and not enough excitement either. We are not suggesting that we build another Kursaal, but in the days of the Empire we were a rather prosperous spa town – not as famous as Baden of course – but nonetheless we had a flourishing community and a great many entertainments. Now, what can our visitors do? They walk a little, they rest. They attend the concert hall if they are lucky enough to visit when a concert has been arranged. And then they go home to Vienna and think no more about us.'

He had become quite heated. There had even been a note of unexpected sarcasm when he referred to the Kursaal, and the Direktor found he was mildly amused.

'So, Herr Zimmermann. What are you suggesting?'

'We do not want to change Hochhauser from what it is. Our town has always been a place for the Viennese to come in the summer – the mountains, the forests, the pleasant walks by the river and up into the hills. The spa waters for the elderly, the mountains for the young. But we lack . . . colour, excitement. What we need is our own Hochhauser Season – five months of operetta in our own theatre. It is most particularly suitable because we can claim, here in Hochhauser, two great figures from the world of international music.'

The Direktor rapidly ran through the birthplaces of the famous in his mind and couldn't think of one composer who had been born in Hochhauser.

'I don't think . . .' he began.

'Why, yourself of course, Herr Busacher!' Burgermeister Zimmermann had beamed over his spectacles. 'You were not born here, but you have chosen Hochhauser as your home for many years.'

'You said two "great" figures?'

'Karl Gesner, the tenor. He was born here. His father was a cheesemaker. His farm was on the western slopes of the mountain. His cheeses were quite famous in these parts. Perhaps you didn't know that.'

'No,' said Franz dryly. 'I didn't know that.' He stored the information away at the back of his mind for the next time he visited Vienna. Gesner, one of the most unpleasant singers in the business, had always implied that he was the bastard son of an aristocrat and a famous diva whose name he could not divulge. Curiosity, diverting him for the moment, made him ask, 'Who was his mother? Was he illegitimate?'

Willi Zimmermann looked shocked. 'Certainly not, Herr Busacher. His mother was Frau Gesner, a most respectable woman. She used to help in the cheese business.'

Busacher began to laugh and then, surprised, realized he hadn't laughed for several months. He found he was relaxing slightly; the ghosts of melancholy were being pushed into the background by this ludicrous little man.

'So. In what way can I help you with your operetta company?' he asked more genially. Willi Zimmermann swallowed hard, beamed, and blurted out,

'We would like you to be the Direktor of the new Hochhauser Operetta Company.'

The sheer effrontery of the man made the Direktor begin to

laugh again. He thought of the approaches he had had in the past, the political lobbying at the *Staatsoper*, the delicate negotiations over contracts, the careful timetables so that new productions in Paris and Berlin should not overlap. He laughed so much that tears ran down his cheeks, he started to cough and had to reach for his wine to soothe his throat. Willi Zimmermann began to laugh too, his cherubic round face crinkling up into moons of mirth.

'Yes, it is comical, is it not?' he chuckled. 'They all said I was impertinent, that you would laugh, or perhaps even be rude. But I said, so, what harm does it do to ask? If we must start somewhere, let us start at the top. I will approach them both, I said, I will speak to Gesner and to Herr Busacher, and if we are lucky one or the other will accept, and if we are very lucky, both will accept.'

The Direktor wiped his eyes. 'And what did Gesner say?' he asked weakly.

'Gesner said yes.'

'What?'

'Gesner said yes. He will open and be the star of the Hochhauser Operetta Company. He is going to announce that Hochhauser is his birthplace and that is why he is coming back. He is to have casting approval and lead billing.'

The Direktor felt a sudden surge of very professional anger. 'It is up to the Direktor to agree those things, Herr Burgermeister. You should have asked me first.'

'I did not realize, Herr Busacher . . . Does that mean you accept?'

'No of course it doesn't!' he snapped. 'I'm retired. You know that. If ever I did decide to come out of retirement it would be to do something in Vienna or Salzburg. I cannot think what Gesner is doing agreeing to come here. He is an international singer and is, moreover, well aware of his position. I cannot think he was serious.'

'Herr Gesner has not worked in the theatre for two and a half years, Herr Busacher,' said the Burgermeister dryly. 'I think he accepted because he has not been asked to appear anywhere else.'

No, thought Busacher to himself, and neither have I, but that is rather different. I have retired. Gesner has not.

'You see, Herr Busacher,' the Burgermeister continued, leaning anxiously across the table, 'it is not so outrageous as it first appears. All over Europe small cities and towns are setting up their own companies, their own music festivals. Look at Glyndebourne in England. Who would have thought, all those years ago, that Glyndebourne would have become world famous? We all have to

51

begin somewhere, and we would be starting very well indeed if we had two great names on our side.'

'No,' said Busacher. 'It is ridiculous. I am retired. I had to leave Vienna because I was tired – ill. Do you have any idea of the work involved in starting a new company? Even a small one? And – presumably – you would have very little money. I know from experience that when there is little money it means a great deal more work.'

'We have been promised a State grant – not big, but something to begin with. Hochhauser itself will, of course, guarantee as much as it can. And, hopefully, the tickets will pay for the rest. And, forgive me, Herr Busacher, I know you retired for reasons of ill health, but I think you are well again now. And you would have the winter months to rest. Also you are not old enough to retire. When people retire too young they become melancholy.'

The Direktor stared at Zimmermann, a curious sense of life surging in his veins again. Of course the scheme was ridiculous – taking on the responsibility of what would amount to an amateur venture, wrestling with problems of finance and general logistics that he hadn't had to cope with since his early days. He was insane even to consider it.

'I must think on all this,' he said tersely. 'Perhaps you would come and see me tomorrow evening – no – Saturday evening. You know where I live?'

'Of course.' The Burgermeister rose, extended his hand and bowed over his round little stomach. 'Everyone knows where the Herr Direktor lives.'

'What would you use for a theatre? The Concert Rooms aren't big enough and there is no proper room backstage.'

'The old Spa Rooms – you may remember the ballroom there? For many years we have rented it to the bicycle factory for storage space. Now we have withdrawn their tenancy – they are building a new warehouse next to the factory – and we have employed an architect to see what can be done. He has been most encouraging. The auditorium would need very little work. The end wall behind the platform will have to be moved back and a stage put where the platform is. But there is plenty of room, and all the old changing and bathing rooms at the back can stay as they are for dressing rooms. It will need refurbishing of course, but there is already a small gallery running round three sides of the ballroom – you remember the gallery? The most expensive structural item will be moving the platform wall and building the stage. And the auditorium will need to be raked, of course. The work will start as

52

soon as the snows clear. We hope to have it all completed by the end of the summer.'

What astonished Busacher more than anything else was how much had already been done. When the Burgermeister had first spoken to him he had thought it was a vague inconclusive plan, thoroughly unrealistic, a typical piece of small-town nonsense. But it appeared that they had already been organizing themselves for some time. They had a theatre, they had a State grant, they had Gesner. They had Willi Zimmermann, Burgermeister of Hoch-hauser too, he thought, who was not quite such a funny fat little man as he appeared to be.

'I will see you on Saturday,' he said abruptly. 'I must leave now. Good evening.'

Striding up the hill towards his home, he thought again how ridiculous it was that he should even consider the proposition. How they would laugh at him in Vienna to hear he was thinking of starting a second-rate operetta company in the provinces, not even a town that was on the tourist map. But why was Gesner doing it? He tried to remember what he had heard of the tenor's career over the last few years. The man had always been disliked. He was arrogant, ill-mannered, greedy and mean. But he did have a wonderful voice and there were many great singers whose personal offensiveness did not prevent them from being in constant employment. Of course, there was the time he had refused to sing half an hour before the curtain went up. It had been announced that he had a sore throat but the truth was he had just learned the name of the replacement tenor taking the second lead, a young man who had received serious acclaim from the critics and hysterical applause from audiences.

Then Busacher remembered hearing of another cancellation just after he had retired. And wasn't there some talk of a broken contract in London? Aha, he thought. Gesner has committed the one unforgivable sin in the theatre – unreliability. Even Callas had not been allowed to cancel erratically without her career suffering, and Gesner was not in the same league as Callas, good though he was. If the bigger managements were banning him, unofficially, from their theatres, he obviously saw Hochhauser as a way back to his career. And with casting approval he could make sure there were no bright young tenors coming up to challenge him.

And if I needed anything else to make me realize I am mad even to consider this proposition, he thought, it would be the thought of working with Gesner for five months. I'm certainly too old to cope with that.

By the time he went to bed he saw things in perspective again. There was no need to wait until Saturday. He would tell the Burgermeister tomorrow that, while wishing his venture all good fortune, he wanted no part of it. He would make some gracious gesture, of course. Take a permanent box – if there were to be boxes in the converted Spa Rooms – and perhaps give a party on the opening night. That would be quite sufficient.

The following morning on his usual walk, he found that his legs seemed to have carried him inadvertently in the direction of the old Spa Rooms. The building was in a rather pleasant part of the town, on the outskirts where the hills ran up towards the Hochhauser range. There was a beautiful backdrop of forest and rising slopes behind the Spa Rooms and, unbidden, into his mind came the memory of Glyndebourne. A picturesque setting, a small theatre, a few famous names, and who knew what might happen . . .

The yellow stucco was flaking away from the front of the building but many of the old features still remained – a wide and well-proportioned flight of steps led up to the double doors (they would need to open up the walls on each side of the doors for extra entrances if the foyer was to prove practical) and there was a pretty arrangement of balustrades and wrought iron at first-floor level.

The doors were locked but he wandered round the side and found the huge opening that had been knocked into the wall, presumably for the bicycle factory to load and unload. Big wooden doors stood slightly ajar and he slid quickly inside, hoping no-one would see him. The loading bay led directly into the ballroom.

Willi Zimmerman was right. It wouldn't take much to convert it. The raised orchestra dais at one end, now covered with empty packing cases, would have to be replaced with a proper stage and the whole of that end of the building remodelled. But the gallery that ran round three sides could be used partly for seating and partly for lighting units. There was a huge fitment in the centre of the roof where a chandelier had once hung. He must remember to ask Willi Zimmerman if they still had it.

He stood in front of the raised dais where the stage was going to be, and paced off fifteen feet to allow for an orchestra pit. There would still be room for about four hundred seats and a few extras in the gallery. With a sense of growing interest he realized just how pretty a theatre it was going to be. He was sure they could get a restoration grant from the local Province. It was at least a hundred and thirty years old. He took an old envelope out of his pocket and wrote down 'chandelier', and underneath that 'restoration grant'.

54

Backstage – it was actually the old bathing rooms but the waters had long been diverted when the building had been used as an army depot in the Second World War – he counted the dressing rooms and decided how many could be divided and subdivided. No room for a scenery bay – they would have to extend out at the back – but a nice big lofty room up in the roof for a wardrobe department or perhaps, if necessary, an extra rehearsal room.

He had never, in all his years in the theatre, been involved in the actual creation of a new company. He would be in total control right from the beginning – well – as in control as anyone could be with Karl Gesner in the company. He would have this enchanting little chocolate box of a theatre and a government grant to give it official and State blessing. He would have that surprising little man, Willi Zimmermann, to accomplish things that could not be accomplished.

'So, what do I want to do?' he said out loud in the echoing ballroom. 'Go back to my house and sit there brooding about my life, my son, Marta, the things I didn't do and should have done? Is that what I want to do? Sit and stare out of my window at the mountains until I turn into even more of a crazy old man than I already am?'

He had walked straight out of the Spa Rooms into Willi Zimmermann. He grasped Willi firmly by the arm. 'Come, my friend,' he said. 'We will take coffee together at the Franz Joseph. We have much to discuss.'

Together they had swept along the road, the tall, gaunt old impresario in the billowing black cloak, and the fat little man in loden green and a feathered hat. Willi had to run every few steps to keep up with Busacher. They looked amazing and comical together. It was a sight Hochhauser was to see many times in the years ahead.

That had been nine years ago, and since then they had become Willi and Franz to each other, had juggled finance, quarrelled over the choice of productions (for Willi had a tendency to interfere in things that were not strictly his concern), sympathized with each other over Gesner, and spent long hours on the terrace of the Franz Joseph discussing productions, singers, dancers, and – constantly – how to squeeze a little more money from the State, from the Hochhauser *Gemeinderat*, from anyone. Willi, for a short time, had ceased to be Burgermeister, then had bounced back. It made no difference to his involvement with the Hochhauser Season. Whatever his civic status, Willi was always in charge of theatre business and, indeed, no-one else could, or even wanted to cope with everything the way Willi did.

There had been many anomalies as there always were when starting a new theatre company. The grant for restoring and converting the old Spa Ballroom had proved magnificently generous. It had transpired that one of the more revered architects of the early 1800s had built the Spa Rooms and suddenly the Province authorities were anxious that every piece of stucco, every swag and urn should be restored to its full munificence. The result was that they had an exquisite jewel-box of a theatre, the excellence of which was out of all proportion to the performances that were played there. The State grant for the running of the theatre had, as Willi said, been small. It had, alas, never been increased. Inflation and a general tightening of the economy had resulted in repeated refusals for their grant to be raised. Gesner was expensive, so was the orchestra. There had been a suggestion at one point (from Willi) that perhaps the town band, strengthened by a few expensive outside musicians, could be utilized but Busacher, after listening to them once, had firmly stamped on the idea. Apart from problems with the musicians' union, he said, a weak orchestra was the surest way to disaster.

He found that all the old tricks from his youth were coming back to him. He remembered where you could economize, and where you could not. With a good orchestra and with stars in the central roles, you could afford to save on much else. He remembered how to form a strong supporting cast that was cheap and yet had expertise – a mixture of highly skilled elderly professionals, and energetic, attractive youngsters who romped all over the stage with no skills or experience at all. All the sets and costumes had had to be hired from second- or third-hand productions or, in some cases, even older performances. There was no question of lavish new productions of their own. Some of the costumes and sets were overly familiar to Busacher, who had seen them years before when they had been new – all of them were now past their prime and verged on the tatty.

There was another point where he and Willi had quarrelled. Willi had wanted to use a local electrician as the lighting man – he could soon learn, he said, how to specialize in theatre work; after all he had managed beautifully when floodlighting the Schloss at the town's annual *son et lumière* festival. But Busacher was adamant that a good lighting man should come to Hochhauser for the summer months. Clever lighting concealed a multitude of sins: shabby costumes became romantic, sequins and paste glittered a little more, and lines and wrinkles smoothed away into youthful complexions under the flattering tints of Surprise Pink.

The problem that had worried the Direktor most was that of Gesner. If Gesner was to be the big draw, they could not afford for him to be erratic and unreliable over his stage performances. Neither could they afford a good understudy, which would be necessary if Gesner was going to be temperamental over appearances. But, as they began work on their first production, Busacher came to realize that Gesner's two and a half years of unemployment had frightened him. He was still loathsome, conceited, a bully, and destructive to anyone who seemed in any way a threat, but he knew that if he failed to be reliable in this, his one last chance, he was lost for ever. And as the Hochhauser Operetta Company started to make a small but sure mark on the tourist season, as year by year their position became more secure, Busacher began to suspect that Gesner actually liked being the star of a small and somewhat undistinguished company. He didn't have to strive, to work too hard, and his supremacy was undisputed. He had begun to get bookings again for the winter months – not very good ones, a Wagnerian debut in London had proved disastrous – but he always came back to Hochhauser for the summer. He liked being the biggest, greenest, and slimiest frog in Hochhauser's tiny pool.

The last three or four years had seen changes coming to Hochhauser, for suddenly the English and American tourists had discovered the town. And what drew them was the theatre, the magic of seeing Viennese operetta performed in a charming, romantic old theatre in a charming romantic old spa town (the *Gemeinderat* had paid for the planting of several bands of fast-growing pines to shield the bicycle factory from public view. It was, as lucrative industries usually are, rather unsightly). Three new biggish hotels had opened up as well as several small but superior *Gasthäuser*. A surfeit of elegant after-theatre restaurants abounded in the vicinity of the Spa Rooms, all of them sporting violin orchestras or gypsy bands.

And undoubtedly the biggest draw of the Hochhauser Operetta Company was Gesner, tall, broad, handsome, magnificent. When Gesner walked on to the stage one sensed the change in the audience. The rich American and British matrons flocked into Hochhauser season after season, drawn by his strong sexuality and his smouldering brown eyes (the fact that they were rather too close together was noted only by the most discerning).

Gesner began to 'acquire' some rather nice presents which were usually handed up on stage during the curtain call. It had become somewhat embarrassing and Franz had had to start organizing small bouquets for the leading lady, who tended to stand there with a fatuous smile on her face while Gesner preened and bowed with an armful of packages. The presents ranged from gold watches to silk ties and he was doing quite a brisk trade in re-sales.

But the matrons weren't the real problem, for while Gesner was prepared to accept their gifts and their expensive after-theatre dinners, he drew the line at entering into more intimate liaisons with them. Matrons were fine for presents, but his sexual tastes ran to young and pretty girls who were naïve enough to be dazzled by him. Inevitably this meant the company's dancers who, by their very calling, were younger and sillier than anyone else. Season after season Busacher watched yet another pretty young thing having her heart broken by Gesner, who promptly discarded her at the end of the Season. Last year he had excelled himself, but with rather unfortunate results, for one month after the end of the Season the girl had turned up again, pregnant, and accompanied by her father who, to everyone's horror, proved to be a famous and very successful Viennese advokat. Busacher was appalled, so was Willi Zimmermann but Gesner, after the first shock, was indignant and felt himself very hard done by indeed.

'How dare a successful advokat let his daughter become an operetta dancer!' was his outraged cry. 'Dancers usually have only mothers who are as silly as they are. What is the world coming to when professional men allow their daughters to go on the stage!'

Fortunately, a few hours in Gesner's presence had convinced the advokat that to force Gesner into marriage with the girl would only be compounding one disaster with another infinitely worse. The sobbing girl had been returned to Vienna and Gesner had been threatened with public exposure. The girl, in the first flush of her despair, had made a rather ineffectual attempt at suicide when Gesner had disclaimed all responsibility – all of which made for highly delectable gutter press news. Only the combined pleas of the Direktor and the Burgermeister, and the payment of a large sum of money, had kept the affair out of the newspapers.

'So,' said Busacher to Willi, still lost in his trance. 'If I have now solved the problem of my soprano, and it is by no means definite, I still have the lesser problem of finding a dancer who will not be seduced by Gesner. And a few other problems as well.'

This season Hochhauser was to have a new production. For the very first time in their impecunious history they had found enough money to stage a production of *The Count of Luxembourg* with their own specially designed sets and costumes.

A rather prickly and reserved English woman (from her forbidding outward appearance it was difficult to believe she was capable of such frothy and colourful stage work) had been hired by Busacher because she was a) cheaper than a home-grown designer because of the current international exchange rates, b) had a particular aptitude for designing apparently lavish musicals on a lower than average budget, and c) spoke very good German, which was essential if she was to work with Austrian scene builders and costume makers. Franz Busacher was very pleased to have got her, but their consultations to date had not exactly helped to lift his general depression. Madge Grimsilk replied to his questions in monosyllables, never smiled, and on her preliminary visit to Hochhauser had studiously rejected all invitations from both himself and Willi Zimmermann to eat a meal together or even share a morning coffee at the Franz Joseph. In the old days, when he had worked on productions in Vienna and Salzburg, it was customary for the Direktor and the designer to spend many cheerful hours together before the production dates, exchanging ideas, discussing new and outrageous angles that could never possibly be put into practice (*The Merry Widow* in a New Orleans jazz cellar?) but out of which came a sparkling of something new, a fusion of ideas between direction and design which would give, eventually, something different, hopefully brilliant, to an old and slightly stale operetta theme. With Miss Grimsilk – neither he nor Willi had dared address her as Madge – there had been no such interflow of ideas. He had talked at first in German, then in English when he appeared to be getting no response, and she had listened with an expressionless face. He was waiting now for her first sketches and designs, and waiting with a sinking sense that he might have made a terrible mistake in employing her. In his worst moments he imagined a *Count of Luxembourg* set in a Carmelite monastery with everyone wearing costumes of black, grey and brown. There was still time to get rid of Miss Grimsilk and employ another designer but the expense would be more than their little company could stand. If worse came to worse, he thought gloomily, they would have to hire the old sets and costumes from Vienna as usual. It was just one more problem in a sea of complications.

'You see, Willi, even if we can get over all the hurdles of persuading Gesner to accept Therese Aschmann, we still have this problem of a dancer. And I have the formidable Madge Grimsilk about to submit her gloomy designs, and on top of everything else, the accountants are coming in on Thursday to go through the budgets and warn me about extravagance. Ha!'

Willi still didn't answer.

'Are you all right, Willi?' Busacher asked.

'Oh, yes.'

'Not feeling ill?'

'No.'

'So what do you think? Will it work with Aschmann? If we give her every encouragement and support her throughout the Season, do you think it will work? I'll get Madge Grimsilk to design something special for her – we'll find a bit extra out of the budget for her wardrobe. She'll need all the help she can get. Hans says she is only about forty-four but she looks nearer fifty.'

'She was the most beautiful woman I ever saw!'

'What?'

'Therese Aschmann. I saw her three times, in *Manon*, in *Die Fledermaus* and again in *Gypsy Baron*. She was the most beautiful Saffi I ever saw – the most beautiful woman I ever saw – after Gerda, of course.' He spoke in tones of tender eloquence. Willi was very emotional. He often cried in operettas, even the badly performed ones.

'Yes . . . well. You must understand, Willi, that the years have not dealt kindly with her. She's been short of money, and fairly badly shattered by the husband. God knows what those years following the débâcle were like, sheer hell one imagines.'

'Nobody can change that much. She may be a little older, but nothing could diminish that kind of beauty. I cannot believe she is coming here, to Hochhauser, to our little theatre, our little season. Aschmann . . . I cannot wait to see her.'

'Now look here, Willi. There's no use expecting someone you saw twenty years ago. You'll only hurt her if you expect that and then let her see that you hardly recognize her. I didn't recognize her at all.'

'I shall,' said Willi instantly.

'She's not beautiful any more, Willi,' the Direktor said in tones of exasperation. 'I keep telling you, she's fat, and has faded hair and a sort of grey look about her. She was lovely as a girl. I remember that. But it's all gone and we have to start from there. Not try and pretend she's what she used to be.'

'I shan't have to pretend,' said Willi, and the Direktor wanted to slap him.

'I hope you're going to be a little more constructive about the productions this season than you are about Aschmann,' he said testily. 'We have many more problems to sort out than usual, and you're not really being very much help, just sitting there mooning about Aschmann like an adolescent boy.'

Willi, with one of his effervescent, chameleon-like changes of character, suddenly broke into a mischievous grin and filled his glass from the wine bottle.

'I have a suggestion to make about one of your other problems, Franz. While you have been gallivanting in Vienna with Therese Aschmann, I have been giving serious consideration to the question of a replacement dancer for the season.'

'Oh yes,' said Franz morosely.

'Let us examine. What is our perennial problem with regard to the opera dancer?'

'Don't be pompous, Willi. You know the problem as well as everyone else in the company. Gesner.'

'And why does Gesner always manage to seduce our dancer, making her either pregnant – in this day and age too! – quite incredible – or attempt suicide, or merely weep all over the stage in the final production?'

'Why?' Busacher shrugged. 'Because dancers are like that, I suppose. Eighteen-year-old girls who have spent most of their lives in a dance studio aren't used to men; they're usually naïve, and just, well, young, I suppose.'

'Young. Away from their mothers – who are often as silly as they are – and very susceptible to a persuasive older man.'

'I don't see how you can solve that, Willi.'

'I am suggesting Suzi Hoflin, who runs the children's dancing school in the town, who is not exactly a professional ballerina, but quite good enough for our productions and has had proper training and all the right bits of paper. She is very pretty. She lives with her mother and father, whose farm is next to mine, and she has a very handsome boyfriend whom she will eventually marry.'

'Who is that?'

'My son.'

The Direktor was silent for a moment, considering.

'How bad is she? The dancing I mean.'

'Quite good enough for a few gypsy romps and some pretty solos. She is very athletic, has a beautiful figure – quite remarkable legs, my son is very fortunate – and her mother, although a farmer's wife, had rather grand ideas. Suzi, against her father's wishes, spent three years at a school in Vienna that specializes in music, dancing, and the theatre. She wouldn't be good enough for the *Volksoper* but she's quite good enough for us. She organized the dancing at last year's festival at the Schloss, you may remember. You said how pretty it all looked.'

Busacher recalled the *son et lumière* at the Schloss – a quite efficient little masque and some folk dancing that was reasonably proficient.

'It might just do, Willi,' he mused. 'Parents on guard, home each night to mother, in love with your son. It might just do.'

'She's also quite a good dancing teacher. She'll be able to line up the young chorus singers into a bit of ensemble work, could probably also bring a few of her older pupils in if we needed some crowd dancing. You used some of her girls for the children in *Countess Maritza* the year before last.'

A resident choreographer was another luxury Hochhauser had had to do without. Busacher had picked up enough experience over the years to stage a few waltz scenes, and muddle through. Once or twice he had hired as cheap a choreographer as he could find just to design some new groupings and dance routines, and had then used them again and again, every time they brought back an old production. He was rather inclined to think that, providing you had some pretty girls in bright costumes, you could slide through the dance routines if you took them at a fast enough pace. They probably wouldn't have to pay too much for this girl either. He began to feel quite cheerful. If Aschmann came, and they took on this dancer, that would only leave all the normal problems, like Gesner, and finance, and sorting out the combination of his geriatric and infant singers, and trying to make Ingrid better than she was. And of course, the new production and the worry of Madge Grimsilk. He gave Willi an approving smile.

'Tell this little girl . . . Suzi Hoflin, you said? Tell her to come and see me tomorrow. At the Spa Rooms. She can dance a couple of little pieces for me and we'll see if she'll do. Thank you, Willi!'

But Willi was gazing into his wine glass again, looking back twenty years at the memory of Therese Aschmann.

As the little Burgermeister left the road for the mountain track which led to his farm, he was conscious that, for once, the sense of desolation that usually overtook him as this point was missing, curiously submerged in the excitement of Aschmann. He was ebullient, fat, jolly, and he made everyone laugh. But like most clowns, most extroverts, he had moments of misery, ranging from just sadness to profound despair. He hated coming home each night to a house empty of Gerda. It wasn't an empty house, for

Georg was usually there, but there came a point on the mountain track every night when he looked up and saw the light in the window and knew that when he entered the kitchen it would be empty, the house would be scrupulously tidy, and Georg would be working in the office. Since Mitzi, his dachshund, had died, there was no-one to come forward and welcome him, no-one even to say good evening, for if he wasn't there promptly at seven every night to eat his supper with Georg, his son would lock himself away with his record sheets and milking charts and not emerge until it was time for bed. Willi hated walking into his lonely home.

But tonight the memory of Aschmann, the possibility of her coming to Hochhauser and staying there for a whole season, blotted out the depression of the silent house.

He and Gerda had seen Aschmann together. They had gone up to Vienna for a little holiday and every night they'd gone to the *Staatsoper*, the *Theater an der Wien*, or the *Volksoper*. Georg had stayed with Frau Hoflin, and he and Gerda had had the most romantic week of their lives, a sort of delayed honeymoon.

When they'd first got married they had no money and no time for a honeymoon. They had just bought the farm and were worried about their debts and loans from the bank. They couldn't afford any help and he and Gerda had worked alongside each other, Gerda doing as many of the rough, hard jobs as he did, desperate to make their small farm pay. Then, when Georg was nine, they had taken their little honeymoon. He'd bought Gerda a late engagement ring that he hadn't been able to afford before, and they'd stayed in a good hotel with a private bathroom and one night they'd had supper in their room. It had been the most glorious time of their lives. And Therese Aschmann embodied the whole of that wonderful lazy week when he and Gerda had felt young, and glamorous, and romantic.

There was a part of him, the practical part, that knew that he and Gerda had never been glamorous and romantic, at least, not on the outside. He had always been short and tubby, and he had lost his hair quite young, so that now he had just a frill of wiry brown curls round a bald crown. He'd always been able to make people laugh, though, the way he bounced about like a rubber ball and struck comical attitudes. Gerda too, if truth be told, hadn't really been beautiful, just as short and round as he was, a neat well-scrubbed little mountain girl who was an excellent cook – they both loved food – and a tireless farmer's wife.

But beneath those prosaic exteriors lurked the Willi and Gerda they both longed to be, wildly romantic, he handsome, she beautiful, both filled with poignant, vague longings for the kind of emotional riches that only happened to beautiful people. Sometimes, in the evenings, after they'd discussed the cows and the pastures and the milk yields and the bank loan, he would open a bottle of wine (not the best) and they would sit in the firelight listening to their favourite opera and operetta music. If they weren't too tired he would pull her to her feet and they would waltz round the room singing to one another the words they knew by heart. They would dream of all the wonderful places they were going to visit one day, when they had the money and the farm could be left. Paris, Venice, Rome, all the places they knew from operettas. The trip to Vienna was just the first of these magical trips. Bitterly, it had proved to be the last as well, for the following year Gerda had died, quite swiftly, in his arms, out in the chicken run where he'd seen her fall. She just had time to say, in a surprised voice, 'Oh, Willi, I *do* love you,' and then she'd died, her heart worn out by the heavy work she had so happily shouldered over the years.

He had wanted to die too. He'd found that the grand passions of opera, of romantic tragedy, of Manon dying in Lescaut's arms, of Tosca standing by the body of her dead lover, didn't help him at all when it came to Gerda going away, leaving him and little Georg in the empty farmhouse. He missed her, and it wasn't the romantic things about her that made him cry. It was the sight of her old shoes by the kitchen door, the ones she slipped on to go and feed the hens, and the sight of her neat handwriting on the labels of cherry jam.

He survived. Funny little fat men don't die of broken hearts, not when they have a farm to run and a ten-year-old son to raise single-handed. The loneliness had been almost more than he could bear, but gradually the terrible searing despair had faded, leaving just a sad nostalgia that struck him from time to time. The years had brought him compensations. His farm had done well, he had become a respected and highly valued figure in Hochhauser, serving on many councils and committees, finally being voted on to the *Gemeinderat* and elected Burgermeister. He had bought more land and Georg had grown into a fine young man, a good son with advanced ideas about farming. Georg didn't want to go off to the city like so many other young men these days. Georg wanted to stay and build the farm into an even bigger property.

He'd been to Vienna many times in recent years, on business, as head of the theatre committee of Hochhauser, to get grants for the theatre, but somehow he could never bear to go to the opera houses in Vienna, not without Gerda. He'd been to theatres in Baden and Salzburg, and thoroughly enjoyed them, but in Vienna he always arranged to have business dinners in the evening so that he wouldn't have to think about seeing *Manon* and *Die Fledermaus* with Gerda. A silly and sentimental little relic of the past.

And now Therese Aschmann, who meant more to him than just a lovely voice and a great artist, was coming to Hochhauser. He was excited, strangely close to tears, and longing to talk to someone about it.

In the kitchen Frau Trauffer had left his supper ready, some cold veal and potato salad and one of his own ripe cheeses, but he walked straight past the table, through the large pine-panelled living room which was now hardly ever used, and into the farm office on the far side.

'Georg!' he said exuberantly. 'What do you think? Therese Aschmann is going to come to Hochhauser as our leading lady for the Season.'

'Good,' said Georg, not lifting his head from the pile of invoices he was busy checking against an account book.

'She was a big star, you know, in Vienna. Your mother and I saw her there twenty years ago – a very big star, and a wonderful voice. You never heard a voice like Aschmann's.'

'Good.' Georg spiked an invoice and then frowned over an entry in his ledger. 'Have you eaten, Papa? Frau Trauffer has left your supper. And Papa, do you realize the top pasture did not give nearly enough winter feed last year? I told you how it would be if you put the cows up there again in August. That field needs to be left fallow at the end of the summer months. The soil isn't good enough up there – too thin, too rocky to support sustained feeds.'

Willi gazed sadly at his son. Sometimes he wondered how he and Gerda had managed to produce this tall, strong, beautiful young man. Georg was everything to look at that his father longed to be. Over six feet tall, with strong, lean features, brilliant blue eyes and crisp blond hair, he looked as romantic as Willi felt. But there the matter ended, for Georg was not musical, didn't like the theatre, and was a computer bank of facts, farming statistics, pasture productivity and down-to-earth common sense. Willi was always telling himself how very lucky he was that Georg was such a sensible young man. He had never, to Willi's knowledge, drunk too much, experimented with drugs, or got into trouble with a girl. He had done well at school, and on the business and farming course he had taken at college. Sometimes Willi wondered if Gerda and he could have done anything, when Georg was little, to make him less prosaic. He had sadly come to the conclusion that Georg had been born the way he was and would never change.

'Georg,' he said sadly. 'Don't you care about the Hochhauser Season?'

Georg raised his head, shocked. 'Of course I do, Papa. Don't you think I realize what a difference it has made to the town? Why, we all depend on our tourist turnover for our increased prosperity. Look at the orders we get for our creams and cheeses and eggs from the hotels. And there is a new one opening up on the other side of the valley. I heard about it this morning. As soon as we know who the catering manager is we must put in our tender for supplying them.'

The Burgermeister sighed. 'Then why don't you ever go to the theatre?' he asked. 'Why have you never taken Suzi? She would love it.'

'I do not like the theatre, Papa,' Georg replied, neatly closing his ledger and placing a paperweight on the pile of invoices. 'I never could understand all those foolish games they play on the stage. They all seem so ridiculous. And Suzi is sensible like me. She knows I wouldn't like to waste money on nonsense.'

'Perhaps you'll come to see Suzi in the operetta,' Willi said mischievously. 'The Direktor is auditioning her tomorrow, to see if she will fill in and take the dancing roles for the Season.' He couldn't help it – he took a mildly malicious delight in seeing Georg's face. He loved his son dearly, but for such a young man Georg did have a tendency to be pompous.

'I don't believe it!' said Georg, shocked.

'Well, it isn't decided yet. He still has to see her. I called in on my way home and told her all about it. She was very excited.'

Georg pushed his chair back from the table and reached for his jacket. When he stood he towered over his father.

'I must go over there at once,' he said. 'I cannot think Suzi knows what she is doing.' His face was quite flushed and he sounded cross. Willi hadn't seen him so discomposed since a new strain of bacteria had got into the processing of one of their cheeses. They'd had to destroy the entire batch and get the Health Department in to sterilize the dairy.

'It's not so very terrible, is it, Georg?' he asked, smiling. 'It will only be for the summer months, and not even for every operetta. It will just mean a little extra money for her – and the pleasure of working in the theatre, of course.'

'It is outrageous,' Georg answered angrily. 'Look at them all down there – lying about sleeping all day and making fools of themselves at night. And what about that man Gesner? You told me all about that trouble last year, the girl he got pregnant. You think I want Suzi mixing with people like that!'

He flung out of the door, two bright spots of colour on his cheeks. Willi followed him, wishing he hadn't spoken but at the same time finding Georg's puritanical righteousness hilariously funny. As he walked behind Georg he puffed his cheeks out and went 'Pouf! Pouf! Pouf!' in time to Georg's angry footsteps. But Georg was away and out of the kitchen door, up over the track towards the Hoflin farm. Willi poked a plump desultory finger into his cold potato salad, decided it was unappetizing, and thought he would cook himself some fried potatoes instead.

Georg, striding angrily up the mountain track, felt again the frustration that constantly beset him when he tried to deal with people like his father, and Suzi. He loved his father, he loved Suzi, but why did they always present him with such difficult . . . such ridiculous situations? Everything was so simple if only people would do the obvious, the straightforward, the decent and honest things that made life worthwhile – cultivating land, breeding herds of pedigree dairy cows, expanding the dairies, looking forward to the day when there would be a Zimmermann cheese factory in Hochhauser. Suzi and he would live in the farmhouse but it would be enlarged out at the back, where there was a flat piece of ground that would take a two-storey extension and turn the old farmhouse into a luxury mansion.

In his mind, without wanting either Suzi's parents or his father to die, he could envisage the day when the two neighbouring farms would be combined into one, his and Suzi's. Of course, strictly speaking, at the moment it wasn't his farm and Suzi's wasn't hers. But as only children they would one day inherit, and when that time came the holding would be a magnificent one. He had already decided about the houses. The Zimmermann farmhouse was the better, slightly old-fashioned but with the extension and some modernization it would be wonderfully efficient and luxurious. The Hoflin farmhouse would be used for a farm manager and for a secondary dairy until the time when he could realize his factory project. It never occurred to Georg that he was being calculating when he made his plans. He loved Suzi's parents. As a small, lonely boy, missing his mother – his wonderful, practical mother who was so sensible and . . . unromantic, so unlike his father – he had gravitated naturally to the Hoflin household and had found in Frau Hoflin a steady, constant figure who was always the same, whilst the women who came up to clean and cook for his father constantly changed.

He and Suzi had grown up together. He had eaten there, shared in their family treats and festivals, and taken his cuts and bruises to Frau Hoflin. Suzi had been his playmate, his disciple, his adoring young acolyte who had always done whatever he had told her to do. At some point, and he couldn't remember quite when it was, he had realized that he and Suzi would one day marry. It was unthinkable that they should marry anyone else when their land lay side by side, when he was a farmer's son and she a farmer's daughter. There could be no-one else for either of them.

As Suzi had grown up she had presented him with problems. For instance, there had been the three years in Vienna. Frau Hoflin had silly ideas sometimes. She wanted, she said, Suzi to have some fun, to learn to do something frivolous and pretty. He hadn't approved of that at all, but Frau Hoflin had had her way and Suzi had gone off to school in Vienna to learn French and English and music and dancing, and she had come back looking extremely pretty and graceful and waving a few certificates and medals, and announced that she was going to set up a little dancing school for the children of Hochhauser. She would have done much better, if she had wanted to go away to school, to go to the agricultural college, as he had. In her sweet, pretty, acquiescent way, she had agreed with everything he said, then gone ahead and set up her dancing classes. After a while he'd grown used to it. She was tactful and didn't keep talking about it, and he supposed she had to earn a living at something while she was waiting to get married. But the thought of her prancing around on the Spa room stage, mixing with the theatre riff-raff, was more than he could take.

He crossed over the top pasture, the one he and his father had disagreed over last summer and, on impulse, although he was in a hurry, he walked a few paces up the mountain and climbed on to an outcrop of rock. From this point he could look down and see both farms, both farmhouses. Here, as a boy, he had sat, wishing his mother hadn't died, and deriving comfort from the fact that he could see the Hoflin farm, where Frau Hoflin lived. Here, when he was twelve, he had brought the six-year-old Suzi and showed her the two farms. 'We have the best farms in the valley, Suzi,' he had said. 'And our mountain is the best mountain, and our cows the best cows.' And all the way back to the Hoflin house Suzi had joined in the game, singing 'our hens are the best hens' and 'our fields are the best fields' right through to the milking buckets and ploughs and feed corn and every single thing on the farm.

He stood for a moment on the outcrop which was covered in a very thin sprinkling of snow. It was a clean, crisp night. The stars were clear and a light breeze, chilly, touched by ice, blew down from the top of the mountain – their mountain – his and Suzi's. This was their land and he never wanted to leave it. Suzi and the land went together. Without one he couldn't envisage the other.

He saw the lights in the Hoflin farmhouse, thought of Suzi drifting away from him in the silly world of the theatre, and had to fight down a blinding rage. He began to bound down the mountainside, not bothering to find the track, jumping in the snow and the wet patches of mud where the snow had melted. His father would have been surprised to see him behaving so impulsively.

He knocked on the kitchen door and walked in. There was no-one there but he could hear voices from the living room, and then Frau Hoflin called out.

'Is that you, Georg? Come in.'

'Suzi . . .'

Suzi's face was flushed and her eyes bright. 'Have you heard the news, Georg? I am to audition for the Direktor tomorrow – for the Operetta Season. They need someone to do the dance spots. You see! Those three years in Vienna weren't wasted. I shall be paid a salary and be a proper part of the company! Aschmann is coming. I haven't heard of her but your father was very excited because she used to be a big star.'

For a moment he couldn't speak, couldn't think. It was on occasions like this that Suzi and his father became totally incomprehensible to him.

'Suzi! It's ridiculous. I won't let you do it!'

Herr Hoflin stood up and turned the television off. Both he and Suzi's mother were looking at him rather oddly.

'What's ridiculous about it?' asked Suzi coldly.

'Well – you – to dance, prance about on a stage with hardly any clothes on. You're a farmer's daughter. You can't behave like that.'

'I have no intention of prancing about with hardly any clothes on. What do you think the Hochhauser Season is – the *Folies Bergère*? And if Herr Busacher and the theatre committee think I can be taken seriously as a dancer then it surely doesn't matter whether I'm a farmer's daughter or a . . . or a . . .' she spluttered away into silence.

Georg began to feel sick. He knew it would be all right in the end: Suzi would see how silly it all was and would agree with him. But he had never encountered such defiance from her before.

69

'But Suzi, you cannot agree to this. You cannot consider it for one moment.'

'I have considered it,' she snapped – Suzi never snapped at him. She was calm and capable like her mother. 'And if I am offered the spot I shall take it.'

'But, Suzi. We do not like that kind of thing, you and I. We have no time for the theatre. We do not like it.'

'I like it very much,' said Suzi rudely. 'I have always liked it. In Vienna I loved the theatre. I went as often as I could. And I never thought that anyone would ask *me* to dance in Lehar and Strauss. Do you realize there's a brand new production of *The Count of Luxembourg*? And I shall have my own solo in Act Two?'

Frau Hoflin came across and stood by her daughter. 'I don't really understand, Georg. You came with us to the *son et lumière* at the Schloss, when Suzi led the masque. You enjoyed it.'

'That was different. It was history. And everyone in the town took part. And it was to advertise the anniversary of the town. It was different.'

'I'm sorry, Georg, but we don't see that it's different at all.'

There was a tense silence in the room. Then Georg said, 'I would like to speak with Suzi alone please. Suzi, get your coat.'

For one dreadful moment he thought she was going to say no. Then she shrugged and went out into the hall. He helped her on with her coat, watched while she thrust her long elegant legs into boots, and followed her silently out through the door. When they were outside he tried to take hold of her arm but she shook him off.

'Why didn't you ask me before you agreed to go for this ridiculous test tomorrow?'

'Georg, if you use that word ridiculous once more I shall hit you.'

'Why didn't you ask me?'

'Because I knew you'd say you didn't want me to do it. Because I knew I'd have to go through all this.'

Georg tried to muster all his self-control. 'Well, you'll just have to tell him you don't want the job. Herr Busacher will have to find someone else, because I forbid you to do this foolish, embarrassing thing. You're a farmer's daughter, not a dancer, and when we're married I don't want people remembering that my wife once pranced about on the stage of the old Spa Rooms.'

'Ha!' shouted Suzi, her temper finally snapping. 'Who said anything about us being married?'

He was so astonished he couldn't speak.

'I have no intention of marrying you!' she shouted, even louder.

'But of course you will. Everyone knows that. We've always known it.'

'I don't know it,' she cried. 'You've never asked me. You've never even said you love me. You don't even have time to take me out properly.'

'That's ridiculous,' he spluttered. 'We've always known we would get married. You know I love you. Would we marry if I didn't love you?'

She was suddenly quiet, worn out by the swift fight, by the effort of trying to make him understand.

'But you see, Georg, I'm not really sure that I love you any more.'

'Suzi . . .'

'I can't imagine my life without you in it, because you've always been around, ever since I can remember. You were good to me when I was small. You always looked after me, you were never impatient, but I think we've grown up now. I know what you want, Georg, the life you plan for us, the future all neatly docketed and entered into one of your ledgers. But you don't know what I want. You've never taken the trouble to find out.'

He was trying not to take any of this seriously. He knew it was all a stage-struck fever brought on by the malaise of the wretched theatre.

'I don't believe any of what you're saying, Suzi. You were always happy with me before. It's just this operetta nonsense. It's made you doubt all the things we'd planned for the future, being married and . . . the farms . . . everything . . .' he choked suddenly, then braced his back and stood rigid.

'Georg,' she said gently. '*We* never planned anything. You did all the planning. You never asked me to marry you. You've never said you loved me. You've never asked me what I'd like for the future. You've never really seen that I've grown up. You still treat me as though I'm six and you're twelve. You still order me about and tell me what to do. Georg, even if you ask me to marry you, I don't think I could. I'm going back now. I don't want to talk about this any more because we'll both of us say things that will hurt. I just think we need some time as two separate people.'

'Suzi!' he cried. 'Please, be sensible!'

She didn't even turn her head. 'I'm tired of being sensible, Georg,' she said softly as she walked away. 'I'm tired of sitting watching television with you, of our once-a-month visit to the cinema, which you don't really enjoy either. I'm tired of being

71

given books about farming and cookery and cheesemaking for my birthday. I'm tired of never having a compliment paid to me, except that I'm sensible. I'm tired of never going out for a meal with wine and music because you can't spare the time from the farm and don't want to waste your money. And Georg . . .' she had arrived back at the house, and with one hand on the latch she turned and looked back at him. 'I'm tired of cows. I hate cows.' She went in and shut the door very carefully and quietly behind her.

He stared at the door, his world smashed and lying about him.

He felt the same terrible sense of disorientation he had felt when he was ten and his mother died. But this time he couldn't run to Frau Hoflin.

CHAPTER FOUR

Busacher and Hans Kramer got to Sachers well in advance of the other two. They needed to do a bit of private plotting before Therese and Gesner met.

'What did she say about *Luxembourg*?' Busacher asked, waving the waiter away with a 'Later . . . later . . .'

'A little *bouleversée*, I think. I only spoke with her on the telephone and she asked if she could ring me back. I think she wishes it were not that particular operetta, but she finally sounded quite determined and said there would be no problem.'

'And did you speak to Gesner personally, when you set up the meeting?'

'Yes. He knew of her, of course – he's quite a bit older than he makes out, isn't he? – but they never worked together in the old days. She was bigger than he was at that time. He knew, vaguely, of the scandal, not the details, but just that there was some scandal. He didn't seem too interested in that.'

'Yes . . . well . . . he has plenty of scandals of his own to occupy him,' said the Direktor dryly.

'However, he said that he did want to hear her sing. Suggested coming to my studio with her, but I managed to fumble through that one.'

'If he insists on hearing her sing, we shall have to let him.'

'I think I've solved that particular problem. I sent him a tape of her singing the Bach chorale in the cathedral.'

The Direktor smiled approvingly. 'Clever,' he applauded. The chorale wouldn't hide the quality of the voice, but by its very nature the work brought out the purity, the control, the lack of emotional passion. The chorale wouldn't give any indication of what that voice could do in an acting role.

'What exactly was the problem with Hanna Brunner last season? We all know she refused to work with him, that he had behaved even more appallingly that usual, but what made last year's débâcle worse than any other season's?'

'Hanna was getting too good,' the Direktor shrugged. 'You know last winter she sang in London and Munich? She's been getting excellent notices and she has also acquired some striking stage techniques. Gesner's no fool. He could tell the audiences were beginning to like her as much as him. Nice-looking singer too. Once or twice she made him look his real age.'

'Hmm.'

'At least there won't be that problem with Therese.' The Direktor sighed and thought for a moment how good it would be to be back in Vienna, taking his pick of the best singers and actors, not having to think about the problems of making two middle-aged soloists look like young lovers. Then he thought about *his* theatre, *his* company, his undisputed dictatorship over the whole of the Hochhauser Season (well, apart from Gesner's casting approval and Willi Zimmermann's tendency to interfere in matters of production) and realized that, like Gesner, he rather enjoyed being the large frog in a small pond, especially when he had created the pond in the first place.

'Here she comes,' said Hans, and the two Viennese rose to their feet. She was wearing the blue suit again, the one she had worn for the audition, but rather surprisingly, draped over her shoulder was a brilliant shawl, a whirl of colours, blues, reds, purples, greens. It made her look younger than she had at her audition. Busacher bent over her hand, and Hans pulled out a chair. Therese smiled, and the Direktor was struck once more by the incongruity of the youthful smile on the tired face.

'Now, Therese, all I ask is that you will be quietly pleasant to Gesner. He can – sometimes – be quite charming, but it is more likely he will be impolite. But just remember that when you get to Hochhauser you will be surrounded by old friends. Not just myself. Alfred Bahr is our baritone, Freddi Bartmann the basso, and Luiza our mezzo – you remember Luiza, yes? And many of our chorus will be known to you. The youngsters you will not know, Ingrid, our soubrette, and Rudi, our second tenor, but they are nice children, very enthusiastic. We all work very happily together.'

'I shall enjoy it very much, Herr Busacher.'

'Shall we order? Karl is sure to be late.'

The pastries had arrived, and Therese was pouring the tea, when there was a slight stirring from the other side of the restaurant. The Direktor saw him at once and had to concede, not for the first time, that Gesner had presence. He was able, within a few seconds, to make every eye turn towards him. The buzz of conversation in the café died down as everyone's attention was focused on the tall figure in the theatrical cloak standing just inside the entrance. A waiter hurried over but Gesner flung one hand towards Busacher's table, managing, at the same time, to reveal a flash of scarlet lining, and the waiter bowed himself away. As he came towards them he began to unbuckle the large silver clasp (a gift from a devoted female fan) that held the cloak over his magnificent shoulders. He crossed to the table and stood, towering over them, looking down. Therese, studying for the first time the man who was to be her partner for five months, felt dwarfed and insignificant.

'Madame!' He bowed very slightly, extended a hand towards her but removed it quickly before she could reach out her own.

'Hans. Herr Direktor.' He flung himself carelessly into the remaining chair and stretched out strong, elegant legs into the space between the tables. A waiter tripped, recovered, mumbled '*Bitte um Entschuldigung*' and grovelled away.

Busacher cleared his throat. 'Therese, this is Karl Gesner, our tenor, and Karl, Therese Aschmann.'

The arrogant dark eyes ran slowly over her face, then down to her body, or what he could see above the table. He swayed to one side and looked down at the part of her below the table. Then he raised one eyebrow.

'So,' he said, and shrugged.

'Would you like some tea?' Therese asked, flushing. She felt shocked at his rudeness, but was determined to be cool and unaroused.

'No.'

Hans cleared his throat, raised his cup to his mouth and gave a nervous noisy slurp. 'You received the tape I sent you?' he asked.

'Yes.'

An uncomfortable silence fell over the table. Gesner suddenly saw someone he knew on the other side of the restaurant, rose, strode across and there were five minutes of effusive kissing and greetings and protestations of undying friendship and future meetings. Then he returned, making a great point of not looking at Therese.

'Therese has been absent from the stage for some time.' The Direktor thought it was time to call him, very gently, to order. 'But of course, in the old days she worked with me many times. *Manon*, *Traviata*, *Fledermaus*, *Hoffman*, and several of the Lehar and Kalman operettas. She is most interested in returning to the operetta stage. For my part,' he smiled towards her and placed his hand over hers, 'I should be delighted to work with her again.'

Gesner shrugged. 'If you wish to have her in the Company I see no reason why you should not. We have several of your old singers with us, what is one more? But what of my leading lady?'

'Don't be so bloody rude!' said Hans angrily. Gesner was not one of his clients so he had nothing to lose. 'You know very well why you're here . . . to meet Therese and approve her – or not – as your lead soprano.'

Therese fumbled for her handbag on the floor beneath her chair. 'Excuse me, Hans, Herr Busacher.'

'Please don't leave, Therese.'

White-faced she stared at him, and he suddenly realized she was very, very angry. 'I am not leaving, Herr Direktor. I am going to the cloakroom. I shall return in a few moments when I am . . . calmer.' She stared at Gesner who was still pointedly ignoring her, looked as though she were going to speak, then pursed her lips together and walked away.

'Karl! How could you!'

'And how could *you*! Do you want to make me look ridiculous on the stage? What kind of joke do you think you are playing – how will it look, Karl Gesner making love to a fat old Frau, the romantic Karl Gesner trying to waltz his mother around the stage? You might as well give me Luiza!'

'You are being deliberately difficult. You know what lights and costumes will do. You had Anna Latti three years ago – she's no chicken. We managed to make it work.'

'Latti was quite well preserved. Compared with that . . . that lumpy old hag, Latti was a girl. I shall be laughed off the stage!'

'For God's sake, Franz,' Hans said. 'Why don't you get rid of the man? I'm damned if I'd have him singing on any stage of mine.'

'I sing where I like!' Gesner had worked himself up into one of his rages and several of the people sitting near were staring at him. 'They can't get rid of me. I'm too important. Who do you think attracts the audiences?' He thumped his chest. 'Me. Who do you think manages to pull that pathetic bunch of amateurs and worn-out old pros into a company? Me. If I didn't sing, there would be no Hochhauser Season.'

'And if you don't have a soprano there will be no season,' retorted Busacher. 'We have to have someone who can sing. If you think you'll look ridiculous acting with a . . . a fat old Frau . . . then reflect how much more ridiculous it will be with someone who can't sing.'

'You can get me someone else,' he shouted. 'There are plenty of sopranos. Just get me a reasonable singer who doesn't look like my grandmother.'

He became aware that people around him were looking towards them with interest, but he was totally unperturbed. He turned his head slowly round the restaurant, glaring scornfully at the staring faces until they quickly averted their eyes and began to fumble with cups and pastry forks.

'All right,' said Hans silkily. 'I guess it will have to be Hanna Brunner again.' As the Direktor raised his eyebrows Hans frowned very slightly at him. 'She has had some excellent offers for next season – Covent Garden has come forward, I hear, and the *Staatsoper* is considering a major role for her. But that will not be until September. She is prepared to come to Hochhauser for the first four months. That will give us time to find someone for the end of the Season. And, of course, with Hanna's growing reputation, you would have a quite brilliant opening. It wouldn't matter too much if the end of the Season tailed off a little.'

'I do not want Hanna,' said Gesner sulkily. 'We do not get on. We are not suited temperamentally on the stage. She cannot act, she cannot dance.'

'Come now, Karl,' said the Direktor, thinking to himself that Hans, in many ways, earned his ten per cent. 'You know that is not true. You only have to think of her notices last season, and her calls. She was one of the most popular sopranos we've ever had at Hochhauser. I only wish we could count on her for every production. It might give a new direction to our season.'

'I do not want her. Find me someone else.'

'There is no-one else, Karl. You must understand that you are not very . . . popular in our profession.' Gesner prepared to bristle. 'Oh yes, the audiences love you, but the singers do not. I have tried every agent in Vienna, and all we have offered to us is Aschmann . . . and Hanna, of course. I cannot think why she is prepared to come again. You were most unpleasant to her last year.'

'She likes the mountains,' mumbled Hans weakly.

'Why can't you give Ingrid the roles?' Gesner asked with the air of one who knew it was a stupid question.

'You know very well why. You yourself complained last year when she had to take Hanna's roles for three nights. Her voice cracked and she couldn't maintain her performances. She's all right for one or two second leads – we might even try her in a lead spot of her own this year if that is what you want. But if she had to sustain a whole season she wouldn't have a voice at all.'

'You are seeing Aschmann at her worst.' Hans was now prepared to be conciliatory. 'She has been ill for some time. In fact she is only forty-four.' He ignored Gesner's guffaw of incredulity. 'She is most certainly going to lose weight and you know yourself what wigs, costumes, make-up can do. The voice will not let you down. Think of those duets in *Luxembourg*. If you have a weak singer it will make you seem off balance. And, in any case, it is better to have a partner who is too old, than one too young. Better that your adoring fans should say you are waltzing with your mother than with your daughter.'

Gesner's eyes narrowed and there was a long silence while he glowered at the table. 'She looks so old,' he grumbled finally. Busacher sensed they were on the home run.

'Everyone looks old at the end of the winter. And she's been ill, as Hans said. Karl, you really don't have any choice, believe me. I have searched, hunted, for weeks. It is either Aschmann, or Hanna again.'

'I do not want Hanna.'

'Then you will have to settle for Therese.'

Gesner picked up a pastry fork and stabbed it savagely into a piece of strudel. 'I suppose I shall have to have her then. At least I can take comfort – some comfort! from the fact that a woman as lifeless as that will not have any prima donna tricks. She will know her place. Are you sure she's a competent singer? That would be the last straw, if the voice wasn't up to it.'

'You heard the tape.'

'Yes.' A faint frown crossed his face. 'Yes. That was all right. Uninspired, but that's what she is. But I suppose it was quite good for her age.'

Just wait until you hear her singing lyric roles, the Direktor thought to himself gloatingly. You're in for a shock, Gesner old friend. Oh, what a surprise you're going to have!

'So,' said Hans equably. 'Shall we return to my office and sign the contract?'

They saw Therese, with an excellent sense of timing, making her way back through the tables. She had renewed her make-up and recovered her equilibrium.

'Therese,' Busacher stood, holding out his hand. 'It has been agreed. You are coming to Hochhauser.'

She looked at Gesner with loathing. She had decided that the only way she was going to be able to work with him, to prevent him from totally demoralizing her, was to hate him, consider him less than dirt. But already the old stage skills, the gift of acting was coming back. She smiled. It was a mirthless smile, but nonetheless a smile. The contract wasn't signed yet.

'I'm honoured,' she said. 'It will be a great privilege to sing with the famous Karl Gesner.'

'Yes,' said Gesner. 'It will.'

The day wasn't done for the Direktor. Madge Grimsilk had flown in from London that morning with her preliminary designs. He was feeling tired. A bout with Gesner always left him exhausted and he would have liked to climb on the train and sleep his way back to Hochhauser. But they couldn't afford to let more time slip past before putting the building of the set and the creation of the costumes into production. Madge Grimsilk had come out to Hochhauser at the beginning of January to see the theatre and spend a little time with the production team. It was during that week that Busacher and Willi had begun to wonder if they'd made the right decision. Miss Grimsilk's portfolio had appeared to be impressive and her price was low, but what a sour lady, said Willi, who could usually manage to winkle some smiles out of the most forbidding characters.

Franz had met her once since then, in London, a brief and equally oppressive meeting when she had given him a timetable of dates, and when she would submit first drawings, second drawings, the model, when she would arrive in Hochhauser, when the set would be finished. Franz had been horrified. Designers didn't work like that, as though they were civil servants or mathematicians. In his experience, although they had a degree of reliability, they were usually late turning in the final designs and often did a great deal of tweaking about in the later stages, not knowing quite *when* this costume would be finished, or putting last touches on to the set at the dress rehearsal or even just before the curtain went up on the first night. His blood ran cold at the awful English efficiency projected by Miss Grimsilk.

Because Hochhauser was paying for her trip to Vienna, she was staying at a very cheap hotel on the Wiedner Gürtel, right opposite the sidings of the *Sudbahnhof*. As he waited in the tiny reception area the noise of the trains, and of the tram terminus outside was deafening. When he was sent up to her room he found it was even more deafening. Her window, at the front of the hotel, looked out right over the station.

Her room was very small and had one chair. Madge Grimsilk had left it free for him and was perched primly on the edge of the bed as though, he thought with a flash of humour, she was suspicious of being alone in an hotel room with a Viennese, even one as old as he.

'Miss Grimsilk,' he said, taking her cold hand in his for a second. 'Did you have a pleasant flight?'

'Thank you.'

'The hotel is comfortable, I hope?'

'Thank you.'

'And you've done your drawings for the production?'

This was where the designer usually burst into descriptive prose. Flights of fancy came bursting forth . . . 'I have taken my inspiration from a flower garden in Provence – you will see the scheme carried through in colours and symbols.' Or, 'I thought we should stress the humour of this production and base it on clowns and tumblers.' Madge Grimsilk said absolutely nothing. She undid the tape on her portfolio and left him to open it and turn the pages himself. Then she walked over to the window and glared out. With a sinking heart he turned to the first sketch.

At first he was puzzled. She had drawn not just the stage, but the whole of his little theatre, as though standing at the entrance at the back of the stalls. Then, as he looked, he saw that his theatre had changed. The chandelier in the centre of the ceiling was surrounded by hanging icicles, diamonds, spheres. Garlands of ribbons were swathed all round the front of the balcony and down the pillars at the sides. He turned the page. It was the same view but in colour, beautifully drawn and painted in water colours. The ceiling was turned into one mass of glittering light with his chandelier as the centrepiece. The colours of the cleverly constructed ribbon garlands suggested huge swags of flowers covering the walls. At the bottom of the sketch, in Madge Grimsilk's neat handwriting was the noted description:

'Swathes composed of dyed gauze and synthetic lining fabric, folded to suggest flowers. Cheaper than artificial flowers.'

And why couldn't she have told me that, he thought, puzzled. It's quite beautiful, and clever. Why didn't she begin by telling me she wanted to turn the whole theatre into a ballroom?

He turned the page again. It showed the stage, which had become an enchanted alcove, part of the whole ballroom that was his theatre. The alcove, festooned with more garlands and gauze, looked out on to an enchanted forest floating in mist. It reminded him of a fairy ballet set. It was ethereal, magic, very different from the usual type of set designed for a Lehar production. For the first time Miss Grimsilk spoke without being asked to.

'You said you had a difficult and limited cast to blend together. I thought we'd make the whole thing look like a fairy tale or fantasy, a Cinderella ballroom; that way the characters could be anything you wanted them to be, old, young, funny, fat, unreal. I know Lehar is supposed to be full-blooded and erotic, and, in a romantic way, quite realistic. I thought we'd leave out the full-blooded bit, concentrate on the erotic and make it all slightly other-worldish.' Her German was faultless. Much later he realized that, strangely for an Englishwoman, it wasn't German, but Austrian. How had she come to speak the idiom of Vienna rather than correct English college German?

He turned the page again. Act One: The usual Paris street scene was a simple front cloth, but again painted to look like a scene from a medieval fairy tale. It was Paris all right – but the Paris of Perrault. She had drawn a set of figures dancing across the front of the stage, funny masque-like figures, right for the carnival scene, but even righter when you realized that some of the figures were fat elderly goblins and others were dressed liked burghers' wives from the Pied Piper of Hamelin.

'What about the artist's studio? The screen scene. Where are you going to fit that?'

'In the alcove of the ballroom. The Act Three hotel foyer will be there also. Lighting will change the backcloth view. You'll see, if you turn over, that back lighting will make the same forest scene look different every time. You said you couldn't afford anything too ambitious. There's only one backcloth; a front cloth and the dressing of the alcove will provide all the other scene changes.'

He couldn't believe it. Page after page revealed something infinitely refreshing, different. He looked across at the dour, forbidding Madge Grimsilk and wondered how these magical ideas had emerged from that unsmiling, unanimated face.

'You also said you didn't do too much dancing in your productions, so I haven't worried about space apart from the Act Two ball scene when we open up the whole stage. In a theatre as tiny as yours we can keep some of the other scenes quite intimate. I would suggest that at the end of Act Three, the hotel foyer, we suddenly open out again into the ballroom. Take poetic licence and move everyone back into fairyland.'

He found he was suddenly breathing quite quickly. It tended to happen when he was excited and he made a conscious effort to control the tension. It had been a long day and he was tired. He turned the pages again, came to the costumes, again the fairy-tale theme carried through, some of them quite grotesque, others pure fantasy, some just hazily beautiful. It was the perfect answer for his mixed bag of a company. Always before they had had to push themselves into the standard hired costumes of earlier productions, trying to make everyone look like the original Viennese cast, whatever their size or age.

Gesner was going to look superb, like the hero of a Russian fairy tale.

'They're magnificent,' he said quietly. 'I would like to take them back to Hochhauser and study them a little. Perhaps, if you have no other commitments, you could come out and stay a couple weeks with us, to meet the cast. Some of the costumes – perhaps a little too fantastical. When you meet the cast you will understand what I mean.'

'I think that will be convenient. The model will be ready in a month. I'll bring it out and stay for two weeks.'

'Thank you.' His heart was still pumping and it wasn't just tiredness, but excitement. In his great days he'd had famous designers and wonderful stages. But they were taken for granted – in a famous theatre you expected the best. This, his first new production at Hochhauser, could be as exciting as anything he'd done before and no-one would expect that on a provincial stage.

'I think you'll find I'm well within budget,' said Miss Grimsilk.

'Good. If there is anything over we shall need to spend it on our lead soprano. We have a problem I wasn't able to warn you about before.'

'Yes?'

'We have a singer making a comeback, a new début after eighteen years away from the stage. A wonderful lyrical voice but some problems with style and appearance. I don't think,' he said wryly, looking down at Gesner's costume drawing of a bravura prince, 'that we can quite carry the fairy-tale theme through. Therese Aschmann will be a divine singer, but there is no way you can make her look like Cinderella or the Sleeping Beauty.'

'I will redesign her costumes after I have seen her.'

'That would be wise.'

He leaned back in the chair and closed his eyes for a moment. 'I

82

would like to ask you to dinner, Miss Grimsilk, but I am afraid I must get back to Hochhauser this evening.'

'Thank you. I'm not free for dinner. I have arranged to see the set-builders and costume-makers. I wish to set up all arrangements early so that I can keep to my timetable.'

He forgave her much, because of what he had just seen. She had brought a new concept to *Luxembourg* on a cheap budget. But he wished she had a little more warmth. These thin, stringy, Englishwomen were always cold fish, he thought. If she had been more human he would have asked her to help him downstairs and call him a taxi.

'I will go down and ask the receptionist to call you a taxi,' she said coolly. 'Perhaps you would like to sit there until I come back.'

After she had left the room he turned the pages of the portfolio once more. Ideas began to come into his head, fired off by her drawings. The lighting outside the alcove could be faded into cloud, suggesting that all the intimate scenes were taking place in a private fantasy world. The Lehar quality of sensual romanticism would still be there, but it would take on a dreamlike quality.

When she came back she had brought the hotel manager to help him down the stairs.

CHAPTER FIVE

Willi, at first, couldn't see the appeal of the designs submitted by Madge Grimsilk. 'Lehar is always Viennese,' he protested. 'Even when the operetta is set in Paris or St Petersburg, it is always Viennese in style, with traditional Viennese costumes and turn of the century sets. You can't have a Lehar operetta with the audience sitting in a fairy ballroom. Think of those wonderful productions at the *Volksoper*! I am told that even in London, at Sadler's Wells and the Coliseum, they copy our Viennese style.'

'Oh, Willi! All those red velvet curtains and golden tassels, and settees with little golden legs. Aren't you tired of those productions?'

'No,' said Willi stubbornly. 'I like *Luxembourg* to be the way it always has been. It doesn't have to be quite the same, one doesn't always have to have red and gold. But the style should be the same.'

'With our budget it would be a thin imitation of the *Volksoper* productions, Willi. You know how much all those lavish ballgowns cost, all those urns and chandeliers and marble staircases and pages in imperial livery. Miss Grimsilk has found a way of giving us something exciting and original at very little cost. It was more than I could hope for. Just look at the carnival scene. Luiza will be a stout elderly witch instead of a Columbine. Much more suitable. And your little dancer, Suzi Hoflin – you were quite right about her legs – she will make the whole thing look enchanting as a watersprite or a dragonfly instead of a ballet dancer in a mask.'

'I should never have done that,' Willi said gloomily. 'Suggested Suzi as our dancer.'

'Why ever not, my friend? It was a good idea. She's not exactly

Pavlova, but what do you expect from a country girl who runs a dancing class? But she moves well and is very pretty.'

'Georg is very angry with me. He is very cold when he is angry, very polite and correct. He and Suzi have quarrelled and Georg believes it is all my fault.'

Busacher shrugged. 'Children! Mere children having a lovers' spat. You mustn't let your son intimidate you, Willi. You are always telling me tales of him rebuking you. It is your farm, after all. You shouldn't let him depress you like this.'

'It's all right for you. You've never had any children. You don't know the emotional hold they have over you.'

The Direktor was silent and when Willi looked at him he was staring down at his glass, a disconcerted expression on his face as though Willi had said something embarrassing.

'Is something wrong, Franz?'

'No, no.'

'I expect I shall get used to the designs in time. You know more about these things than I do.'

'Of course.'

'And Georg will come round . . . I hope.'

'Yes.'

They were sitting in the Direktor's music room, overlooking the mountains. It was the middle of March and the snow had receded even further up the slopes. The winter had been mild and in the Direktor's garden the green sheaths of daffodils stood well above the ground. The two men were waiting for Gesner, the production manager, and the two members of the *Gemeinderat* who were on the theatre committee. Six chairs had been placed around a small antique card table and in front of each chair were papers topped by a sheet of figures. Willi removed the top sheets from one pile and placed it in his briefcase. 'That's Gesner's place. No need for him to see the balance sheet.'

'I don't see that it would do any harm,' said the Direktor glumly. 'It might make him accept a cut in his fee – out of sheer good will and concern for the Hochhauser Season.'

'Ha!'

'The figures are only here to prove one thing. Our other three productions for the Season can have very little spent on them. We shall have to do three old ones from the last couple of years and get the costumes and sets from Vienna as usual. We'll have to use all our rehearsal time for *Luxembourg* too – we can't possibly afford to have the full cast up here for longer than three weeks and we'll need that for the new production.'

85

'What about Aschmann?'

'She is coming next week. Once I know what the other operettas will be, I shall work with her every day. Some of the older ones will come a little earlier at their own expense. Luiza and Freddi haven't worked all winter, so feel they might just as well rent out their Salzburg apartment and come up here to wait for rehearsals to begin. I might see if I can persuade them to do some practice bits with Therese.'

'Next week! She is coming next week? Where will you put her? At the Franz Joseph? – no, that wouldn't do, Gesner stays there in the summer. You will have to try one of the other hotels. Perhaps I should book a suite for her, as Burgermeister, you know. I can insist that she has the very best attention . . .'

'Willi . . .'

'The Franz Joseph is our grandest hotel, of course, but after that . . . I suppose the Hochhauser Palace is not too bad. It is not very close to the theatre but we can arrange for a car to take her back after every performance.'

'Willi – she is staying at the Goldener Adler with Luiza and Freddi. No need for a car. It is very close to the theatre.'

'Therese Aschmann? Staying in a Gasthaus, with the rest of the cast?'

'She says she will be quite comfortable there, and of course it is very inexpensive. As a matter of fact she asked to be with Freddi and Luiza. They are friends from the old days.'

Willi looked very dubious, but at that moment they heard voices in the lobby outside. Frau Schmidt came in and said the gentlemen were here and please, should she bring coffee in now or later.

'Now, please, Frau Schmidt. We should like the coffee as soon as possible.'

The committee men slapped Willi on the shoulder, shook the Direktor's hand, stamped around the music room a bit, making flattering remarks about the view and the garden. Stefan, a thin, grey-faced, middle-aged man with stomach ulcers who had been production manager since the Hochhauser Season had begun, sat down at the table, looked at the balance sheet and the final sentence at the bottom and took a bottle of tablets from his pocket.

'Stomach still bad, Stefan?' asked the Direktor kindly, and his production manager nodded. 'Got some new tablets to get me through the Season – supposed to be revolutionary – solve all problems.'

'Frau Schmidt will be bringing you your usual glass of milk in a moment. Gesner is late, of course. We may as well sit down and begin with sorting out what we can afford.'

The committee men took on a new authority. In Franz Busacher's villa they were always slightly awed. It was the best private house in Hochhauser, and after all, he was an internationally famous name. Artistically they felt out of their depth here, but when it came to spending the town's money they knew a lot more than Herr Busacher did. And they weren't having him go over budget, as he had six years ago.

Willi Zimmermann took the chair. 'We've been financially solvent for the last five years, and the surplus has all been allocated to the new production of *The Count of Luxembourg*. The State grant remains the same, although in view of our rising reputation there are rumours it might be increased next year, especially if we make a success of the new production.' A gratified rumble went around the table.

'For the rest, you see in front of you where the money goes. Singers' fees have had to be raised a little to keep pace with inflation and union rates. Maintaining the building is covered by the State grant, but there is very little left over for anything else.'

'Can't we raise the price of the tickets?' one of the committee men asked.

'We did that last year. I don't think we can do it again so soon without a very noisy protest from the Tourist Board.'

'So,' said Stefan. 'We come to what we more or less knew in the first place. It's three revivals of previous productions involving as little work and expense as possible.'

The door opened and Karl Gesner entered with a flourish, turned, took the tray from Frau Schmidt who was just behind him, and placed it on the table.

'My dear Frau Schmidt! Allow me. Gentlemen – forgive! I am late. I drove down from Vienna. And here, a little something to enjoy with our coffee.' He took a bottle of schnapps from his pocket. The Direktor relaxed slightly. Gesner had decided to be charming, which was a relief. Stefan looked at the schnapps and winced. He reached out his hand for the glass of milk and took a large gulp.

The committee men shook hands with Gesner and preened. He too was a star and it was pleasant to be able to mention that they had drunk schnapps with him at Direktor Busacher's house.

'You've missed the depressing bit, Karl.'

'We have no money, as usual?'

'None to spare. It will have to be *Luxembourg*, and three old ones that we've done quite recently, so that we don't have to waste too much time rehearsing them.'

'No problem.' Gesner opened the bottle of schnapps. Frau Schmidt twinkled in again, this time with a tray of glasses, and Gesner smiled up at her. 'I hope you've brought one for yourself, Frau Schmidt. You must take a glass back to the kitchen to drink whilst preparing the Direktor's lunch.'

Frau Schmidt looked gratified but slightly overwhelmed. 'Well no, Herr Gesner, I didn't bring a glass . . . I didn't think . . .'

'Have mine,' said Stefan through his milk.

The schnapps was poured, the glasses dispensed, and Frau Schmidt sent simpering back to the kitchen. Willi spooned several dollops of thick whipped cream on to his coffee and studied the *Gugelhupf* on the tray. 'Shall I cut it?' he said, and sliced eagerly in without waiting for an answer.

'So,' said Gesner, smiling affably round the table. 'Which three productions shall we resuscitate?'

'*Fledermaus* is out of the question. It was four years ago and Ingrid couldn't cope with Adele. I think we shall have to look at just the last two years.'

'*Gypsy Baron*,' said Gesner blandly, staring into his coffee. The Direktor gave him a sharp glance.

'Impossible, Karl. You know very well Therese could not play Saffi. It's a very young role and she has to lead the gypsy dance routine. It's an energetic part even for a young singer. Therese couldn't possibly manage it.'

'I'm sure she could,' Willi said vehemently, brushing crumbs from his stomach. 'I saw her play Saffi twenty years ago at the *Volksoper*. She was miraculous. I would love to see her play Saffi again. And it is Strauss! It is always good to open the season with a Strauss.'

'And it is one of my most popular roles,' purred Gesner. 'Every seat was sold out for every performance when we did it last year.'

'I repeat, Karl,' said Busacher coldly. 'There is no possible way Therese could play Saffi.'

'Then let her sing Arsena,' smiled Gesner. 'Ingrid will make a gallant attempt at Saffi, I'm sure, and Therese can stand quite still by the farmhouse, thus saving her energy, and sing Arsena as best she can.' He knew, and the Direktor knew, just what sort of gallant attempt Ingrid would make. It would do – just – although they would have to shorten some of the solos and adapt the range. She would look all right and would throw herself into the dancing with undisciplined enthusiasm. With luck it would be a mediocre performance. It was the kind of situation Gesner loved. With Therese – who might or might not be able to sing – tucked away into a thoroughly unsuitable but static role, and Ingrid struggling along opposite him, there would be nothing, but nothing, to remove attention from Gesner. He would flow unchallenged through his role of the Gypsy Baron, his ego fed on the ripples of admiration seeping back at him from the auditorium.

The committee men rumbled approval. The Direktor felt, not for the first time, deeply resentful of the fact that they had any part in choosing the programme.

'You did say, in Vienna,' Gesner reminded him, 'that you would be prepared to let Ingrid have a lead role in one of the productions. You obviously have Therese in mind for Adele in the new production of *Luxembourg* – so much more suitable for her, an older woman – I would have thought you could let poor little Ingrid have her moment of triumph in *Gypsy Baron*.'

'I don't see why Aschmann can't play Saffi,' repeated Willi with dogged persistence.

'Well she can't!' snapped the Direktor. 'It is out of the question. All right. We will let Ingrid play Saffi and Therese will sing Arsena. And then we will follow it, quite naturally, with *Countess Maritza*. It is always best to do the two together – *Gypsy Baron* followed by *Countess Maritza*. The audiences love the connection. Half the English and American ladies don't realize until they've seen it that it is linked to the *Baron*, and if we make a feature of that in the advance publicity we can suggest double bookings for consecutive nights. You're quite right, Karl, when you say that every seat was sold out last year for *Gypsy Baron*. So, if we advertise the two linked operettas on consecutive nights we shall sell out for *Maritza* as well.'

'It is not one of my favourites.' Gesner was caught and couldn't think quickly enough how to veto Busacher's choice. One of the committee men came to the Direktor's assistance.

'Quite *my* favourite of all the Kalman operettas,' he said enthusiastically. 'And how would it be if we offered a slight reduction for buying the two tickets together? That would make it a very attractive proposition.'

'I don't like *Maritza* – all that Hungarian music is so banal. And the screeching violin solos. I was quite embarrassed when we did it two years ago.'

Yes, my good man, thought Busacher maliciously. And you may well be embarrassed this year too, though not because of the violin solo. Therese could be rather good as Countess Maritza. It was a sophisticated role. The Countess, like the Merry Widow, could be played at almost any age providing she was elegant. And Maritza had the best solos too. Possibly the twenties costumes wouldn't be too kind to Therese, but they'd do something about that when the time came.

'Good,' he said quickly. 'That's a splendid idea, about the ticket reduction. So that is settled, *Gypsy Baron* followed by *Countess Maritza*, and *The Count of Luxembourg* for our new production. Just one more. Any suggestions?'

'*Der Zarewitsch*,' Gesner put in hurriedly, and Busacher's heart sank again. Gesner was obviously determined to sabotage the whole Season. The man was a fool . . . did he think it would do his reputation any good to appear in weak productions? He'd been so adamant in Vienna about not looking ridiculous with the 'fat old Frau' and now he was suggesting productions that were totally unsuitable.

'Not a good role for Therese,' he said wearily.

'Then perhaps Ingrid again?'

'No,' said Busacher. 'You know she doesn't have the voice, and she'll already be covering two heavy roles if she is to lead in the *Baron* and sing Juliette in our new *Luxembourg*. That's as much as her voice will stand, and we'll have to cut quite a lot of those anyway if she's going to get through the Season intact.'

'*Zarewitsch* is a cheap production,' said Willi thoughtfully. 'Virtually a two-hander – one doesn't have to put a chorus on stage unless one wants to. We could save a lot on costumes if we did that. Trim it down a bit from two years ago.'

The Direktor prepared to fight, and then he recalled that brilliant clear voice singing '*Einer Wird Kommen*' at the audition. The melodies of *Zarewitsch* were some of the loveliest and most powerful Lehar had ever written. Not household-humming tunes like *Merry Widow* or *Luxembourg*, but surprisingly moving. And because they were not so well known the audiences were always enchanted and wondered why they had never heard them before. Of course, Therese would look ridiculous in the part – nothing they could do about that, a boy's costume was a boy's costume – but the voice, that electrifying voice rippling up and down through the registers without effort. And if Gesner could forget his jealous ego and sing the way he was capable of singing, it could prove a powerful musical piece. Suddenly he decided to take a chance: somehow they would get Therese on to the stage in that ridiculous boy's costume and let her sing.

'All right,' he said. 'Therese shall sing Sonja.' Gesner was surprised.

'You're happy about that?' he asked. 'Perhaps one of the new singers would be better – that little creature who did small parts last year, dark hair, pleasant little tinkling voice?'

'No. Therese can sing Sonja. She's coming to sing the leads, and sing them she will.'

Gesner looked suspicious. He had the feeling he had been outmanoeuvred but, on the face of it, he seemed to have come out quite well. *Maritza* and the new *Luxembourg* were better for Therese than he liked, but he'd got her pushed out of the *Baron* – and she would really look very silly singing Arsena, which was the juvenile role even if it was fairly static – and she would be even more ridiculous playing Sonja in *Der Zarewitsch*. He decided to bide his time. Once rehearsals started it would become obvious that Therese couldn't support a romantic juvenile lead like Sonja, and they would have to do something. If not Ingrid, then the little thing from last year. There were several youngsters in the chorus playing understudies who would jump at the chance of having a stab at Sonja.

'So that is settled. Stefan, can you see about ordering the old sets and costumes? I'll give you the cast list but it is more or less the same as last time. A couple of new young ones in the chorus, but that's about it.'

'I shall not require the hired costumes this season,' said Gesner. Stefan darted a suspicious glance across the table at him.

'I had the chance to purchase, very reasonably, a full set of operetta wardrobe from the *Volksoper*. Some slight alterations needed. Stefan, perhaps you would be good enough to arrange for them to be collected from my apartment in Vienna and brought down here for the wardrobe woman.'

'But they won't look right with what we're hiring,' said Stefan.

'They will look magnificent,' said Gesner. 'They belonged to Mandrika.'

Busacher blinked. Mandrika had been one of the giants of the *Volksoper* and the *Staatsoper*. Like Gesner he had been a big handsome man and his costumes had been lavish and spectacular. He had retired last year and was now only doing concert work. How on earth had Gesner persuaded the *Volksoper* to sell him the costumes?

'I was intending to ask the committee for something towards my purchase.'

'Forget it,' said Busacher sharply, and thank God, this time the committee men and Willi thundered in behind him. Phrases like 'unauthorized purchase – not the responsibility of the company' rumbled around the room.

When, finally, Gesner and the committee men and Willi had left, Stefan and Busacher began the arduous and long overdue task of organization and paperwork.

'We must get the advance billing done as quickly as possible,' Stefan said reprovingly. 'They're embarrassingly late. The Season opens in May, and apart from the fixed *Luxembourg* dates we've made no other announcements.'

'Unavoidable. We nearly didn't have a season at all until we got Aschmann.'

'Do you want me to put her billing in the advance announcements – Aschmann starring as Adele in the sensational new *Luxembourg* – that kind of thing?'

The Direktor hesitated. Things could still go wrong, even at this late stage. Only one thing was certain. Gesner.

'No. Just announce the productions and give a vague whooflepouffle – something like, four enchanting productions starring Karl Gesner, world famous tenor. Then list the rest of the cast below but put Therese's name at the top, same size lettering as Alfred's. He still brings in a few of the old fans. And Stefan, try to write up the *Luxembourg* so that the emphasis is on that and it detracts from the fact that we're resurrecting those three tired old numbers we've so often done before. You can make a great point of the exciting English designer, say something like – a revolutionary departure: English artist brings fresh and startling look to classical Viennese works.'

'That will ensure she gets bad notices,' said Stefan gloomily. The Direktor thought of Madge Grimsilk's totally impassive face and personality. Would that passionless person mind if she got bad notices?

Stefan pulled out his folder of balance sheets. 'We can more or less estimate the costs of the old productions now,' he said. 'It will be the same as last year, plus about five per cent. I went through everything last night. Knew we'd have to do the old ones, so I dug out all the figures of the last two years' productions.'

Stefan was invaluable. They really couldn't have managed without him.

'Orchestra rates have gone up,' the glum voice continued. 'But I had to book them in January. Couldn't leave it any later.'

'Splendid, Stefan!'

'And – I suppose it's true? Gesner's fee is bigger this year, as always?'

'I'm afraid so. But on the whole I think so far we've brushed through quite well with him.'

Stefan grunted, rummaged in his folder, and produced yet another sheet of figures.

'We've been approached by some welfare organization about group bookings. You know, the handicapped and people in institutions. They undertake a booking of a minimum of fifty seats once a week if we will give a special price. They take care of the transport and looking after the invalids. I thought it a good idea.'

'So it is,' said Busacher approvingly. 'We're by no means sold out for every performance, in spite of Gesner. Fifty guaranteed seats once a week will give the advance bookings a most healthy look. Well done, Stefan. What would we do without you? Stay and have lunch with me. I have quite a few exciting things to tell you about this year's season. I think you will be pleased.'

Stefan belched. 'Could I have another glass of milk, Herr Direktor?' he asked, and Busacher knew the Season had really begun.

CHAPTER SIX

On the morning of the day when Therese Aschmann was due to arrive in Hochhauser, Willi spent a long time getting ready before he went to meet her at the station. The Direktor had suggested that it was not necessary for Willi to go, that in fact it would be much better if it were just him, Busacher, and no-one else. Willi had been deeply shocked.

'It would be quite disgraceful not to meet her! A great star like Aschmann arrives in Hochhauser and there is no-one from the theatre committee to greet her. The entire committee should be there!'

'No, no, Willi. She would hate that. She is very shy. She does not want to be treated like a star.' He had given up trying to explain to Willi that Therese was no longer a star, had not been a star for eighteen years, and even then had only been a small rising star. He could never quite work out whether or not Willi was being deliberately naughty. He'd told Willi the plain facts. Willi had appeared not to listen. But he'd done this before and then suddenly, by a single comment, Willi would reveal that he had been playing a game all along. Willi also had the most appalling memory when it came to forgetting things he wanted to forget.

'One cannot have the star of the new Season arriving, and the Burgermeister and Founder of the Hochhauser theatre not there to greet her.'

'All right, Willi. As you wish.'

And so Willi was squeezing himself into his best suit, the one he wore for daytime ceremonial occasions, and had spattered himself lavishly with after-shave cologne, and spent a long time arranging

94

the frill of curls round his bald crown. When Georg came in to lunch, covered in cow muck and mud, the converging smells caused Frau Trauffer to wave her hand in the air and give a disgusted 'Phaw!'

'I don't know which is worse,' she said plaintively, dumping the goulash down on the table and turning to the sink to strain the noodles. 'I'm not fond of the smell of cow dung, but at least it's an honest smell – where did you get that scent, Herr Zimmermann?'

'In Vienna. It is French. Very expensive.'

Frau Trauffer grunted. Georg ignored them both and padded across to the table in his stockinged feet.

'Georg,' said his father nervously. 'Are you busy after lunch?'

'Why?'

'I wondered if you would drive me down to the town in the van.'

'Why don't you take the car?'

'Because I want to collect a bouquet from the florist. It will not fit into the car. If you would take me to the station, passing the florist on the way, it would be very helpful.'

'Why don't you take the van yourself?'

'Because I do not know if I shall be coming back this afternoon. I may persuade Fräulein Aschmann to join me for tea at the Franz Joseph. And the last time I did not return with the van in time for evening milking you were very cross.'

Georg dug savagely into his plate. That morning he had walked over to the Hoflin farm and asked Suzi to go to the cinema with him that evening, after her class. He had found himself begging and it made him feel undignified. Suzi's answer had not been one of unalloyed enthusiasm.

'I will come with you,' she said kindly. 'Because I do not want us to stop being friends. There is no need for us to quarrel and I see no reason why we cannot – occasionally – go out together. But you must understand that it really isn't any fun spending an evening with someone who is cross all the time.'

And now, here was his father also accusing him of being cross.

'What do you mean, Papa? Cross? I am never cross. Just because I don't go around laughing my head off all the time or . . . or spending money on bunches of flowers too big to fit into the car, it does not mean that I am cross.'

'Of course not, Georg,' his father smiled fondly at him. 'Just serious, eh?'

'Someone has to be serious, Papa.'

'And you are serious enough for both of us. I am very lucky – you do all my worrying for me.'

As that was exactly what Georg thought, several times a day, he felt slightly mollified.

'So will you drive me to the station, past the flower shop?' His small round face crinkled up like a naughty baby and, through his irritation, Georg found himself having to stifle a grin of his own. He always felt that if he allowed his father to see that he could wheedle Georg, it would be the thin end of the wedge.

'Very well, Papa.' He refused to smile but – he told himself – he was by no means cross. Why did everyone accuse him of being cross?

When they got to the florist and Georg saw his father emerging he really *was* cross, so cross he leapt out from the driver's seat and intercepted Willi on the pavement.

'For God's sake, Papa! What on earth have you got there? How much did it cost? Wouldn't a normal bouquet, even a large one, have been enough? Do you know how much flowers cost at this time of the year? Not even spring flowers! Hothouse flowers! Carnations, in March. And lilies!' He poked a frantic finger into the blooms as he spotted a huge madonna lily, and then another. 'How many lilies are there? Two, three . . . six! Six lilies, and all the rest. There must be a month's milking money there!'

'Can you open the back of the van, Georg. If I let go the wind will blow it over.'

Georg's mouth firmed into a thin, disapproving line. There was no point, no point whatsoever in saying anything now. They couldn't take it back to the florist. It was quite obvious they had been ordered specially in advance. Grimly he opened the back of the van and made no effort to help whilst his father tried to manoeuvre the basket across the rest of the pavement. The basket was about a metre deep and the back of it had been built right up high so as to support the bank of flowers. The offending lilies and several branches of mimosa were about level with the top of Willi's head.

'You look absolutely ridiculous, Papa. Have you any idea how silly a short man looks trying to carry flowers bigger than himself? You're making an absolute fool of yourself.'

'Thank you, Georg.'

'And what is she supposed to do with them?'

'They will cheer up her room at the Goldener Adler.'

Georg slammed the door shut, climbed back into the driver's seat, started the engine, and put his foot on the accelerator even before his father was properly in. In thunderous silence he raced to the traffic lights and had to brake hard as the lights changed.

'George, are you happy?' asked his father mildly.

'No. Not when my father spends good farming money to make an ass of himself over an actress.'

'I am not speaking of the flowers, Georg. I'm speaking of every day, every week, your life. Are you happy, Georg?'

'Of course,' he snapped.

'That's good,' said Willi. 'I am very happy, nearly always. I would like you to be happy too.'

Suddenly Georg hated his father, hated Suzi, hated Suzi's parents, and most of all hated the theatre and this wretched actress who was arriving. He pulled into the station car park, slammed on the brakes, and made no effort to get out of the van. In his rear mirror he watched his father struggle with the doors and manhandle the basket on to the ground. He steadied it with one hand whilst with the other he slammed the doors, then, holding the handle of the basket, he tottered away. His right arm, the one on the handle, was completely submerged in blooms. From the front you probably wouldn't even be able to see him. It would look as though a mountain of flowers was moving through the car park all on its own.

The flare of hatred vanished, to be replaced by the now familiar wave of misery that had descended on him when he had broken up with Suzi. For a moment he allowed himself to slump forward over the wheel, wanting to blame the world for his despair but knowing, because he was not unintelligent, that the despair stemmed from something lacking in himself. He was constantly ashamed of his father, embarrassed by him, infuriated by him. He was always surprised to discover that other people didn't feel this way about him. He couldn't understand why his father had been elected Burgermeister or the head of the theatre committee. He constantly came across people who adored his father and he couldn't think why they did when he was such a silly little man who made such a fool of himself. Why did everyone like his father?

He took his handkerchief from his pocket and blew his nose. Willi had vanished. So had the flowers. Slowly Georg got out of the van, looked around to make sure there was no-one who knew him, then he walked quickly across to the station restaurant, entered, and hid himself quickly in a booth that had a view of the rails.

Luiza and Freddi were there, Luiza muffled up in a huge and unflattering beaver lamb coat that had seen better days. As they stamped their feet against the cold, Busacher strode towards them, and behind him Alfred, the company baritone who had sung with Therese in *Die Fledermaus* twenty years before. Willi staggered round the end of the car park, puffing, red-faced and sweating in spite of the cold wind.

'*Magnifique!*' breathed Luiza, looking at the flowers. Willi beamed, righted himself and the basket, keeping one hand lightly on the edge to balance it, and rubbed some pollen from the shoulder of his overcoat. In the distance along the line, the train took shape. Franz Busacher glanced at Willi and tried, for one last time, to prepare his friend for the shattering of an illusion.

'Willi, don't let her see if you think she's badly changed. Twenty years is a long time. Don't let her see you're disappointed.'

Willi tweaked a carnation out of the basket, broke the stem off with his teeth, and tucked it into his buttonhole. 'Here she comes,' he said happily.

The train stopped, doors slammed, a man further up the line lifted out two suitcases and placed them on the ground. Therese appeared, stepped carefully down from the train, smiled at the man who had helped her, then looked about her.

It was six weeks since Busacher had seen her, and she'd certainly fined down, not a lot, but enough to make a difference. Her face was thinner, not altogether a good thing, and she'd had her hair coloured too, a sort of pale version of the colour it used to be. It had been styled rather well, as though she'd gone to a really good hairdresser and it suited her, was soft over her forehead and short at the back. She wore the blue suit and the bright shawl and carried a rather shabby grey coat over her arm. She smiled as she came towards him.

'Dear, dear Franz!'

He kissed her warmly on both cheeks and caught again that elusive scent that was special to her. He felt excited and happy that she was here. They had spoken several times on the telephone and he had rediscovered many things about her, things he had forgotten – her pleasant manners, her humour, her gentleness, and above all her dedication to her music. He knew he would be able to work with her the way he liked to, not a barnstorming nonstop battle which was the way he had to work with Gesner, but an exciting exploration of just what new heights could be achieved. Mostly, he supposed, he was happy because she was going to be the most startling singer he had put on to the Hochhauser stage. He couldn't wait to begin.

'Some old friends, Therese!'

'Luiza. And dear, dear Freddi. How long it has been, but really, you look just the same. And Alfred! It is such a reception committee. I feel quite like a star, all these old friends!' She was filled with happiness, although during the past six weeks she had suffered from indecision and doubts. Once she had signed her contract, fear had overtaken her. Supposing she couldn't do it? Supposing she let them down after dear Franz Busacher had connived and wheedled to make her acceptable to Gesner? She had frightened herself still further by asking those of her friends who knew the theatre gossips what the latest *on dit* was on Karl Gesner. Story after story had followed, each one more ghastly than the last. Even allowing for delicious exaggeration it still added up to a horrifying picture and she began to wish she hadn't even tried to get into the company. Strangely enough it was a tiny thing that suddenly gave her confidence again – her hair. She had discovered the name of a really good – and expensive, but never mind! – hairdresser. He had tutted and twitched and tweaked, then proceeded to do more for her than she had thought possible. It was foolish, just to feel different because of her hair, but excitement had begun stirring within her. Now, at last, here in Hochhauser, looking her best, with her dear, dear friends from the past, she knew it was all going to work.

'Therese, this is Willi Zimmermann, Burgermeister of Hochhauser and founder of the Hochhauser theatre. He is a great admirer of yours. Willi, Therese Aschmann.'

'Well, of course it is Aschmann,' cried Willi. He stared at the divine creature of his dreams and twenty years vanished. 'Madame . . . I cannot tell you . . . so many years ago . . . the happiest time of my life.' An unexpected, swift and quite sharp longing for Gerda swept over him. It was almost a physical pain and for a moment he felt shocked because it had been many years since the agony of losing Gerda. He couldn't speak, and, to his horror, he felt tears welling up in his throat. Aschmann was looking at him, slightly puzzled but smiling still. He pulled himself together and gestured with his free hand towards the flowers.

'Dear Madame. These are for you, from the grateful town of Hochhauser. And as well as our gratitude, please accept from the Burgermeister the humble admiration of . . .' He felt the presence of Gerda so strongly he couldn't finish. What a silly old fool he was.

Therese held her hand towards him. 'How beautiful, how kind of you all. I did not expect such kindness . . . I promise to sing for Hochhauser as well as I can. Such a lovely old town – I know I shall be happy here.'

He was a comical little man but as she smiled and tried to say the right things – 'Oh! Mimosa. How lovely. One of my favourite flowers. And lilies and carnations . . . in March . . . How wonderful' – she had a vague feeling of comforting familiarity, as though she had known him before. He bounced and bowed and smiled, and suddenly she thought, Uncle Dimitri! Of course, that's who he reminds me of, dear Uncle Dimitri. I wonder if his father . . . but no, he is older than I am. He could not possibly have a Russian father. But it gave her another flare of confidence, this elusive and somehow warming reminder of her childhood. It was a good omen, surely it was a good omen?

'And now, it is too cold to stand here. Therese, you would like to settle into your room. We have a car waiting. And perhaps, later, we could all meet for tea at the Franz Joseph. Willi, I am sure you would like to join us.' Willi nodded emphatically. Franz pulled Therese's arm through his and began to lead her up the track towards the car park, but she stopped and looked back.

'My flowers. I must not forget my lovely flowers.'

'Allow me.' Willi plunged his hand back into the blooms and began to retrace his steps to the station car park. The basket wouldn't fit into the back of the Direktor's car, nor into Freddi and Luiza's Volkswagen.

'No problem,' said Willi nobly. 'You go ahead to the Gasthaus. I will have them delivered at once.'

'So kind!'

Georg had sat and watched and glowered. He couldn't hear anything, but he could see his father covered in pollen and then he had watched the actress get off the train and a lot of kissing and hugging, and everyone behaving the way theatre people always did behave. And it was obvious the actress thought his father was ridiculous. She was laughing at him. He distinctly saw her laughing when she first caught sight of Willi covered in pollen. Why should Willi always make himself look so ludicrous so that people laughed at him? He watched, felt indignant but also justified because he was right. And then, as they all stood laughing and chattering in the cold wind, the sense of desolation swept over him again. It was like watching a party to which he hadn't been invited. They all looked so happy, the fat old girl in the fur coat, and the new actress, and all those old men. He didn't *want* to be invited to the party but it would have been nice to have friends like that who came to meet you from Vienna and were delighted to see you. Of course, he'd never had time to make friends. He'd been working too hard in college, and even harder since he'd been running the farm. Supposing, he thought, with a stab of fear, he was never going to have any friends? He watched them disappear from his view, his father still waddling along with that bloody basket. How was it that his father could make friends and he couldn't?

He came out of the station restaurant into the bitter wind and strode across the car park. Willi was standing alone, rather nonplussed, with his basket.

'Wait here, Papa,' Georg said wearily. 'I'll bring the van round. I suppose you would like me to deliver it to the Goldener Adler.'

Willi beamed.

Every day they worked on the old scores. Therese had been studying them as soon as the Direktor had telephoned her with the news of the productions and her roles. At first they worked in the Direktor's villa, then moved to the icy theatre, where his last fear was removed. Therese's voice, in a theatre, was even bigger, more fluent and lyrical than he had hoped. The liquid notes rose and flowed round the chandelier, already removed from its dust bag ready for the Season. Some days Luiza, Freddi and Alfred joined them and they began to walk her through parts of the productions. Without Gesner and the rest of the cast they couldn't do a great deal, but the *Maritza* scenes with Freddi could be rehearsed and several other small fragments of the three old operettas. She had taken, without comment, her secondary role in *Gypsy Baron* but even then, when he heard her sing Arsena, he felt that familiar surge of excitement. All right, many of the audience would find it puzzling to have a middle-aged woman playing the juvenile role, but some of the audience would recognize just what they were hearing. For the music lovers, the serious devotees, Arsena's music would dominate the entire production.

Willi frequently turned up for the sessions where Therese was working with Luiza, Freddi and Alfred. Willi often did turn up for rehearsals, had often done so. In the early days Busacher had tried to discourage him. He did not approve of 'amateurs' attending rehearsals. But the Burgermeister, usually so jovial and noisy, had proved to be exceedingly sound, never saying anything at all at the rehearsal other than to praise the faint-hearted at the very end. Later, over their wine at the Franz Joseph, he would make the odd tactful comment to Busacher.

'Our poor Luiza didn't look too happy paired with Rudi in the ball scene.' Something Busacher should have noticed for himself, but which he had been too busy to observe. Of course Luiza shouldn't be paired with the lanky and very young tenor; they'd have to replot the run-up to that part so that she came into the ballroom with someone else. They were always tiny points that Willi raised, but useful, and Busacher, over the years, sometimes found himself asking Willi's opinion on a production. On four separate occasions when the problems involved finance, Willi had somehow managed to wheedle an emergency sum from the *Gemeinderat*. He was excellent at charming wardrobe ladies, new young chorus members straight from music school, and surly, battered old musicians in the orchestra pit who had seen it all before. He had, during one terrible crisis, taken off his coat and acted as Sparks to the electricians and stage crew without causing any kind of trouble with the unions.

Just once or twice, when he remembered, Busacher wondered how Willi managed to find the time to do all these things, and be Burgermeister, and put in at least a modicum of hours on his farm. He presumed that that surly young son of his did most of the running of the dairy business.

He was quite happy for Willi to sit through some of Therese's practice sessions, for Willi's overwhelming admiration for Therese's voice – and Willi, in spite of his romantic overview, did understand about voice – was doing wonders for Therese's confidence.

The Direktor stopped going home for lunch. So did Willi. Every day a group of them, sometimes Luiza and Freddi, sometimes Alfred and Stefan, sometimes the entire party, would troop off to the restaurant. Every day Busacher watched Therese growing a little more animated with her friends, a little more confident, a little more like the girl she had once been. She had lost nearly a stone in weight and her face looked somewhat drawn, but she laughed a lot, especially when Willi was around.

On the day he was going through *Der Zarewitsch* with her, Willi didn't turn up. There was no need for the others; nearly all her numbers were either solos or duets with the absent Gesner. Although it was the end of March, a swift late fall of snow made the theatre icy. Therese was huddled in nearly every garment she possessed, slacks, jumpers, her shabby grey coat and the multi-coloured shawl. A small electric fire stood near the piano on the stage. Busacher had his cloak pulled round his legs and at intervals held his hands in front of the fire to thaw them out before playing again.

'Just the duet, once more, Therese, then we shall finish for today.'

He began playing and let Therese go through it once on her own. Then, because he was feeling happy, confident and delighted with the speed at which she had learnt everything, knew, musically, all her roles, he began to sing Gesner's part himself in his cracked old basso voice. Therese grinned at him. They'd had a long, hard, cold morning's work and levity took over. He boomed out, slipping in all the glottal stops and nasal sobs of an appallingly melodramatic tenor. He didn't have a good voice but he was never off-key. Therese sang back, matching every sob with a shrill one of her own and giving an extra heartrending tremolo here and there. Busacher put in a few whirly violin runs on the piano and crescendoed unnecessarily loudly, paused too long, gasped, she joined him, and together they sailed into the finale and burst out laughing. A frantic round of applause came from the back of the theatre.

'Bravo! Bravo!' cried Willi. 'I couldn't have done better myself!'

'I think you probably could, Willi,' said Busacher dryly. Willi, surprisingly, had rather a pleasant tenor voice. 'Now, I must leave. The divine Miss Grimsilk has already arrived in Hochhauser – at her own request, unmet and unheralded – and will be coming to see me at one. Spare a thought for me, dear friends. She will be sharing my luncheon.'

He wrapped his cloak more tightly around him, pulled on woollen gloves, sang a final note into the air, and left the theatre. Therese followed the fire flex along the stage and pulled the plug from the socket. It was the first time she and Willi had been alone together.

'Lunch?' he said, raising his eyebrows.

She hesitated. She had, like everyone else, become very fond of the little Burgermeister. He was enormous fun and there was also that elusive and comforting reminder of Uncle Dimitri. Perhaps that was why she didn't want to lunch with him alone, away from their usual theatre crowd. If she got to know him too well, the Dimitri element would probably vanish. And he was also sometimes a little overwhelming (Uncle Dimitri had been like that too). He was prone to over-effusive compliments which made her feel embarrassed. And – Uncle Dimitri or not – she wasn't sure how to behave with a man near her own age any more, even a nice uncomplicated one like this. She wasn't sure she could cope if he became sentimental or tried to pry into her past.

'I really should go back to the Gasthaus and practise.'

'Nonsense! You must have lunch, even if you work all the afternoon. Come now, today we will abandon the delights of the Chu Chin Chow.' (Luiza had developed a passion for Chinese food and Hochhauser's first and only Chinese restaurant had done a roaring lunchtime trade as a result.) 'Today we shall eat like real Viennese.'

'Perhaps . . . yes, it is most kind of you.'

Outside it was almost warmer than in the theatre and they walked along the road keeping a slight distance between them. Willi was about four inches shorter than she was and tended to take bouncy steps. He was well known in Hochhauser and several times they were stopped and she was introduced to yet another friend, another business or civic colleague. At the Franz Joseph he was greeted with great style and they were led into the terrace restaurant, to a table with a magnificent view over the whole of the Hochhauser valley, once more covered in snow.

They ordered, sipped drinks, and Therese was conscious that it was the first time for years she had eaten a meal alone with a man. A rather awkward silence began to stretch between them and she strove for something pleasant to say.

'Everyone has been so kind in the company. And Hochhauser itself has been so welcoming. Is it always like this?'

'Always. That is why everyone comes back to Hochhauser.'

'It is a little strange . . . that you, the Burgermeister, should spend so much time in the theatre.'

'Not strange at all. One: the theatre is now the most important part of the Hochhauser economy, the tourists, you know. Two: I am the founder of the Hochhauser Season, with my dear Franz of course, and am responsible for seeing that all continues well. And three: I have always loved the opera, the operetta. The best moments of my life have been with music.'

'Did you ever have secret yearnings to be a performer?'

'Never.'

'Tell me of your best moments with music.'

He continued smiling at her but she sensed a slight withdrawal. She was relieved. She preferred there to be a reserve between them, however small.

'Ah! Here is our soup, and the wine . . .' He whisked a pair of spectacles from his breast pocket and studied the label. 'Splendid.'

'Tell me,' she said, fussing with soup spoon and bread. 'Tell me about Gesner. Is he always unpleasant to his leading lady?'

'Always. It will be far worse with you but it will not matter, it will not worry you. You will be above it.'

She wished she shared his confidence. She felt again that slight *frisson* of foreboding that came every time she thought of Gesner. 'Why will it be worse for me?'

'Because you are the greatest voice Gesner has ever sung with. Because you are Aschmann, the star, the most wonderful diva

Hochhauser has ever seen.' She shook her head angrily and said, 'No, no.'

'No? You do not believe so, Fräulein? I cannot think why. Perhaps because you cannot hear yourself, cannot see yourself. I remember, twenty years ago, thinking you were greater than any of them!'

'But Willi! That was twenty years ago. I have changed. And I never was . . . what you thought I was . . . never!'

Willi put his spoon down and stared at her. He had forgotten to take off his spectacles and he peered over the top of them.

'You were the most wonderful thing I ever saw,' he said firmly. 'You were then, and you are now. When you are on the stage I shall be able to see no-one else. It will be as though twenty years have slipped away, and Gerda is sitting by my side at the *Volksoper*, and Georg is at home, a nice normal, cheerful little boy, and our farm is beginning to make money at last, and the future looks wonderful.'

Therese smiled. 'You're talking about youth, Willi. Not me. Your youth, when you were both young and full of . . . the excitement that happens when one is young. Nothing can bring that back.'

'You remind me so much of Gerda, you know that? Not that you are alike, although she was beautiful too. But you were so much part of our youth.'

'What did Gerda look like?' she asked gently.

He pulled out a wallet and took a photograph from it, smoothing it with his fingers as though to keep it perfect. Then he handed it to Therese and she saw a small, round-faced young woman with bright eyes and fair hair and the beginning of a double chin. 'A lovely lady,' she said quietly, and handed it back to him. 'How long is it since she died?'

'Nineteen years.'

'And you never wanted to marry again?'

'No . . . Sometimes I thought it would be nice . . . to have someone. But for a time I could not do that to Georg. When he was little he was very possessive, first of his mother, then me. And by the time he was older, I was old too.'

'Nonsense, Willi. You will never be old.'

The soup plates were removed. Willi's huge knuckle of ham with Sauerkraut and Knödel arrived. He beamed down at his own plate, then cast a glance of concern at hers, a plain grilled escalope with tomatoes.

'Are you sure that will be enough?'

'Quite sure.'

He picked up his knife and fork and looked utterly content.

'You, Therese, were married, were you not?'

She couldn't believe he didn't know it all. She thought everyone in the world knew, then she realized she was, indeed, behaving like a star, expecting not only that her nine-day scandal in the theatre would still be common knowledge after all this time, but also that he would know the details of her life since. It had been in all the national papers, but news is quickly forgotten, and at that time Willi must have been mourning his wife, trying to cope with loneliness and a small son, submerged in his own misery.

'I'm divorced, as you know,' she said briefly. 'My husband was a singer. I expect you know that too?'

'I think Franz mentioned it. Ah, yes. It was bad for you. Now I remember.'

'He became . . . unwell and gave it up, the stage. I haven't seen him for many years.' Even talking about Friedrich made her catch her breath, swallow, bring the shutter down in her head. That was the only way she could cope with Friedrich, by blocking him out from her mind. She pushed her plate away, not hungry any more. Willi was infinitely preferable when they were in a crowd, when he was being the life and soul of the party.

'Some dessert?'

'Thank you, no.'

'Coffee?'

'Thank you.'

'You will not object if I have dessert? They do very special pastries here.'

She smiled.

The tart was brought, a huge confection of pastry, strawberries, pineapple, banana, built round a pyramid of cream. The base was the size of a cheese plate.

'More cream, Herr Zimmermann?' Willi beamed. The waiter placed an enormous bowl of whipped cream on the table and Willi spooned lavishly, then picked up his fork, paused and beamed again. Therese burst out laughing and Willi waved an admonishing fork at her.

'The second happiest moments of my life,' he said seriously, 'have been eating the Franz Joseph's Matterhorn Torte. They are an emotional experience.'

As he plunged his fork into the confection Therese reflected that it was very difficult not to like a man who enjoyed life as much as Willi Zimmermann.

When the Direktor arrived back at his villa Madge Grimsilk was already waiting for him. He opened the door quietly and for one second saw her unobserved, leaning against the stove at the end of the hall, her model on the seat beside her. She looked thin and cold and rather frail. If it had been anyone else the Direktor would also have said that there was something a little pathetic about her. At once she sat up and crossed her hands in her lap.

'Forgive me. I am late. I did not think you would be here so promptly.'

'I took a taxi directly from the station.'

'You haven't yet checked into the Gasthaus?'

'No.'

'Right. Well, I'm sure you are ready for some lunch.'

'I would prefer that you looked at the model first.' Mentally the Direktor raised an eyebrow. He had never been told what to do by a designer before.

'As you wish.'

It had a huge box top over it and she carried it into his study, supporting it underneath. It must have been awkward getting it all the way to Hochhauser from London. She placed it on the desk and removed the lid, then the tissue paper underneath. There was his jewel-box of a theatre in miniature, with a sparkling ceiling and hung with fairy garlands. The stage at the end was an alcove in the ballroom, a big one, but still just a part of the whole. Swathes of coloured gauze separated silver benches, and a twisting staircase on one side had a cobweb of azure spangles hanging over it. Backing it all in the distance was the mysterious forest.

Madge Grimsilk took a small hand torch from her bag, pressed the button and placed it behind the forest at one side. At once a faint impression of medieval city spires and domes appeared in the right-hand corner.

'It's a lighting trick, of course,' she said. 'The buildings have been there all the time on the backcloth but they'll only show up when lit, and the alcove, for Act One, will be altered thus.' She slid all the gauze curtains and silver cobwebs along their runners at the top, removed the benches, popped in a Pre-Raphaelite easel, couch, and a stained-glass window behind the staircase, and it was Brissard's studio, as though designed by Hans Andersen.

'It is brilliant!'

'Thank you.'

'And so economical!'

'I was given my budget.'

Did the wretched woman never smile? He had just given her a triumph and had got no more reaction than if he had held a door open for her. Less. If he had held a door open for a Viennese woman she would have charmed him.

'I've incorporated all the changes you wanted. Is there anything else?'

Busacher gave up. 'Nothing, thank you, Miss Grimsilk. You have done everything I asked most efficiently. Now shall we have lunch?'

'I eat very little lunch.'

'You may eat as little as you please.' She did glance at him then, rather warily, as though suspecting him of trying to ridicule her.

'Some wine?' A silly question.

'No, thank you.'

He poured himself a glass and led the way through to his large music room. Frau Schmidt had set a table in front of the open fire. Frau Schmidt liked to do things properly and was an incurable romantic. When she learned there was a lady coming to lunch she had laid an extremely pretty table, with Hungarian embroidered table linen, the best glasses and a delicate posy of snowdrops and violets. Busacher pulled the chair out for Miss Grimsilk and she suddenly flushed, plonked herself down, and jerked the chair in under her knees.

As she picked at her food he studied her across the table. Difficult to tell how old she was. She could be anything between twenty-eight and forty-eight. He had noticed before how slowly the British matured. The men never looked anything until they were at least forty, and the women, especially the thin ones, went into a condition of permanent desiccation in their mid-twenties. Occasionally they had a brief flowering in old age, but that was it.

Miss Grimsilk had a clean good skin, clean good hair of an indeterminate brown, used no make-up and wore trousers and jacket that were excellently cut and of clean good British wool, but of a miserable dirty slate-grey colour. Her blouse was grey too. How could all those wonderful, light, fairy designs have come from this dreary-looking lady?

'When can I meet Fräulein Aschmann? I have yet to design her costumes.'

'You will meet her this evening. She is staying at the same Gasthaus as you. And if you wish to begin early with your costume-maker you can measure three of our soloists who are also staying at the Gasthaus.'

'That would save time. Herr Gesner's measurements I have already. I have designed for him before.'

'Really?'

'He sang in London the winter before last. In *Rigoletto*. The Duke.'

'Ah, yes.' That would account for the fact that the drawings of Gesner's costumes were so magnificent, so suited to his style and size. She obviously had a flair for putting people in what suited them, not always true of designers.

'Tell me, Miss Grimsilk – I am most intrigued – where did you learn your German? You speak it like an Austrian.'

There was such a long silence that he looked up from his plate. The colour had drained away from Miss Grimsilk's face. Her enormous grey eyes (they would have been rather striking if only she had used some make-up) were staring at him with the expression of a trapped rabbit.

'I learnt German at school, also later at college.'

'But not Viennese German. German, as taught in British schools, is of the correct variety. Not our lazy vernacular.'

'I . . . I once knew someone . . . quite well, who spoke Viennese.'

Ha! A man, could it be a man? No, surely not. Miss Grimsilk had surely never, ever known a man 'quite well' unless it was her father. He studied her more closely. Perhaps he was wrong. Her severity stemmed from self-control, not old-maid prudishness. Her guard was up all the time and she lacked a sense of humour. But perhaps under that stoic, stringy frame lurked a welter of passion.

'Presumably if he spoke Viennese, he was Viennese?'

'He was . . . he had Viennese parents. He is English now.'

So, it was a man. He had cleverly inveigled that out of her without her realizing it.

'Was he in the theatre?'

'I haven't seen him for some time.' And that is no answer, Miss Grimsilk, thought the Direktor. He was quite enjoying his lunch after all. Could it have been Karl Gesner? What a thought. No, impossible. Gesner was only in Britain for fleeting engagements. And Miss Grimsilk was not his type. She suddenly rose to her feet, pushing her chair back and reaching for her bag.

'Thank you for lunch, Herr Direktor. I shall not stay for coffee. I have a great deal to do. I have a meeting with your production manager, and the wardrobe department, and then I would like to meet Fräulein Aschmann. I believe I can also see the girl who will be your lead dancer at some time?'

He was disappointed. But she was here for a little while now, and would be coming back in mid-April to get *Luxembourg* on. If he had any energy left over he might well indulge in a bit more naughty meddling.

'Tomorrow, at the theatre. Her name is Suzi Hoflin, and she and a couple of her pupils practise on the stage from nine until ten. Then Fräulein Aschmann and the other soloists arrive and the dancers have to leave. Karl Gesner and the rest of the soloists arrive next week. The chorus, the week after that. You will have to work from measurements they send in to Stefan. We cannot afford to get them all here for a costume call.'

'I understand. I shall be at the theatre at nine tomorrow morning. Thank you for the lunch.' She shook his hand briefly and left the room. He looked out of the window and, a few moments later, saw her walking down the path to the tall wrought-iron gates that screened his house from the road, clutching her model as though it were a tray of very precious cut crystal.

CHAPTER SEVEN

On the following Monday the other soloists arrived and rehearsals proper began. Karl Gesner was three-quarters of an hour late.

It was still very cold and everyone was muffled up in coats and scarves and gloves. Gesner wore a coat with a fur lining and a Russian fur hat. Stefan, sucking his miracle tablets at the back of the stalls, muttered to the Direktor, 'He's about fifty years out of date. Who does he think he is . . . Gigli? I bet Domingo doesn't dress like that, even in the coldest theatres.'

Gesner didn't bother to greet anyone particularly. He waved a hand vaguely in the air and said, 'Ciao!'

'He does think he's Gigli,' said Stefan viciously.

'Quiet please, everyone. I thought, as it is our first morning and we shall want to get used to each other again, we should run through the score of last year's production of *Gypsy Baron*. We shall be opening the season with the *Baron*. Everyone exactly the same as last year, except Therese sings Arsena, and Ingrid sings Saffi, which she understudied last year. You've been working on it, Ingrid, yes, with your teacher?'

'Oh yes, Herr Direktor!'

'We shall have separate practice sessions from now on, when I have worked out the timetable. But for today we shall go straight through, just to warm up. Everything as last year. There will be no changes.'

He played the accompaniments himself at this stage. Later in the week a *répétiteur* would come down from Vienna to take over the piano and help with individual coaching.

'So, please, Karl. Act One solo, "*Als Flotter Geist*".'

111

The piano sounded thin in the cold theatre, then Gesner's voice, rich, strong, flowed into the auditorium like cream pouring from a jug. It was a good voice, the Direktor thought grudgingly. It was very nearly a great voice and sometimes, when Gesner was on form, when he was forced for some reason to try hard, it *was* a great voice. He darted a brief glance towards Therese and saw she had a surprised little smile on her face, the smile of a professional who discovers she will be singing with a partner well above average.

'Rudi, Alfred, Freddi . . .'

Act One continued, the dialogue between melodies fumbled along but most of it not too bad. He really wasn't too worried about this revival, in spite of the casting of Ingrid and Therese. He and Stefan had worked out a performance programme so that Ingrid wouldn't have to sing two big roles on consecutive nights. He didn't want her cracking up in the middle of the Season.

'Therese.' He gave her a big, warm, encouraging smile. In a way this was her début, in front of the full team of soloists, in front of Gesner, who lounged at the side of the stage talking to Alfred. Alfred, embarrassed, raised his finger to his lips but Gesner took no notice. Therese's pure golden voice lifted into the air, up into the chandelier, effortless, joyful. Gesner stopped talking and turned round, his eyes narrowed. For the first time since he had entered the theatre he looked hard at Therese. It was difficult to see any change in her, muffled as she was in coat and scarves, but one change he did recognize. She had confidence. And that voice was nothing like the voice he had heard on the tape of church music. This sound was richer, more vibrant. This was an acting voice and she knew how to use it. He felt a surge of rage, realizing that Busacher and Hans had played a trick on him.

The voice continued, finished. Nothing was said but he could sense the optimism all round the company. When an operetta company was as . . . thin as theirs was, they depended on their lead tenor and soprano to pull the show together, make it a success. Every single operetta really stood on the lead perform-ances, on *his* lead performances. The rehearsal went on and he watched her all the time. Yes, she had confidence in her voice, but what would she be like when she got out there in front of that terrible voracious animal, the audience? What would happen to her then? And whatever the voice, she was still a tired middle-aged woman with a bad figure.

When they broke for coffee Gesner went over to her, clutching his paper cup in his hand. 'When Franz begins to give you your plotting for Arsena, you must ask him to find you static positioning,' he said without any preamble. 'We have to do that for Luiza – find her a seat or a place she can lean against whilst singing.'

'I think I might just be able to totter from chair to chair,' she said, smiling sweetly at him.

'I was thinking of the look of the thing. You are supposed to be eighteen years old. If you don't move you won't be noticed so much.'

'I shall do as the Direktor wishes.' She managed to keep the smile on her face.

'Have you seen Ingrid dance?'

'No. I have only met her this morning.'

'She's excellent. Very graceful, very lively.'

'Then she will be a very good Saffi.'

He turned and walked away. He felt unsure. Close up he could see how she couldn't possibly be a rival, whatever they did with wigs and make-up, but that voice was alarming; or was it? Perhaps it was just a fluke, perhaps she could sing like that once, and then the voice would tire. He'd come across that before now. He decided to wait and see what happened in the other rehearsals. He heard the Direktor calling them back to work again, and he crossed to Ingrid who was nervously studying her score, her lips moving as yet again she went over the part she already knew in minute detail.

'Our duet, Ingrid,' he purred. 'You are going to be the star of the Season.' It was said loud enough for Therese to hear and he had the satisfaction of seeing a slight flush creep over her face. But her smile still held firm.

They alternated rehearsals that week between *Gypsy Baron* and *Countess Maritza*, the two opening productions of the Season. Gesner was taking a lot of trouble with Ingrid in the *Baron*. In the duets he cheated for her, sang some of her more difficult phrases with her to drown her inadequacies, and frequently stopped the piano to suggest changes of key. Suzi Hoflin came in with two of her pupils and put Ingrid through a reasonable enough gypsy dance routine. It was no more than adequate but Gesner was ecstatic.

'Such lovely girls!' he enthused. 'So pretty and vibrant and energetic . . . and so young!'

Ingrid was in fact twenty-nine, which was young compared with Gesner, but not young for a dancer and she found the routines rather a strain, especially when she had to sing at the end of them.

But she tried. And at least Gesner was determined it would work. The *Maritza* rehearsals were becoming more and more disastrous. When Therese was on stage without him, he talked all the time. Called to order he was silent for a moment, then resumed his loud comments which disconcerted Therese, however hard she tried not to let them.

In the *Varasdin* duet with Rudi, the second tenor, when they were working on a very simple foot routine, Therese caught her heel in the hem of her trousers and tripped. A loud snigger from the auditorium suddenly destroyed her. Her hand went to her mouth and she stopped singing.

'Are you all right, Therese?'

'I'm sorry, Rudi . . . Could we have a short break please . . . my heel.' She walked very quickly to the side of the stage, was absent for two minutes, then returned.

'We'll continue with the waltz duet. Karl, Therese.'

They stood, side by side, wooden, facing the front, Gesner singing splendidly, Therese unsure, afraid. Busacher mastered an urge to knock their heads together.

'This is supposed to be a love song. Could you manage to appear a little . . . involved with one another? Could you begin the song with a gap between you, and Karl, move towards her, your hand outstretched. And Therese, take it slowly, then draw close. And will you please look at each other as though you are in love. Karl, please do it exactly the way you did it with Hanna in the last production.'

They began again. With an air of disdain Gesner proffered a hand on a take-it-or-leave-it basis. Therese clutched it, moved closer, stared bravely up into his face and faltered at the total contemptuous sneering disdain she saw there. The duet dwindled to a finish. Therese stood silent. Gesner shrugged his shoulders.

'That was quite dreadful,' said Busacher quietly.

'What do you expect?' said Gesner derisively. 'I told you how it would be. It is like performing with a potato.' He raised his hand to his face and with careless insolence began to pick his nose.

Tiredly, Busacher realized he would have to lose his temper. It was the only thing that worked with Gesner and he had been saving it for when they went into rehearsal on *Luxembourg*. But perhaps it would be better to tackle this huge problem now before it went any further. He took a deep breath, then slammed the piano lid down so hard the notes reverberated all round the theatre.

'I will not have it!' he screamed. 'I will not have it. I am the

114

Direktor of this Company!' He lifted the piano lid, and banged it again. Boom! Boom! 'I *will* have my singers doing as they are told. I will not have rudeness nor constant undermining of this company. I am finished! I am leaving! Karl, Therese, I shall see you separately this afternoon. Stefan, continue the rehearsal. I do not care what any of you do any more. Please yourselves! Karl, you can do what you want and let the audience think you have gone mad. I no longer care.' He deliberately pushed his chair so that it fell over, walked down the stage steps and up the gangway of the auditorium. His heart was pounding, even though it was all a sham. It was getting harder and harder to fight Gesner. In the foyer he leant against the wall for a moment, breathing deeply. Willi came in from outside, took one look at Busacher's face and walked hurriedly towards him. 'I have my car outside. Come. Get in. I'll run you home; or would you rather have a brandy?'

'A brandy, Willi. I shall be all right in a moment.'

Willi's strong, stocky body inserted itself under the Direktor's arm and he supported him out through the theatre doors towards the car.

Busacher slumped into the passenger seat and sat catching his breath. Willi unscrewed the cap from a metal flask and passed it to him. After a while the pumping of his heart began to slow down. He turned to Willi, but Willi held up a hand.

'We shall just sit quietly for a moment. Say nothing. Just rest.'

'This is getting too much for me, Willi. I used to be able to do this and come out chuckling.'

'Shall I get a doctor?'

'There is no doctor for this complaint, to cure me of Karl Gesner.'

'Say nothing. Just rest.'

They sat quietly. The street took on a sense of unreality, the posters outside the theatre announcing the new Season, a huge photograph of Gesner, some bonbon papers blowing along the pavement, a surly young man sidling up to the front of the theatre.

'Isn't that your son, Willi?' asked the Direktor, his thoughts suddenly diverted. Willi quickly started the car. 'Yes,' he said. 'But he won't be very pleased if he thinks I've seen him lurking. Let's get you home.'

'I'm all right now. I had to lose my temper. As you know it's the only thing that brings Gesner to heel. It is very curious the way it works, but it does.' Willi glanced at him in the mirror and thought he still didn't look too good.

'Don't you think you should go home for the rest of the day? Stefan and old Anton can take the rehearsal.'

'I shall have to go back. I've said I want to see Therese and Karl at separate interviews this afternoon. Therese, of course, needs nothing but another injection of confidence and some sympathizing over Gesner. Gesner needs his usual are-we-going-to-have-a-season-or-aren't-we lecture.'

'Why don't you go home anyway, and I'll tell Gesner he must report to your house at a certain time. That will make it seem even more serious. In fact I think it would be a good idea if I was there, and possibly Gaston and Julius from the theatre committee. We could all sit in a row behind your big table; impress the gravity of the situation upon him.'

A little colour came back into Busacher's face. 'I ought to be able to handle him on my own, Willi.'

'No. He's been getting steadily worse for years. I think we need a concerted attack this time.'

'It would have some impact,' Busacher agreed gratefully. 'Could you arrange it, do you think?'

'Of course. It's settled. I'll take you straight home to rest and I'll organize Gaston and Julius to come just before five, and I'll tell Karl he is to report promptly. No need to worry about Therese. I'll look after her.'

'Thank you, Willi.'

They drove silently to Busacher's house and Willi helped him indoors, relieved to see some of the old vigour returning.

'May I use your telephone, Franz?'

Busacher waved his hand towards the study and disappeared into his studio. Willi paused, thought for a moment, then dialled his own number, spoke to Frau Trauffer, then dialled his friend the florist and then Gaston and Julius. He felt rather pleased with his organization. Just before he left he opened the door to look at Busacher. Franz was seated in an armchair with a glass in his hand. He smiled reassuringly, said, 'Thanks, Willi,' and smiled.

Back in the theatre the entire stage was silent after Busacher had slammed out of the auditorium doors. He didn't lose his temper very often, but when he did it was always with Gesner, and it was dramatic. There was a sense among them, even the innocent ones, of naughty children who had gone too far and had been abandoned by their parents. Even Gesner, the star, looked a little sheepish. They couldn't have a season without him, but quite definitely they couldn't have one without Busacher either. And it was fine when Busacher was paying him attention, rebuking him for talking

116

during someone else's numbers, railing at him for rudeness, for lack of participation. It was all right providing he wasn't ignored and abandoned. It was all the fault of that bitch they'd brought in. How could they expect him to perform with someone like that? It was all her fault.

'Therese, Freddi, Rudi, your Act Three opening.' Stefan knew he couldn't cope with the traumas of continuing where they had left off. He was only the company manager. It wasn't his job to try and get Gesner and Therese to sing together. Anton, the old *répétiteur*, even older than Busacher, sat down at the piano and the thin embarrassed voices began to tingle into the air, picking up a little courage as they went on. It was something, thought Stefan, darting a quick glance at Gesner, who looked very slightly uncomfortable, that for once he wasn't talking. At least the Herr Direktor had accomplished something.

Therese, under the fixed smile and the determination, was beginning to wonder if she ought to withdraw now, before they got too far into rehearsals. She didn't really know if she was going to be able to take any more, and still give a worthwhile performance. It was difficult, even though she had been told all the problems of Gesner, to continue to hold oneself together in the face of such blatant hatred. To feel oneself so disliked, so vulnerable, never knowing what new piece of venom would manifest itself next, needed someone more arrogant, more . . . theatrical than she was.

It had all gone – the thin veneer of self-confidence, the determination that she had been so proud of acquiring and nurturing since that first audition in Vienna. She had tried, but the rehearsals had gradually taken on the menace of trials of endurance. On the days when she knew she had to practise duets with Gesner, she lay awake the night before in a sweat of fear. It was more than just fear of Gesner's contempt. Similarity with that other man who had tried to destroy her threatened to break down the shutter in her mind with which she blanked out memories of Freidrich.

Of course, one didn't drop out of an engagement simply because one was not strong enough to take insults and hatred. But her very presence seemed to be wrecking what chance the company had of any success. Look at the Herr Direktor this morning. Exploding into a temper, the sort of temper she had never seen in him before. She was suddenly afraid, not just of Gesner but of the catastrophes that might occur to the whole company because of the tension.

She got through the rest of the morning as best she could. Stefan was very careful not to rehearse any numbers that she and Gesner had to perform together, but she still felt afraid. If he went on like this she wasn't even sure she would have enough composure to return to Vienna and resume her church and radio work. All she longed to do at this very moment was run back to the Gasthaus and hide in her room. Pride and a sense of dignity kept her from letting any of them see how terrified she was. She sang as well as she could, hitting the right notes – she never had any problem with that – but it was pretty dreadful singing, so lifeless and uninspired, not the way she had been singing during the weeks before Gesner's arrival. When they broke for lunch she left the stage very quickly, anxious only to go back to her room. Footsteps followed her. It was Luiza, trying to hurry in spite of her hip.

'Therese . . . shall we go to the coffee shop . . . have a sandwich?'

'Thank you, no, Luiza. I can't.'

'Don't let him do this to you, dear. He's a bastard. We all hate him really . . . just that our jobs depend on him . . . but we're all on your side. We really are, love.'

Therese swallowed hard. She didn't want anyone giving her sympathy, otherwise she'd be blubbing all over the stage. 'Thanks, Luiza. It's not your problem. And I don't want anyone taking sides. This is Hochhauser, not the Middle East.'

'Well, I just don't want you getting all upset. You're so good . . . we all think so . . .'

'Thanks. I must go now.' She almost ran to the stage door, opened it, leaned on the outside.

'Oh, no!'

Willi Zimmermann was standing by his car door, beaming, holding it open.

'No. I must go back to my room. Thank you, but please leave me.'

As she went to walk past, Willi grabbed her by the arm and pushed her, quite roughly, into the passenger seat. Foolishly, the roughness from one who had been so kind was the last straw, and tears suddenly welled into her eyes. Willi took no notice but walked around to his seat and started the engine. He said nothing at all and she averted her face, staring out of the window, hoping he hadn't noticed. As they set off she realized they weren't driving back towards the restaurants of the town centre and Willi's beloved Franz Joseph hotel, but up to the mountain road that led over the pass and into the next valley. Willi changed into a lower gear. She hadn't even noticed, locked up in the theatre with

Gesner and her misery, but it was a glorious day, cold, with a huge blue sky, not a cloud anywhere on the mountain tops, and the pines of the tree line glowing green against the snow. They went higher, up the steep winding road, snow banked high on either side of them and no traffic at all coming down from the pass.

Twenty minutes later Willi pulled the car into a clearing and got out. She stared stonily ahead until he opened her door and beckoned her forward.

'Come. I want to show you the valley.'

Because it would have been childish to refuse she stepped out and went to stand beside him on the snow. In front of them the valley dropped sharply away from the road. Tiny fields, green and white where the snow was melting again, led down to the outskirts of the town. It looked quite small from this angle and one could see all of the bicycle factory.

'You see that building there, on one side of the ridge, with the big barn and the red roof?'

'Yes.'

'That is my farm. All the land on that side of the ridge is mine. It belonged to my grandfather, but he lost it when the *Creditanstalt* crashed in the twenties. He lost all his money and had to sell the farm and go and work in an abattoir in Vienna. He hated it, my grandfather. He'd always been a dairy farmer, you see, like I am. He hated butchering cattle. He was the one who brought me up, more a father than a grandfather.

'My father was called up when the war broke out. He died in Russia. I was only four when he went away so I don't really remember him. Mother went to visit her relatives in Hungary, near Szeged, and got caught there when the Russians advanced. She never came back. My grandparents were my parents. I wish the old man had lived to see me get the farm back. He left a little money, he had managed to save a small amount, though God knows how in the war and just after. And then I worked in an hotel in the Tyrol as soon as the tourist industry opened up and saved some money to put with Grandfather's. Gerda and I got a bank loan, and I was able to buy the farm back. We've more land now. We bought the section running down on the east side eight years ago.'

She looked at the smoke coming out of the Zimmermann chimney. On the lower slopes was a large herd of cows. 'Are those cows all right in the snow?'

'We bring them inside in the bad weather. You see the smaller farmhouse, on the other side of the ridge?'

'Yes.'

'That is the Hoflin farm . . . where Suzi Hoflin lives with her parents. Georg is hoping to marry her and unite the farms.'

'A very practical young man,' she said politely. She was feeling calmer. Up here, on the top of the pass, Gesner and the theatre didn't seem so important – not important at all when one thought of losing one's farm and parents in a war.

'Yes, I'm afraid he is,' said Willi gloomily. He stared down at the Hoflin farm, then clumped back to the car.

'Get in,' he said. 'Now we shall go and look at my farm.'

They drove slowly back down the mountain road until they came to the track that led up to the Zimmermann farmhouse. The ground was soft and squelchy when she got out of the car, and she felt mud oozing over the top of her shoes.

'Do you want me to walk round the farm?' she asked, alarmed. Willi chuckled.

'Straight indoors. I'll clean the mud from your shoes when we're inside.'

He opened the kitchen door, and a cheerful middle-aged woman gave Therese an inquisitive stare.

'Frau Trauffer. Here is Fräulein Therese Aschmann from the theatre who has mud all over her shoes.'

'Off at once, please,' said Frau Trauffer sharply. 'You must go through in your feet.'

Willi led her into a huge living-room with a window looking over the valley. A table was set for two. A bottle rested in an ice bucket, and on one of the settings was a posy of spring flowers.

'My son was very cross with me for burdening you with the basket of flowers.' He winked at her. 'So here is a more modest offering.'

Slowly she picked up the flowers, not knowing what to say. Willi was busy undoing the wire round the champagne cork.

'There are some days,' he said, 'when champagne is not for celebration, but for bracing the spine, putting back heart, restoring the ego. Today is such a day.' The cork popped and Willi skilfully caught the first fountain in a glass. 'I do not want you to say a word until you have drunk at least two glasses.' He took a large gulp from his own glass and gave an ecstatic sigh. 'Excellent. One feels so depraved drinking champagne in the middle of a working day.'

She felt curiously distanced now from all the problems of the morning. Up here, in Willi's mountain farmhouse, with no shoes and her old rehearsal clothes, it was all very unreal.

She was tired, emotionally and physically tired, and the champagne made her cease to worry about whether she was right

120

to allow the Burgermeister to cosset her with flowers and champagne. She stretched back in her chair and blocked the morning out of her mind. She was good at blocking things out.

'You are very kind to me.'

'Do you want to talk about Gesner?'

'No.'

'Then we shall not. I shall tell you, instead, of the time Gerda and I saw you on the stage in Vienna.'

She didn't really want him to recreate the past like that. There were too many shadows between that time and this, but as she listened it wasn't her past that came back to her, it was his. She got a glimpse of a different life, a different marriage between two good, kind, ordinary people – perhaps not so ordinary when one thought what they had done with their farm. She began to see herself, the self of those twenty years ago, as just a part of Willi and Gerda's pleasure. She had done what actors and singers were supposed to do – provided enchantment for a brief passage of time. To Willi and Gerda she had been no more than a romantic inspiration, a cardboard figure of tinsel who ceased to exist when the curtain came down. What became real to her was not Therese Aschmann, but the tiny diamond and garnet engagement ring Willi had bought in a shop at the back of St Stephen's Cathedral, and Gerda's delight, and the luck they had had in getting two cancellation seats at the *Staatsoper* for a performance of *Figaro*, and the elegance of their hotel, and the toy truck they had bought for Georg, which had been so large they'd had trouble getting it home. She felt transported into their safe, happy world, felt as though she were part of it.

'So you see, dear Therese, when I learned you were to come here, and then I saw you, exactly the same as you were twenty years ago, you can perhaps understand how I felt . . .'

It was embarrassing, the way he kept on about her being the same as she was twenty years ago. His foolish exaggeration made her feel uncomfortable. In any other man it would have seemed like meaningless and artificial flattery, but Willi was incapable of being artificial. As she studied him closely over her coffee cup she wondered why he said those things, then decided he could no more help it than he could help having three portions of everything. Willi didn't know the meaning of restraint, not in any aspect of his life.

By the time he had taken her back to the theatre she felt totally removed from the morning, quite calm, controlled, almost as though she was nothing to do with the Hochhauser Season but had just come back from a week in Vienna staying at a luxury hotel.

The row of figures behind Busacher's desk disconcerted Gesner for a moment. That fool, the Burgermeister, was there, and the two members of the theatre committee. But he had no intention of letting himself be intimidated. He flung himself into a chair without waiting to be asked. If they thought he was going to stand in front of them like a naughty schoolboy, they were mistaken.

'I thought we were to have a private discussion . . . about Aschmann,' he said insolently.

'No, Karl. We are not having a private discussion about Aschmann. We are here to have a committee meeting about the Season, and about your attitude, and indeed about whether we can go on with the Season at all.'

'I cannot go on with that hideous old Frau. You have made a very bad decision and something must be done. She must be got rid of.'

'Very well, Karl. I have already telephoned Hans about your attitude, which I anticipated would result in this kind of ultimatum. Hans has announced his intention of suing the company, and also you. Your signature is, of course, on the contract we all signed in Hans's office.'

'I was trapped into it!' blustered the tenor.

'No doubt that will all come out in court, also the fact that you refused to rehearse with Aschmann past the first week. The case will, naturally, destroy the Season entirely. Hans has announced his intention of fighting for as big a settlement as he can get. He has said he does not care what it costs him, he is standing on a matter of principle. I expect you know he has no love for you . . . your reneging on the Munich contract some years ago meant several of his singers lost work. He thinks you are an unreliable and subversive influence in the theatre, and he will be only too pleased to make an example of you.'

'Ridiculous,' stammered Gesner. 'All over the little problem of changing the soprano.'

'That is not the problem. You know that quite well, Karl.'

'Pay her off. Give her the fees.'

'We can't afford to do that,' said Gustave, scandalized. 'Neither can we afford a court settlement.'

'You are deliberately undermining the morale of this company because you do not want to work with Aschmann,' Busacher continued. 'You know very well, because you are not a fool, that we cannot use Ingrid any more than we are doing already. Our

122

audiences put up with a lot, but they will not accept total inadequacies for every performance. You also know we have no chance of getting anyone else. That has been made quite clear, categorically clear, by everyone in Vienna. Apparently Hanna Brunner has offered to come forward and give evidence in court about your behaviour to your fellow artistes, and Hans has said he is making it plain to all the other agents that none of his clients will be allowed to sing in Hochhauser and he recommends that they do the same.'

There was a shocked and disapproving cluck from the committee men.

'So, Karl. Will you please tell me what you are trying to achieve? Is it your wish to totally destroy the Company in a lawsuit that will bankrupt us?'

Gesner didn't answer.

'Is it your wish to so demoralize Aschmann that she cannot perform and you are therefore left without a leading lady for three operettas?'

'Understudies . . .' muttered Gesner, knowing he was being ridiculous.

'Understudies . . . yes. You know about our understudies. You know the standard. You are happy to appear in a season of rapidly declining productions? You do not mind your reputation disintegrating along with the rest of the Company? I have to say that I *do* mind about *my* reputation. If Aschmann becomes unable to perform – as a result of your deliberately destructive influence – I would at once have to issue a statement making it plain that from now on I disassociate myself entirely from the Hochhauser Season.'

There was an agitated rumble from the two committee men, who weren't entirely in the picture. Willi had given them the briefest of explanations for their presence being required but they were becoming as alarmed as Gesner by this talk of lawsuits and the resignation of Franz Busacher.

'Surely it would be simpler to get another tenor!' panicked Gaston. 'If Herr Gesner is unhappy, perhaps it would be simpler to let *him* leave.'

'Then I shall sue!' shouted Gesner.

'Yes. You have sued before, have you not, Karl? Litigation is not unknown to you. You have quite a reputation in our profession for providing the catalyst of many a legal battle.'

Gesner was extremely frightened. He could not think what had happened for things to have become so out of hand. His efforts to destroy Therese had been purely instinctive: a fear of the star quality of her voice, a distaste for her appearance, the fact that he would appear foolish performing romantically with her. He wasn't quite sure what he wanted . . . Therese kept down, in the background, her voice modulated into no more than competence . . . Busacher indulging him, letting him do as he wished as usual . . . everyone treating him as the saviour of Hochhauser. He couldn't afford another lawsuit. He couldn't afford any rumours getting out that he had deliberately destroyed the Hochhauser Company. That would be the end of any engagements elsewhere, just when he was beginning to get back on the international circuit.

'I don't understand what all this is about,' he said, in the tones of a reasonable and patient man. 'All I want is to sing in Hochhauser as usual. I wish we had someone better than Aschmann, but if that is the best we can do, then we shall have to manage. I do not understand why – because of her little temperaments in the theatre this morning – we are having all this talk of lawsuits and resignations. I just do not understand at all.' He shrugged and raised his hands with the air of a man prepared to be tolerant and forgiving. He smiled charmingly at the two committee men. He even smiled at Busacher and Willi who did not smile back.

'Good. That is settled then. There will be no more talk of Aschmann leaving and from now on rehearsals will be conducted professionally.'

'It was not my fault this morning . . .'

'There will be no more talking and laughing during Therese's solos. No gratuitous rudeness.' Busacher knew that was almost impossible to implement. Gesner was a master of the devious insult. 'And some serious attempt at convincing performances with Aschmann. That will be all. You can leave now. Rehearsals promptly at ten tomorrow. You will not be late. We shall go through all the *Maritza* scenes with you and Therese. I shall call no-one else.'

Gesner groped for a suave exit line, something to make him feel the star of Hochhauser again, but the four serious faces were all staring at him blankly, totally devoid of any warmth or admiration. He gave another little shrug and muttered 'So ridiculous!' then left the room. All the way back to the Franz Joseph he blustered to himself, justified everything he had done, and thought how dreary and provincial they all were. But he was conscious too of a small knot of apprehension in his stomach. He was, of course, totally capable of dealing with the situation. If they wanted him to sing with that ugly old bitch, then sing he would. But he would have to try and be a little more compliant, throw a little more charm around. It was easy enough to do.

He went straight to the bar in the Franz Joseph. He needed a drink and that old swine Busacher hadn't offered him anything at the villa. Sitting up at the bar was Ingrid and the little dancer – two pretty girls, just what he needed.

'The most enchanting sight I have seen today . . . may I join you?' He was sensible enough to know he couldn't get away with flip, funny conversation, trying to compete with the young. His style was older, smooth, charming, experienced and no-one had laughed at him yet. He was well aware that he made young men look badly dressed and ill-mannered. Ingrid smiled at him a little tenatively. Like the rest of the Company, she knew Gesner could be a swine. But he was being jolly nice to her and she really couldn't think of anything else except her first leading role. She ate, slept, and drank Saffi. She was sorry for Therese Aschmann, but she had no energy left for anything except getting through her own part. She was beginning to experience the soloist's panic of realizing that the success of the show rested on her shoulders.

'Suzi and I are going back to her dance studio and she's going to put me through the dance routine again.'

Suzi, leaning against the stool, smiled at him more warmly. He was extraordinarily handsome and he was the star of the Season. She had missed the worst of the scene this morning. Gesner decided she was about twenty-two or -three, younger than Ingrid, who looked quite good until you saw her against a really pretty girl, like this one. His eyes wandered down. Marvellous legs too.

'Your dance this morning was delightful,' he said, to Suzi more than Ingrid. He smiled into her eyes, then lightly touched her under the chin with his finger.

'You are very talented.' Suzi blushed.

'Thank you.'

'And very, very pretty. I think you have some Hungarian blood. Am I right?'

Suzi blushed even more deeply. 'No . . . I don't think so. My parents were both born here, in Hochhauser.'

'Well . . . I'm quite sure there is a Hungarian great-grandmother somewhere. The high cheekbones,' he ran his finger from her chin to just below the eye. 'The heart-shaped face. The eyes that tilt slightly at the corner. Enchanting!' He waved to the bartender, knowing that he couldn't expect her to make any coherent reply to such compliments. She just sat there flushed, slightly embarrassed.

'What would you like to drink? Ingrid? Suzi?'

'Oh, no, we don't want any more. We're leaving now and going to rehearse again.'

'I was going to invite you to share my dinner here.'

'We'll be working.'

'We won't be working for the whole evening, Ingrid,' said Suzi quickly. 'You can't possibly do more than an hour, not after a full day's rehearsal. You'll be exhausted tomorrow. We could always come back in about a couple of hours.'

Gesner looked at his watch. 'Eight-thirty . . . yes?!' Suzi dimpled up at him. She really was exceptionally pretty.

'That would be lovely, wouldn't it, Ingrid?'

'Yes. Thank you.' He *was* the star and it was really terribly nice of him to buy her dinner for her, and at the Franz Joseph too. She didn't earn much and dinner was usually a bowl of soup and a cold platter at the small restaurant next door to the Goldener Adler.

As they hurried away he saw Suzi look back over her shoulder, as he'd known she would.

The rehearsals continued, subdued but in an orderly way. Gesner totally ignored Therese when they weren't on stage together, but he at least kept reasonably quiet when she was performing, and if he passed derogatory comments about her at least they were audible only to those close to him. On stage there was a professional if uninspired attempt at singing together. There were odd moments when, for no reason, the two voices lifted off, as though they were nothing to do with the two people who didn't like one another. When that happened Busacher began to hope again. Those two voices were incredible, and could be sensational if they both forgot everything except the performance.

On Friday Madge Grimsilk was sitting at the back of the stalls again. She had been there a few times throughout the week but Busacher frequently forgot her. Sometimes she wandered quietly about with measures and notebooks, but mostly she just sat and watched and listened. At the break on Friday she approached him with her drawing pad.

'May I speak with you, Herr Busacher?'

'Of course. Are you well? I'm afraid I have had little time to entertain you or introduce you to Hochhauser. I hope you have not been too lonely.'

'Not at all. I've been busy. I have a great deal to do.'

'Of course. What did you wish to speak of?'

'The designs for Therese's costumes. In *Luxembourg*.'

'Splendid.'

'You were right, of course, about it being impossible to carry through the fantasy look and dress Therese as a fairy heroine. But we *can* make her look part of the magic theme. See . . .'

It was almost an exact drawing of Therese. She had caught the tired nervousness, the apprehension in the face. She had also caught the very faint remnant of warmth, gaiety, that he thought no-one but himself had recognized from the old days. There was something vaguely familiar about the costume.

'I've seen this before,' he said slowly.

'I've based it on the photograph of Rosa Ponselle as La Gioconda. Therese cannot be Snow White or Cinderella, but she *can* be Queen of the Night. She's quite tall, and she has good legs. And Angèle Didier is supposed to be an opera singer, an experienced woman of the world. There is no reason why she shouldn't appear older, and slightly wicked! I've designed all her costumes in either dark sapphire or emerald. That way she'll stand out from all the light colours around her.'

The drawing reminded him not only of Rosa Ponselle's photograph, but also the wicked queen in *Snow White*. It was high-necked and had long tight sleeves and a straight line to the floor, where it flared out at the back into a huge swirling fishtail train. There were points of light, glass stones he supposed, all over the dress, and the neckline and tail of the train were heavily encrusted with glittering theatre tat. The finishing touch was supplied by a high pointed tiara. In the drawing Therese appeared to be about seven feet tall and not at all overweight. It was a clever illusion, but it was more than that. This was the way Therese would have looked if she had never left the stage, never married Friedrich, never had years of misery and failure.

'That is for the ball scene. This is for the marriage scene.'

The same line again, but in blue and silver, a huge swirling cloak that swept out several feet behind her, the ends weighted with silver stones. She was the infinitely alluring, forever mysterious older woman who knew everything there was to know about love, sex, and romantic liaisons. She was every adolescent schoolboy's dream.

'And, Herr Busacher, I think something must be done about her costumes for the other productions. I know you have no money for anything but the hired costumes and I am prepared to waive my fee for designing extra clothes for her. If she has to wear the hired 1920s costumes for *Countess Maritza* it will be disastrous.'

Busacher was taken aback. 'That's very kind of you, Miss Grimsilk.'

'I think I shall be coming in a little under budget on *Luxembourg* so perhaps any surplus could be spent on the other productions.'

'Certainly *Maritza*,' he said. 'You are right. That could be one of her best roles, but the twenties costumes will not be kind to her. Arsena in the *Baron* . . . it does not matter. The hired clothes will have to do. But . . . if you could look at *Der Zarewitsch*? The boy's costume in Act One. If there is any way that could be modified?' He smiled at Madge who had suddenly revealed unexpected human traits. 'That boy's costume defies the most skilful of designers.'

Therese suddenly appeared above them on the stage. She seemed quite cheerful.

'Are you looking at Madge's drawings, Franz? Aren't they incredible?'

'You've seen them?' She shouldn't have done that. Not before he had seen them.

'My fault, Franz. I wheedled a look out of her after we'd shared a bottle of wine last night.'

Madge Grimsilk's face didn't even flicker. It was as impassive, as cold as ever. She flapped her sketch pad shut.

'If that is satisfactory then, Herr Busacher, I'll have the costume-maker begin work on those designs.'

'Thank you,' he answered, bewildered, and was even more surprised when Therese called down from the stage, 'Coming for coffee, Madge? I've got a cup here for you.'

'Excuse me,' said Madge, and left him alone pondering on the strangeness of women and of Madge Grimsilk in particular.

CHAPTER EIGHT

As the first night of the Hochhauser Season approached, Suzi Hoflin found herself increasingly torn between dread and a curious sense of wild exhilaration that was only partly to do with the excitement of appearing in a professional production. Many times, in the middle of the night when she could not sleep, she was faced with the slightly guilty realization that she was behaving rather badly, but in the daytime it didn't seem to matter. She pushed all serious thoughts to the back of her mind and climbed back on to the helter-skelter of excitement and self-confidence induced by the undisguised admiration of Karl Gesner.

She had never wanted to hurt Georg. She had spoken the truth when she said she couldn't imagine her life without him. He had always been there and when she was little she had worshipped him with all the adulation of any little girl for a big, brave, older brother. She wasn't being quite fair either when she said – to herself – that that was how she thought of him, as a brother. Even when she was tiny she hadn't really thought of him that way, and when she was older, about thirteen, she had secretly been terribly proud in front of the other girls when Georg, who had never seemed to go through a spotty adolescent phase like other boys, used to wait for her outside school so that they could walk up the mountain road together. Once, when he had been late and a crowd of louts from the factory had started to shout at her, calling out about her legs and what they'd like to do to her, Georg had come storming down the road on a bicycle, jumped off, and knocked two of them down before the rest ran away. She'd felt like a princess.

She couldn't quite remember when it was that she'd realized Georg took it for granted they'd get married as soon as she was old enough. Possibly it was when she'd said how much she'd like to go to school in Vienna and learn how to dance. Georg, walking along beside her, his hand resting in a comradely way on her shoulder, had laughed. 'Dancing is no use to a farmer's wife,' he'd said, but even then it wasn't a surprise. Somehow, over the years, without ever asking her, he had made it plain that her future was mapped out. And it was then, when she was thinking about going away to Vienna, that she had begun to feel trapped. She loved her parents, and her parents' farm, and she loved Uncle Willi, and Georg, and their farm, and she would hate that world to change. But when she thought about the future, about staying at home, then marrying Georg and just moving over the ridge, and starting there and then to have babies and spend every day in the dairy the way her mother did, a terrible sense of panic overtook her. Surely there was more to life than that? Every time you looked at a magazine or newspaper, or turned on the television, there was the world of the young as it was today. The world belonged to the young. Their music dominated all other music, their lifestyle was brave and fun and independent. They went around the world with backpacks and no money, and they left home and lived together without getting married, and many of them became superstars when they were still only in their teens. And what had she, Suzi Hoflin, ever done? Stayed at home. Passed her school exams, played with Georg, helped her mother in the dairy, and never given either of her parents a moment's worry.

Frau Hoflin, a sensible woman, old-fashioned, but not so old-fashioned that she couldn't see the signs of rebellion beginning to germinate, pressed for the safest 'revolt' she could think of. Three years at a nice school in Vienna, not *too* liberated, but at the same time not a convent school. A rather lively and interesting school, as it turned out, with quite a few theatrical sons and daughters as pupils and an emphasis on the performing arts. Frau Hoflin knew her daughter well. Suzi was never going to backpack round the world or become a rock star, and if she had been forced to go and live away from home – to study nursing, for instance – she'd have mouldered away from homesickness. But at the same time she *was* young, and she wanted to have some fun before she became exactly like her mother.

In Vienna quite a few of them had gone around in a crowd together, boys and girls. She'd had a couple of little fumbling and innocuous affairs, nothing serious, and she never dared breathe a word to Georg. In fact, the reason they had never become anything more serious than fumbles was because, compared with Georg, the boys seemed very young and silly. Still, it had been the most enormous fun, the café groups in the mornings, the theatre parties, the concerts they'd put on themselves. There had been a time when, like everyone else at the school, she had said she wanted to be a professional dancer, or an actress, or anything else that was exciting and totally different from working in a bank or being a dairy farmer's wife. But when it came to it, when she had to make the decision about leaving home for good, throwing herself into the wide world and trying her luck, she felt unhappy. Leave Hochhauser for good? Those wonderful mornings in summer when the larks rose high over the mountains and you woke to the sound of cowbells and the sun streaming in through the window? Leave all her friends, the ones she had known all her life? Leave Mama, and Papa, and Uncle Willi, and Georg? The principal of the school had suggested the answer. She had passed all her dancing exams. She had acquired her teaching certificates. Hochhauser was becoming an increasingly affluent little town with a new emerging middle class who were prepared to spend money on life's smaller luxuries, so why not begin her own little dancing academy? With relief Suzi had departed back to Hochhauser, feeling she hadn't altogether lost face amongst her fellow students – after all, her choice of career was still quite artistic and adventurous, it was still 'show business' in a way – but also overjoyed to be going home.

And then Georg had closed in on her, a grumpier, more disapproving, hectoring Georg. A Georg who was constantly finding fault and who, in some curious way over the three years of her absence, had become *mean*. When she thought about living the rest of her life with that bad-tempered, stingy, humourless Georg, she felt like bursting into tears. The Hochhauser Season had come along just at the right time, a time when she needed a little excitement, a little glamour, a little of the old camaraderie that she had known with her friends in Vienna. The Hochhauser Season had given her the courage to defy Georg – not to quarrel with him, she didn't want to do that – but to make it plain she was now her own woman, with her own life to lead, a life that might or might not include him.

She had never, in a million years, meant to take Gesner seriously. She knew all about Gesner – he'd got a girl pregnant last year and everyone in the Company said he was appalling to the new leading lady, although she hadn't noticed it herself. She was rarely there for the full rehearsals. She took her dance calls with the chorus, and had separate sessions coaching the soloists. She'd done a bit of elementary choreography for Therese and Gesner, but he seemed to be all right, a bit standoffish and dignified perhaps, then then he *was* the star.

It was *because* she'd never taken him seriously that the whole thing had come as a surprise. Like everyone else even remotely connected with the Hochhauser Season (and over the years she had listened to quite a few of Uncle Willi's stories) she had accepted the image of Gesner the seducer, the monster of conceit, the arrogant and selfish star of the company. It had come as quite a surprise to discover he was charming, very generous, and enormous fun to be with. She began to wonder if all those other stories about him had been not a little exaggerated.

The evening he had taken her and Ingrid to dinner had been wonderful. He'd bought them champagne. He'd been funny, telling stories against himself of fiascos he had survived in the theatre, and he'd been flattering in a subtle way. Several times she'd caught him staring at her with a warm, smiling expression in his brown eyes, and if she hadn't been so sensible it would have made her feel quite wobbly.

The following morning, in her pigeonhole at the theatre, had been a sealed envelope.

'I *adore* Ingrid, but I *do* spend a lot of time making love to her in the *Baron* and a man needs a change. Your turn. Can you get away at five? We'll drive over to Baden for dinner and I promise to get you back before your mama realizes that Big Bad Gesner has abducted you over the mountains.'

The note had made her giggle and she'd seen absolutely no harm in going. After all, he was only one of the Company and if she could go out and eat with Ingrid or Rudi, why not with Gesner? And the thought of swooping all the way to Baden in his Alfa Romeo was quite dreamy. It made a change from Georg and his old van.

Gesner had flirted with her quite outrageously during the dinner (more champagne) and had made no secret of his intense interest in her life, and particularly of the men in her life. He wanted to hear all about Georg and about the boyfriends in Vienna. He asked her, smiling over the top of his glass, if she had ever been to bed with a man and when she said 'not exactly' he had burst out laughing and touched her cheek with one strong brown hand. He really had very nice hands, large but well-shaped with just a shading of dark hair on the back of his wrists. She had quite expected him to stop the car on the way home and make a grab at her and she was all prepared to cope with it, had her little speech ready about what a wonderful evening she'd had but at the moment she was concentrating on her career and didn't really want to waste time on that kind of thing. So she was relieved, but at the same time a little chagrined when he didn't stop the car at all but drove her to the bottom of the footpath that led up to the Hoflin farm.

'I will happily drive you to your front door, little one,' he said dryly, 'but I have the feeling you would prefer not to waken your parents with the noise of the vulgar Alfa revving off into the night.'

'Er . . . Oh, it's no distance at all up by the path, only a few moments . . . yes . . . I think that would be better . . . and thank you, it's been a lovely evening, wonderful!'

Gesner beckoned her forward to the open car window. He pointed to a place on his cheek. 'I am not quite the Hochhauser rapist I am made out to be, but I expect a little peck, just here, on the cheek.' She leaned forward and kissed him quickly. He smelled of something very expensive and sophisticated. Nice.

The following evening (that was three expensive dinners in a row, which made a contrast to Georg's grudging once a month treat at the cinema) she had insisted that this time they talk about him. After all, she was grown-up enough to know that to please a man you needed to listen to him, and in fact it was no hardship at all to listen to Karl (unlike Georg, who spoke only of the farm). He had met many famous and exciting people, he'd had a rich and varied life, some of it rather sad. He told her he'd been married once, long ago, but had been so bitterly hurt that, although he loved women, couldn't live without them, he had never been pre-pared to trust his life to one ever again. She would have loved to know what the erring Frau Gesner had done, but he had suddenly looked so stern, so sad, that she hadn't the nerve to ask.

They'd seen each other every day since then; sometimes, because of rehearsals and because Gesner had so much work to do, it was only for a drink at the Franz Joseph. Other times it was dinner; twice he took her dancing, the smoochy old-fashioned sort of dancing, not a disco, the sort where she was right up against him and his hands held her in a strong, commanding kind of way. When he finally did kiss her, properly kiss her, she was more than ready.

Inevitably, the rest of the company, the rest of Hochhauser knew what was going on. They couldn't avoid being seen together and she braced herself for the blast from Georg and from her parents. But Frau Hoflin, who had been infinitely wise in her daughter's education, was equally wise on this occasion. She prevailed upon Suzi's father to keep his mouth shut and she said, just once, laughing, 'I never thought the infamous Gesner would conquer you, Suzi! He really must be a remarkable man! I can't wait until he gets round to me – I must be the only female in Hochhauser not on his list.'

'Mama, really!' Suzi was shocked.

'I'm not that old, Suzi. I might even be younger than Gesner. There's no reason you should be shocked at the thought of him taking me out. We're of the same generation.'

'Mama. You're married!'

'Of course I am, darling.' Frau Hoflin patted her daughter's cheek. 'I'm only joking.'

She had said no more. She had made her point – that Suzi was one on a long, long list, and that Gesner was her parents' generation. She only hoped the affair hadn't gone too far for those things to cease to matter.

The interview with Georg, too, while unpleasant, hadn't been as terrible as Suzi had feared. She still saw him, made a point of popping over to say hullo to Uncle Willi and sought out Georg in the dairy or the office. Georg was prickly and proud.

'I hope you're coming to see me on the first night, Georg. I can get you a ticket if you like.'

'Thank you. No.'

Suzi sighed. 'I would like you to come, Georg. You are my oldest and most special friend. I would really like you to come.'

Georg turned his back to her, clamped down the lid of the sterilizer and switched it on.

'I see enough of you and Gesner racing around in that appalling car of his without watching you prancing together on a stage.'

'Actually, Georg, we don't perform together on the stage. We are hardly on at all together. I only have very short appearances. He is the star.'

'So I understand,' said Georg bitterly.

'We're only friends, Georg,' she said gently.

'You mean you and I are only friends? Or you and he are only friends?' He turned and glared at her and for a moment she thought the old Georg was going to start carping and nagging and telling her what she ought or ought not to do. But his mouth suddenly tightened and he turned back to the sterilizer in dignified silence.

She suddenly realized she didn't know what she *had* meant. She was hopelessly confused, not wanting to lose Georg, but at the same time obsessed with the pull of Gesner. She couldn't stop thinking about Gesner; every moment of her life when she wasn't working she was thinking of him, reliving what he had said, what he had done, how he had kissed her, what he would do next time. What she would do if he tried to take her to bed. She knew she ought to tell Georg it was all over between them, that it was finished for good. But somehow she couldn't. She wanted to eat her cake and have it, put Georg away in a little box for the future, when she'd finished having a good time.

'We're still friends, aren't we, Georg?' she asked.

'Go to hell!'

She didn't know why that hurt, but it did and her eyes filled with tears. She was tired and off balance. She hadn't had an early night for ages and when she did get to bed she didn't sleep but just lay there thinking about Karl. Georg looked at her and for a moment she thought he was going to grab her, thought he was going to cry himself, but he suddenly stormed out of the dairy and began to stride up towards the lower pasture. 'I've had enough,' he shouted in a choked voice.

She was upset, but later reflected it hadn't been as bad as it could have been. At least he hadn't interrogated her in his awful 'Georg' way. If he had really started asking questions she wouldn't have known how to answer them.

Three days before the opening night of the Season, Gesner – rather embarrassingly – stopped the rehearsal when he saw she was slipping out of the theatre to go home.

'Carry on without me for a moment,' he said, waving his hand in an imperious way, which Suzi found funny and Busacher found infuriating. 'I just want to have a word with Suzi.'

Everyone watched him stride up the aisle towards the door at the back of the auditorium. Everyone looked from him to Suzi. They were all too kind to snigger but Suzi distinctly saw fat Luiza shrug her shoulders in a gesture of fatalistic despair. Suzi dodged outside the door into the theatre foyer. 'You shouldn't have done that,' she said nervously. 'Everyone will blame me for you stopping the rehearsal.'

'They don't matter. What they think doesn't matter. Tonight is our last free night before we go into production. It's non-stop rehearsals from now on. I think we should go somewhere special tonight. I want to be alone with you – it will be the last time for several days.'

He had her penned up against the wall, both arms stretched out, imprisoning her in a cage of his body and arms. She shivered. The oppressive power of him was overwhelming.

'I can't come tonight. It's Uncle Willi's party. He always has his party on the last free night before production.'

'You're not a little girl. You don't have to go to Uncle Willi's party.'

'Oh, but I do. I've always gone. And this year, with me being in the Company for the first time, I really must go.'

Gesner smiled down at her. 'But I want you to come to my party, pumpkin. I thought we would have a special party, just the two of us.'

Suddenly she realized what he was saying, just what he meant. She felt totally confused, totally lost. If she could have gone to bed with him at that moment it would have been all right.

'I can't,' she faltered. 'If I didn't go to Uncle Willi's party, everyone would know . . .'

'Know what, pumpkin?' he purred.

'Know . . . where I was . . . with you.'

'Would that matter?'

In spite of her shaking legs, of the heat swamping up from her stomach, of the overwhelming desire to throw caution to the winds and not think about anything else, she was also conscious of the fact that if she gave in, went out with Karl, Uncle Willi would be unbearably hurt, and that she couldn't cope with. It was very strange that she didn't mind too much what her parents thought, or even Georg, but Uncle Willi so loved his pre-production party, and this year was really excited about it, that she just couldn't let him down.

'I really couldn't disappoint Uncle Willi,' she said faintly. 'I must go. Perhaps if I asked Uncle Willi, I could bring you.' Even as she said it, she knew it was an outrageous suggestion. Uncle Willi's pre-production parties were very, very special, small, and select. Only his close friends were asked. Karl Gesner had never been invited.

Suddenly Gesner took his arms away from the wall.

'As you wish,' he said coldly. 'I had forgotten what a silly little girl you still are.' He pushed through the swing doors and was gone, leaving her close to tears and frantically worried that she had upset him for ever.

All the way home she agonized about what she should do. Should she go back and tell him she'd changed her mind? But how could she? She would have to speak to him in front of the entire

Company. She could hang around up at the Karl Joseph and hope to catch him when he went back after rehearsal, but the same applied – everyone would see her. And what about Uncle Willi? How could she make excuses to Uncle Willi? Uncle Willi, she was sure, would totally understand about being in love, even though he was Georg's father, but he wouldn't understand that you had to be in love on the one night of his party, not when you'd had all those other evenings with Gesner. She drooped miserably into the farmhouse, dropping her bag of rehearsal clothes on to the floor. Frau Hoflin took one look at her and refrained from asking her to pick them up and put them in the washing machine.

'Upstairs and into the bath,' she said. 'Papa has already had his. I've pressed your dress for you. Uncle Willi wanted us to dress up specially this evening, because of Therese Aschmann coming.'

'I'm sick of Uncle Willi's parties!' she said irrationally and not a little spitefully. It was all Uncle Willi's fault that Karl was so angry with her. Her mother was suddenly still, said absolutely nothing.

'I don't see why I have to go. There's never anyone else my age there. And it's foolish of him to have it when we're all about to go into production and we're so tired.' Her mother still didn't answer.

'If he didn't make such a fuss about it, make you feel guilty if you didn't go, I would never go to one of Uncle Willi's parties ever again.'

'Suzi, if you don't want to go, that's fine. I will ask you to write a little note to Uncle Willi and I will take it with us when we go. That will be sufficient. But if you do go, I would ask you not to spoil Uncle Willi's evening with a long face. It will be quite bad enough with Georg sitting there glowering at everyone. If there are two bad-tempered miserable guests, poor Uncle Willi will be very upset.'

Suzi burst into tears and hurried up to the bathroom.

It was a measure of Willi's popularity that, even though his pre-production party was known about by nearly everyone who was anyone in Hochhauser, and even though the guest list was extremely small, no-one ever felt slighted because they hadn't been invited. Willi rang the changes a little every year. This year, as well as his old regulars, the Hoflins, Busacher, and old Anton, the *répétiteur* from Vienna, he had invited his friends on the theatre committee who had assisted so nobly in quelling the Gesner revolt, and Luiza, Freddi and Alfred, who came nearly every year but not so often they took it for granted. Therese, of course, was the special guest, the one he was most looking forward to having. Aschmann in his house, all dressed up for a festive occasion, the most glamorous lady in the theatre, was going to make it a party like no other. She had promised to sing for them later in the evening if she wasn't too tired.

Busacher arrived first, looking grand and archaic in full evening dress, white tie and tails. Willi had, somehow, over the years, forced everyone into the custom of dressing as though it were a State ball instead of a private dinner party in a prosperous farmhouse.

'I'm getting too old for this kind of caper, Willi,' Busacher said testily. 'Far too much to do this year, with the new production and Gesner worse than usual. I'm amazed any of us have time to come.'

'Oh, pouf!' said Willi. 'You say that every year. My pre-production party is part of the tradition of the Hochhauser Season. You would be very cross if I stopped giving it.' He popped the first bottle of champagne and poured a glass. 'Drink that, you grumpy old man, and get into the party spirit.'

Busacher snorted, drank, and wandered over to look at the long table which had been set up right down the centre of Willi's big living room. Willi's dinners were always good and he liked to see how many courses his host was serving.

'Sixteen place settings, Willi? More than usual. Who else is coming?'

'Julius is bringing his wife. And as we seemed to be rather overweighted with gentlemen I have also invited Ingrid – it is her first time in a major role – and the enchanting Miss Grimsilk.'

'She accepted?' The Direktor was startled.

'It seems that Miss Grimsilk and our own adorable Therese have become firm friends. Therese said Miss Grimsilk was a very nice lady who is at present a trifle unhappy. She said it would be a kindness to invite her. So I did. Also, I was conscious that my little friend Suzi Hoflin is usually the only young one at these evenings, so I thought a couple of extra women nearer her own age would make her feel less conspicuous.'

And, thought Busacher to himself, it would also help with the awkwardness of Suzi and Georg no longer speaking and everyone knowing that the little Hoflin was currently messing about with Gesner.

'Your little idea didn't quite work out, did it, Willi? Your plan that taking on Suzi as the dancer would avoid the Gesner problem.'

Willi looked glum, then quickly downed a glass of champagne. 'I refuse to be depressed this evening,' he said firmly. 'Not by Suzi, and not by Georg. I am going to enjoy myself.'

'You always do, Willi. You always do,' murmured Busacher as Willi bounced away to welcome Gaston, Julius, and Julius's large wife who, overwhelmed by the invitation to one of Willi's famous parties, had gone to Vienna and bought herself a long brown satin dress with a purple sash swathed round the middle. 'Looks like an Easter egg,' murmured Busacher to himself and heard a snort behind him. He turned. Georg was standing there and although Busacher had no time for the disagreeable young man, he had to concede that Georg, in dinner jacket and black tie, was extremely handsome. Pity he can't sing, act, and has no charm, he reflected. He would make a wonderful Alfredo if only he would smile. All those looks are quite wasted on a farmer.

'Good evening, Georg. How nice to see you at this kind of gathering. I know theatre people are hardly your choice of party companions. Indeed, I know you do not care for parties at all.'

'Obviously I would be present at a party in my own home,' said Georg stiffly. 'You are all very welcome.'

'Thank you.' Busacher inclined his head slightly, noting the 'my own home' and not 'our'. My friend Willi is going to have severe trouble with this one, he thought. It is patently apparent that young Georg has forgotten just who owns the Zimmermann farm. He cast about desperately for something to say. Making small talk with Georg was not easy.

'I hope you will be coming to our opening night next Tuesday, Georg.'

'I'm afraid I do not care for the theatre.'

'No. Of course. I had forgotten.' What a boor the young man was. One would have thought Willi would have drummed some kind of graciousness into him. And who am I to criticize, he thought wryly to himself. Willi has done a better job with Georg than I ever did with Peter. These days he tried not to think of his son too much. It was unproductive.

The crowd from the Gasthaus arrived and the party began to lift. They were all old troupers and knew the importance of entering on a high note. Freddi and Alfred and the ancient Anton all wore their 'stage' tails. Luiza had decked her inevitable blue with a piece of tat borrowed from the wardrobe, and Ingrid wore black silk trousers and a gold waistcoat and very little else. Therese was magnificent in a swirling confection of crimson that Busacher didn't recognize from the wardrobe department at all. Had

Therese spent a large part of her salary on a dress she would never wear again? Willi bustled forward.

'My dear, dear friends! And . . . Therese!' He clasped his hands together. 'Silence, everyone!' Over by the door Busacher saw the Hoflins sidle in. Suzi was pale and had obviously been crying. He did hope Gesner hadn't done anything to interfere with the opening production next Tuesday.

'Dear friends – how honoured I am to have you at my party for another year, a very, very special year in many ways. Our first new production in two weeks' time, our very own original *Luxembourg*, designed by our very own designer from England, and chor-eographed' – that was really a somewhat over-splendid description of Suzi's little dance steps – 'by our very own special Hochhauser girl, our little Suzi.' Everyone smiled at Suzi then looked hurriedly away as her mouth began to tremble. 'We have Ingrid, making her début in a leading role, and above all, my dear friends, this season is very special because, for the first time, we have a soprano of outstanding quality, a soprano who was, and is, truly a great star. Friends, before we do anything else, I would like you to raise your glasses and drink to our leading lady, and to the Hochhauser Season.'

'Therese, and the Hochhauser Season!'

Thank God for my old professionals, thought Busacher. Without them the toast, and the evening, would have fallen flat. The Hoflins looked uncomfortable. Suzi was close to tears, Georg was scowling, and Madge Grimsilk, in her grey suit, looked prim and forbidding. Willi bounced about filling up everyone's glasses; more corks popped. He managed to co-opt the gloomy Georg into circulating with more champagne and everyone averted their eyes as Georg drew near Suzi and refilled her glass.

Willi bustled over to the dresser that stretched along one side of the room and picked up a huge basket of flowers. He had always done that at his pre-production party, given everyone a carnation to wear, but this time he had overreached himself.

'Very special corsages for my delightful lady guests!' he cried. Oh dear, Willi could be such a fool. 'I have had a wonderful time trying to select flowers that will complement each of you. Madame!' Julius's wife in the Easter egg dress was presented with a gardenia. Well, at least it was dignified. Willi padded round the room with his basket, a balding, rubicund Eliza Doolittle. Carnations for Luiza, irises for the sensible Frau Hoflin, red camellias for Ingrid (she would love the tenuous connection with *La Traviata*), cream and yellow roses for little Suzi Hoflin, a spray of mixed violets and primroses – rather clever – for Madge Grimsilk, and finally, with a flourish . . . 'For a prima donna there is only one flower. I know the other ladies will understand – but for our leading lady there can only be orchids!'

Two spotty, purply-pink flowers that looked appalling against Therese's crimson dress. She smiled radiantly and allowed her eyes to widen slightly. 'My dear, dear Willi! How luxurious. I only hope the Season will prove that I have deserved your wonderful orchids.' She pinned them bravely to the shoulder of her dress, touched the blooms lightly with her fingers and said to the room at large,

'Aren't they absolutely wonderful?'

Therese had changed. She had come to Hochhauser in hope and desperation and Gesner had nearly destroyed her. But since the day when Willi had brought her up here, to his farm, she had won back something she hadn't had for years, a sense of balance, of proportion, a sense that there were a great many other things, other people in the world other than Therese Aschmann and her problems. She had realized that she, who had always been so outgoing as a young singer, had been verging on the brink of obsession with her own failures, her own abilities or lack of them, with Gesner and his personal vendetta. She had never been to lunch or any other meal alone with Willi since that day, but she was wholeheartedly indebted to him for his kindness, his common sense, his consciousness of the world outside one's own personal situation.

Since that lunch everything had taken an upward swing. She and Madge had begun a guarded friendship based on a similar sense of humour and a past that both of them skirted around. Gesner, since that terrible day, had been, if not co-operative, at least not openly antagonistic. She had looked around the company and seen that she was not out of place at all. They were a ragtag crowd and she was as good – or as bad – as the rest of them. She had, for the first time in eighteen years, recovered her equilibrium. And she had also begun to observe what a miracle the whole Hochhauser Operetta Company was – a miracle that stemmed from two people. Direktor Franz Busacher, and Burgermeister Willi Zimmermann. She had seen what huge uphill problems they faced and she was determined to support their heroic effort to the best of her ability.

As the party noise began to dominate the room, the hum of voices, glasses clinking, laughter from the old guard, who were not going to allow any tension to spoil their evening, Busacher came over to Therese.

141

'You look . . . quite splendid, Therese. Apart from Willi's orchids, of course.'

'Ssh.' She smiled and touched the flowers again with her fingers. 'Dear Willi. And in some ways they are quite right with this gown. You remember, Franz, how I always liked bright, even garish colours? I often wore the wrong things together, just because I couldn't resist them. I think Willi has put his finger on the essential me!' She laughed.

'The gown is certainly you, Therese. Have I seen it before? In my own wardrobe department?'

'Madge brought the material back from Vienna the last time she went on a buying trip – it is not part of the *Luxembourg* budget, I hasten to add – and, wonderful creature that she is, she threw it together on an evening when Wardrobe weren't using one of their machines.'

'Madge? Madge Grimsilk?'

He put his arm through Therese's and drew her into a corner of the room.

'I am quite bewildered by all this, Therese. Bewildered, and fascinated. Do you realize that Madge Grimsilk has never, not once, shown any sign of . . . humanity in my presence? I have done everything. I have praised her effusively for her work – quite rightly – I have given her lunch at my villa – she refused the wine, though I observe she is guzzling Willi's champagne without a shudder. I have exerted myself to be as charming as I can be – perhaps you will reassure me, Therese, that I can still be charming when I try?'

'You are the perfect Viennese, Herr Direktor.'

'So why has Madge Grimsilk never offered to run me up a quick ball-dress on the wardrobe sewing machine?'

'Madge is . . .' she hesitated, 'a very private person. Not the kind of character to wear her heart on her sleeve. That is a very English expression. It means . . .'

'I know what it means.'

'She has been hurt, let down I think, by a man, some man in England. I don't know the details but I recognize the symptoms. She's very reserved. I know he was in the theatre. But that is all I know.'

'How old do you think she is?'

'Not sure. Thirty, thirty-seven, difficult to tell.'

'It did go through my head – a wild surmise – that the man might have been Gesner. He did that season in London last year.'

Therese began to laugh. 'Gesner? And Madge? You should hear

142

her talking about Gesner. You should see her doing her impersonation of him; one of the funniest things I've ever seen.'

'Madge Grimsilk? Impersonations of Gesner?'

'Quite wonderful!'

Busacher stared across the room to where Madge was standing talking to the two committee men and the Easter egg. She wore her corsage of violets and primroses pinned to the lapel of her grey suit. She wasn't smiling but she was obviously being polite, nodding and asking questions and pretending to be interested in the answers.

'Why does she wear no make-up?' he asked distastefully. 'And why has she come to Willi's party in that dreadful suit? Did you not tell her that everyone dresses up for Willi's party? If she made a dress for you, she could have made one for herself.'

'I'm not sure,' Therese answered thoughtfully. 'It is something to do with not wanting to be noticed. It is very strange. She understood at once about me – how I always loved bright colours, outrageous clothes, unsuitable jewellery – but she seems to prefer to be invisible. And you know, Franz, sometimes designers get tired of clothes. They have to invent so many for other people they just can't be bothered when it comes to themselves.'

Busacher suddenly shrugged, dismissively. 'Englishwomen,' he said sadly. 'Someone should teach them how to be gracious, how to accept compliments prettily, how *never* to wear a grey suit to a party however bored one is with designing clothes.'

'I won't hear a word against her, Franz. She has designed the most wonderful costumes for me and she's been a good friend. And I think Willi is about to sit us down for one of his gargantuan dinners.'

Willi, slightly tipsy, but still wonderfully in control, was marshalling people to the table. Georg next to Frau Hoflin – hard on his old friend, but at least Georg was comfortable with her and she would be motherly and kind to him. Suzi with Alfred, who although ancient was still an entertaining man who took pleasure – and patience – in making a pretty girl enjoy her dinner. Frau Trauffer and her daughter began to bring in the first of six bountiful courses.

There is something quite atavistic about a group of people sitting down together to a good dinner. Even the awkward, the misfits, the discontented, feel a lessening of their misery when they realize they have a place, specially set for them, at a dinner which has been the subject of much thought, care, and several hours of preparation. One becomes a privileged member of the tribe. If one did not sit down at the table there would be a gap, an empty space that would spoil the symmetry of the host's table. Therefore one is important. One has been chosen.

Willi's magic began to work as the meal progressed. His old friends, the Hoflins, looked a little less worried. Suzi smiled a couple of times at Alfred, Georg began to feel rather proud at hosting a dinner of such magnificence. And Madge Grimsilk was seen to lean back in her chair instead of sitting upright and swallow a surprisingly large quantity of Willi's excellent wine. Therese, sitting at Willi's right, felt a sudden surge of pure, undiluted happiness wash over her. I never expected to feel like this again, she thought. Never. Even if nothing nice ever happens again, I must remember this.

Willi had carefully seated Georg and Suzi on the same side of the table, but at opposite ends, so that they could not see one another and could relax. Willi made another speech, so did Busacher, so did both of the committee men. The Easter egg, overcome by heat, too much food, and an excess of wine, had to go and stand outside the door for a little fresh air, but came back full of verve and ready to tackle some of Willi's bonbons that were scattered about the room in dishes in case anyone felt the need of more to eat. Willi was already nibbling.

'And now,' said Willi, 'I shall ask Therese to sing for us, and because this is my house and my evening, I shall accompany her myself and ignore criticism from the professionals. Therese?'

'What would you like me to sing, Willi?'

'*Traviata*. Act One. The waltz.'

'It's a duet, Willi.'

'You can sing it all.'

The golden, fluting, essentially *young* voice filled the room. Frau Trauffer and her daughters came out of the kitchen wiping their hands on their aprons. The voice seemed to seep through the seams of the farmhouse, echo up the mountains and ripple back around the flowers and empty champagne bottles.

Her teacher had been right all those years ago, reflected Busacher. He'd said it was a natural voice, one that didn't have to be nursed or conserved or constantly disciplined. He remembered her in the old days, singing at parties for hours and then turning up for rehearsal next day without any sign of strain or tiredness in her voice.

There were enough singers in the room to finish the chorus lines with her, then Luiza rose from her chair.

'Help me over to the piano, young Georg. I intend to play some waltzes and you shall all dance.'

144

Gaston, the committee man, who had been eyeing Ingrid the entire evening, trying to discern if she was wearing anything at all under the gold waistcoat, hurried over and pulled her to her feet. Julius danced soberly with his Easter egg. Freddi grabbed Therese and, amazingly energetic, whirled her round and round with surprising control. Therese was a good half-head taller than Freddi and when Busacher caught her eye, she winked at him.

Willi made his way over to Madge Grimsilk, coughed, hesitated, then bowed in a very old-fashioned and courtly way. To Busacher's astonishment Madge Grimsilk rose to her feet and placed a hand on Willi's shoulder. The next moment, stiff as a beanpole but smiling, actually smiling! she was pivoting round with Willi, stumbling, tripping, but nevertheless dancing. Busacher was so riveted by the bizarre sight that he failed to see what was happening with Georg and Suzi.

Suzi had been conscious of Georg the whole evening, even when she couldn't see him. She often forgot how handsome Georg was, especially lately when he always seemed to have a scowl on his face. But tonight he looked splendid in his dinner jacket, groomed, combed, and really being rather charming to his guests. He wasn't as handsome as Gesner, of course, and at the thought of Gesner the misery of the evening threatened to engulf her again. She felt reckless, off balance. She didn't want Georg back but she wanted to hurt him the way Gesner had hurt her. She didn't know what she wanted and she'd drunk too much. She walked across to Georg and looked at him the way she looked at Gesner.

'Dance with me, Georg.'

'You know I don't dance.' She looked pretty and provocative and very, very sexy. He'd never seen her look like that before, and when he thought of *why* she looked like that he wanted to throttle her.

'Oh, come on, old sourface. You can surely stand up and just put your arms round me.' She laughed rather shrilly, grabbed his hands and tried to pull him up against her.

'Stop it, Suzi!'

'Come on!' She pulled harder, dragging him out into the path of a waltzing couple, trying to wrap his arms round her waist.

'Sour old Georg. Aah!' For suddenly Georg's control had snapped and he pushed her hard, violently and savagely away from him so that she spun across the room, hurtled into the table, and nearly fell. Some glasses crashed to the floor. There was an

145

appalled silence in the room, broken by a choked sob from Georg, who suddenly ran out of the door.

And at that moment Madge Grimsilk gave a gentle hiccough and passed out cold upon the floor.

CHAPTER NINE

In the following three days they had to get through two complete run-throughs, two technical rehearsals, and one dress rehearsal. The dress rehearsal for *Countess Maritza* was left until the Wednesday morning, after the opening night. There was no time or energy for anyone to do anything but get through the long gruelling hours and fall into bed, usually after midnight and on the night before the opening, at three in the morning.

Gesner was in a foul mood again and Therese took the brunt of it. He didn't totally sabotage the production but during the technical run-through – when the cast spent a lot of time just standing about waiting for lighting and scenery and props to be adjusted – he made a point of whispering to Ingrid, putting his arm around her, making her giggle, while they both looked over at Therese. As the opening production was *Gypsy Baron*, where Ingrid was taking the lead and Therese had to play the role of an eighteen-year-old village maiden, it wasn't hard to guess what most of the jokes were about. When they came to plotting the lighting for *Countess Maritza*, Therese's first starring role, he became very aggressive. He had absorbed enough knowledge of lighting in his career to know who was being given the best spots, and he fought all the time to get Therese pushed out when he was on stage. It was also observed that he was fairly cool with the little Hoflin girl, who seemed to be mooning miserably about the theatre with a pale face, even when she wasn't needed. He wasn't rude to her, just cold and polite. Idly, without a lot of interest, the company wondered if he was planning to take Ingrid to bed instead of Suzi although, as Luiza pointed out, Ingrid wasn't really his type. Too old.

On the Monday night the orchestra arrived ready for the dress rehearsal of *Gypsy Baron* the next morning. Busacher tried, as far as possible, to get the same musicians every year, those who knew, as he put it, 'our funny little ways'. This meant that on some occasions they would be conducted by Busacher, on others by Anton, the old *répétiteur*, and in emergencies by their own lead violinist. They were also used to bursting into unexpected crescendos of sound when Ingrid's voice cracked or Freddie lost his pitch, and infilling with fiddly bits when some backstage hitch caused long pauses. They were worth every penny of the large chunk of the Hochhauser budget they absorbed.

The dress rehearsal was fairly dull. They were all tired and Ingrid was, by this time, thoroughly frightened and didn't want to use her voice too much. Gesner, sniffing the advance of his adoring fans, suddenly became smug and rather patronizing. He walked through his role, yawning and refusing to sing any of it.

'La, la, la,' he said dismissively, waving his hand in the air. 'We all know what I sing here. We have all heard it many, many times. Same old tunes, same old singers, same old operetta.'

'Perhaps I may remind you, Karl,' said Busacher waspishly, 'that the choice of this revival was yours. You were very anxious that Ingrid should star in it.'

But he was really too tired, like everyone else, to get angry with Gesner. He knew the man would be magnificent when he got on to the stage that night. He always was.

The dress rehearsal finally ended at four in the afternoon and everyone went home to rest. The young members of the company were more exhausted than the old. Busacher had noticed that before. They tended to wear themselves out with too much excitement. On the way home he checked with Stefan on the evening's bookings.

'Not sold out, but a couple of coach parties from Vienna – you know, the usual thing, group booking for early dinner at the Strauss Inn and straight back into the coach after the performance. Same tomorrow, and the following night is the first charity block-booking of patients from the Elizabeta Hospital. All sold out for first four performances of *Luxembourg* next week.'

'Good. Good.' Stefan was in the front booking office; not really his job but the front of house manager had given up and gone home to bed. Stefan looked particularly grey and was frantically scrunching indigestion tablets.

'New pills not working, Stefan?'

'Be all right once we get started – get Ingrid and Aschmann on the stage without hitches.'

Buscher knew exactly what he meant. It was the same old production of *Gypsy Baron* they'd done last year, but there were two huge question marks over this year's production: two new débuts, Ingrid and Therese.

Therese, lying on her narrow bed at the Goldener Adler, was fighting overwhelming panic. She was exhausted and she wasn't even taking the lead in tonight's performance. If she was this tired, how did she think she'd be able to survive *Maritza* on the following night, and *Luxembourg* next week? Eighteen years away from a stage, eighteen years and she'd forgotten until now that terrifying gut-wrenching dread of stepping out in front of several hundred people and making a total fool of yourself. Supposing Gesner pulled a trick, or she fell over. Supposing the audience laughed at her playing a soubrette role. Supposing she forgot what she was supposed to do, missed her entrance, let them all down. The Direktor had taken such a chance on her. Supposing she let him down?

When she got to the theatre she found her dressing room was full of flowers – Willi again. The Zimmermann farm was in danger of bankruptcy if Willi didn't control himself. She donned her white dress, the wig of blonde ringlets, and began to put on her make-up. She looked absolutely ridiculous and she knew it. Busacher knocked on the door and came in.

'To wish you good luck, my dear!' He was deliberately playing it down. She didn't have the lead but it was still a big part and it was her first time on the stage since the scandal. But he certainly wasn't going to encourage her to indulge in nerves or old memories.

'I hope I'm not going to let you down, Herr Direktor,' she said through tight lips. 'I'm beginning to wonder if this was such a good idea.'

He was deliberately offhand. 'It doesn't really matter what you do, my dear. You are not the lead. Ingrid is. I am much, much more concerned about her voice lasting out for the evening. You need to do nothing except stand there and sing your numbers. No-one will notice you. Everyone will be watching Ingrid.' He saw the colour flow back into her face.

'Of course,' she said. 'I must go and wish her luck.'

Ingrid was defiant but shaking. She refused the offer of a glass of schnapps. He didn't approve of singers drinking before they went on stage, but he could see that Ingrid was in a very bad way.

'You are going to be quite splendid, Ingrid,' he said briskly.

'I know. I'm quite confident. No worries at all.'

'Good.'

'Karl has sent me a good luck card. Wasn't that kind?' Kind and unprecedented! Karl Gesner had never done that before to any member of the company.

'Karl will see you through, Ingrid. You know you can rely on him.'

'Yes. But I'm quite confident, Herr Direktor.'

He closed the door, paused outside Gesner's dressing room, then decided not to go in. The man had nerves of steel and didn't need anyone's good wishes.

There were many times in the past years when he had wondered why on earth he had involved himself with the Hochhauser Season, times when he was worried, exhausted, furious, and prepared to consign the whole company to hell. But when he stepped up on to the conductor's rostrum for the opening production of a new season, he was – every time – filled with a sense of sheer elation. It had always been a moment of pure magic to him in the theatre, the consciousness of the huge rustling animal behind him, and the hush as the house lights went down, the pause of utter stillness, silence, and then as he brought his baton down, the incredible surge of excitement as music smashed the silence, created instantly the illusion of that otherworld that didn't really exist. Every time it happened he was conscious of the audience being captured, ensnared into his world of fairy tales. They didn't always stay ensnared; often they were lost when a performance was bad and didn't sustain the magic. But always, for that one first moment, there was a hope, a promise of a few hours of enchantment. At that moment he loved the theatre.

The curtain rose to the usual restless flutter of the audience, the last coughs – audiences were as predictable as the performers in their reactions – and the chorus began their opening song. OK, just. Gesner would be on in a few moments and then the thing would lift off.

It was when Gesner stepped on to the stage – on this occasion looking unbelievable in his Mandrika costume successfully altered by Wardrobe – that Busacher forgave him, nearly, for all the trouble he caused. The man dominated the stage. Superbly self-confident, exuding sexuality, he captured the audience in the space of two minutes. Busacher relaxed. They were away again for a new season. Freddi did his Zsupan number with all the expertise of an old professional – miraculous! – what did it matter if his voice had gone – and then, Busacher swallowed hard, realizing his heart was

150

pounding dangerously fast, Therese made her entrance and began to sing.

The audience, many of whom knew the operetta well, were puzzled. She didn't look as bad as she had done in the dressing room but she was obviously not young, not slender, not a girl. It was very odd casting and they couldn't quite work it out. But as she sang, the voice seemed to lift itself out of the setting, out of the plot, and become a performance in itself. Probably the audience, most of them, didn't realize what they were hearing except that it was . . . different, something one didn't expect on the stage of Hochhauser. What Busacher *was* suddenly aware of was the orchestra. They'd heard her a little at rehearsal, but not properly, not consistently, and not without interruption and background noise. Professional musicians are mostly a cynical lot – they've heard it all before and played it all before too. They know the tricks used by most singers and are expert in helping out or not as the case may be. Even Gesner was very careful not to be rude to the orchestra. Now Busacher sensed a sharpening all around him, a tightness, an awareness that something was happening. Without realizing it, their orchestral accompaniment fined itself to the quality of her voice. I wasn't wrong, Busacher thought exultantly. I wasn't wrong. They've recognized it.

She got a round of applause when she'd finished, a modest round and Busacher suspected it had been started by Willi. But even so, in Hochhauser not many of the second soloists got rounds.

Ingrid was still shaking when she came on. He just hoped they couldn't see it from the stalls. Her performance was about what he'd expected but they brushed through without anything too awful happening. Her hair looked wonderful as she darted about the stage and she was at her best in the gypsy dance. Backed by Suzi, who did most of the energetic stuff, Ingrid strutted and flounced and flung her hair about. It was all very Hungarian and high-spirited. Went down well, all things considered.

By the end of the evening all had come together very nicely and the Direktor knew the performance was 'set' for the rest of the Season. Gesner had made it better than it was and had carried Ingrid through most of her numbers. Luiza, who was always very happy singing Czipra as she spent most of the evening sitting on a gypsy log, had been in superb voice and Therese – Busacher gloated – Therese had made one or two of the more discerning wonder what she was going to do in some of the other productions.

No-one really had time to celebrate that night. The dress rehearsal of *Countess Maritza* was the following morning, but still they all found time to make a fuss of Ingrid, who was now smugly self-confident instead of defiantly self-confident. Busacher gave Therese his own private accolade. Willi was ebullient.

'You heard it, Franz? You heard what happened? The audience recognized it and so did the orchestra.' Busacher had at one time been surprised at Willi's musical perception, but was no longer.

'The orchestra were very kind,' Therese said. 'One or two of them came and spoke to me afterwards. They remembered me from the old days.'

'You were wonderful, Therese! Wonderful, wonderful! Even Rudi sang better when he was with you!'

She couldn't stop smiling. Even knowing she looked ridiculous, she'd enjoyed it after that first entrance, had loved being on a stage again, singing with the company. She had to keep reminding herself to behave with dignity and not whoop round the dressing room like Willi.

'And tomorrow, *Maritza*!' gloated Willi. 'Just wait until tomorrow!'

Gesner, turning up for the dress rehearsal the next morning, was rather bored. His opening night had been his usual triumph. It had been amusing to get Ingrid through it, just to spite Busacher and keep Aschmann in a supporting role, but now he had to sustain Ingrid through the rest of the Season. No effort or trouble, but it would become irritating in time. The conflict with Aschmann was over. She was no threat, he'd seen that last night. Oh yes, her voice was good, but voice alone wasn't enough in operetta. She was never going to look right and she didn't have any stage style, no attack, no panache. Even Ingrid had stage style, a certain energy that made her project something over the footlights. Aschmann had none of that. She was just going to be rather tedious from now on.

The Hoflin affair hadn't worked out quite the way he'd planned either, although he'd spent a lot of time and money on the little thing. He debated whether Ingrid would do. She was terribly grateful to him at the moment and it wouldn't require any effort on his part. But, he reflected idly, the little Hoflin thing had been so much prettier, so much more uncritically adoring. She was still mooning about the theatre, gazing at him. Probably it wouldn't take much to reactivate things, but on the other hand, if she was one of those drearily perennial virgins it wasn't really worth the effort.

He wandered into his dressing room, climbed into his costume – really, buying Mandrika's old wardrobe had been the best investment he'd ever made. The rest of the hired costumes looked appalling by comparison – and strolled out towards the stage.

'Good God! That's not the hired costume.'

Therese was standing on the stage, Madge Grimsilk on her knees crouching and doing something to the bottom of Therese's costume, which was most certainly *not* the hired costume.

'There were no twenties costumes in my size,' said Therese sweetly. 'I'm too fat to fit any of the stock *Maritza* costumes.'

He glared at her. Was she being funny? Sarcastic? But another look at her face, just blankly polite, made him decide he had imagined the irony. He certainly hadn't imagined the costume, however. She stood there in a full, swirling coat of silver-grey silk. Actually it wasn't silk. It was the cheapest, thinnest, shiniest material that Madge could find and she had told Therese it would just about last out the Season before you could start shooting peas through it. It didn't matter. Under the clever lighting it fell in folds of shimmering silver round her knees. It was caught up at the neck into a huge thick collar of silver fur. On her head was a large Russian hat of the same fur, and on her right hand a muff.

'It looks very silly against all the other costumes. It isn't twenties at all.'

'That's why I'm shortening it,' said Madge Grimsilk from the floor.

He stared at the hemline which was being taken up to Therese's knees. She had, whatever the rest of her figure, very good legs, long and slim. He didn't remember noticing her legs before. She'd worn slacks all through rehearsals and the only other times he'd seen her she'd been wearing that dreary suit. She also wore extremely high-heeled shoes that made her legs seem even longer. From the auditorium he heard Franz Busacher's voice.

'Excellent, Miss Grimsilk. Very good indeed. Therese, could you come down here for a moment? And Miss Grimsilk.' As Therese walked forward towards the stage steps the silk coat swung out around her, catching the light, drawing attention to her legs. Framed by the silver fur her face took on a glow that emphasized her high cheekbones. Madge held the folds of material away as Therese climbed down from the stage.

'You're going to be hot in that fur, Therese,' she murmured. 'It's not fake. I found an old coat in the flea market and cut the good bits out. It's real and hot. You'll be a greaseball by the end of Act One. And it will probably give you some horrible skin disease too.'

'I don't care,' said Therese firmly. 'I don't care if I dissolve into a puddle the minute the curtain comes down. The whole thing is a miracle.'

It *was* a miracle. She looked rich, stylish, elegant. Busacher lowered his voice.

'Brilliant. Do we have some paste in the wardrobe, Miss Grimsilk? A few diamonds perhaps. I think a large diamond pin of some kind up near the collar, and those glittery sort of earrings, and perhaps several bracelets to flash when she moves the muff.'

'I'll see what we have, Herr Direktor.'

'And Therese . . . I think perhaps, for the dress rehearsal, more of a walk through? Not too wise to let . . . everyone see exactly what you can do.'

Therese grinned. 'I quite understand, Herr Busacher.'

It was unbelievable what the costume had done for her. She had nothing else quite so effective to wear for the other two acts, but this, for her first entrance, for establishing herself as Countess Maritza, did absolutely everything.

'You . . . you and Gesner,' said Busacher a little apologetically. 'You look rather splendid together. The rest of the costumes do look a trifle . . . stale. You make a handsome couple.'

'Thank you, Herr Direktor.' Her mouth twitched.

'Now. On with the rehearsal.'

They got through quite quickly. Chorus numbers were sung in full, and the Hoflin girl's little solo in Act Two was performed from beginning to end, but Ingrid, who was singing Lisa – not such a heavy role, but she still had a couple of solos – was resting her voice again, and the rest just walked and hummed their roles. Gesner seemed rather wooden and he kept giving Therese a speculative scowl.

That evening she felt no nervousness at all, just excitement, controlled excitement. She knew just what she had to do, knew the music perfectly, could sing it in her sleep, but now she felt, for the first time in years, she could bring something of herself, her personality, into her singing.

It was a wonderful entrance. Busacher wanted to cheer. Willi nearly did. The music of Maritza's entrance was always a gift to any singer, good or bad: the rising crescendo from the orchestra that tells the audience a star is about to come on stage. And tonight the orchestra, intrigued by the vibrations they had picked up of something unusual happening this season, gave the entrance a full-bodied flourish of emotional sound, a build-up of chord and melody that culminated with Therese, shimmering, a mass of silver and flashing diamonds, swinging her way down to front stage,

154

smiling, radiant, totally in control, moving quickly, gracefully around her stage guests, a wave of her muff to this one, a kiss blown to that. Busacher was suddenly blinded by tears. It was the old Therese, the happy, extrovert Therese, the golden girl who had lit up the stage of the *Volksoper*.

Of course, she still wasn't as good as Gesner, she didn't steal the show from him by any means. She was uncertain in some places, still finding her way, upstaged by him whenever they were on together, but the rippling golden voice never faltered, and in the Varasdin duet with Freddi she took flight again, gave the whole scene a sense of gaiety and even kept Freddi on key for once.

'I'll be all right by the time we come to *Luxembourg* next week,' she said confidently to Franz and Willi at supper that night. They had found a small restaurant away from the theatre circuit where there was no chance of bumping into Gesner. 'By the time I've done the rest of this week, two *Gypsy Barons*, and two more *Countess Maritzas*, I'll be totally on top of everything. You've no need to nurse me along any more, Franz. I've been, oh, so aware that you've been more than generous, with your time, your coaching, your support against Gesner. From now on you don't have to worry. I can do it myself and you can go back to being the Direktor of the company instead of my protector. I can manage Gesner myself.'

'Be careful. You've seen how spiteful he can be; possibly even dangerous.'

'Nothing can hurt me now,' she said blithely, reaching out her hands one on each side towards them. 'With my two dear, good friends who have brought me this far, nothing can go wrong now.'

It was the uncles again. That was how she felt – as though those dear supporting figures of her childhood were once again hovering over her. She had always prided herself, as she got older, that she wasn't a bit like her mama, but perhaps she was. The uncles had looked after her when she was young, then her professor and Hans Kramer and Busacher had begun her on her career, and then she had fallen in love and it had all gone wrong. And the years when she had had no-one to look after her had been disastrous. So perhaps she was, after all, like darling Mutti (now married to a Hungarian doctor and living an extremely respectable old age in Budapest). Perhaps she was incapable of standing on her own and needed the encouragement of supportive males. It was all very pathetic and she didn't like the thought of it at all.

'No,' she repeated. 'I can cope with him on my own now. Nothing can go wrong.'

Busacher, under the spell of an unexpectedly successful evening, began to feel quietly confident that she was right.

Karl Gesner, not frantically worried, but conscious of a slight worm of discontent at the back of his mind, bought Ingrid an indifferent supper and decided to take her to bed. He needed a little boost to his ego and she was better than nothing.

CHAPTER TEN

By the end of the week the company had played themselves in and the two opening productions were soundly established. *Countess Maritza* had moments of brilliance, and even in *Gypsy Baron* Therese had improved. The casting was still incongruous but, because she had gained enormous confidence, she began to look better, held herself tautly, lightly, and, by the Saturday matinée, gave a convincing performance of an eighteen-year-old girl.

Gesner was becoming increasingly angry. He knew that, somehow, he had been fooled. He watched her, listened to her getting better and better in *Countess Maritza*. She was receiving curtain calls nearly as long as his and on the Saturday night performance a spontaneous (spontaneous – ha – Willi Zimmermann was in the house again) burst of cheering broke out when she took her call. He began to think about Therese Aschmann – could she be dangerous? A threat to his position of total supremacy over the whole of the Hochhauser Season? He began to try to remember things he had heard about Aschmann. He'd been conscious of her in the old days of course, although he kept quiet about that. He didn't want anyone to realize he was – well – as old as he was. He had worn well, unlike her. He still looked like a romantic lead. She didn't. And he'd also clocked up several more years on the operatic stage than she had. And why was that? He tried to remember the details of the old scandal – something to do with a scene on the stage that had stopped the performance, and after that she'd never appeared again, until now. That was very odd indeed. He was not a fool and he recognized that what came out when Therese opened her mouth was a unique sound that could, if she had continued in her youthful career, have taken her right up to the top, to the international opera houses of the world. Something had happened to make her vanish, all those years ago.

He woke late on the Sunday morning after their first week, sent Ingrid back to her Gasthaus, and wandered down to the coffee shop where several of them came and ate a late breakfast. He looked around for someone who would fill him in on the gossip. Luiza and Freddi were there but he knew they would be hopeless. They clammed up like leeches when anything about Therese came up. Then he saw Stefan, blue round the chin, sitting down with a plate of rolls and butter and a jug of milk.

'So, Stefan. May I?' He pointed to the chair on the other side of the table.

'Please yourself.'

'Stomach any better, Stefan?'

'Terrible.'

'It's been a trying time, warming up to opening. Our new leading lady hasn't helped either – needed more work than usual to get her going.'

Stefan grunted and gave him a sharp look.

'Very promising now though, don't you think?' Gesner said hastily. 'I do believe we have a leading lady of some merit.'

'Sounds good to me,' said Stefan guardedly.

Gesner waved for some coffee and helped himself to one of Stefan's rolls.

'Seems a shame she hasn't made a comeback before,' he said genially. 'Good voice – and she must have been very attractive when she was young. What a waste!'

Stefan began to thaw a little. He was a strange, rather lonely man with a lonely job that was highly pressured and didn't leave him any time to make friends or indulge in theatre gossip. When he was given a chance he enjoyed it as much as anyone else.

'I believe she tried a couple of times. The managements were very wary of taking her on, of course. Couldn't risk letting that kind of thing happen again. She was in disgrace for a while, not her fault though.'

'Ah yes – it was the husband, was it not? Something to do with a scene on the stage that stopped the show?'

'He was a drunk, a jealous drunk. He rushed on to the stage with a knife, tried to kill her. Rest of the cast fought him off but the tenor got cut about quite badly and had to go to hospital. Curtain brought down. Couldn't go on with the performance even with the understudies because of the police coming in. And the stage was in

158

a terrible mess, all blood and vomit, and the scenery all smashed up. Was in all the papers.'

'But of course everyone's forgotten it by now?'

'Well, naturally the old ones remember it. And the managements. But it was a long time ago and other things have happened since.'

'But nothing quite as . . . sensational as that.'

'No. But she's a plucky lady. She stood by him in court. He wasn't given too long a sentence providing he agreed to go into a clinic – you know – to be dried out and cured. And she stuck by him through all that.'

'Presumably he's dead now?'

Stefan hesitated. 'Not sure. Never liked to mention him and I don't think anyone else does either. He's certainly not around any more and she doesn't wear a wedding ring – not that that means anything these days.'

'Who was he? The husband?'

'A singer. No-one ever remembers his name. He wasn't a very good one, I suppose.'

Idly Gesner finished eating Stefan's rolls. He wasn't sure just how worried he ought to be by Therese Aschmann. She was good as Maritza, but still no threat to him. He wasn't even prepared to admit to himself that he'd had to work hard to keep her down. Absolutely no threat. She'd be dreadful when they came to *Der Zarewitsch* in three weeks' time; like playing Arsena again. But he was very much afraid she was going to be rather good in *Luxembourg* – it was a role not unlike that of Countess Maritza. He wasn't too worried about the stagecraft. He was an old hand at knowing how to steal his audiences; he'd managed to do it with Hanna Brunner last year and she *was* experienced. This one, after a gap of eighteen years, didn't even remember how to hold her place in the lights when he started to manoeuvre her upstage. But what really concerned him was the voice. It was good, and it was getting better, and no matter what he did, all the old tricks that had always worked so well, the talking in the wings, blocking her when she was on stage, that voice never faltered. Even when the audience couldn't see her because he'd managed to move across and mask her, holding centre stage for himself, they could still hear that effortless, golden sound spinning round every prism of the crystal chandelier in the middle of the theatre. When he thought about that voice he felt he would like to murder her with a knife himself.

The entire cast were excited about the dress rehearsal of *The*

Count of Luxembourg, even the blasé old orchestra catching some of the anticipatory delight that stemmed from the new production. The sets were marvellous and Madge Grimsilk had devised a quick and efficient way of implementing her transformation of the whole theatre into a fairy ballroom. Huge stiffened but graceful garlands were hung from twenty-four tiny hooks set round the gallery parapet, and were constructed so cleverly that they gave the impression of winding around the gallery pillars. The transformation of the ceiling was brought about with two simple pulleys, almost on a clothes-line principle, that took a tent of diamonds and icicles up around the chandelier. The garlands that swathed the proscenium arch took the audience right on to the stage – in spirit. But the most exciting thing of all was that, after eight years of hired costumes, old, stale, tired costumes from ancient productions, everyone in the cast was dressed in an outstanding design that really fitted.

Gesner was pleased with his own clothes, and had to confront the realization that Therese's would be no less effective. He'd seen what Madge Grimsilk had done for Therese in *Maritza*, and had savagely braced himself to give no sign, no indication of anything when he saw her *Luxembourg* costumes. Even so, it took all his self-control not to lose his temper with Madge Grimsilk, for Therese, in the dark sapphire Rosa Ponselle gown, studded all over with flashing blue stones and with the huge peacock train spreading out behind her, was outstanding, so outstanding that the rest of the cast, pleased with their own designs but quick to recognize a 'star' outfit, burst into a little patter of applause. Gesner felt an actual furious pain in his gut. She didn't look fat at all, not even a bit plump. Her wig, a soft gold colour, was dressed to sit high on her head, emphasizing once more the high cheekbones and the slightly slanting eyes. The pointed tiara flashed as she moved. She looked mysterious and quite, quite beautiful.

'You seem to have fallen from the top of a Christmas tree, Fräulein,' he said spitefully.

'Thank you, Karl.'

'Will you be able to breathe, and sing, with all that corseting?'

'No corsets, Karl,' she said sweetly. 'I've been losing quite a lot of weight since I came to Hochhauser. The strains and stresses, you know.'

The rehearsal was a mess of stops and starts. In spite of the technical run-through the day before, Madge Grimsilk's front and back cloths kept sticking and not coming down when they should.

The little Hoflin, who had her speciality showpiece in Act Two, did it very badly and finally tripped and fell. Everyone tried to help, reassuring her that this was a good omen, she would be marvellous when it came to the actual performance, but it was fairly obvious she was in a bad way. News had spread that some kind of scene had occurred at the Burgermeister's pre-production party. No-one was surprised. They'd seen it happen before to Gesner's dancers, but not usually so early in the Season. But even though the rehearsal was, if not exactly bad, then most certainly inconclusive, nothing could dull the sense of wild excitement that gripped the entire company. This was *their* new production, and an electric charge went through them, intensely fuelled amongst the younger members because they had heard that Hans Kramer, the Viennese operatic agent, was coming specially to Hochhauser to see Therese. Nothing like that had happened before in the history of Hochhauser. Each one of them envisaged the scene where Hans Kramer, overwhelmed by *their* particular performance, begged to represent them in the international field.

The entrance foyer was packed when Georg sidled in that evening, hoping that no-one would see him and recognize him. He knew his father would be backstage, interfering, and Suzi's parents had arrived much earlier in order to park their car and get to their seats in good time. In any case they were sitting upstairs in Willi's little loggia (the gallery of the Spa Rooms had not lent itself to conversion into boxes, but parts of the curved balcony had been sectioned off with wrought-iron grills into small loggias for distinguished guests).

He didn't know why he had come, hated himself for coming, but had by now tormented himself into a state of mind where he was deliberately looking for fresh spasms of anguish. He couldn't understand how his world had collapsed and although he said to himself, several times a day, that it was all the fault of the theatre, that sick, all-pervading fever that seemed to turn everyone foolish and mad, in his heart he knew it was more than that. Something had gone wrong between him and Suzi that was nothing to do with the theatre. Every time he saw her it hurt him, and he knew it would hurt him even more tonight, to see her cavorting with her lover on the stage. He didn't know what was happening between Gesner and Suzi any more, hadn't seen either of them since the Season began, since that dreadful scene at Willi's party, but he knew he had to submit himself to yet another bout of torture and watch them together on the stage. He pushed his way through to the box office and thrust a handful of money through the window.

161

'One seat. In the back stalls.' It was a sign of his distress that he didn't care what it cost, hadn't even looked to see the list of seat prices posted up by the side of the window. He wanted back stalls because he'd be right under the gallery and no-one would see him.

'No seats at all for this evening. All sold out long ago.'

Georg stared. 'But I must have a seat for this evening. I've come specially. I'll stand.'

'Standing room all gone too.'

He felt himself begin to tremble. 'What about tomorrow?'

'Nothing at all this week. First available is next week – Saturday.'

He'd forced himself to do this, sneak down here, humiliate himself because he had to see her now, this evening.

'Well, do you want a ticket for Saturday week or not?'

'Yes.'

'It's more than that. I'll need thirteen schilling more.' Blindly he pushed more notes through the window and turned away.

'Don't you want your ticket?'

He crammed it into his pocket and bludgeoned his way rudely through the first-night crowd. One or two people spoke sharply to him as he elbowed and trod on feet. When he got outside he turned to the right, up to the mountain road leading to his home. He had walked all the way down and he began to walk back. The May evening was warm and filled with a golden light, and as he passed the Maria-Therese gardens the scent of the lilacs hit him with an almost physical pain. He clenched his teeth, pulled back his shoulders and began to stride up the road. When he reached the branch-off track to the farm he looked up at the farmhouse. It had never seemed such a lonely, sad place since the day his mother had died. Even the sight of the herds, grazing gently on the new young grass, failed to cheer him. He wished his father was in the house. He felt the way he had when he was eleven, coming back to the farm after school, knowing his mother wasn't there and trying hard not to cry.

Busacher, after careful thought, had decided he would conduct the orchestra himself this evening. In some ways it would have been wiser to remain backstage, allowing his presence to be felt, the sight of him reassuring everyone. But Stefan had everything under control and he could not resist the temptation to open his first new production on his own rostrum. And in any case, he could control the things that mattered very well from there. Any nonsense from Gesner and he'd have to fight the orchestra.

He went around the dressing rooms, wishing everyone good luck (even Gesner) and congratulating everyone on a magnificent effort. This was not the moment to tell Ingrid to strain less in her upper registers, or to remind Luiza to allow plenty of time when she had to walk on in the ball scene. A special accolade for Stefan, that prodigy of a man who virtually single-handed got everything together on time, and then, just as he was about to go through the orchestra door he saw Madge Grimsilk, the headdress of a rat under her arm, hurrying up to the wings.

'Err . . . Miss Grimsilk?'

'Herr Direktor?'

'No problems?'

'No, Herr Direktor. Max had broken the strap on his mask. It's mended now.'

'Good. I . . . we . . . You have made a major contribution to this production, Miss Grimsilk. You must be aware of the excitement we all feel about this evening. Quite a large part of that excitement is due to you, to your designs, and, also, if I may be forgiven for mentioning something so personal, for the way you have helped and befriended Therese. I like to think that you have truly become one of the Hochhauser Company.'

Miss Grimsilk's face didn't crack, although he did perceive – perhaps – the very faintest of flushes creeping up from her neck.

'I hope you have enjoyed working with us,' he persisted.

'Good luck, Herr Direktor,' she said impassively, and he gave up. He had assisted in lifting her from the floor of Willi Zimmermann's living room when she was blindly unconscious. He had helped drag her to a chair, and had watched Julius and Willi carry her out to a car and take her home. Never once had she referred to it at all. He wondered if he had imagined it. He watched her hurry away from him as though she was terrified he was going to say more, and then the sounds of his orchestra tuning up took him through into the pit.

A full house, wonderful, and an excited one. All the committee were there and most of the *Gemeinderat*, a few interested specialists from Vienna, friends and relatives of the performers, the editor of the local newspaper and the top echelons of Hochhauser.

And then his own special moment of elation: the overture, the rustle, the curtain up, and suddenly his tacky, ragtag little chorus was out there, looking wonderful, moving well, even *singing* better! Something had happened to them – they were charged for just a while into being better than they were. This time he didn't have to wait with trepidation for the entrance of Gesner. This time his chorus was good!

Gesner, as Luxembourg, carried the excitement up several notches, as though realizing that tonight everyone was better and in order to shine he would have to exert himself. When Therese came on the entire evening lifted into top gear. She shone, both physically – Madge's dress sent prisms of sapphire light flashing across the stage – and artistically. Her voice began to dominate Gesner's, controlling him in the marriage scene. He couldn't upstage her, for the piece was carefully staged so that bride and groom were hidden from each other, one each side of the screen and Therese, radiant, controlled, confident, set the atmosphere of the whole scene. Busacher could feel, hear, Gesner fighting. He was superb but she was better and the voice coated the entire stage, the entire production with a quality never before heard in Hochhauser.

And then, just when the Direktor was congratulating himself that nothing could go wrong, Gesner refused to take it any more. Instead of staying carefully on his side of the screen – '*She goes left, I go right*' – he suddenly stepped forward, centre stage, out of his position, out of the whole plot of the operetta, threw out his arms in the great expansive sexual gesture that never failed to work with the audiences, and began to sing in front of Therese, ignoring the screen, ignoring the action, making a total mockery of the whole theme of a bride and groom who marry without knowing who they are.

'Get back!' Busacher hissed, but Gesner was in charge now. He had centre front stage, his voice projected forward over Therese's, and he ceased to make any attempt to act out the plotted movements with her. He was giving one of his best solo Gesner recitals, whilst totally blowing the sense of the scene. Busacher was livid and Alfred and Freddi were obviously lost. If those old pros didn't know how to get Gesner back into the plot, how to adjust and improvise the act, then nobody could.

Therese, on her side of the screen, totally masked by Gesner, suddenly peeked round his shoulder and gave a gay little smiling wave to the audience, then she tapped Gesner on the arm. Startled, he turned, but Therese had darted, scooping her peacock train up over one arm, back around behind the screen, to the side he should have been on. Again she tilted her head at the audience, still singing. Gesner moved to mask her again, and once more she darted round the screen, suddenly making great play with the peacock tail, holding it up to hide the lower part of her face, managing to pretend never to see the front of Luxembourg's face, and never to let him see her.

The duet continued, with Gesner planted solidly in the middle of the stage, and Therese whirling and gliding around him, managing never to confront him face to face, and with wit and grace stealing the scene totally back from him. The audience, through the music, were beginning to laugh, and Busacher, sacrificing one of Lehar's most romantic and loveliest passages of music to the emergency of the moment, speeded up the orchestra, gave the melody a light-hearted rather than a passionate lilt, and swore to himself that he would murder Gesner in the interval. The duet ended to a roar of applause and laughter. Gesner looked angry. He was conscious that Therese had been engaging in 'business' but hadn't appreciated how it had looked from the front until it was too late to do anything about it. He fumbled back to his position to the right of the screen and somehow Busacher got them all through the rest of the act.

Backstage they were all screaming at Gesner; Stefan – 'You do that again and I'll bring the curtain down' – Alfred, Freddi, Ingrid, Rudi, everyone was shaken, aware that he had nearly wrecked the entire production, and afraid that he still might.

'Karl,' Busacher said. 'Into your dressing room, at once.'

He was shaking with rage and this time it wasn't a deliberately contrived rage. It was a dangerous one he knew he mustn't release. His wretched heart began to pump ominously again and he closed his eyes for one second, tried to breathe slowly, tried to control himself.

'Karl, you do that once more and you will never work on my stage again, you understand?'

'Without me you have no company. Don't make foolish threats to me, old man. They don't care whether I stand on the side of a screen or front stage so long as they can see me, hear me, Karl Gesner. Without me you have no company.'

'Don't be too sure, Karl. Who do you think was making the audience laugh while you were giving them the full force of your personality? Who turned the scene round, made it work so that the rest of the operetta is not totally ridiculous? Who kept singing, and what a voice! I shouldn't be too sure that you are indispensable, Karl!'

'She's ruined this company! Everything's gone wrong since she came here. No-one likes her. I told you at the beginning how it would be. We were all good friends until she came!'

'Chaa!' Busacher's voice cracked on a derisive laugh.

165

'I refuse to sing with her again. You will have to choose between her and me! It is impossible for me to work the way I want to work when she is on the stage.'

Busacher was so enraged that diplomacy, tact, talking Gesner down into finishing the performance, all vanished into the maw of his rage. He opened the dressing-room door.

'Stefan!' He'd been hovering anxiously outside and stepped in at once.

'An announcement to the audience – there will be a slightly longer interval and Herr Gesner, due to an indisposition, will not be able to continue his performance. Tell Rudi to get out of his Brissard things, and get Edouard out of the chorus and into Rudi's clothes. Rudi will take over from Karl.'

'I refuse! You cannot do this!'

'I can and will. You either go on and sing with Therese, the way it has been rehearsed, or you do not go on my stage, at all, not tonight, not any night.'

'I shall sue!' screamed Gesner.

'Go ahead. I, the committee, and Hochhauser will probably sue you for refusing to go on, thereby breaking your contract!'

Stefan, white-faced, looked from one to the other.

'Hurry, Stefan. I've told you what to do.'

'Wait. All right. I'll finish the performance. I'll finish this one performance. But tomorrow she must go, other plans must be made, someone else found.'

'There will be no alterations in the plans for the rest of the Season. Aschmann remains. If you wish to break your contract I will inform your agent of your decision tomorrow morning.'

The dressing room was charged with venom, jealousy, spite, and also total and undisciplined panic, which stemmed mainly from Stefan, who had been through most things with Gesner in the course of the various Seasons, but never anything like this; never before an open confrontation between Gesner and the Direktor in the middle of a performance.

'Act Two – Beginners please,' said a tremulous voice from outside the door. Everyone in the company knew something was going on, and when no sound came from the dressing room the tremulous voice said again, 'Beginners please.'

'Get out of my dressing room!' Gesner said angrily. 'I haven't even begun to change yet.' It was a capitulation of sorts.

'Remember what I said, Karl! There are to be no further scenes on the stage, no deviations from the rehearsals. If there are, I shall instruct Stefan to bring down the curtain.'

'Ha! In the middle of your new production? The production you've waited eight years for? You'd be committing suicide and you know it.'

'No, Karl, I don't know it. And in any case I am so angry – I have never been so angry! – I am prepared to commit suicide if it would mean the end of your career! And I would take good care to see that it *was* the end of your career.'

'You cannot survive without me!' screamed Gesner. 'You cannot survive without a star!'

'No. We cannot. But I believe a new one is beginning to emerge. Think on that, Herr Gesner!'

He turned and walked from the dressing room with as much control as he could muster. Outside, he turned to Stefan. 'Stefan, do you think you could find me a brandy from somewhere?' He felt so ill and exhausted he didn't know how he was going to get through the rest of the evening. But get through it he must, and from the conductor's rostrum. That was the best way of controlling Gesner for the two remaining acts – through the orchestra. If the worst came to the worst he would cut his numbers, take the orchestra straight over Karl's sections and leave him standing. Please God it wouldn't come to that.

'Are you ill, Herr Direktor?'

'A brandy and a short rest will put me right. Extend the interval. No-one will notice. Give me another ten minutes.'

He wanted to go and see Therese, thank her, warn her, but now had no energy for anything but getting to his office, sipping his brandy, and sitting back with his eyes closed, trying to steady his breathing. The pain in his chest began to lessen, his legs stopped shaking. Idly, in a detached way, he wondered what would happen if he collapsed in the orchestra pit, dropped dead in the middle of his new production. But he couldn't do that. He couldn't let them down like that, his brave little company who had battled their way, despite enormous odds, into a precarious success.

Therese, conscious, as was everyone else, of a row of gargantuan proportions going on in Gesner's dressing room, was blithely uncaring. She felt totally in charge, totally confident, able to cope not only with herself but with any emergencies that might crop up. The Act Two ball dress, the emerald gown with the huge stiffened collar embroidered with pearls, looked even better than the Act One dress and she realized that, without knowing quite how, she had quelled Gesner – not for reasons of rivalry but because she had had to get the production back on course. If she could do it once, she could do it again. She saw him in the wings just before she went on stage and she chose to ignore whatever had happened in the interval.

'It seems to be going very well, Karl. Good audience.'

He turned his back, as she had expected. It wasn't going to make it any easier playing the love scene, but she could cope. If necessary she could do it without even standing close to him. She could make it quite convincing just by throwing yearning smiles across the stage and focusing her gaze at a point just over his left ear, so that the hard brown eyes didn't impinge on her concentration.

'Thank God for Madge,' Busacher reflected grimly as the curtain went up and the enchanted ballroom brought a round of applause from the audience. He felt slightly cheered. Nothing could detract from the atmosphere that Madge's set created, an otherworld of romantic fairyland, all silver and white and iridescent greens.

It went better than Busacher had hoped. As lovers they were not exactly vibrant, but their voices and Lehar's music more than made up for that. They were both singing well, not exactly together, but not destroying each other either and, as he listened, he realized that once again it was Therese who was making it work, adapting slightly, but still dominating the sounds as they came over the footlights. The little Hoflin didn't fall over and looked extremely pretty, and when the curtain came down he leaned for a moment on the rostrum and took a deep breath. Act Three was short and musically not too demanding, just tied everything up without putting Gesner and Therese into a strained situation. They made it to the winning post fairly creditably.

Backstage, in Therese's dressing room, all was excitement and congratulations – Willi, old Anton, Alfred, the entire Hochhauser Theatre committee complete with the Easter egg – the expensive dress had found an occasion worthy of a second showing – and Hans, a smugly self-satisfied Hans who sat in the only chair sipping a glass of champagne provided by Willi. Busacher desperately wanted to go home and rest, but he daren't let any rumours of his frailty get around. As soon as the congratulations were over he could go.

Hans, under the cover of general triumphant noise, raised both his glass and an eyebrow at Franz.

'Congratulations, my friend. I came prepared to be mildly pleased – one or two rumours have trickled back to Vienna, you know – and find myself overwhelmed. The entire production was . . . very good.'

'Thank you, Hans.'

'A rather novel production, of course. That Act One marriage scene – I don't think I've ever seen it played that way before, as a comedy number.'

'You know very well, Hans, that was *not* intended,' Busacher remarked dryly.

Hans sniffed. 'Well, I did wonder – rather suspected that Gesner was behaving very naughtily. Also I knew it was most unlike you to sacrifice one of the loveliest passages in the whole operetta to a comic routine. But it was . . . different.'

'And what do you think of our diva? Did you recognize her – that poor crushed creature we saw in Vienna, did you recognize her?'

Hans looked even smugger. 'The voice I recognized – oh yes – that will never change, please God, and you have nothing to do with that, Franz. But for everything else I give credit where it is due. To you. You have created a star, in a small pond at the moment, but by the end of the Season Aschmann will be a highly commercial plum. Mozart next, I think. I shall begin to put out a few delicate hints. Salzburg perhaps. Glyndebourne, that level. A winter working on Mozart, perhaps a few concerts, and then we'll see.'

'I think you owe me one more Season, Hans.'

'Perhaps. Well, yes, perhaps you are right. We'll see.'

Busacher pushed his way over to Therese, kissed her on the cheek, then excused himself. Willi followed him out of the dressing room.

'I'm going to drive you home, Franz. You're ill.'

'But Therese . . . the party?'

Willi looked slightly wistful. 'She has all her old friends from Vienna to take her out to dinner. It will not matter if I am not there.'

He felt Willi was wanting to be reassured but he was just too tired and ill to bother. With relief he gave up trying and allowed Willi to see him out, into the car, and home.

CHAPTER ELEVEN

He felt considerably better the next morning and, upon reflection, decided to cope with Gesner by doing exactly nothing. Karl was not unintelligent when it came to his own interests, his own career. He had got the message quite clearly last night. He could stay and sing with Aschmann, or he could break his contract. There was no need to reiterate it all this morning, and it might be unwise to force Gesner into losing any further face. Karl was a master at ignoring unpleasantness, situations he had brought about by his own actions. Busacher rather thought they would rub through the next few days without an open revolt from Gesner.

They were performing *Luxembourg* for the remainder of the week. He had found, over the years, it was always better to play a new piece in several times before ringing the nightly changes. By the end of the week *Luxembourg* would be nicely set, and next week they would return to the *Baron* and *Countess Maritza*, finishing up that week with *Luxembourg* again. And the week after that, the last of the Season's productions, *Der Zarewitsch* from last year, could be reintroduced into the programme.

Willi came up to see how he was during the morning.

'I know there was some trouble backstage last night,' he said. 'But I don't want to know too many details. Just assure me it won't affect the rest of the Season.'

'I hope not, Willi. Gesner threatened to walk out unless Therese was fired. I made it quite plain he would go before she did, and I rather think he has accepted the status quo. What we will do next season I dread to think. In fact I refuse to think about it at all.'

'Will we . . . I mean is there any chance we shall have Therese next season?' Willi asked tentatively.

'Perhaps. I think, from the way Hans, her agent you know, Hans Kramer, was speaking last night, we may effect some kind of compromise. Therese for part of the Season.'

'She will go back to Vienna then?' asked Willi.

'Her agent was speaking of Salzburg – Mozart. A good idea I think. Then perhaps some work in Munich before returning to Vienna and the *Staatsoper*.'

'I'm not terribly fond of Mozart,' said Willi glumly.

'Willi, we cannot keep her here. She's too good for us. We have done exactly what I wanted us to do – brought a great singer back into the difficult world of the performer. And we shall have a wonderful season, and possibly a wonderful season next year. But we cannot hope to keep her here for ever. It would not be fair.'

'No,' said Willi.

'But it has been a great triumph for Hochhauser, Willi. Therese, the new production, Madge Grimsilk, all have helped to make the Hochhauser Season an outstanding one. Our grant will surely be increased next year. Better singers will be attracted to us. We are beginning to be well known, Willi!'

'Yes,' said Willi grudgingly.

'And we still have the rest of this season, Willi. It has only just begun.' Really, it was like consoling a small child. And Willi was usually such a tower of strength.

'That's true,' said Willi, cheering up. 'A magnificent season – and *Zarewitsch* still to come. *Der Zarewitsch* has always been one of my favourites.'

How absurd it seemed – that they had been worried about Therese in *Zarewitsch*. It was, of course, still an unsuitable role for her, a seventeen-year-old dancer disguised as a Circassian boy. But now, with the triumph of *Countess Maritza* and *Luxembourg* behind her, it seemed unimportant. It wouldn't be the pick of the Season, but Therese's marvellous and emotive voice would be a joy to listen to, no matter how uncomfortable the casting. And it had always been one of Gesner's greatest roles. It was – almost – Lehar's most operatic piece and Gesner had always found he couldn't fuff his way through it. He had to sing properly in *Zarewitsch* and one was reminded yet again that he could have been a great singer if only he had tried.

'When is Miss Grimsilk leaving us, Willi? Is she staying on for another couple of *Luxembourg* performances? Just to see us safely in?'

Willi had revealed that, since the night of Madge's fall from grace, she actually socialized with him, accepted the occasional invitation for coffee and, whilst not exactly chatting effusively about herself or her private life, indulged in fairly normal conversation with him.

'She has said she will be staying on, at her own expense of course, until the opening of *Zarewitsch*. Apparently she likes it in Hochhauser and intends to take a little holiday here – as we have already paid her fare from London.'

'How fascinating, Willi! And what do you think she will do on her little holiday? Get drunk and pass out every night?'

'Apparently she walks. She, Rudi, Elisa, and some of the young ones go out every Sunday, up on the Hochhauser. They rather like her.' Willi paused, then said apologetically, 'Actually, so do I.'

'Why, Willi?'

'I don't know why. She's very quiet, of course, reserved. But she's very kind and she can be very funny, when she's had a drink or two.'

'I am rapidly coming to the conclusion,' said Busacher thoughtfully, 'that it is something personal with Madge Grimsilk and me. She does not like me. Still . . .' he shrugged. 'What matters is that she has given us the most glorious production we have ever had at Hochhauser. She is a genius, and we shall use her again. And now, my dear Willi, I would ask you to make just a little overture of . . . friendship, to Gesner this evening. Oh, nothing much,' he hastened to say as Willi made protesting noises. 'Just a little to keep him sweet before the curtain goes up. Karl Gesner has had to swallow quite a few blows to his ego over the last few days. Just a kind word, a *flattering* word, Willi, to help us all out.'

'Oh, all right,' said Willi. 'But if you saw how miserable my poor Georg is, and how he has upset Suzi, to say nothing of my friends the Hoflins . . . well, I shall find it very difficult to be nice to him.'

'Just try, Willi,' said Busacher closing his eyes. 'Just think of the Season and try.'

As the week's performances of *The Count of Luxembourg* continued, it became increasingly obvious who was the star of the company. Every night Therese sang better, dominated the stage, laughed, bubbled, and sailed through the part with a charm that delighted the audience. They reinstated the waltz with Gesner and it was observed that it was Therese who was the light, lithe dancer, whirling around the stage, pulling Gesner with her, making him dance in spite of himself. Gesner fought a bit but it didn't work.

When he tried to upstage her she sauntered down to the front of the stage and such was her control over the audience now, he had to back off, otherwise it would have been he who looked ridiculous. Offstage she was scrupulously polite to him, an exercise that was totally wasted as he continued to ignore her. It made for a somewhat strained atmosphere, but as a company they were used to that. It was worse than last year, with Hanna Brunner, but the high spirits of the company, knowing they were creating quite a stir, knowing they were good, all of them, made it bearable.

Ingrid was the one who found it most awkward. She was Gesner's girlfriend. That was how she described it to herself, although what it really meant was that he took her to bed whenever he felt like it and occasionally gave her an absent-minded smile backstage. She'd hoped, thought, it would be nice if he had taken her to lunch sometimes, or let her stay to breakfast in his room at the Franz Joseph instead of pushing her out early and sending her back to the Gasthaus. But the most she got was a hasty and inexpensive meal after the evening performance on the nights he wanted her to go to bed with him. Still, she *was* his girlfriend and he was wonderful to her in *Gypsy Baron* and also in *Maritza*. She had a duet with him in the latter that she couldn't have managed if he hadn't carried her through. But she also liked Therese, who had made a point of introducing her to Hans Kramer, the big Viennese agent. She sometimes felt she was walking a tightrope, wanting to be friendly with Therese, and yet terrified of upsetting Karl.

The week of that first production of *Luxembourg*, Karl had been absolutely beastly to her – really hurtful about her performance as Juliette which, as she was desperately saving her voice for the other productions, she tended to talk her way through. Herr Busacher had said that was fine, perfectly all right, so she didn't know why Karl was so scathing about it. One evening he had almost made her cry. 'You'll never be a singer, however hard you try. What will you do if you have to manage in the company without me, eh? How would you manage without me to carry you through?'

She'd been upset by that. She told herself that he didn't really mean it, that he was just angry about the way everyone was praising Therese, and about the applause and cheers that she got. That was what it was, but it hurt just the same, his open contempt of her.

Then suddenly, after the Thursday night show, he was wonderful again. They went back to the Franz Joseph together – she liked everyone to see them walking off together when the performance was over. It made her feel that he didn't mind everyone knowing she was his girlfriend, and he was really sweet to her in bed, told her she had lovely hair and said she must never, ever cut it, it was so beautiful, and then he began to talk about Therese, saying how cruel it was that he had carried the company all these years and now, just because she was the Direktor's favourite – he snorted at this point and said he really did believe Therese must have been old Franz's mistress years ago in Vienna – he was being treated like a pariah, no consideration, everyone being rude and unkind to him, Therese allowed to do just what she liked on the stage even though she'd been no-one before she came to Hochhauser.

'She *was* a singer, years ago, in Vienna. Luiza told me.'

Karl stroked her hair and murmured, 'So pretty.'

'Actually, it's terribly tragic, Karl. Her husband became an alocholic and they had to put him away in a clinic.'

'Are you and Luiza good friends?' he asked.

'Well . . . yes . . . we were. Until, you know, until you and I . . .'

'Of course – but if you were to go to Luiza and pretend to be friends again . . . you could tell her you didn't like me any more.'

'Oh Karl! That's not true!'

'I know it, sweetheart. But if you told Luiza you were finished with me, then perhaps you could find out about Therese Aschmann for me.'

'But what more do you want to know, Karl, and why? What does it matter if you know about Therese and her husband?'

'Because . . . because she has hurt me, Ingrid. She has been very rude and unkind to me. She has made my position here in Hochhauser untenable. You must see how appallingly she behaves on the stage. Makes no effort at all to work with me, just thinks of herself all the time. She's not thinking of the company, Ingrid. You must see that? She's just concentrating on making everyone say how good *she* is. That's not going to help us as a company, is it? We want everyone to work together.'

'Yes . . . I suppose you're right.'

'The way you and I work together – some of the *Baron*'s a bit difficult for you, isn't it? Oh, no fault of your own, it's a very tricky role. But do I take delight in pushing you down, making you worse? I help you, don't I?'

'You're marvellous, Karl! I couldn't have done it without you.'

'You wouldn't like me to have to leave the company, would you?'

174

'Oh, Karl. There wouldn't be a company without you!'

'Well, Ingrid. I'm going to tell you something I don't want repeated, not to anyone.'

She felt really wonderful when he said that. Usually he never bothered to talk to her in bed, but this was what real lovers did, told each other their fears and worries, confided in each other, helped each other.

'That first night of *Luxembourg*, when she turned that marvellous duet into a slapstick comedy routine and I complained to the Direktor about it – you knew I complained about what she had done to the duet, didn't you, Ingrid?'

'Well, I wasn't sure exactly what had happened,' she breathed.

'I said it was terrible, to ruin one of Lehar's most wonderful love songs like that, and Ingrid, he made it quite plain that if I didn't fall in with Therese's wishes – *exactly* – I would be thrown out of the company.'

'Karl! I don't believe it.' She was really upset. She couldn't imagine the company without Karl. How would she cope?

'I never wanted there to be a war between us, Ingrid. But that's what it has come to. And I know that's what she's planning to do – get me thrown out of the company that I've helped to build, taken a reduced salary. I could have worked all over Europe, Ingrid. I could have gone to New York, but I chose to stay in Hochhauser because I believed in the company and wanted to help them. And now Aschmann is planning to get rid of me!'

'Oh, Karl, how dreadful. I had no idea she was like that. She always seemed so nice . . .'

'So you see I've got to protect myself. I've got to find out everything I can about her. That's the only way I can hope to fight back and keep my job.'

'But I don't think there's anything else to know about her,' Ingrid faltered. She was thoroughly upset now, angry with Therese for being so two-faced and injuring the man who had, more or less, founded the company single-handed. 'Luiza told me, when Therese first came up here, that she was divorced and the husband was in a clinic over near Mayerling – the Schubert Clinic – I remembered that because I thought it was a funny name for a clinic.'

'You knew that and you didn't tell me?' Gesner suddenly shouted at her.

'I didn't think it was very interes—'

'You sly little trollop!' he cried, grabbing her hair and pulling it so hard she nearly fell out of bed.

'Karl!'

'God preserve me from foolish and deceitful women,' he said, letting her hair go and falling back on the pillow, his arms raised angrily above his head.

'Karl! I wasn't being sly or deceitful. I wasn't. I didn't know about all this, about Therese trying to get you out of the company and . . . and everything.'

'Oh, get dressed and get out,' he snarled. She began to snatch up her clothes, brushing her hand across her eyes. This time he really had made her cry.

'Do you still want me to make friends with Luiza?' she choked. 'I didn't understand . . . I see now it's important to you. I'll do anything I can to help.' He eyed her speculatively across the room, stupid bitch, then decided he ought to be careful.

'Sorry, Ingrid. You see how all this has upset me. Aschmann has really ruined my life. No, don't do anything about Luiza. I'll tell you if I want you to do anything.'

'Would you like me to stay?' she asked tremulously.

'God, no! I mean, you can see what I'm like this evening. We don't want to have a quarrel, do we? You go back and have a good night's rest.'

'Good night, then, Karl.'

''Night, pumpkin.'

When she had gone he took his bottle of schnapps from the bedside cupboard and poured himself a glass, then lay back against the pillows, thinking about what to do next. Ingrid was pathetic, disgusting. He should have continued with the little Hoflin girl. Maybe if things worked out he'd start that up again. He drank, and then began to think how he could use the information he'd just been given.

Stefan didn't room with the other members of the company in the Goldener Adler, nor in any other Gasthaus close to the theatre. He had a room in a private house some way out of the town. It took him longer to get there after the performance but he was away from all the problems of the rest of the company. He'd tried, the first year, rooming with the others, and had found they still came up to him all the time with their queries – 'They've sent me the wrong costume for *Gypsy Baron*. Will you sort it out with Wardrobe?' – 'My parents are coming all the way from Linz and the box office say they've sold out. Can you do something, Stefan?' – 'I've got the chance of an audition in Vienna early on Wednesday morning but it will mean I'll miss the Tuesday night show. Can you make it all right with the Direktor?'

He didn't have much time in his lodgings on the outskirts of the town, but when he was there he was able to lie down in his quiet, quiet room and totally relax. His landlady was very kind to him too. She had put a small fridge in his room and she kept it well stocked with milk. He had a nice room. The house was quite high on the slopes and he could see the main road down into the town, and behind that the mountains on the other side of the valley sweeping up into the changing skies. It was very restful and he'd moved his furniture around so that he could lie on his bed and look at the view.

He was appalled, late on the Friday morning, to glance out of his window and see Karl Gesner striding up the road towards his house. It had to be his house. There wasn't another beyond this, and Karl Gesner wasn't one to take mountain strolls in the morning. He debated whether to dart out and tell his landlady to say he wasn't in, but he had underestimated the speed of Gesner's long, athletic legs. He came straight up to the open window and smiled.

'Hullo there, Stefan. Hoped I'd find you in.'

'I'll be at the theatre after lunch. Couldn't it wait until then?'

'That's why I came. I'd like to buy you lunch.'

'No thanks. Too busy. And I don't feel like eating out today. Frau Gess has promised to make me some creamed chicken and steamed potato. I'm looking forward to it.'

'I thought these wonderful new tablets were supposed to solve all your troubles?' He smiled kindly and Stefan felt a twinge of alarm shoot through him.

'They've solved the ulcer problem for nearly everyone, but for one in a hundred it doesn't work. I'm the one in a hundred.'

'Tough. Can I come in?' He vaulted cleanly through the open window, brushed his hair back and sauntered around Stefan's room, picking up his record book, his razor, his hat.

'What do you want?' asked Stefan nervously.

'Just a chat. I was thinking about those poor people we had in last week – the charity group. You know, the wheelchairs and white sticks.'

'It's a block booking. There's another one tonight. There's nothing wrong with them. Their own organizers look after them. Nobody else has complained.'

'Stefan! Why should you think I'm complaining? I felt sorry for them, thought it was quite a decent thing to do. I wondered why we didn't do a bit more for them. Meet them after the show or something. Give them a really good night out.'

'They have to get back after the show. There is a sort of refreshment thing organized beforehand, in the small studio at the side of the theatre. They give them about an hour there before the curtain goes up. I checked with the Direktor and he said it was quite OK. The Franz Joseph have the catering franchise. It's just cakes and coffee. There's no harm in it.'

'Of course there's no harm in it! I just wondered if we couldn't do more. Who runs the whole thing?'

'Fräulein Hubert.'

'And she'll be there tonight? Before the show?'

'I suppose so.' Alarm bells were ringing frantically in Stefan's head.

'I think I would like to meet her. To discuss what more we could do. It would be nice, for instance, if some of the cast went in in costume before the curtain went up – to wish them well, hope they enjoy it, that sort of thing. Make it more glamorous for the poor wretches.'

'I don't know. The Direktor would have to decide. You know he doesn't like that kind of thing before a performance.'

'Still, even so, perhaps I'll wander in early this evening. Have a little chat with this . . . Fräulein Hubert.'

'I don't think that would be a good idea.'

'Stefan! For God's sake – what do you think I'm going to do? Steal their white sticks? Sabotage the wheelchairs?' He laughed rather ruefully. 'Everyone in this company seems to think I'm incapable of doing anything even halfway decent for anyone. I do get a bit tired of being the permanent Big Bad Wolf. I have occasionally been known to be kind to an old lady and I don't kick *every* stray dog that comes across my path.'

'No, I know,' said Stefan stiffly.

'You needn't bother to introduce me to Fräulein Hubert. I can sort her out for myself. Presumably she'll be the one without a white stick.' He chuckled. 'Nice room you have here, Stefan. Nice and quiet. Can't blame you for getting away from everyone. They're a motley crew, aren't they?' He climbed back out of the window. 'Enjoy your lunch now, Stefan. See you later.'

Stefan waited until he had gone some way down the road, then rushed out to the telephone. He didn't know what Gesner was up to but he thought he'd better tell the Direktor.

That night Gesner got into his *Luxembourg* costume early, slid out of the stage door and into the outside entrance of the small studio. He didn't want anyone to see him walking through the theatre. He looked as amazing as he always did in his stage

178

costume, twice the size he was on stage, twice as powerful. He stood in the doorway and smiled around him. More wheelchairs but no white sticks tonight. Several crutches, though, and quite a few people who didn't apparently have anything wrong with them, helpers or nurses, he supposed. He stared at the women. There was one in a loden green suit with a felt hat – in May! – and terrible legs. She was in that indeterminate middle age that lasts for ever with unattractive women. It must be Fräulein Hubert. He smiled even more widely and went across to introduce himself.

Young Suzi, in the depths of her misery, knowing it was making her worse, still couldn't keep away from the theatre, even during the day, even on Sunday when no-one was there. Like Georg, she felt the need to submit herself to the possibility of seeing the one she loved who had rejected her. She was deeply ashamed of the way she had behaved with Georg, drink, misery, badly upset hormones, whatever it was she knew that from now on she must keep right away from him, let him get over her, meet someone else, someone interested in farming and cows, and be happy again. At the thought two miserable tears wandered down her face. She imagined Georg happy and married to some nice girl, while she went on in this gulf of misery for the rest of her life, hanging around waiting for glimpses of Gesner, spending every night reliving every moment they had been together, all the wonderful things he had said to her, the magic of his hands when he touched her – she shivered. She could see no way out of her present despair. The excitement of taking part in the Hochhauser Season had totally gone, swallowed up in the misery of losing Karl. She hadn't even been nervous on the first night, not in the way other people were nervous. She wanted to do well because of Gesner. Perhaps if he saw her looking wonderful, dancing beautifully, he would realize that he needed her as much as she needed him.

On Sunday she rose late. She didn't ever get to sleep until the early hours now and she woke up heavy and lethargic. She wandered into the kitchen, poured some coffee and slumped down at the table. Her hair was limp and needed washing, her face was pallid and there were dark stains under her eyes.

'Try to eat some breakfast, Suzi. You told me once that it was important for a dancer to eat plenty of protein.'

'I'm not hungry.'

Frau Hoflin fought an overwhelming desire to slap her daughter. But it would achieve nothing. Gesner was the one who ought to be slapped, but he had at least done the decent thing in abandoning

Suzi. She was miserable now but inevitably she'd recover from her first heavy affair. Frau Hoflin hoped it *hadn't* been an affair, but even if it had, well, things were different these days and it didn't matter too much as long as it was over.

'Are you going out today? Would you like to come to church with Papa and me?'

'No.'

'So what are you going to do?'

'I'll wash my hair – and then I'll go out for a walk.'

'Why don't you go and see your old friends? You haven't seen Eva and Manni for ages. You've rather neglected them since you became involved with the Season.'

'I don't seem to have anything in common with them any more.'

'That's because you've dropped them. It doesn't do to drop old friends, Suzi.'

Suzi made patterns in the sugar with her spoon. 'Oh well, I might.'

But when she had washed her hair and dressed – in a new pair of designer jeans and a silk shirt that had been a Christmas present and which she'd never worn before – it wasn't to Eva's house that she went but back down into the town, towards the theatre and the Franz Joseph. It was a glorious morning. All the snow had gone from the tops and the sun was really warm. The parks and main avenue were awash with trees in full blossom, and when she looked back up towards the farm she could see patches of cloudy pink where the apple trees were in bloom. Usually in Maytime she liked to walk up into the high mountain meadows to see the wild flowers, but this year she had no heart. And anyway, the big meadow was the one on the ridge, the one that separated her farm from Georg's. It would be awful if she met Georg up there.

She hung around for a while, looking aimlessly into the shop windows, wondering if she should go and have a coffee in the Franz Joseph, just in case he was there. She bumped into Rudi, Madge Grimsilk, and some of the young ones. They all wore mountain shoes and had packs slung over their shoulders.

'Hi, Suzi. We're off to see how high we can get up the Hochhauser. Come with us. We've enough lunch for you.'

'Oh . . . thank you. But . . . well, I haven't got the right shoes on or anything.'

'We can go up the long way, past your farm, and you can nip in and change. We don't mind waiting a bit.'

Should she go? For one moment she thought what fun it would be with them all. No-one very serious about anyone else, just a crowd of friends all having a good time, walking up the mountain on a lovely day, drinking the spring water and having a picnic. She hesitated, just about to say yes, and at that moment saw Karl coming slowly down the steps of the Franz Joseph pulling on his driving gloves.

'Thanks,' she said quickly. 'But I've promised to look up some old friends I haven't seen for ages. Have a good time.' She waved them on and quickly walked away, terrified they might hang about and try to make her change her mind. Karl certainly wouldn't stop and speak to her if she was with a crowd from the theatre.

Should she walk towards the car park? No, that would look too obvious. Better to stroll back the way she had come, then perhaps she would cross over the road and look in the souvenir shop.

She didn't even have to cross over. The miracle happened: she heard the car slow down and stop beside her. She turned and tried to look surprised.

Karl was smiling at her, the first time for over two weeks.

'Hullo, little one. Where are you off to?'

'Oh, nowhere special.'

'Where have you been hiding yourself? I haven't seen much of you lately.'

'I've been on stage every night,' she said sharply, surprising herself with her own effrontery at speaking that way to Karl.

'Oh, the performances!' He shrugged carelessly. 'Everyone's so paranoid in the theatre these days it's impossible to actually *see* anyone there. I meant, why haven't I seen you outside the theatre? Why haven't you come to lunch with me? Where have you been?'

'I . . . er . . . well, you haven't asked me.'

'I could hardly ask you if I didn't see you, could I?'

She was faintly conscious of being manoeuvred into a defensive situation she didn't deserve, but Karl had one arm hung over the side of the car, his sleeve rolled up to reveal a hard masculine arm and his brown eyes were smiling, one eyebrow slightly raised in an amused sort of way.

'I thought you . . . didn't like me very much.'

'I like you too much, pumpkin. That's been the trouble all along.'

She felt a throb somewhere in the region of her midriff, a throb compounded of relief and a dawning hope. Perhaps it really had all been a terrible misunderstanding.

'I wanted to come with you that night,' she said earnestly. 'The night of Uncle Willi's party. I just didn't know what to do. I've been so miserable.'

'Me too,' he said softly, reaching out his hand to touch her face. 'Are we friends again, little one?'

She could hardly speak she was so relieved. She couldn't believe that it had all stopped, the misery, the anguish, the self-recrimination. It was all right again, it was wonderful again. She waited for him to invite her into the car and out for the day. It was such a marvellous brilliant day! A day to go out with Karl, sweep over the mountains in his fantastic car, the top down and the sun shining on them. She waited, but nothing happened. He patted her cheek again, then put his hand back on the wheel and started the engine.

'I'd like to ask you out, pumpkin, but I've got rather a lot to do today. I have to drive over to Mayerling and see someone.'

'I could come, just for the drive,' she said breathlessly. 'I don't mind waiting in the car, however long it takes.'

He hesitated. 'I don't think so, sweetheart. It's business, may take a long time. And I've lots of other things to do. I'll see you in the week, eh? We'll have lunch one day.'

'That would be nice,' she said bleakly.

'Bye now, pumpkin. Don't forget me, will you?' He put his foot down and roared away. He could see her in his rear mirror, standing on the pavement looking wistfully after him. He was very tempted to hurry developments along in that area, but with things as they were he decided he ought to play it very carefully. Ingrid was a bore but he wasn't sure he might not need her again. It had worked very well last night with Fräulein Hubert, better than he'd hoped, but he ought to be careful until his plans were all consolidated, then he could dump Ingrid and carry on where he'd left off with that lovely little thing. She really did have the most fantastic figure.

On Monday Busacher made Stefan go over again every word of his conversation with Gesner. Like Stefan he was highly suspicious, but he couldn't see quite how Gesner could use the charity bookings in his quest for glory.

'Did you get a chance to look in at the side studio, when they were there last Friday? Did he go in?'

'Yes. I couldn't stop for long, not just before the show. But he didn't *seem* to be doing anything awful. That Fräulein Hubert was taking him around, introducing him to the group, and he was being – oh, well – you know, like Gesner, laughing, shaking hands, holding the women's hands too long, you know the kind of thing.'

'I know.'

'Fräulein Hubert said, when they were getting them back on to the coach after the show, what a wonderful man he was. How he'd made their evening for them.'

'He likes to be adored of course, and maybe he's just lobbying for an extension of his fan club, but I wouldn't have thought he was that desperate. What the charity groups think of him is hardly going to make or break him in the operatic world.'

'Unless he's going all out to make people think he's a really nice fellow.'

'Hmm. When's the next group in, Stefan?'

'End of the week. Saturday evening performance. *Luxembourg* again.'

'We'll watch him. I think I'll ask Willi to go into the side studio and see exactly what he's up to. And we'll keep a very careful eye on him this week. He'll be all right at the beginning, *Gypsy Baron* and *Maritza* again. We can cope. But we'll watch very carefully for the three *Luxembourg*s at the end of the week, just in case he's planning a fresh revolt on the stage.'

But Gesner behaved beautifully all that week. He gave a magnificent performance in *Gypsy Baron*, and a nearly magnificent performance in *Maritza*, in which he was overshadowed only by Therese. Offstage he was fairly quiet, preoccupied. Twice he was called to the telephone just before the curtain went up and he had long intense conversations with his hand over the mouthpiece. He also, Busacher observed, seemed to be playing a curious double game with both Ingrid and the little Hoflin – being charming to both of them and he was seen lunching with them on alternate days. But in the evening, after the show, he vanished, alone, back to the Franz Joseph and, presumably, a celibate bed. He still ignored Therese offstage, but was – surprisingly – quite civil to the rest of the company.

'I really think I felt happier when he was being his normal, rude, arrogant, bullying self,' said Busacher gloomily to Willi one evening. 'I feel very uneasy about this well-behaved Gesner.'

'No need,' said Willi with confidence. 'He's been badly frightened. That first row, when we got the committee up to face him, that frightened him, and then it was made quite plain that Therese was here to stay. And now she's become the star he realizes that he may be out of a job if he doesn't behave. Before this season he always knew that we couldn't survive without him, but now we can, now we have another star. I think he's trying to be sensible and doing it all wrong.'

'Perhaps you're right, Willi. Perhaps you're right.'

'And if we all watch him, Stefan, you, I, he can't do anything fatal. Three against one should be enough of a match for Gesner.'

'Of course,' said Busacher, relaxing slightly. 'I'm probably being neurotic. But still, my friend, I think we ought to watch him, the three of us.'

But by Friday the three had been reduced to two. Frau Gess telephoned very early in the morning to say that she had just called the doctor. Stefan had begun haemorrhaging in the night. His ulcer had finally blown up and the doctor was rushing him to hospital. The theatre would have to manage without him, and Busacher suddenly had more than enough to do without watching Karl Gesner as well.

CHAPTER TWELVE

By Saturday morning Gesner was feeling complacently triumphant. He felt he had learned something from the whole of this
season's events. Sometimes, instead of acting on the spur of the
moment, it was better to lie very low, plan carefully, think things
through. Nothing would go wrong now, and even though old
Busacher would probably be furious with him, there was nothing
he could do. The company had to have a star, but only one. There
certainly wasn't room in this company for two, and he had to make
sure which star survived. He felt a sense of general benevolence to
all the people who had helped him, even Ingrid, who had really got
on his nerves this week but whom he could now write off. He knew
exactly how to write off an unwanted appendage like Ingrid – the
icy disdain, the scrupulous, cold politeness. He supposed he'd still
have to prop her up on stage, but that was all to the good. She
wouldn't dare make even the slightest reproach when her very
stage life depended on his good will.

In a spirit of general good humour he dropped some flowers into
the hospital for Stefan who had been operated on the day before.
He didn't feel he could face going up to the ward to see him – too
dreary – but he did feel he'd behaved very generously about the
flowers. And then he had invited Suzi to lunch at the Franz Joseph,
where everyone could see. He was spending a lot of money but he
calculated that it was a worthwhile investment. A nice leisurely
expensive lunch – plenty to drink – then straight up to his room for
the afternoon (he realized he'd played that wrong before, warning
her in advance that she was going to be deflowered in the evening)
before his complete and absolute triumph on stage in the evening.

He hummed a few phrases from *Luxembourg* to himself as he waited on the terrace for Suzi. Because it was unusually warm they had begun serving lunches outside and he had booked a table right on the corner, looking out across the valley to the mountains, everything high, blue, and beautiful, the way he felt himself.

Suzi arrived looking breathless, eager and, thank God, she wasn't wearing jeans or trousers but a pretty dress with a short skirt that showed her legs to even better advantage. There were quite a few tourists already booked into the hotel for the start of the Season and, as he led Suzi to their table, he was conscious of the admiring glances – at her for being so extraordinarily pretty, at him for acquiring such a delicious young plum. The champagne was already cooling in the ice bucket.

'To us,' he said, raising his glass and gazing at her, a mixture of humour and admiration, in a way that he was well aware reduced her to a state of melting acquiescence. 'No more misunderstandings, eh?'

'Oh, no, Karl.'

'We've wasted so much time, little one, when we could have been friends. I've missed you. It really has been unutterably dreary without you.'

'Has it?'

He chuckled, warmly, deep in the throat. 'You know it has, pumpkin. I don't have to tell you that.'

'I thought . . . well . . . you and Ingrid . . .'

'Ah yes,' he sighed and shook his head a little. 'Poor Ingrid. A brave girl, Ingrid, but very frightened, very insecure. I've done what I can. I help her in the production as much as I can.'

'Yes . . . but everyone said, well, not everyone, and not to me, they wouldn't say it to me, but I overheard Luiza saying that you and Ingrid . . . And you took her to supper some evenings . . .'

He sighed again. 'When did people not say things like that about me? Every little kindness I do, every time I try to help someone, it's turned around to Gesner being a swine again.' He thought he might have gone a bit too far, sound too sorry for himself, so he laughed, winked, and continued, 'Poor little me!'

'But you and Ingrid . . .'

'Pumpkin! Do stop carping on about Ingrid!' He watched her flush, then dipped his finger in his champagne and ran it down her nose. 'I felt sorry for the girl. She can't sing, she can't act, she's only been able to dance since you took her in hand' – (that wasn't strictly true, Ingrid wasn't too bad at the dancing) – 'and she's terrified in case her voice doesn't last for the performance. I've done my best to prop her up. I've spent hours, bought her supper, talked to her, trying to boost her confidence. But I really can't spend the rest of my life trying to turn Ingrid into a performer. Sometimes I want a little time to myself, to take someone special out to lunch. I don't think that's unreasonable, do you?'

'Oh no, Karl.'

'But it would be lovely, Suzi baby, if for this one special lunch, with the prettiest and most charming girl in the company, we didn't have to talk about Ingrid.'

She dimpled back at him, picked up her fork, and dug joyfully into her quenelles. He foresaw no further problems.

Georg had coped with his misery the only way he knew – by total immersion in frenzied and grinding work. It was the best time of the year for working fourteen hours a day. The herds were giving maximum yield. The upper pastures had to be fertilized. Cheese production was in full flight, with the extra girls taken on needing supervision. A new extension was being built on to the side of the dairy and, in addition, this was the time when his father spent nearly all his time at the theatre, messing about a bit on the farm during the day, but constantly dashing off for emergency consultations with Franz Busacher or – Georg's gut twisted bitterly – spending good cheese money and time in delivering bloody great bunches of flowers to Therese Aschmann. About the only thing he did still do on a regular basis was the deliveries – and that was only because they took him round and about the town and he could talk to all and sundry about the performances at the theatre. And, on this particular afternoon, when Georg was so frantically busy, and the Franz Joseph rang up for an urgent delivery of butter, cream and cheeses, Willi was off somewhere, visiting the production manager in hospital or something. It was typical, Georg thought savagely, as he loaded the van. Never here when he's wanted, leaving everything to me.

He'd got used to feeling sour. It was with him all the time now, a sort of dull, dour acceptance of things as they were, a consciousness that from now on he was on his own and that was the best way to be. He obviously wasn't the type to mix with other people and he didn't intend to spend the rest of his life belly-aching about it. That's what he was. That's what he was going to be. The richest and most hardworking man in Hochhauser.

He drove down into the town, then up the other side to the Franz Joseph. They had a big account there and one of the reasons it was so big was because they always delivered promptly. He drove in through the gates, up the drive and round to the service entry. As he turned off he glanced up towards the terrace and, with a sense of bewildering pain, saw them together, laughing, their heads bent across the table, their hands clasped. It all seemed to happen in a frozen tableau. He didn't brake or slow down, he hardly realized what he had seen until he was round the back, but the picture was projected clearly into his mind, the laughing intimacy, Gesner raising Suzi's hand to his lips.

In numbed shock he unloaded the van, took the slips into the store room and waited while the chef checked the delivery and signed the invoices. He'd known, of course, that she was going out with Gesner, but knowing it was different from seeing it. He went outside, back to the van and for a moment leant against the rear doors, his fists clenched, his face screwed into pain. Then he suddenly walked away, back towards the front entrance, not knowing what he was going to do but unable to go away and leave them.

They had gone. Their table was empty, used glasses, dirty coffee cups, an upended wine bottle in a cooler. He paused, then walked towards the swing doors and pushed through. No-one spoke to him as he strode into the centre of the reception foyer. He was just in time to see the lift doors closing on them. Gesner was towering over Suzi, his arm possessively on her shoulder. She was gazing up, leaning against his body. Georg closed his eyes and felt sick. He ran towards the lift, pressed the button, but nothing happened. The light showed that it was stopping at every floor and suddenly he raced back to the desk clerk.

'Gesner's room . . . what number is it, what floor? Karl Gesner!'

'Shall I see if he is in, sir?'

'I just want to know the number of his room!'

The face of the desk clerk froze into bland politeness. 'I'm sorry, sir. We don't give the numbers of guests' rooms. I can telephone and see if he is in. What name shall I say?'

Georg stared at him, unseeing. He remembered the little girl she had been, chubby-faced, golden-haired, trying to keep up with him, racing after him. 'Dord . . . Dord . . .' That was what she'd called him when she was little and she couldn't manage to say his name properly.

'What name shall I say, sir?'

He realized it was hopeless. What could he do or say now that would make her change her mind? It wasn't Gesner. She'd told him, before Gesner, that he had no place in her life. If it wasn't

Gesner it would be someone else. He turned and walked back through the foyer, telling himself it made no difference. She wasn't his girl any more. But as he drove back to the farm a brooding hatred for Gesner began to fester in his gut.

He didn't work that afternoon. He sat alone in his office, staring out at the mountains, no longer in control. His stoic acceptance of life's misery had been absorbed into a mindless rage. At some point he heard his father come back and call to see if he was in, but he didn't answer. He just sat there, and finally he got the ticket out of his desk, the ticket for this evening's performance, and placed it in his pocket. He was still wearing his farm clothes, but he didn't care. When it got to seven o'clock he went out and climbed back into the van, then drove down to the theatre car park and waited behind a coach and several cars that were unloading people in wheelchairs and on crutches.

He didn't know the way in through the stage door but numb, sick, he followed the people in wheelchairs through a door into a small hall, and then he went through a door on the other side and found himself in the theatre. He studied the stage. It was easy really – under the far end of the balcony was a door that said *Eintritt Verboten* and so he just pushed his way through, up a few steps, into a mess of ropes and pulleys and cluttered space, through again to the back where several staircases led off a central area. There were a lot of people milling about and no-one took any notice of him. He stood, waited. Once, someone – the thin Englishwoman who'd come to his father's party – stared curiously at him so he managed to give her a polite smile and then he turned and began to read the notices on a board, read them without seeing them. He heard, in the distance, the noise of the orchestra tuning up, and a lot more people in costumes clattered down the staircase. And at last came Gesner, strolling carelessly down, adjusting a dark blue velvet cloak over one shoulder.

Georg waited until he had reached the bottom step, then sprang forward. He didn't shout or say a word, but everyone else suddenly screamed. He hit him hard. Gesner was a big man, but Georg was just as big and much younger and spent his days working hard on a farm. He managed to hit him twice – two really good ones – before a surge of people behind pulled him off. The first blow was full in the left eye and Gesner cried out and staggered back. The second was right bang on the nose, and as Georg felt his arms pinned to his side he saw with satisfaction a spume of blood surge from Gesner's nose and splash all down the front of his costume. Gesner, one hand to his eye, the other to his nose, shouted again and several people rushed towards him. Georg, standing passive and acquiescent, felt the hands on his arms and shoulders relax and he shrugged them off, shook his head a little, then went back the way he had come, getting his ticket out of his pocket. He would have to hurry if he was to find his seat before the play began.

Gesner, blood spilling from his nose, was screaming with rage. The terrified stage manager rushed down to the orchestra door to tell old Anton, who was conducting tonight, to stretch out the overture. When she came back Gesner was lying flat on the floor holding a towel to his nose. Madge Grimsilk hurried forward with a large pack of ice cubes and pushed them – none too gently – on to his face. The Direktor suddenly appeared from the other side of the stage.

'Oh my God! What's happened?'

'It looks as though Gesner finally got what he deserved,' said Madge Grimsilk dryly. 'I guess it's Rudi for the *Count of Luxembourg* tonight.'

'Doh,' said Gesner from the floor. 'I'll doh on.'

'You can't go on like that, man. You probably won't even be able to sing with a nose like that.'

'I'll ding. The beeding's stobbed.' He sat up, very gingerly, and took the towel away from his face. The left eye was red but the nose was redder. Madge wiped his face with the towel and blood smeared messily all over his chin.

'Elisa,' she said. 'Run up to Wardrobe and tell them to bring me down some strips of silk, anything dark, blue, black, anything like that. Karl, use the sink in the office, no time to go back upstairs again. Douse your face with cold water. I'll come in and disguise the blood marks down your tunic. It's a damn nuisance you're on first.'

'I still think you shouldn't go on,' Busacher said. Madge waved him away.

'No time to argue now. You know it takes time to argue with Gesner. If he wants to go on, let him. If he can't sing and packs up halfway through, he'll have to get himself out of the mess. He'll cope somehow.'

Gesner got shakily to his feet and, with Rudi supporting him under the shoulder, made his way over towards the office.

'Where's the schnapps?' Madge Grimsilk asked Busacher.

'In the cupboard.'

'Give him a large shot just before he goes on. Ah, here are the bits from the wardrobe.'

She followed Gesner and Rudi into the office, waited while he washed his face, then sat him down and proceeded to make a swathed drape down the front of his tunic. Busacher handed Gesner a glass of schnapps. 'You're sure you're OK to go on, Karl?'

'Nothing would stop me from going on,' said Gesner through clenched teeth. 'Not tonight. You'll see, all of you. I've had enough of being pushed around. You fixed that up, didn't you! Wanted to get me out of the performance, out of the way. Well, you didn't – I'm fine and I'm going on. And you'll regret this. You'll all regret every bloody thing you've done to me in this theatre!'

'The man's insane,' said Busacher. 'I don't believe what I'm hearing!'

'Shut up, both of you. There's no time for all that. Anton can't keep the overture going any longer. Karl, do you feel ready to go on at once?'

'Yes,' he gritted.

'Fine.' She called to the stage manager, who dashed down to the orchestra door again.

'Front of house lights?' said Madge.

'Mitzi's doing them. Says she thinks she can manage.'

'OK. Off we go then.'

The house lights dimmed, the overture came to an end, the curtain went up. Georg sat back in his seat, calm, relaxed. He felt strangely at peace, with a sense of fatalistic acceptance about the future. He looked forward, in a detached, abstract sort of way, to seeing what would happen on the stage.

Backstage there was an atmosphere of nervous agitation in the air. The company, inadequate and badly understaffed, had already been feeling insecure with the loss of the tired but reassuring presence of Stefan who, under the loose heading of company manager, did more than any one man was capable of – superintending the young and inexperienced stage manager, the front of house manager, the prompt, the stage hands, the wardrobe, and who was capable of acting in almost any capacity other than that of actually going on the stage and singing (although he had once, in an emergency, gone on as a waiter in *The Gypsy Princess*). The fight, if one could call it that, just before the curtain was due to go up, made everyone feel shaky and tense.

Busacher, who had deliberately asked old Anton to conduct because he felt he would be more use backstage in Stefan's absence, went from performer to stage manager, from lighting man to stagehand, trying to exude serenity and confidence, endeavouring to reassure them all that nothing could go wrong. When he had seen the chorus on, and then Gesner – singing in a strained and somewhat nasal tone, but still singing – he hurried up the stairs as quickly as he could to Therese's dressing room. At the top of the steps he clutched the rail for a moment and leaned forward. If he was honest with himself, the other reason he had asked Anton to conduct this evening was because he hadn't felt too well and thought he might find it hard to get through the performance. Now, he reflected wryly, it looked as though the orchestra pit was going to be more restful than backstage. He knocked on Therese's door and went straight in when she answered.

'You've missed the dramatic events that have just occurred downstairs,' he said dryly. 'Willi's belligerent young son somehow got through the pass door, punched Karl in the face and knocked him down. His nose has bled all over his costume.'

Therese stared at him blankly for a second and then a smile of utter delight spread slowly across her face, to be replaced almost at once by an expression of responsible concern.

'Franz, I am sorry! Well, no, I'm not sorry. If it isn't too bloodthirsty of me, I'm delighted. But I am sorry it's happened just before the show. You're under enough pressure with Stefan being ill without that happening. So I'm singing with Rudi tonight?'

'No. We've cleaned Gesner up, given him a schnapps, and sent him on. He insisted. Was furious – very angry with almost everyone – but insisted on going on.'

'Oh dear!'

'He's not in best voice. Thought I'd better prepare you. You may have to carry him in the duets.'

'Thank you for the warning,' she said, resigned.

'He really is very angry indeed – vowing melodramatic vengeance on one and all,' said Busacher apologetically.

'It's going to be a heavy evening,' she said glumly. 'But don't worry, Franz. We'll get through somehow.' She fixed the tiara firmly in place, scooped her peacock train up and over her shoulder, and led the way from the room. He followed her at a slower pace down the steps, feeling suddenly ill again, with an unpleasant nausea in his stomach and an ache down his left arm.

In the screen scene Gesner's nose started to bleed again and he had to turn upstage – he did it quite well, as though he was overcome with emotion – and hold a rag hard against his nostrils.

192

Through the bleeding he managed to speak the song and occasionally hit a note. By the end of the act he'd picked up again and the curtain came down to a more or less normal finale. Therese, in the wings, spoke to him.

'Are you all right, Karl?'

'Just wait. I won't forget what you've done, you and the rest!'

'I had nothing to do with this . . . débâcle,' she said angrily. 'If you do not realize why that young man hit you on the nose, you're a bigger fool than I thought. This is one thing I refuse to be responsible for!'

'Therese . . . Therese!' The Direktor, hurrying up, had caught the exchange and was just concerned with getting his two singers through to the end of the evening. He thought with longing of his bed and a brandy. 'Can we manage to leave all recriminations until later? We've a difficult evening to get through. Karl – go and lie down in your dressing room for ten minutes.'

But Gesner had stormed off, and not in the direction of his room but towards and out of the stage door. Therese and the Direktor looked after him, puzzled.

'Perhaps he wants some fresh air,' she said slowly.

The stage manager came up at a run. 'Herr Direktor. Luiza's leg has suddenly gone again. She asks if she can get on stage before the curtain goes up and stay there. She doesn't think she'll be able to walk into the ballroom at the same pace as everyone else.'

'Tcha! And what is she going to do for the rest of the act? Sit on the stage like a duenna while the love duet is going on?'

'I don't know, Herr Direktor.'

Busacher flapped his hand, irritated. 'I'll come. We'll have to sort something out for the beginning of the act at least. And I'd better have a word with Anton about adjusting some of Gesner's music. The orchestra will have to help him out.'

He walked off. Therese went back to change, and general chaos took over as the stagehands began to move the set. Ten minutes later, Gesner came back through the stage door. He had a rather nasty smile on his face, the only time he'd smiled the whole disastrous evening, but nobody who mattered was there to see it.

Act Two began well. They'd solved the problem of Luiza, or at least Madge had solved it with an extension to the silver curtain and a bit of backing which revealed or concealed Luiza more or less as required. Therese, in the emerald dress, came on looking and sounding wonderful. It was one of her favourite moments of the operetta, mostly because she was on without Gesner and could relax. The chorus were a bit ragged – nerves and worry always made them disintegrate – and Busacher, who had decided to stay in the orchestra pit for the opening of the act, signalled to Anton to speed it up a little. A short piece of bad singing was always better than a long piece of bad singing.

Gesner came on, voice much better, although his left eye was beginning to close. Hopefully it didn't show too much from the auditorium. To the Direktor's growing alarm he began to play the scene differently from the way it had been rehearsed. Up until now, apart from the waltz, he and Therese had enacted their love scene with a space between them. Now, suddenly, he moved up close to her, very close, and when she tried to move away he captured her hands in his, acceptable to the audience, but alarming to Therese who felt, for the first time, a fear of the actual physical strength of the man. She tried not to look at his face, but then, while she was still singing, he raised one hand to her chin and forced her head round. She refused to let the sight of the venom in his eyes distract her from singing but she felt an increasing sense of panic – panic that came from not knowing what he was going to do next, fear that she wouldn't be able to control him. Her chin, gripped hard in his hand, was turned upwards. He bent his face down as though to kiss her and, through the reprise of the orchestra, she heard him whisper,

'Look into the wings – past me and into the wings . . .'

It was like a replay, a horrifying reenactment of a scene she had forced herself to forget, a scene that had kept her awake at night for years, made her break out into a sweat in the middle of restaurants or shops when it came into her head without warning. There was a split, mindless, horrifying second when she thought she had gone mad and was imagining what she could see. A surge of pure undiluted panic burned from her stomach into her throat and her voice trailed away. She recognized him at once, even though she hadn't seen him for five years. He was bloated, fatter, more obscene than he had been when she last visited him, but still she recognized him. It was Friedrich, slumped grotesquely in a wheelchair, the grisly representation of the nightmare her life had been for so long, a figure of sheer and appalling horror that totally tore away the mental curtain which had screened her terror for the past few years.

In the deep recesses of the pitiful creature's mind, some obscure spark awoke in a brain which rarely had consciousness. Some vague glimmer of a past no longer remembered, alerted perhaps by the sound of familiar melodies or the surroundings and smell of a theatre, made the huge hulk in the chair reach an arm out towards her. She could do nothing. She was held, paralysed by fear, by the realization that she had descended into a black world where the same dream was going to occur again and again. Some fusing between them made that creature, who had once been her husband, gather impossible strength to repeat a scene that had never been completed. The outstretched hand fell on to the arm of the wheelchair and, with a mighty groan he tried to drag himself up and forward. He managed one violent surge towards her before collapsing on the floor, one arm stretched forward, just protruding on to the stage.

She couldn't scream, not as she had that first time when she had seen the blood running down the arm and chest of the man who had stepped forward to save her. She had screamed then, but this time she had no scream in her, only a terrified whimper that no-one except Gesner heard.

When her voice had first faltered away, Busacher realized at once that something was wrong. He hissed at her from the orchestra pit, even though he knew from the way she was standing and staring that she was oblivious to anything happening around her. Something dreadful was taking place in the wings and he raced for the orchestra door and up the stairs. At first he couldn't see what had caused the hiatus. It was all very confusing, and he could only think, with considerable irritation, that Stefan – no, of course, Stefan wasn't there – had allowed one of those charity people to bring a patient backstage. There was a wheelchair, a male nurse in a short white coat, the sound of Anton slowing the music in the hope that Therese would pick it up again, and the slight murmur of the audience realizing something was wrong.

He stared out of the wings at Therese and saw from her face that she had retreated into some private world of terror, and at the same moment he heard the nurse cry out and saw that the figure in the wheelchair was now thrusting forward to crash on to the stage and lie there, only partially concealed by the curtain. He still didn't know what had happened but an overwhelming panic came up from deep in his stomach, and with it rose a pain, a violent, blacking, grinding pain that spread like an opening flower across his chest.

'Get him off the stage,' he tried to say, but nothing came out and he twisted forward, leaning over the back of the wheelchair, bent almost double with pain, unable to speak, to move, to control the agony that moved in great tides across his chest. He was dimly conscious of a flurry of movement behind him and then he felt an arm round his waist.

'For God's sake! The man's having a heart attack – can't you see? Get him down on to the floor, quickly.'

'But my patient . . .' faltered the nurse, totally confused at everything that had happened so unexpectedly.

'Bugger your patient!' spat Madge Grimsilk. 'You're supposed to be a nurse. Do whatever you're supposed to do when someone has a heart attack.'

The man blinked once, then put his arms under Busacher's shoulders and lowered him to the floor.

'Rudi! Go and telephone for an ambulance at once – it's very, very urgent.' She knelt beside Busacher and, suddenly controlled and quiet, said, 'You'll be all right. Try not to be frightened. An ambulance is coming.' In a strange, awkward gesture she placed her hand over his and patted it gently. Through the pain he tried to speak.

'The stage . . .'

'Don't worry. We'll keep it going somehow. Don't think about it. I'll sort it out.' She turned her face up to the nurse and hissed, 'Isn't there anything you can do?' Busacher's head and shoulders were supported on the lap of the crouching man.

'Keep him at this angle – upper torso propped up. It would be better with cushions.'

She stared round, a trifle wildly. 'Ingrid, you go and find . . . no, you can't, you're on next. You,' she pointed to one of the stagehands, 'go and find what you can: rolled-up coats, costumes, chair seats, whatever you can.' Under her hand she felt Busacher stirring again.

'The stage . . .' he gasped.

She looked back over her shoulder, saw the gross, prone figure lying half on stage stir feebly, and suddenly got to her feet, seized his ankles and began to heave. Incredibly she managed to move the figure back a couple of feet, just enough to get him out of the audience's vision. Busacher, through the sea of pain that washed over him in great waves, now receding a little, then surging up again so strongly it nearly obliterated everything else, found himself operating on two curious levels. One was just pain, but at the back of that was a tiny thread of consciousness that said how very curious it was that Madge Grimsilk should be strong enough to pull a man off the stage like that.

Rudi came hurrying back, followed by the stagehand who carried several opera cloaks bundled up. Madge and the male nurse packed them carefully under the Direktor's head and shoulders. He felt the pain recede again, just a little.

'The ambulance will be here in just a few moments,' Rudi whispered. 'What do you think we ought to do? Bring down the curtain?'

She had time for one brief glance towards the stage. Dimly, in the background, she had been aware that Gesner was singing on his own. Now she saw that Therese was standing quite still, her eyes mesmerized by the figure Madge had just dragged from the stage. She seemed to have totally retreated from the world about her. Gesner was singing her lines as well as his, but even though old Anton had slowed everything down the duet was about to end.

'No. It's all right. You and Ingrid are on next. I think we can trust Gesner to get her off the stage. Go on and do your best. Once she's off I'll cope with her.'

The stage manager, who was far too young to be a stage manager, suddenly appeared in a state of total disintegration. 'What shall I do?' she hissed. 'What shall I do? Shall I bring the curtain down?'

'Where the hell have you been all this time?' snapped Madge, suddenly furious with the whole bloody company for being so understaffed, so generally incompetent. I'll never work with a tinpot, ramshackle outfit like this ever again, she vowed to herself.

'Luiza,' faltered the young stage manager, nearly in tears. 'I had to move the curtain so that she wouldn't show . . .'

Madge felt a surge of hysterical laughter begin to rise in her and fought it back. In some ways that was all the whole farcical evening needed – the designer going into hysterics over two prostrate bodies in the wings. She took a deep calming breath, then looked down at the Direktor. He was a ghastly colour, but he seemed to be breathing more regularly and his eyes were open, looking at her.

'The ambulance will soon be here,' she said quietly, reassuringly. 'And I promise you I'll make sure the show finishes. Even if I have to sing Adele myself it will finish.' His lips twitched as he tried to smile, a feeble acknowledgement of a weak joke that wasn't a joke at all.

'What shall I do?' bleated the stage manager. Madge recognized the mounting hysteria in her voice.

'Go down to the orchestra pit and tell Anton to give Rudi and Ingrid an extra reprise when they go on, then tell him we'll be sending Suzi on early to do her dance. Tell him just to try and keep up with what's happening on the stage. Then go and find the Burgermeister in the audience and tell him to come backstage.' The terrified little creature scurried off. The wings seemed to be packed with frightened faces. She picked out Alfred and Freddi, and young Suzi Hoflin in the background.

'Alfred, Freddi, once Rudi and Ingrid have finished, lead everyone on for the ball scene, but don't do the waltz. Suzi will do her dance first. OK, Suzi?'

'Yes.'

'In fact, do it twice. That will give me time to sort out Therese – I don't know what's happened to her. Will someone . . .' she glared round and picked out the hapless stagehand again, 'will someone go round to the other side of the wings and bring Therese here? I'm terrified what might be going on over there with Gesner.'

'What about . . . him?' Freddi nodded towards the prostrate figure of the man who had been in the wheelchair. 'I don't think she ought to see him.'

'Who the hell is he?'

'I think it's her husband . . . her ex-husband,' Freddi said slowly. A slight *frisson* of delighted terror went round the little group in the wings.

'He's my patient. I'm supposed to be looking after him. I'm not supposed to leave him.'

'You should have thought of that before you brought him round here,' Madge snapped. 'What the hell did you think you were doing?'

'He said he was an old friend,' the man stammered. 'We were specially invited. He said it was all arranged – a nice outing.'

'Get rid of him.'

The nurse, Alfred, and two young members of the chorus in full stage regalia, managed to get the huge torso raised and back into the chair. It was grotesque – he had been conscious all the time, moving slightly, but incapable of controlling himself in any way. Settled again in his chair he was humming in time to the orchestra, waving a bloated hand in the air. On his face was no sign of intelligence or a realization that anything had happened to him.

'Put him in the office. We'll sort it out later.'

'The ambulance is here!' someone cried.

'Thank God!' She bent over Busacher again, once more putting her hand over his. 'I can't come with you in the ambulance,' she whispered. 'Not if you want things running here. But I'll come later, after the show, just to let you know it's all right.' He tried to smile again, and then he was lifted carefully on to the stretcher and taken away. She followed him to the stage door and allowed herself a moment to watch him being carried into the ambulance. He was such a big old man, so craggy and ancient, it was as though a vast tree had been felled. She bit her lip and hurried back to the stage. Therese had been brought round and Willi Zimmermann was giving her a glass of schnapps. Therese was shaking, a curious kind of shaking, cheeks, mouth, neck, as well as body.

'What have you done with him?' she choked. Thank God, at least she was out of that catatonic trance.

'In the office with the nurse. Who was he?'

'Friedrich.'

It was extraordinary what had happened to her. She still wore the same dress, the tiara, the make-up, but now she looked ten years older. Her face was sagging and even through the make-up you could see that all the colour had gone.

'You'll have to go back and finish, Therese. You know that.'

'Yes.'

'Has Willi told you . . . about the Direktor?'

'Yes.'

'Once you've finished this act you'll be all right. You don't have too much in Act Three. Everyone will help you get through somehow. But you must finish this act – the scene with you and Gesner – you must finish that.'

'I didn't have to do that before,' Therese said dully. 'They brought the curtain down, so I didn't have to finish the act. They had to bring it down. Luxembourg was bleeding – Friedrich had got him in the neck and chest – meant for me, of course – but I didn't have to finish the act. Not that time.'

Willi Zimmermann moved closer to her, filled her glass again, and then very gently put his hand on her shoulder. She spun away from him. 'Leave me alone,' she hissed.

'Therese, it doesn't matter if you just walk through it, say the lines instead of singing them, but you must finish.'

'I'll finish,' she said tautly, then laughed. 'I'm a professional, aren't I? One must always be professional, mustn't one? Whatever happens one must be professional.'

'The Direktor's very ill,' said Madge sharply. 'I promised him we'd finish the show. It was the last thing I said before they put him in the ambulance.'

'I'm so sorry,' said Therese bleakly. 'So sorry. He was so kind to me. It didn't work. I shouldn't have come. But he was so very, very kind. And now . . .'

Madge, her antennae half on the music and half on the sound

199

coming back from the stage, said, 'Suzi's finished her dance. Can you go on now?'

'Oh yes.'

Her cue came, muddled out of the score by some frenzied juggling on old Anton's part. She tensed her shoulders, grimaced, and then walked on to the stage. Madge offered up a silent prayer and waited. It was a shrill, near hysterical performance but she did it, followed all her cues, sang her songs, walked through her stage directions. When the curtain finally came down the applause was polite but no more. The whole act had been a mess, out of order, and the confusion backstage had communicated itself to the audience. Madge turned to Willi.

'What do you think? Should I go and talk to her again?'

'No.'

'That's what I think. What about Gesner?'

'No. We'll sort him out later. At the moment things are just holding together. Leave everyone alone. No more dramas, no recriminations, just let things be still and continue as best they can.'

'Will you sort out that poor creature in the office? Find out from the nurse exactly what happened – how they got in here. And then get rid of them.'

'Don't worry. I'll see to all that.'

'And I promised the Direktor I'd go to the hospital as soon as the curtain comes down. Please God he's all right! Will you look after Therese? Or shall I ask Luiza and the old crowd who know her?'

'I'll look after her.'

'I think I'd like a glass of schnapps.' Willi reached behind a float and picked up the bottle. He refilled Therese's glass and handed it to Madge. She drank and coughed. 'I don't really like schnapps,' she said calmly. 'Right now I'd give my entire fee for a bottle of Scotch whisky.'

Willi just smiled at her, rather sadly. His ebullience had gone, but he still sent out a reassuring aura. She felt he was the only one who could help her get through the rest of the evening.

Once the final curtain had come down, the entire company disintegrated into solitary units and small groups. Madge took one look at the chorus, huddled into unhappy bundles, whispering amongst themselves, and then she watched a group of solid protection – all the old ones – form itself around Therese, and they moved up the stairs in a dense group. Gesner disappeared, so did

200

Rudi and Ingrid, so did Suzi Hoflin. They all slunk out of the theatre in an almost guilty way, as though each of them were responsible for the disasters of the evening – which indeed perhaps they were, Madge reflected tiredly.

She went into the office, dreading that the catalyst who had begun it all would still be there, humming to himself in his wheelchair, but Willi had done his work well and the nurse and his patient had gone. Madge sat down and began to dial a London number, then she telephoned locally for a taxi to take her to the hospital. She felt wrung out, and only her rigid self-discipline kept her sitting bolt upright, determined not to descend into exhaustion before the evening's work was done.

At the hospital she had an argument with the nurse in reception, which she could have done without. The officious woman tried to fob her off with medical platitudes and it took half an hour of reasoning and a stubborn refusal to leave the desk before a tired young doctor came down to see her.

'I know he must be kept quiet,' she assured him. 'But he won't be quiet until I've seen him and assured him that everything at the theatre has gone well.'

'I can tell him that.'

'He won't believe you.'

'We've just given him morphine so that he'll rest.'

'He won't rest until he's seen me.'

Finally, after another ten minutes, they let her in to see him. She was expecting him to be all wired up, the way you see people in films who have had heart attacks, but he wasn't, not that you could really see. There was a screen to one side of the bed, but she deliberately didn't look at that. His eyes were open, following her as she came in. She bent over him and smiled.

'All well,' she said. 'Therese finished. Not one of her best performances but competent.' She knew there was no point in lying to him. She'd be no better than the doctors and he wouldn't believe her. 'Gesner's voice seemed to get stronger as the evening went on, although you couldn't hear his words too well. And it's Sunday tomorrow. No performance, so everyone will have time to calm down and rest, and get well before Monday. Willi is looking after everything.'

He smiled and closed his eyes. She paused for a second and then said, on impulse, 'I've sent for your son. He's flying out tomorrow. He'll be here in the afternoon.'

The deep-set, tired old eyes flew open again, regarding her with disbelief, and she smiled reassuringly and put her hand over his.

'That's right,' she whispered gently, 'Peter will be here tomorrow. And now you must sleep.'

He closed his eyes again, and two tears wandered slowly down his face. She wiped them gently with her fingers, then walked softly from the room, the young doctor following her.

'How bad is he?'

'Are you his next of kin?'

She hesitated. 'I'm the best he's got until his son arrives tomorrow.'

'It's a bit too soon to tell. We'll have to do some tests, but I don't think it's a bad one, not this time. He didn't lose consciousness, did he?'

'No.'

'I think he'll get through this one all right.'

'Thank you.'

She staggered downstairs. It was late now, raining hard, and there were no taxis about anywhere. She debated whether to go back and try to find a telephone to ring for one, but she was too tired. She pulled her jacket collar up and began to trudge through the pouring rain towards her bed.

She was trying very hard not to scream at them, her old friends, Freddi, Alfred, Luiza. That's what she wanted to do, scream at them to leave her alone, let her be, let her sink like an animal into a dark hole, where no-one could see her shame and fear. They were being so cheerful, so supportive. They meant well, wanted to be kind and she had to keep telling herself that they were nearly as pathetic as she was and she had no right to spurn their kindness. She was conscious, even in her obsessive misery, that Luiza's hip was bad and that it had taken her an enormous effort to get up the stairs with the others to Therese's dressing room. So she had to pretend to be grateful, to thank them, assure them she was fine, refuse their invitation to supper but at the same time promise them that she would eat something and not go into a decline in her bedroom. And finally, after half an hour, they went, reluctantly, still showing concern and worry, but they went and she was able to send the dresser away, sag down at her dressing table and shudder.

She wanted to do many things at once: give way to hysterics, weep, curl up in a tight ball and die, but most of all she wanted to go where no-one could find her, and she suddenly tore the tiara and wig from her head and began to get out of her costume, shivering so hard her teeth chattered, but driven by the need to run and hide. She pulled on slacks and a shirt, grabbed her jacket and ran down the stairs and out of the theatre. It was raining but she didn't notice. Thank God it was dark now, dark and silent except for the spattering rain. She began to walk, then panic overtook her, a mindless panic, for she knew Friedrich couldn't possibly be after her. She had seen him sprawled helplessly on the stage, but the terrible fear spawned out of years of violence and humiliation surged in her stomach – all those times she had *had* to run from him, the times when even a locked door had not prevented him from getting at her – and she began to run, away from the theatre, away from Hochhauser, up towards the mountain, a less-frequented route than the roads around the town.

Then the fear subsided, and shame took its place, shame, and disgust with herself for letting her life become the travesty it had, for not being stronger, braver, for letting that awful scene on the stage tonight actually happen. In her mind she replayed it the way it should have gone – she should have looked at Friedrich – she shuddered even now at the thought of his name – and then have spat in Gesner's face, and sung even more brilliantly. She gave a choking cry that was somewhere between a sob and a laugh at the thought that she could have done any such thing. Her confidence – she had been so proud of the way she had rebuilt her confidence, coping with Gesner, getting her figure back, her voice back, her stagecraft, acting, everything. She had really thought she could cope with anything, but her confidence had been as useless, as precarious, as much of a sham as everything else in her life. She tried to pull down the curtain again, the curtain she had used all these years to block out the nightmare, but now it didn't work. The nightmare just had an extra dimension to it: an obese sprawling figure trying to reach her from a wheelchair, the disintegration of a performance, another public humiliation on a stage. She began to run again, this time not from Friedrich but from herself, from the disgusting, pathetic creature she had become. She didn't even want to think about it, never wanted to think about it again, never wanted to see anyone who knew who she was, but just get away, run and exhaust herself so that she was so tired she would die, not be able to think any more, remember. Run, just run, sobbing, trying not to scream, but sobbing, hoping by her flight to leave everything behind, most especially herself.

A car came up behind her on the road, slowed, then passed, slowed again, and she stopped running and tried to walk purposefully as though she were a sane being who knew exactly where she was going. A track appeared on the right and quickly she turned towards it, and saw with relief the car speed up again and vanish up the road. She was tired now, but not tired enough, and she strode on, as fast as she could, up the rough track which finally petered out into a mountain trail. She was drenched. It was heavy mountain rain that had soaked right through her thin jacket and trousers. Water was running from her sodden hair and down inside her collar and suddenly the fear, the panic, the frenzied self-loathing gave way to a violent despair, a descent into sheer, apathetic misery compounded by coldness and physical discomfort. She sank down on to a rock, bent her head over into her hands and began a terrible and desolated weeping, rocking backwards and forwards, to and fro, a crazed, demented creature of a woman. The path turned into a stream running across her feet but she didn't notice, didn't care.

'Therese.'

Earlier she would have screamed at the voice to go away, but she was beyond that now. She didn't even bother to look up. She was aware that the voice belonged to Willi Zimmermann but she was beyond caring about that too.

'Therese.'

'Go away,' she said dully.

'No. I can't go away and leave you like this. You will be ill if you don't go home and get dry. This is no good, sitting here like this. You must go and sit in your room if you want to be alone.'

The rain had stopped but it still ran down the mountainside in streams and rivulets. A thin, watery moon shafted through a tiny break in the cloud and she raised her head and looked at Willi. His spectacles were wet and he wore a plastic raincoat that was too small for him. He was standing in front of her, right in the middle of the stream.

'Your feet will get wet,' she said dully, and he gave a little half grin that she sensed rather than saw.

'Shall we go back?' he asked gently.

'I suppose so. There's nothing else to do, is there? I can't sit on the side of a mountain for the rest of my life.'

He put an arm under her elbow and raised her to her feet. 'If you can just walk a little further up the track, we can branch off down to the road. It's quicker than going back and my car is there.'

'Was it you who overtook me? On the road back there?'

'That's right. I was looking for you.'

She made no comment but just squelched on up the track. They breasted the rise and came down the other side, slithering down through mud and stones until they hit the road. Willi's car was parked on the other side, under some fir trees. When they got into the car he reached into the back and handed her a rug. 'Wrap that round yourself and try and get warm.'

Her teeth were chattering but as he went to put the key in the ignition she placed her hand on his and stopped him.

'Put the light on,' she said.

'Why?'

'Just put it on.' He paused, then flicked the switch over the mirror.

'I want you to look at me,' she said bitterly. 'The great Aschmann, that's what you called me the first day I came here, a star, a diva, the most wonderful thing you ever saw on a stage. Were you sitting out front tonight?'

'Yes.'

'So then you saw me as I was, as I am,' she said savagely. 'A performer who should never have tried to return to the stage, a singer who could not sing, an actress who disintegrated yet again, ruining not only herself but the rest of the company too. Ha! The most wonderful thing you ever saw on a stage – that's what you saw tonight.'

She looked terrible, hair flattened into dripping wisps, her stage make-up blotched and running down her face, her eyes crumpled with scorn and misery.

'I saw Gesner pull one of the cruellest tricks of his career,' he said, subdued. 'I saw my dearest friend driven into a heart attack by that trick, and I saw a company, including its leading lady, struggling on somehow to finish the performance in spite of everything.' He turned the light out. He couldn't bear to look at her. They were both silent, oppressed by the events, the rain, and above all by her self-disgust.

'How did he get there?' she asked suddenly. 'How on earth did he get there? He was in a clinic – he's been there for years. How on earth did he get there?'

'Gesner managed to make friends with the woman who runs the charity bookings. He apparently told her he had a very special old friend who didn't get out very often, and asked that if he arranged for the transport and a special nurse, could this friend come in under their group? Then he went over to the clinic and convinced them – somehow – that he was an old friend who'd sung with . . . your husband . . . years ago. Said he'd like to give him a little outing, take him to the theatre, as they'd worked for years together in operetta. Thought he might enjoy it. He got the charity woman to telephone them and vouch for him and all that. How the nurse managed to get him into the wings without anyone noticing I can't say – Gesner arranged it, of course – and with Stefan away and everyone in chaos, events really played into his hands. Well, you know what it's like backstage at the moment. The stage manager is useless and wasn't there anyway. It all seems unbelievable and obviously quite a lot of people from the clinic and the charity group are going to be in very serious trouble. But you know how Gesner can charm when he wants to. And he's a convincing liar too. He had thought it all out very carefully.'

'To hate me so much,' she whispered. 'To hate me so much he would plan all that.'

There was nothing Willi could say. It was horrifying to think of the venom that had driven the man.

'I lived with hatred for so long. I think you all wondered why I couldn't take Gesner's spite, not the way your other leading ladies have taken it. But you see I have lived with it, for years I lived with it, and not just the spite, the constant threats, the violence, the unpredictable violence, the insults, the contempt, the nasty little surprises just to stop you from ever thinking that a day might be normal. It made me . . . afraid, I suppose . . . afraid of men who were aggressive and unpredictable. In time I forgot how to brace myself against that kind of attack. It happens, you see, like someone continually punching you on a sore place. You don't recover, you can't fight back any more. That's why I wasn't able to fight Gesner. And when I did manage to fight him,' she choked suddenly, 'I did it the wrong way. I made him so insanely angry, he did this.'

'He did this because he was jealous of your voice.' He felt her turn her head in the darkness.

'That was why Friedrich did it, too,' she said dully. 'Everyone thought he was jealous because he believed I had a lover. That was the gossip that went around afterwards . . . But it wasn't the truth. He wasn't jealous of another man. There was no other man. He was jealous of me, of my success. He had no need to be. He could have been a successful singer too – he was, at first, when we began together in the same company.'

'How old were you when you married him? *Why* did you marry him?'

'I was nineteen. He was thirty-three, a soloist taking small leads, as I was. It was one of Busacher's productions. I'd been working with Busacher before, several times, but this was the first production with Friedrich. It was all . . . wonderful. So exciting, the beginning of my career, and I was doing so well. Friedrich was very handsome and very . . . well, erratic and moody, I suppose. At the time I thought his behaviour interesting.' She gave a sob of laughter. 'How incredibly foolish one is when young. I remember telling a friend he was just like Mr Rochester, you know, in the film of *Jane Eyre.*'

Willi didn't answer.

'I've watched poor little Suzi Hoflin being dazzled by Gesner, and it has reminded me of myself. I wanted to say something to her, try and prevent the hurt I knew would be inevitable, but I also knew it would be no good. Someone . . . a friend of my mother's, an Englishman, tried to warn me about Friedrich. He obviously recognized the moodiness as instability. He was someone who had known me nearly all my life and he tried to stop me but I couldn't even understand what he was talking about. That's why I knew it would be no use speaking to Suzi. Gesner has it too – that ability to get whatever one wants. Friedrich charmed me just the way Gesner has charmed Suzi – a fatal mixture of glamour, sexuality, humour, and brooding sadness. I had never met a man like Friedrich before. All the men I had ever known had been kind and comfortable, not brooding and mysterious. I was foolish, spoilt, naïve, and incredibly stubborn. Even then I would probably have grown out of him – Suzi will grow out of Gesner – but Friedrich pursued me with such relentless determination I just . . . went down before him. I still don't understand why he was so obsessed with the idea of marrying me.'

'Don't you?' said Willi. 'I do. Anyone would have wanted to marry you then.'

'No, Willi! Don't talk like that. Please don't talk like that. Not now, not after tonight!'

Willi began to answer her, then stopped and they both sat silently for several seconds.

'We had two – nearer three, I suppose – good years, and then he began to change. Uncle Hugh, the Englishman I spoke of, had died and my poor little Mutti was so sad, so helpless, I couldn't talk to her about it. She had looked after me for so many years – now I had to look after her. I couldn't possibly add to her worries. There was no-one I could talk to. I dared not speak to anyone in the theatre in case it threatened his work. It was beginning to deteriorate, you see. He was so hurt, so angry. He thought we would go up together. It is always difficult for couples in the theatre – one always moves faster than the other, but things change all the time. It's like a see-saw, sometimes it is good for one, and then the other begins to do well. I kept telling him this. I kept reassuring him that I was just having my run of luck and very soon he would have his. I asked the Direktor to give him another chance when he wanted me for *Hoffman*, and he did. But that was disastrous too, because my role was much bigger than his and then Busacher had to ask him to leave because of the drinking. He'd always drunk a little too much, but it began to get worse; then he didn't work at all.'

A car came slowly down the other side of the road, the headlights blurring through the rain. Inside their car it was muggy and wet and the windows had steamed up, but still Willi didn't attempt to start the engine. They seemed to be held in a time-warp and neither of them could move.

'I began to be afraid of him then. Sometimes he was violent. Once he locked me in the apartment when I should have been in the theatre and my understudy had to go on.'

'Why did you stay with him?'

She sighed. 'Why? Why does anyone stay with anybody? Guilt is one reason. I had known only happy relationships between men and women in my youth. If this marriage wasn't working, it must be my fault. I kept feeling that if only I could do the right thing, somehow it would be all right again. I just didn't know what that thing was. And then, much of the time, when he was sober, he kept asking me to forgive him. He had become such a pitiful creature – I felt so sorry for him. He would beg me to help him get back into the theatre. Whenever I said I was going to leave him, he would cry – say that I was the only good thing in his life, that without me he'd give up, kill himself. Then it would be all right for a few weeks, and then he'd start again.' She shuddered.

'Then I was asked to sing at the *Staatsoper* and there was talk of a contract with Covent Garden, but before any of that happened he . . . he came on the stage, that night . . . you know what happened.'

'Don't talk about it,' Willi said quickly. 'No need to talk about it. But why didn't you leave him then?'

'How could I?' she cried. 'He was my husband. He had no money, no job. We were both in disgrace, the scandal of Vienna. It was on all the front pages of the newspapers. He was put in prison for a short term and they let him out with the provision that he went straight into a clinic to be cured. I had to give an undertaking that I would be responsible for him.' She gave a brief contemptuous laugh. 'Even when he was in prison and then in the clinic, when I was safe from him, I still couldn't get back to singing. I was so spineless, so pathetically, futilely spineless, I couldn't get my

208

nerve back. They all tried to help me, Busacher, Kramer, all of them, but I didn't have the guts to try again. The only thing I was grateful for was that my mother had already left Vienna, before the fiasco. She married a Hungarian and went away. She knew of the scandal of course, she offered to come back, but I pretended it was all right, nothing to worry about. I never told her the truth, then, or later. I just said Friedrich was ill.'

'What did you do? How did you live?'

'Taught piano. At that stage I couldn't even teach singing. Worked as a telephonist. Waited for Friedrich to come out of the clinic. Even then,' she said bitterly, 'even then, I was so stupid, so naïve and maudlin, that I hoped, once he came out, we might be able to start again. Go somewhere else perhaps, where the scandal wasn't known. France, or one of the smaller German companies where we might be able to work together again.'

'But that didn't happen?'

'No.'

'How long before . . . you gave up?'

'I don't remember. A lifetime,' she shuddered again. 'Sometimes I look back and wonder how I let myself descend into that . . . that pit. It's so difficult to explain to someone who hasn't experienced it. It starts gradually, you see, and all the time you think it will be better, that if you try really hard you'll be able to do something. And after a while, after your friends have drifted away because you cannot be honest with them, because you're always trying to hide from them exactly what is happening, then you find yourself isolated, totally isolated with this malignant incubus whose sole intent is to destroy. And what is so very, very strange,' she said, almost to herself, as though she had forgotten Willi was there, 'what is so strange is that, even then, even in that terrible nightmare there are moments, brief passages of time, when you look at him and suddenly see the face of the man you once loved, the man who loved you. And you have a sense of guilt because you cannot believe you are not responsible for this horrible decay.'

'When did you send him away, for good?'

'Nine years ago. I used to go and see him at first but it was . . . upsetting for both of us. Then he deteriorated and became . . . as you saw him tonight.'

The atmosphere inside the car was oppressive. Even Willi could find nothing to say that was positive or reassuring or offered a gleam of hope. He turned on the windscreen wipers and a watery picture of the road ahead came into view.

'Gesner . . . he isn't like Friedrich, not really. He's much stronger than Friedrich ever was. But what is the same is the hatred. It's frightening to encounter that kind of hatred, not once, but twice in your life. And when you meet it for the second time, when you are older, I'm not sure if you can ever recover from it.'

Willi desperately wanted to say something kind, to put right everything that had been done to her this evening, but his heart was burdened with the misery of her life and he had no comfort to give. He felt all the cruelty and sadness and worries of the world pressing down on him and he could say nothing.

She spoke just once more.

'And the worst thing about all this, about my life and what happened tonight,' she said quietly, 'is that you become self-obsessed. You grow increasingly to think about your own fear, about your past and your future. You become neurotic, selfish, concerned only with yourself and your own misery. Do you realize I've been sitting here, talking about myself, and Franz Busacher is in hospital, and not once have I suggested we try and find out how he is?'

'We don't know yet,' said Willi. 'I telephoned the hospital before I left the theatre. They're doing everything they can. He can't have any visitors. They'll let us know as soon as there is any news.'

They sat in silence for several moments and then Willi started the engine and began the slow, sad, wet drive back down into the town.

CHAPTER THIRTEEN

Gesner woke very late the next morning, feeling ghastly. His nose was swollen and very red and he found difficulty in breathing through it. His left eye was closed and surrounded by bruising and he had a headache, only partially the result of his battered face. He'd drunk quite a lot of brandy when he'd returned to the hotel the night before. He had wanted to blot out some aspects of the evening's events and also to deaden the ache in his nose. But perhaps the brandy hadn't been a good idea.

He rang down for some coffee and aspirin, then staggered into the bathroom, looked at his face in the mirror, and winced. Gingerly he touched his nose. It was lucky it wasn't broken, he thought, and tried to feel angry, but in truth felt only nervous. Of course right was on his side and he was sure that, if he bothered to look into it, he could bring a case of assault against Georg Zimmermann. But that wouldn't stop the young thug from attacking him again if he felt like it and also, in the circumstances, it might not be a wise move to take the son of Burgermeister Willi Zimmermann to court. He had to tread very carefully at the moment and not antagonize anyone who might matter.

His coffee and aspirin came and he lay down for a while after he'd taken them. He was beginning to feel sick, but after half an hour, after having dozed, he got up again, had a shower, and then took all the ice from his room fridge. He filled the basin with water and ice cubes, and sat with his face in it. Then he dressed with great care. He wasn't sure what he was going to do today but he wanted to be ready for anything that might happen. And that was what was so worrying. What was going to happen?

It wasn't that his plan had misfired. It hadn't. On the whole, in spite of the vicious attack before the curtain went up, he'd been able to carry things through pretty well. He'd known there would be hell to pay afterwards – had accepted he'd be hauled before Busacher like a naughty schoolboy, warned by the committee, frozen out by the rest of the company – not that that worried him. They didn't dare be too antagonistic towards him, they relied on him for their jobs. But in spite of all that he knew, and they would know, that he'd won. However angry Busacher and Willi Zimmermann and the rest of the committee were, they still couldn't manage without him.

The company had to have a star to survive and he'd taken great care to ensure that *he* was the ongoing star, not Aschmann. Anyone who had seen her last night, watched her total disintegration, knew she was finished. He'd always sensed that her confidence was paper-thin, had detected that her voice, her performance, came from a very recently acquired veneer that had been pasted on by Busacher. And that confidence had gone, was totally destroyed and he doubted it would ever come back, and certainly it wouldn't come back here, in Hochhauser, not when she had to go on singing against him, never knowing what he was going to do next. No. All that had been very successful, more than successful. It had been an extra bonus, one he hadn't thought of, when the creature fell out of the chair on to the stage. He felt quite satisfied with the way it had gone with regard to Aschmann. It was just that other things, more serious things, had superimposed themselves over that little affair.

He got up, suddenly restless, and moved over to the window. It was after midday, and through the trees at the front of the hotel he could see the main road in the centre of Hochhauser. It seemed to be deserted, as though everyone in the town, not just the theatre people, was keeping out of the way, just waiting very quietly to see what was going to happen next. His stomach was churning. Why hadn't anyone telephoned him and told him what was happening? Why hadn't anyone told him how Busacher was? And if Busacher wasn't all right, then who was going to run things for the rest of the Season?

He paced up and down, beginning to feel sick again, but this time the sickness came from fear. It wasn't his fault that the old man had had a heart attack – it was ridiculous even to think that way. But what would they do if he wasn't there? It had very nearly been a disaster last night after the old man had been taken ill. With no Busacher, no Stefan, a stage manager who was useful only when she was told what to do, and a leading lady who – most fortunately – was no longer any use, they needed someone to take charge, make decisions. Who was going to sing in Aschmann's place? Who was going to look after things, get them out of the messes they were constantly in? There was the Burgermeister of course, but he wasn't any use backstage. What would happen tomorrow night? Why hadn't anyone told him what had been arranged?

His nose began to throb again. He went to the telephone and lifted the receiver, then replaced it. Whom could he phone? If he telephoned Willi Zimmermann there was always the chance he might get Georg. He bit his lip. It was that woman who had taken control last night, the English designer. She'd seemed to be running things. He could telephone her at the Goldener Adler. Maybe she'd have some news.

There was only one telephone at the Gasthaus and it rang for a long time before anyone answered it. When he heard who it was he swore softly to himself, then tried to force some charm – he had never felt further from being charming – down through the wires.

'Ingrid? My dear! What a night it was. How are we all this morning?'

'What do you want?' She sounded rather cool, most unlike Ingrid.

'Well, I really just wanted some news of what was happening. Is Madge there?'

'No.'

'Ah . . . I wonder where she is?'

'Gone to the hospital, and then off to the station to meet the Direktor's son. He's arriving on the afternoon train.'

'His son?'

'That's right.' Ingrid was monosyllabic and growing more and more acid.

'Has anyone heard . . . I mean, how is our dear Direktor?'

'Still alive.'

'I see.'

'I think what you did last night was filthy. I'm glad Georg Zimmermann hit you in the face. I hope he does it again. We really hate you here – every single one of us. We hate you!' The receiver was slammed down.

He'd pay the little trollop back, just see if he didn't. Who did she think she was? Just wait until the next *Gypsy Baron* – he'd show her she couldn't talk to him like that. But all the same, as he put

213

the phone back on to the cradle, he was conscious that his stomach was beginning to churn again.

Madge, waiting for the train to come, felt a curious sense of disembodiment. It was three months since she had seen him and their parting, which had been her decision, had been unhappy and destructive. She still wasn't over it and, in any other circumstances, the thought of seeing him again would have strung her out like a piano wire. But so much had happened here in Hochhauser, she was so emotionally exhausted, that she felt as though it were someone else waiting to meet him. If she had any emotion left in her at the moment it was all concerned with that old man lying doped to the eyebrows back in the hospital, and that surprised her. She had kept her distance from him very carefully, for obvious reasons. She had come prepared not to like him, determined to keep the entire relationship a professional one. And somewhere along the way a small core of affection had grown, unsuspected until she had seen him lying on the floor last night, fighting his pain.

It was really the first moment she had had to herself all day, and as she stood by the track she closed her eyes for a second and breathed deeply. The air was marvellous here. She really loved it, specially at this time of the year. It was clean but warm and the gentle mountain wind carried all kinds of elusive scents. She had an amazingly acute sense of smell. Peter had always laughed at it: she could tell before he came into the room whether he had eaten garlic, and a favourite trick of his – in the early days at least – had been to bring her a bouquet, make her close her eyes, and tell him what flowers he held in his hand. She had never failed. Even the non-scented varieties had a scent for her. That was one of the first things she had noticed about Therese – the delicate soft smell on an otherwise unattractive woman. It had been that which had made her look more closely at Therese. Study her, and realize what she could be. And now that . . . that animal had done this to her! A brief spurt of rage vanished almost at once in her tiredness. She could only sort out one thing at a time.

The train wound around the mountain pass in the distance and she thought, how curious, in a few moments I'll see him again. I really didn't ever expect to, but I think it will be all right. We can be civilized. We can be friends.

The train stopped, and he was the only passenger who got off. From the other end of the platform he looked like his father, large, rawboned. When she had first met him eight years ago he hadn't been attractive at all, but now, in his late forties, he was growing into a kind of grand dignity, the same kind that Busacher had. He walked slowly up the length of the track and they stood silently facing each other.

'Madge.'

She smiled and put out her hand. She thought for a moment he was going to kiss her, but he didn't, just took her hand and quickly released it.

'I've hired a car and booked you a room at the Franz Joseph. It's the grandest hotel in the town and you'll be assured of your privacy there. I thought we'd go there first, then on to the hospital.'

'How is he?'

'Holding up. He hasn't had a second attack and apparently that's a good sign. They've done some tests and have more to do, but they seem to think he'll pull out of this one.'

They walked to the car. He put his case on the back seat and climbed into the passenger seat.

'I don't know why I came,' he said. 'I really don't know.'

'Because, whatever you think of him, he's your father and he might have died. He might still die.'

He didn't answer. Just stared out of the window at the pretty golden buildings against the backdrop of the mountains.

'I hate Austria,' he said grimly.

'I know. It's time you grew out of it. Some Austrians are quite nice. The theatre people are nice – theatre people usually are – most of them. And it's ridiculous, a man of your reputation in the theatre never having done anything in Vienna.'

'I get offered enough work around the world to choose where I want to go.'

'Oh, Peter! Don't be so grand!' She thought she'd gone too far; after all they weren't on those kind of terms any more, but suddenly he laughed and started to say, 'Oh, Madge . . .' and then stopped. She was glad he had. There was absolutely no point in resurrecting any of the past. Nothing had changed.

'You'd better tell me what happened,' he said. 'It all sounded very melodramatic on the telephone last night, what little you did say. Like something out of a very bad Hollywood movie.'

'You don't know the half,' she said wryly. 'You won't believe the set-up here. If I'd known what I was in for I would never have taken the job.'

'I told you not to. I told you not to come here.'

'By the time you told me it was too late. I'd signed the contract.'

They were getting on to dangerous ground and, as though they were both conscious that their present civility was fragile and wouldn't take too much strain, they fell silent.

'You'd better tell me what happened,' he said at last.

She sighed. 'I'll tell you everything, from the beginning. But it will take time. Have you heard of Karl Gesner, the tenor!'

He wrinkled his face up. 'Mmm. The name is vaguely familiar. Wait a moment . . . good voice . . . unreliable. That's all that comes up in my mind.'

'Well,' she said. 'He's the star of this tinpot company, and now I'll tell you exactly what happened.'

It wasn't until she began to go through the whole story, step by step, from the beginning, that she realized just how appalling it all was, and how involved she had become with a company that, in the ordinary way, she would have walked right away from. She couldn't understand her own behaviour. Why had she stayed on once she'd got *Luxembourg* staged? Why had she made such a point of championing Therese? Why, she thought, with a curious sense of pity, had she got so fond of them all?

'My God!' said Peter when she'd finished. 'I can't believe it! It's just surprising the old man hasn't had a heart attack before. And this company manager, this Stefan, where is he now?'

'Still in hospital. The same hospital as your father. There's only one in Hochhauser. I alternate between the two, visiting them and reassuring them that the show will go on without them.'

'Will it?'

She shrugged. 'I don't see how. There's the old *répétiteur*, Anton; he can just about keep the orchestra going. They're good, by the way, they almost keep themselves going. But he couldn't possibly cope with the company. The stage manager's about twenty – does the best she can, but nobody ever takes any notice of her really. The stagehands are experienced. They do more than stagehands ever should do – probably be trouble with the union if it ever got found out, but, no, there really isn't anyone who could keep it going, not until Stefan's fit and well again, and who knows how long that will be?'

'What about this Zimmermann man?'

'He will certainly keep the business side running, budgets, salaries, services of the theatre and so on. But not the backstage stuff.'

Peter made a disapproving tck-tck. Madge paused and said, diffidently,

'I know it sounds extremely odd, as though I'm off my head or something, but the curious thing is that, in the ordinary way, it

216

really does seem to work. In fact, they're rather good. There's a sense of . . . enthusiasm . . . excitement . . . I don't know what. When I first came and saw the ramshackle cast I had to dress, I thought it was going to be appalling. But it wasn't. It was . . . well . . .' she laughed sheepishly, 'rather marvellous.'

He turned his head and stared at her. 'Are you mad?'

'I suppose I am. One gets mad working with this company. But in some ways I've never enjoyed a job more.'

She pulled into the forecourt of the Franz Joseph and he got out.

'I'll wait for you here. Take as long as you like. Oh, and I'd better warn you. Gesner stays here too.'

'That's all right. I won't even know him.'

'But he'll know you. You've forgotten how famous you are. For an impresario who is a fanatic about privacy you have a very high public profile.'

He shrugged distastefully and pulled his case from the back. 'I won't be long.'

She sat quietly in the car. It had been all right, meeting again. In some ways they had slipped straight back into their old easy intimacy, an intimacy based on shared interests, mutual respect, and a reverence for each other's reserve. They neither of them found it easy to share things with other people, Peter because of his background, she because, she supposed, she was a typically buttoned-up Englishwoman. That's what he'd always said. It was amazing that they had both managed to break through their inhibitions and come to love one another.

He came running down the steps and, silently, they drove to the hospital. She managed to park the car and they went upstairs.

'You'll come in with me, won't you?' he said suddenly.

'No. For one thing they won't let me. Only one visitor and that has to be family. And apart from that, you must go in and see him alone.'

'I can't, Madge! I just can't. Please help me, please come in with me.'

She sighed. 'All right. You'll have to make it right with the nurse. I've had too many fights with the staff already.'

The old man wasn't asleep, but his face looked calmer, more relaxed. His eyes were fixed on the door and never moved from Peter's face once he had stepped into the room. Peter looked grim, but Madge knew him well enough to know he was discomfited. He didn't know what to do or say, or how to look.

'Papa?'

Again, as they had last night, two tears welled from the old man's eyes. His nose began to run. Madge fumbled for a tissue and handed it to him. Slowly he raised his hand to his face.

'How are you, Papa?'

Busacher tried to smile. 'It was good of you to come, Peter.'

He nodded gravely at his father. 'I'll stay for a few days, just until they're sure you're out of danger. They think you're going to be all right, providing you rest.'

There was a long pause. Busacher's eyes were still fixed on Peter's face. Then he said, rather timidly, 'That would be nice, if you could stay. You have no commitments at the moment?'

'No. I have a recording session next month, then I need to plan the new production in New York. It doesn't open until November, but I'm not sure about the designer and I want to make quite a few alterations to the existing book.'

'Opera?' said Busacher hungrily.

'*Manon Lescaut.*'

'Domingo?'

'No. Not this time. There's a new tenor who I think is going to be rather good. American.'

'How did you find him?'

Madge, standing quietly by the door, watched the two of them, saw Peter relax and the old man's face light up. It was so sad. They still had this in common and when they started to talk about it everything else was forgotten. She let them go on for about five minutes, then she moved forward and put her hand gently on Peter's arm.

'I think we should go now,' she said. 'They said just a short visit, then plenty of rest.' The spark between them, the old man and his son, died away.

'Of course.'

'Peter . . .'

'Yes, Papa?'

Busacher's face moved slightly on the pillow. 'My company . . . my season . . . who is going to run it?' Peter was suddenly very still. Madge stepped forward again.

'It will be all right, Herr Direktor,' she whispered. 'We'll manage somehow. We'll get them on tomorrow and it will be all right.'

'No.' He stirred restlessly. 'There's Gesner, and Therese, and the revival of *Der Zarewitsch* next Saturday. And my poor Stefan will not be well for some time. What will happen to them all, my company?'

'We'll manage,' said Madge grimly. 'Willi will help us. He's suggested that we try and get someone down from Vienna to run things for a while.'

'It won't do. Whoever it is, they won't understand.'

'I'll stay on,' said Madge recklessly. 'I'll do my best.' But both she and Busacher knew she couldn't control them. She could do a great deal. If the company had been a normal one she could probably, with a bit of help, have kept things going. But not this company, not with Gesner, and Therese in shock, and the young dancer's boyfriend liable to start backstage fights at any time.

Busacher's tired old eyes were fixed on Peter's face again.

'No, Papa,' he said.

'If you're going to stay on for a few days . . .'

'I don't know anything about them, Papa.'

'Madge will help you. And my friend Willi Zimmermann. Just for a few days, just to get things running again. You could do it – Gesner would do what you say.'

'And what will happen when I have to leave? I'm recording in London next month.'

'I'll be better then. I'll be able to sort something out. I'll be able to decide what we should do. But for now . . . there's the bookings . . . and *Der Zarewitsch*. And many problems. Madge will have told you, many problems. It is just . . . I do not want the theatre to close because I am in hospital. That would be disgraceful. It would make the company seem so . . . so unprofessional . . . so pathetic.'

She felt Peter's body tense as a steel girder beside her. She touched his hand again.

'We must go,' she whispered. 'He's getting upset and very tired. We must go. Tell him you'll think about it.'

'I'll think about it, Papa,' he said, in a voice totally devoid of expression.

'Thank you.' The face relaxed slightly and his eyes closed. Madge pulled at Peter's arm. He seemed to be set there, just standing looking down at the bed. She tugged again and he moved with her to the door. In silence they went down the stairs and out to the car.

'You'll have to do it,' she said grimly.

'Don't be ridiculous.'

'You must. You heard what he said. He knows quite well the whole thing will probably close down – the way it's run at the moment, anyway. But he just doesn't want it closing because he's let them down. If the Hochhauser Season is to be wound up, he wants it done legitimately, in a planned and orderly way.'

219

'And what of my reputation? What sort of fool will I look, taking over a half-baked, second-rate provincial operetta company?'

'I would have thought your reputation was big enough to stand it,' she said dryly. 'It wouldn't appear too insane, to help your father out in an emergency.'

'No-one knows he's my father.'

'Perhaps it's time they did.'

'I hate people knowing anything about my private affairs,' he said angrily.

'You're telling me this? I, who was another of your private affairs no-one was supposed to know about? All right, so we solved the problem of me! But you can't get rid of a father quite so easily.'

'Shut up.'

'No. You're neurotic and a misanthrope, but you were never selfish before. You used to be quite kind to people who weren't as famous and successful and godlike as you were!'

'Shut up!'

'You know the way you're going to end up? Like him, in a hospital bed, lonely, pathetic. Only he at least has some friends and a company – a half-baked, second-rate provincial company who love him in a feeble theatrical sort of way. You won't even have that. You'll be so damned private no-one will even know you're there!'

They were standing beside the car, shouting, glaring at one another, all the careful façade ripped away, a replay of the last time they had met and separated.

'Oh, go to hell!' she said, and threw herself into the driver's seat. Shaking with rage he climbed in beside her. She slammed the car forward and flung it out on to the road, just missing a van coming towards the hospital gates.

'You're driving on the wrong side of the road,' he said tersely and, furious with herself, she wrenched the wheel over and got into the right lane.

When they reached the Franz Joseph she slammed on the brakes so hard they both jolted forward. He made no attempt to get out of the car, just sat there staring stony-faced, straight ahead.

'All right,' he said. 'I'll do it. If that's what you want, I'll do it. But I'll do it my way.'

'That's OK by me.' She was suddenly limp with relief and couldn't think why it mattered so much to her. She hadn't known the company very long. Why did she care about them so much?

'I'll just try and organize them into surviving for a few more weeks. And I'll look into things, figures, bookings, budgets, to see if it's feasible for them to continue at all.'

'You're very good at all that,' she said ironically and he glared at her.

'Well, I suppose you'd better come up with me and we'll go through everything in detail. I want to know just what kind of a mess I'm taking on. And get that Burgermeister along. And I'll want an entire company call at the theatre tomorrow morning at nine. And tell the understudies to spend the evening preparing for understudy rehearsals.'

'I presume you would like me to operate as your assistant?' she asked sweetly and had the gratification of seeing him flush.

'It's because of you I'm in this mess in the first place,' he snarled, and suddenly she felt happy. Somehow, in eight years, she had managed to make a tiny dent in that impregnable personality.

Suzi got the news about the company call that Sunday evening. It was Uncle Willi who telephoned her. He sounded tired.

'Are you all right, Suzi?' he asked. She wasn't sure if she was imagining it but she thought he seemed slightly distant.

'Yes thank you, Uncle Willi. How is Herr Busacher?'

'Better than we thought. But he has to have complete rest at the moment.'

'Oh . . . good.'

'Everyone at the theatre at nine tomorrow morning. The Direktor's son is going to take over during this emergency and he wants to see everyone then.'

'Oh . . . oh yes . . . I'll be there.' She wanted to ask how Georg was but found she couldn't. She was too embarrassed.

'Goodbye, Suzi.'

'Goodbye, Uncle Willi.'

She wandered back into the kitchen and picked up the coffee pot, not yet cleared away after supper, to see if there was any left. Her mother followed her.

'Did you want some more coffee, Suzi?'

'Oh . . . er . . . not really.'

Frau Hoflin gazed thoughtfully at her daughter. Something had happened, that was obvious, but possibly something quite good and positive. Suzi had been very quiet all day, but not in a sulky way. She'd stayed in and helped with the lunch, washed some tights, gone out for a long walk on her own up the mountain, and come back and helped with the supper. She had seemed almost pathetically eager to become part of the household again, which was a refreshing change from her recent behaviour.

'What did Uncle Willi want?'

221

'What? Oh, just a company call tomorrow. And Herr Busacher is much better.'

'I see.'

'I think I'll go out for another little walk. It's still very light. A shame to waste this lovely evening indoors.'

Frau Hoflin wondered if perhaps she was hoping to meet Georg, but no. After Uncle Willi's disastrous party Georg and Suzi had hardly spoken to one another.

'I shan't be long.' She flung a sweater round her shoulders and wandered out through the kitchen door. Frau Hoflin watched her meandering up the mountain track.

Suzi hadn't dared venture down into the town in case she saw anyone from the theatre. She was too embarrassed, too anxious to know what to say to anyone. She was dreading seeing them all tomorrow morning. They must all know why Georg had punched Karl on the nose. Before they'd left the theatre last night, Ingrid had given her a very funny look, and Suzi had begun to wonder if Karl had actually told her the truth about his relationship with Ingrid. She'd missed the actual fight, but she'd seen the Direktor having his heart attack, and she'd overheard enough to know what Karl had done to Therese Aschmann's husband. She'd thought about it all day and now she felt slightly relieved, because she'd realized that the heart attack and the scene on stage really had had nothing to do with the fact that she'd gone to bed with Karl Gesner in the afternoon. But still, it was awful that everyone knew, and in such a crude and violent way too. She felt ashamed, but beneath the shame was another and more depressing sensation, one of total anti-climax and deflation.

Of course Karl was still a wonderfully dynamic man, very handsome and a marvellous singer, and so it was very flattering that he was in love with her but . . . well . . . really, was that all there was to it? All that fuss people made, the things people wrote in books about emotional explosions and complete oneness. And those films one saw where music rose into a crescendo and you saw faces rapt in trances of ecstasy – whereas really it had been hardly any different from those fumbles in Vienna. It had been wonderful until Karl actually took his clothes off, for with their removal he had seemed to shed his charm and adoration too and become just a strong and rather rude pushy male. And what had really disconcerted her was that afterwards, when they were lying side by side, she had turned her head on the pillow and had seen, close up, that at the side of his head the very slightest line of grey showed at the roots of his hair.

'What are you thinking, pumpkin?' he had asked.

'Nothing.' It was quite a distinct hard line of grey, not like her father's hair, where the grey was blended into the rest, but a line that suddenly stopped and became dark. *He dyed his hair.*

She was suddenly conscious of feeling messy and sticky, and she rose quickly, snatched up her clothes and went to the bathroom. When she came out he was still lying there, his arms behind his head, with nothing on. It really wasn't very romantic at all.

'Off so soon, pumpkin?' he asked sleepily.

'I've a lot to do before the show this evening.'

'Bye then, sweetheart.'

She'd shut the door and tiptoed away, feeling terribly embarrassed in case some of the wealthy guests at the Franz Joseph should see her where she had no right to be. That really hadn't occurred to her on the way up.

All this afternoon, mooching about the mountain on her own, she'd been wondering what to do. She didn't really think she wanted to go to bed with him again, but if he was in love with her . . . And also – she felt a slight *frisson* of fear – it was incomprehensible what he'd done last night, that poor man on the stage and Therese Aschmann in a state of shock. If he could do that, what might he do to her if she said she didn't want to go out with him any more? And perhaps he'd think it her fault that Georg had hit him, which, she reflected miserably, she supposed it was.

She hugged her arms around herself and wished she was a little girl again, safe and secure in her parents' protection, with Georg looking after her, defending her from the boys at school. But Georg wasn't the answer either, she thought with a sudden flash of maturity. Just because she wasn't sure she liked Karl any more didn't mean that overnight Georg had changed. Georg was still an old misery, mean with his money and his affections, concerned only with work and dairy products. She decided that if she came through this all right, the embarrassment in front of everyone, extricating herself from Karl Gesner, she would cease to think about men at all. It would be rather nice just to go on living her life without all these complications.

The next morning she was up very early indeed. They had only just begun the morning milking outside, and she sat at the breakfast table debating what to do. Should she slip into the theatre at the very last moment so that there was no time to talk to anyone before Herr Busacher's son took over, or should she arrive very early and face up to everyone as they came in, get it over with?

'That's what I'll do,' she murmured to herself.

'What, dear?'

Suzi rose. 'I'm going to get to the theatre early, Mama. I didn't see anyone yesterday, so there'll be a lot of news to catch up on. I'll go early.'

'Not this early, dear,' said Frau Hoflin dryly. 'It's only six o'clock.'

Like a prisoner getting ready for execution, she dressed with enormous care: clean jeans, clean shirt, hair tied back with a bandeau and her make-up meticulously applied. She was at the theatre at eight-thirty, but even then she wasn't the first. The stage manager was there, so were Rudi, Ingrid, Elisa, and most of the young ones. She got some coffee from the machine and joined them on the stage.

'Hi,' said Rudi. 'Well . . . are we in work or are we not?' Tense, worried faces surrounded her.

'What do you mean?' she faltered.

'No-one seems to know what's going to happen. Is Gesner sacked? Will Aschmann be able to sing? Who will take over from the Direktor and Stefan?'

'But I heard . . . Uncle Willi told me that the Direktor's son was here and was going to take over.' Suddenly every eye was riveted on her.

'We knew his son was coming,' said Ingrid slowly. 'But we haven't see Madge since she went to collect him from the station. We just got the message for the nine o'clock call.'

'I didn't know he had a son,' said Elisa.

'Well, that's what Uncle Willi said, that Herr Busacher's son was going to take over during this emergency.'

There was a sudden lightening of spirits all round her.

'Perhaps it will be all right then,' said Ingrid slowly. 'Perhaps it will all somehow be sorted out.' Suzi realized with relief that no-one was really very interested in her. She also realized, with a faint sense of shame, that they had much more to be worried about than she did. They had jobs to lose. Whatever happened to the company, she was still secure.

'What else did you hear?' asked Ingrid.

'The Direktor's not too bad. He's better than we all thought.'

'Oh good!' The atmosphere took another upward surge.

'I said it would be all right,' said Rudi cheerfully. 'They wouldn't have called an understudy rehearsal if we were all going to be sacked.'

'No. Of course not.'

The stagehands trailed in, the front-of-house people, the older members of the chorus, the soloists, Luiza, Freddi, Alfred, old Anton and the orchestra and, just before nine o'clock, Therese slipped quietly to the back of the stage and sat on a silver *Luxembourg* seat. Freddi went back and stood beside her, shielding her carefully as Karl Gesner, looking arrogantly disdainful, strode through them all and came to centre front of the stage.

Suzi darted a quick glance at him, then looked again more slowly and decided that under no circumstances did she even want to eat a meal with him, let alone get into bed with him. He had a swollen black eye and a huge red nose. And in spite of the arrogant disdain there was an air of general seediness about him. The entire company was silent, then one by one they edged away from him until he was standing alone in solitary splendour. It didn't seem to bother him at all.

And then, at last, exactly at nine, Madge Grimsilk and Willi Zimmermann appeared, accompanied by a middle-aged man who looked very much like Herr Busacher once you knew he was the Direktor's son. He strode down the central gangway of the auditorium and up the side steps of the stage. There was a shocked communal gasp from nearly everyone as he was recognized from all the newspaper articles, the television appearances and the theatre programmes of the last fifteen years.

'Good morning,' he said, in perfect Austrian German. 'My name is Peter Grun. Some of you may have heard of me. As you know, my father is in hospital following a heart attack. You will be pleased to learn that he is expected to recover.'

There was another communal rustle, partially relief, but mostly further shock as the name they all knew was confirmed.

'I have agreed to look into the affairs of the company while my father is indisposed. Herr Zimmermann has agreed to take over all the financial and business matters – your salaries will be organized and paid by him. Any queries to do with that side of affairs and you should go directly to Herr Zimmermann.' He nodded once, without smiling, in Willi's direction. The company was frozen into silence.

'Now, as to other matters. We shall try to keep the scheduled programmes running as long as we can. I am here purely as an interim measure and will be looking into the possibilities for the future. Quite honestly, with the state of affairs at the moment, I don't see how you can continue for the entire Season, not without some strong and expensive new management. It may be that the company, as it stands at present, will have to be disbanded and restructured in a different way. All this I shall be looking into. For the present, your job will be to try and keep the production running, either with or without principals. Who is the stage manager?'

'I am,' piped a thin, frightened voice.

'Well, step forward then!' He sounded irritated and the stage manager scurried to the front.

'Do you have all the understudies here?'

'Yes, Herr Direktor.'

'Anton will take an understudy rehearsal for tonight's performance.' He looked at a clipboard in his hand. '*Gypsy Baron*. And tomorrow there will be an understudy rehearsal for *Countess Maritza*. I shall keep you informed of what is happening. Which one of you is Herr Gesner?' Gesner looked appalled.

'I am,' he said angrily.

'Herr Gesner, I would like to speak to you in the office. Where *is* the office?'

'I'll take you there,' murmured Madge. She led him through the stunned and frightened company to the backstage area.

'They look a pretty hopeless lot,' he snapped. 'Some of them are so old they can hardly stand.'

'That's Luiza. But she has a marvellous voice. It hasn't deteriorated at all, in spite of her age.'

'Was Aschmann there?'

'At the back.'

'I'll cope with her later. We may or may not use her understudy.'

'Her understudy is Ingrid, who doesn't have a strong enough voice to carry all the productions. If Therese flunks out we're going to be in trouble.'

'You're in trouble already,' he said dourly. They entered the office and, with distaste, he removed two paper cups of cold coffee from the desk.

'Get rid of these, Madge!'

'Yes, Herr Oberführer.'

'That is not funny, Madge!'

'Nothing's funny at the moment,' she said, near to tears. 'But I think I might get a laugh if only I could sit in on the interview with Gesner.'

'Well you can't,' he retorted. 'And I'm really not concerned with these company feuds and dramas. I don't really care who upset whom and who won't go on tonight. As long as somebody goes on I don't care who it is. From the look of them there's not much to choose between any of them.'

'I just want you to say that to Karl Gesner,' she pleaded. 'Promise me you'll say that to Karl Gesner.'

'Oh, get out, Madge! You'd better go and talk to this Aschmann woman. See where we are with her.'

She left, and then, without knocking on the door, Karl Gesner strode in. He looked round for a chair but there wasn't one, so he leaned up against a filing cabinet.

'Now, Herr Gesner, I understand you are not happy with the company as it stands. All I need to know for the moment is if you are prepared to sing for as many productions as we can manage, or if you would like to be released from your contract now?'

'Of course I'll sing,' Gesner said. 'There was never any possibility that I wouldn't sing. Even with my injuries I went on and sang.'

'Fine,' said Peter disinterestedly. 'But of course there'll be no more tricks. I think we both understand that. Any tricks at all in my theatre and you're pulled off stage. Understand?'

Gesner was badly frightened but determined to bluff it out. He hadn't really properly assimilated that it was Peter Grun in front of him.

'I don't play tricks,' he said grandly. 'I never have. And once you have seen one of my performances you will realize that it would be disaster to pull me off stage, as you so elegantly put it. Your father will tell you, anyone in the company will tell you, that I am the one who fills the theatre. Without me there is no Hochhauser Season.'

'Well, there won't be for much longer,' Peter said curtly. 'Frankly, as far as I'm concerned, the theatre could and should close tonight, but that would upset my father. I'm only doing this for him. He wants it to close in a proper and professional way and I can understand that. But I think you'll appreciate that without him there can be no company. It is quite, quite incredible that he has held all this,' he waved a disparaging hand round the room, 'together for so long – and, I gather, at a minimal salary. With my father no longer running things it just won't work any more. If the Season is to reopen at all it will have to be with properly paid professionals, good soloists, and sufficient staff to see this kind of fiasco doesn't happen again.'

Gesner was terrified. He was used to flattery, anger, rebukes and downright antagonism, but not this bland indifference. It was like talking to a bureaucrat.

'I shall do my best for the company,' the cold voice continued. 'If we close before the end of the Season – although I gather from

Burgermeister Zimmermann that everyone wants to limp on if they can – but if we close before the end of the Season we will try to arrange some kind of gratuity. One of the things I have to do this week is meet with the finance committee and the union people to see just what we should have to pay out in redundancy. You'll get something.'

Gesner felt his stomach drain away to his feet. He tried to move, think – he had always been so quick at mental footwork, but now his brain was clogged with sheer fright. He was standing here in front of Peter Grun; a golden opportunity. How many singers got the chance of a private interview with Peter Grun? And surely Busacher must have told him how good Gesner was? Even when Busacher had hated him he had always thought he was good.

He tried to smile. 'I'm sure that will be of great comfort to the rest of the company. Gallant little troupe, they have tried so hard. But I shall not be altogether sorry to see the end of Hochhauser. I worked in London last winter – I expect you heard, possibly even saw me. I'd be quite prepared to do more work abroad, possibly in one of your own productions.'

'Absolutely not,' Peter Grun said dispassionately. 'You're a troublemaker, Gesner, and you're unreliable. You may or may not have a good voice. I've never heard you. But I make it a point never to have troublemakers in my productions, not even in the chorus.'

'I wasn't thinking of the chorus,' Gesner stammered, appalled.

'Don't think of it at all. You will never sing in one of my productions.'

The man really looked rather foolish, standing there with his black eye and his swollen nose and his mouth open.

'Will you be able to sing with that nose?' he asked, not unkindly.

'Yes.' Gesner was stunned.

'I don't know at the moment if you'll be singing with Aschmann or the understudy. No, wait a moment,' he consulted his clipboard. 'Tonight is *Gypsy Baron* and Aschmann doesn't sing the lead in that anyway. So no problem there. But I gather it will make no difference to you whom you sing with?'

'No.'

'Good. That's all. No tricks, now.'

As Gesner made no attempt to move, he came round the desk and pushed him towards the door. 'That's all. You'd better have a doctor look at that nose. He might be able to give you some drops or something.' He gave him a gentle shove outside and closed the door. The man was pathetic.

He picked up the telephone and began to dial a number in Vienna. He had to hire a temporary company manager and, if the budget would run to it, a more competent stage manager. That terrified girl was worse than no stage manager at all. They needed more backstage staff, a competent doorman who would keep out aggressive young men, a prompt, and someone to help out with the conducting. That poor old creature wasn't going to be able to run the orchestra every night for the rest of the Season.

There was a quiet tap on the door and he put the phone down before he had finished dialling. 'Come in,' he cried, irritated.

A tall woman with short hair and a plain face. Moved quite gracefully but was obviously nervous.

'Excuse me for disturbing you, Herr Grun. My name is Aschmann, Therese Aschmann.'

'Ah yes. I was planning to speak with you, Frau Aschmann.'

'Fräulein.'

'Of course. Please.' He rose from his seat and placed it round the other side of the desk. She sat. Yes, she did move gracefully.

'Of course, you know all that happened at last Saturday's performance?'

'Yes.'

'Most of what occurred was due to my presence in the company. Your father was extremely kind to me, and gave me every support. Perhaps you didn't know but this was my first time back on a stage for many years.'

'Yes. I did know that.'

'So I feel doubly bad at what took place. None of it was deliberate – obviously I intended none of these things to happen. But because I was in the company, they did happen.'

He didn't say a word. Just waited to see where she was going.

'Of course, I understand the problems of the company and I realize that if I leave now, Ingrid will not be able to support all the productions by herself, and Elisa is certainly not ready to carry all the soubrette roles either.'

'So I understand.'

'So I feel I must remain with the company for the time being. But I would like to be released from my contract as soon as someone else can be found.'

'I see.'

'I know you have a great deal to do, and I also know it isn't easy to find singers in the middle of a season – not to come to Hochhauser, anyway. I will remain here as long as you need me, but it would be better, most especially for the company, if I leave as soon as possible. I think you will find things run much smoother if I am not here.'

'Fräulein Aschmann, in my companies things always run smoothly, otherwise I get rid of the trouble spots.'

'And in this company, Herr Direktor, I am the trouble spot.' She gave him a brief smile, and he suddenly saw the quality that Madge had tried to describe.

'Thank you for coming, Fräulein Aschmann. I shall bear in mind what you have said. But for the moment you are prepared to sing, even though it means working with Karl Gesner?'

She gave a barely perceptible shudder but bowed her head. 'That is correct, Herr Direktor.'

'I can assure you there will be no more trouble. I have not even decided whether he will sing every night. I may well put the understudy on with you in *Maritza*.'

She shivered again. 'With respect, Herr Direktor, that would not be wise.'

'Fräulein Aschmann, I think you do not understand. No-one understands. I do not care who sings what on the stage of this theatre as long as someone does. The days of Gesner, or anyone, running wild in the company are over. I'm very happy for him to leave now and I'm afraid that applies to anyone else. But I am grateful for your offer and I accept. I will release you from your contract as soon as we can find another singer, or we decide to close down.'

She inclined her head again and rose from the chair.

'Please,' she said diffidently. 'Please give my fondest wishes to your father when you see him. I would like to go and visit him but I understand he must have quiet and rest.'

'I shall give him your message.'

She hesitated. 'You know, he was a great Direktor. All those years ago, when I was in his productions, I did not realize it. But since coming to Hochhauser I have observed just how great a Direktor he was . . . is. No other man could have done what he has done here.'

A very brief stab of chagrin went through him and he was appalled at himself. Did he really resent the old man receiving a plaudit from a sad, middle-aged, failed soprano? And then he was honest enough to admit that the swift pang of resentment came from knowing that she was absolutely right. His father *was* a great Direktor, always had been, was in fact greater than himself, although he had become the world famous figure and his father had ended up here.

230

'Yes, I know that,' he said slowly. 'Whatever else he was, or wasn't, he was always a great Direktor.'

She stared at him, curious, and he suddenly moved across to the door and held it open for her.

'Thank you for coming,' he said courteously. He was vaguely interested in hearing her sing. Madge wasn't usually wrong about performers and she had given this one quite a hearty testimonial, although after the other night, of course, the voice and stagecraft were probably all gone. A singer was only as good as his confidence.

Then he picked up the telephone once more and started to sort out the other problems.

In spite of everything he was mildly surprised by the evening's performance. He had expected a shambles, a total disaster, but some pattern laid down by his father held the whole thing together. No-one was particularly inspired and he was held in an appalled fascination by Ingrid's performance. He had never seen anyone with so little talent achieve so much. Gesner, in spite of the nose injury, obviously did have a very good voice, but not good enough to warrant putting up with him in one of his own productions. The old woman who could hardly walk was magnificent. She should have been doing recording and concert work and nothing else. It was obscene to make her waddle over a stage like that, although of course, in this role, she didn't move much at all.

Aschmann was wooden. It was a ridiculous part for her and he couldn't imagine what his father had been thinking of to cast her in that role – although, like everything else in this company, there was probably a sequence of convoluted plottings behind the casting. But when he heard the voice, the clear, bright, pure tones, he understood what his father had tried to do. She was hopeless now, of course, totally passive and the voice had no charge of passion or emotive level at all, but the range was incredible. She didn't seem to have to push or breathe for any of the notes at all. He felt a moment's regret. If he could have had her years ago, he could have created a great diva. She'd be better on recordings and radio too. No stage presence at all.

Madge came up to him at the end of the evening. She'd been standing in for Stefan, looking after everything, most especially the stage manager, who had totally collapsed in terror now that she knew the great Sir Peter Grun was running the company.

'Well?' she said. 'They weren't as bad as you thought they were going to be, were they?'

231

He allowed himself the first smile of the day. 'No. Separately they were all – nearly all – quite dreadful, but together they put on a reasonable performance.'

'And they're all nervous at the moment: Gesner not in voice, Therese lost all her confidence, everyone worried about the future. I wish you'd seen my *Luxembourg*. The first night . . . that was really something!'

'I'm sure it was, Madge. I've seen your work before, remember? I know what your sets and costumes can do for a company. But please, don't get too involved with this rabble. We both know where you belong, working with me and people like me. I wish you'd come to New York and do my *Manon*.'

'No.'

'Well . . . we're both too tired to argue tonight. Would you like to have some supper?'

'And let people see us together? Whatever would they think!'

She wished she hadn't said that. His face froze over and he turned away.

'As you wish, Madge. I'll see you tomorrow.'

'Oh . . . bugger!' she said to herself. 'Why can't I forget it, leave it alone.' But she couldn't, not while she was still seeing him every day. She'd have to get away again once this muddle was sorted out. Take another job off the beaten track where he couldn't possibly collide with her, where they couldn't meet or even encounter mutual acquaintances. She flung her coat over her shoulders and stepped out into the clean June night. Over the Hochhauser hung a huge white moon. She wished she was young and romantic again, but they'd been through all that. She wished she'd gone to supper with him.

CHAPTER FOURTEEN

They stumbled on through the week. Performances were erratic and, in Therese's case, totally mechanical, but surprisingly they were also reasonably competent. A temporary company manager from Vienna arrived on the Tuesday afternoon, a cold, bored man who did everything from a clipboard and spent long hours closeted in the office with Peter Grun. There was a wave of fear around the company when two men with briefcases were seen going into the office along with Willi and the rest of the Hochhauser committee. Trudi – the terrified stage manager – who was constantly taking in paper cups of coffee, reported that they were all sitting around the desk which was covered in sheaves of computer printouts. Both Peter Grun and one of the briefcase men were operating pocket calculators and Burgermeister Zimmermann looked grim.

Every morning at nine there was a company call and everyone, even Gesner, attended, fearing that it might be the notice of closure they were all dreading. On the Wednesday morning the new company manager, not looking at any of them but just reading from his clipboard, announced cast changes for the evening's performance of *Luxembourg*.

'René, Count of Luxembourg – Rudi Woolf. Brissard – Edouard Gilbert. Juliette Vermont – Elisa Maxmilion. Everyone else, the same as before. Rehearsal at eleven with new cast.'

Even in the midst of their general misery they were intrigued enough to look, as one man, towards Gesner. His blotched face grew even more blotched.

'Who the hell do you think you are?' he shouted, but the company manager had already flipped the papers on his clipboard over and was leaving the stage. Someone in the cast tittered. It was a nervous titter but nonetheless it *was* a titter, and at Karl Gesner too. The blotched face suddenly drained of colour and he pushed his way through the cast, striding offstage towards the office. Even though he was afraid, more afraid than he had been at any time in his career, he was still angry enough to walk straight into the office without knocking. Peter Grun and Madge, bent over some papers on the desk, both raised their heads, startled.

'Please don't come in here without knocking,' said Grun coldly. 'If you wish to see me, tell the company manager, and I'll try to find time.'

'What's the meaning of this – allowing Rudi Woolf to sing my role tonight?'

Grun raised an eyebrow. 'There is absolutely no reason why I should give you any explanation at all, but I will. Having watched you for two nights it is obvious you need to rest if you are to sing *Der Zarewitsch* on Saturday. I intend that you will not sing tonight, nor tomorrow. Two nights should enable you to recover from your injuries.'

'I do not need time to recover from my injuries! Even with a bruised nose I can sing better than that young bullfrog.'

'Maybe you can, although on the showing of the last two nights I take leave to doubt it. But you will certainly not be able to sing *Zarewitsch* if you do not improve. Also, if I must be brutal, you look quite ridiculous for a romantic lead. Until the swelling has gone down I think it will be better if you remain offstage.'

'And what if I refuse to sing *Zarewitsch* on Saturday? Are you intending to let Rudi Woolf sing that too? Haa!' It was his last throw, and quite a strong one. *Der Zarewitsch*, the most operatic of all Lehar's pieces, was virtually a two-hander. One needed two really competent and professional singers. There was no way Rudi could sustain it.

Peter Grun eyed him coldly. 'We have three well-prepared operettas available. There is no reason at all why *Der Zarewitsch* should not be cancelled. In fact, Miss Grimsilk and I are discussing that possibility even now. I have been firmly of the opinion that this . . . this overburdened company has quite enough to handle at the moment without launching the revival on Saturday. Miss Grimsilk says we should stay with our announced programme and honour our commitment, however bad the production may be. I think if you decide not to sing on Saturday, it will make my decision much easier. Even Miss Grimsilk will see the sense of cancelling the production altogether.'

Gesner's anger had slowly seeped away to be replaced with a sense of righteous self-pity.

'After all I've done for this company,' he said in a pompous whine. 'To be treated like this . . .'

'You have very nearly wrecked this company, Gesner. You have precipitated my father into a heart attack. You have destroyed the confidence of a fellow singer to the point where it is doubtful she will ever be employable again. You have consistently caused trouble and needless expense with your messy little sex affairs within the company, and you have generally attempted to undermine the morale of the rest of the cast. The only thing you had to offer was your voice and a certain somewhat vulgar stage sexuality. Up to a point these two attributes outweighed your many disadvantages. We have a saying in the English theatre – one should always be a little less trouble than one is worth. I'm afraid your trouble quotient has finally outweighed your worth. Please leave us now. We have a great deal to do.'

Without another word, Gesner left.

Madge suddenly turned to Peter, grasped his face between her hands and kissed him warmly on the mouth. 'Peter, that's nothing to do with us. That's for giving me one of the happiest moments of my life! I only wish we could replay it in front of the entire company.'

He grinned at her, that charming, stylish grin she had been so shocked to see in his father, the grin that had helped to send her back into a total cold reserve in her dealings with the Direktor, the grin that had been one of the first things she had loved about him.

'I never thought,' he said, amused at himself, 'that I would take such a virulent dislike to one person in such a short time. I shall have to be very careful, Madge, that I do not become as emotionally involved with this tacky little company as everyone else.'

If Therese found it a relief that the next time she played *Luxembourg* it was with Rudi, not Gesner, it made little difference to her performance. The only thing that kept her together that week was a determination not to let people see how she felt inside, how she wanted to sit in her room weeping, how, on stage, she was terrified every time she looked into the wings, how the sight of Gesner made the old fear rise up so strongly in her that she felt sweat break out across her breast and midriff. There were times when she was spoken to and had difficulty in controlling herself sufficiently to answer. She asked for, and got a prescription for her old tablets, the ones she had had just after Friedrich had been taken away, when she was on the verge of a nervous breakdown. She had broken herself from the habit of taking them, and she was filled with self-loathing at having to rely on them again, but she knew she mustn't let Busacher down, let the company down. She just took one half an hour before going on stage each night and it helped to get her through the performances.

She knew the fear would go. It had gone before. She also knew that she was still, in spite of everything, basically an optimist and she hung on to that amidst the sweats and the fears and the desire to weep. She knew that one day she would get over it and, would be, if not exactly happy, then calm and reasonably content. But that part of her, the part that knew she would eventually get over it, was also filled with the worry of what she would do, where she would go. The insecurity of the future compounded her general fear and, underlying it all, was a gentle sadness that she would have to leave Hochhauser, the friends, the Goldener Adler, the cheap suppers after the show with the rest of the cast, the occasional elegant dinners with Busacher and Willi, the wonderful sense of belonging again instead of being alone.

The person she felt more ashamed of seeing than anyone else was Willi. Every time she remembered the degrading scene on the mountain track and then in his car, she felt she never wanted to speak to him again, never wanted to see him again. But, of course, he was unavoidable, in and out of the theatre all the time, conferring in huddles with the great Peter Grun. The first time she passed him on the stairs she just nodded curtly and said, 'Good morning, Willi.' She was conscious of him stopping, wanting to speak to her, but she swept on, and after that he made no attempt to involve her in any kind of conversation. He probably felt as embarrassed as she did.

Her performances she went through by mechanical rote. Here I turn to the left, take three steps and smile. Now I stand and sing, clasp Rudi's hand on the second reprise, look up, look down, smile again. Helped by her tablet she was able to get through it like an automaton. She didn't know how she was going to cope with *Der Zarewitsch* on Saturday – an emotional operetta, and on with Gesner the whole time, no real backing from the rest of the company. She would be on her own. The sweat broke out again and she thrust the thoughts of it aside. Just get through each performance as it came.

On Friday, when Madge went in to see the Direktor, she found

236

him sitting up with, for the first time since the attack, a good colour in his face and some of his old animation. He had, considering everything, come through extraordinarily well. He now had a telephone in his room on which he could take incoming calls but which he was forbidden to use for outgoing contact – a wise precaution, Madge thought, as he would otherwise be trying to run the theatre from his bed.

'You're looking so much better,' she said, pleased.

'How is my theatre?'

'Fine. Peter's doing a great job.'

'*Zarewitsch*?'

'Going ahead. Peter's going to conduct himself. He thinks he'll be able to help them both more from the orchestra pit than from backstage.'

'I know that already,' he said smugly. 'Hans Kramer telephoned me from Vienna and told me.'

'How . . . ?'

'There's nothing you can keep secret in Vienna about the world of opera. The whole place is buzzing with the news that Sir Peter Grun has come out to run the Hochhauser Season. Hans wanted to know if all the rumours were correct, that Peter is my son, that there was a débâcle on the stage last week, that Peter has come out particularly to direct Therese Aschmann and prepare her for a debut at Covent Garden, that Peter is thinking of staging a new Wagner cycle at Hochhauser.' He giggled rather naughtily, like a mischievous child. 'That Gesner has been fired, that he has had both legs broken by a jealous lover, that my *Zarewitsch* is a brilliant new production, never seen before.'

'Good God!' said Madge, stunned.

'And,' said Busacher with an air of final triumph, 'a whole army of them are coming down from Vienna on Saturday, to see my *Zarewitsch*.'

'A whole army of who?'

'Kramer, Karl Michael, all the critics, one of the Direktors and some of the management of the *Staatsoper,* Zarintsky, everyone.'

'Good God!' said Madge again.

'It is because of Peter.'

'Yes.'

'All these years he has always refused to work in Vienna or Salzburg. Would never come to Austria in spite of being invited many times. And now he has stunned them all by appearing in Hochhauser, to run my little company. He . . .' Suddenly the old man couldn't speak. She looked at him and saw he wasn't far from tears.

'My son . . . conducting, directing, in Hochhauser. My company . . . my theatre . . .'

She didn't know what to say. For a moment she wondered, uncharitably, if Peter would be furious at the world of Viennese music witnessing him in charge of such a hopeless production. But then she remembered the man she had loved for eight years and knew he wouldn't care. He had an arrogant disdain for what anyone thought of his work other than a few very close and outstandingly gifted fellow professionals. For those few friends and colleagues, amongst whom she was numbered, but above all for himself, his standards were set. She had seen him receive a standing ovation at the Met, at La Scala, and yet come backstage furious and dissatisfied with his own work on the production. And, indeed, Saturday's performance of *Der Zarewitsch* might prove to be rather better than expected, orchestrally at least. If Peter was conducting there might well be something worth listening to, however bad the performances were on stage. She thought he would probably be amused at all the pompous musical aristocracy of Vienna flocking like lemmings to see a second-rate company putting out a tired old revival.

'The company will be pleased,' she said, and then paused. 'At least, I think they'll be pleased. Gesner will, of course, behave outrageously, and Therese . . .'

The old man looked sad. 'I know what has happened to Therese,' he said quietly. 'Even while I lay on the floor, fighting this silly pain in my chest, I knew what it would do to her. But she is a professional. She will get through it somehow. She has managed this week, has she not?'

'Oh, yes.'

'She will manage. And she will also know that the reason they are all coming is because of Peter, not to see how good or bad she is. Whatever happened to her in the past is nothing to the fact that, for the very first time, Peter Grun is conducting in Austria . . . I never thought he would, you know. I remember him, when he was sixteen years old, shouting at me that he hated Vienna, hated Austria and would never come back.'

She sat very quietly. She knew only a little of their past – what little she had gleaned over the eight years – but she didn't want to precipitate any confidences, any memories that might later upset one or both of them.

'How did you come to know my son?' he asked quietly. 'I have watched you standing together by my bedside and you are more than just colleagues, fellow professionals. You are lovers, am I right? Forgive me for asking these impertinent questions. I do not wish to pry into matters which are yours alone, but – you see – I am hungry to know things about my son's life. All I have of him is what I read in the newspapers. I would like to think he had tenderness, affection. His childhood was so . . . distorted . . . I would like to think that now he has some of the things that other men have.'

'We were lovers. We are no longer.'

'I see,' he said sadly.

'It is quite all right. We are both . . . committed to our work. I think Peter does not really desire what other men have. He has his work. That is all he needs, that will be his life.'

'It was my life. It is not enough. For me it is too late, not for him. Is that why he left you? Because of his work?'

'I left him.'

'Because of his work?'

'No! How can you say that – you who have worked with me? You think I would resent his work? It was that that brought us together – shared ideas, shared admiration, shared excitements. We were happy in our work. We only did the one production together a long time ago. But I was never jealous or resentful of his work, nor he of mine.'

'Then why . . . ?'

She thought she had it all under control, the hurt, the rejection, the sense of giving everything and having so little in return. She had done what she did deliberately, not wanting to leave herself vulnerable to further hurts, further rejections, but sometimes she wondered if she had done the right thing. Was the little she had had with him better than nothing at all? The old sore pain began to stir once more.

'It is difficult to explain,' she said slowly. 'For eight years we were together yet not together. How can I make you understand – we discussed our work together, we went to bed together, we told one another that we loved, he gave me presents, we knew each other's likes and dislikes, and yet . . .'

'And yet . . .'

'He never suggested we live together, share our lives as people do who say they love one another. Not necessarily marriage, I didn't particularly want him to suggest marriage, but some kind of pledge, some kind of admission that I was important to him. And even if not that – for he *is* reserved, a very private person – then to

239

be seen to be my partner. He would never even eat in a restaurant with me unless it was tucked away somewhere obscure, in case we should be seen together and people would link our names – begin to think of us as a couple. It became an obsession with him, never arriving at parties together, never leaving at the same time. Once, when someone asked us to a wedding, put our names together on the invitation, he wouldn't see me for three weeks. I asked him once if, for some reason, he was ashamed of me and he told me not to be ridiculous. He said he didn't want us to be forced into any kind of conventional relationship, that what we had was totally unconventional, good, true, and neither of us would be hurt or publicly embarrassed if the affair ended. He said it was better that way. Perhaps it was for him. But I felt . . . unwanted. And of course he was right – about there being no public embarrassment when I ended things.'

'I see,' said the old man bleakly.

'That's all there is,' she said quickly, seeing she had tired him. 'I must go now. There is nothing for you to worry about. We are both perfectly all right and the thing we care about most is that you should get better.'

'Please sit down again, Madge. I would rather we spoke of this now than that I lie here thinking, rethinking, remembering. Did you know that I abandoned his mother? Did he tell you that?'

'Yes . . . He told me that it was the war . . . but that you abandoned her then, and later you left both of them. He never told me any details – just that he . . .'

'That he had no time for me as a father?'

She bent her head and looked down at her hands lying in her lap.

'You know, of course, that his mother was Jewish?'

'Yes. I knew that.'

He smiled rather wryly. 'For someone as reserved as my son, he seems to have told you quite a lot about himself.'

'Facts, just facts. He never really told me about what he felt.'

'His mother was a violinist – not a very good one – in a restaurant trio – the *Kaiserhof* it was, just off the Ring. It was destroyed in the war. There's an office block there now. She was poor, and incredibly pretty and she was playing there one night when we went in from the opera. I was the golden boy of Vienna then, twenty-four years old, just back from Paris, on the staff at the *Staatsoper*, made much of, spoilt. I didn't know much about women. I'd been brought up by my father. My mother left us when I was five. There had really been no women in my life at all, a few casual incidents in Paris, but nothing real. I was a little drunk that night and, for a dare, I went up and sat down with the trio, took one of the violins and played beside her. She was . . . overwhelmed, I suppose. I remember her huge dark eyes fixed on my face as I played. It was very . . . flattering. Afterwards I bought her a meal and took her home. She had a small pathetic room in the tenth district. It reminded me of the kind of place my father and I used to live in.' He paused and said slowly, 'There were a lot of things about her that reminded me of the life I had lived as a child.

'She had no immediate family. An uncle in Linz and a few cousins scattered about, but no-one really close, and finally she moved into my apartment, which was a brave thing to do in those days. People didn't live together as they do now. I think she loved me very much.'

'Did you love her?'

'Sometimes. And then, at other times, I would remember my mother and what she had done to my father and, because I was young, I would confuse the two women: Marta, and my mother. But much of it was happy – she was very pretty, and I was the darling of the *Staatsoper*, and all our friends were young and in the theatre. And then she became pregnant and there was the *Anschluss*. You know about the *Anschluss*?'

'Oh yes. I know about the *Anschluss*.'

'Then you will also know it was a very bad time to be a Jew in Vienna. Such hideous violence in the streets, such savagery. I was ashamed of my city.

'It was a good thing she was living with me – I was able to protect her for quite a while. I kept her hidden in my apartment for those first dreadful weeks and – thank God – no-one in the theatre betrayed us, although later there were some who sold out to the Nazis. We were all of us so stunned at what was happening. Like ostriches we had lived in our world so long – concerned only with music – that we did not understand just how these terrible things had come about. We were, I suppose, very irresponsible young people.

'At first, of course, they took only the rich Jews, the powerful ones whom everyone knew. Even then, foolishly, we thought that we, the musical beloved of Vienna, were separate, safe. The musicians, composers, singers of Vienna have always been the real aristocrats of intellectual Austria. And then we realized that no-one was safe. Rudolph Beer shot himself. Reinhardt and Zemblinsky managed to get out, some of the others just vanished. At that point I was prepared to marry her – to give her protection –

but she was terrified. She said, correctly as it turned out, that marriage to an Aryan would not protect her. She just wanted to get out of Austria. I said I would help her, but I begged her to get rid of the child – it was possible, even in those days – but again she was adamant. She had no-one, she said, and now at last she was going to have someone who belonged to her. She said it and looked at me, and now the dark eyes were no longer admiring but reproachful.

'It got worse in Vienna and I finally did the only thing I could do. I arranged for her to go to England, got her papers, money, and saw her out through Yugoslavia and Greece. I thought it was too dangerous for her to travel through Germany on her own. She told me afterwards, after the war, that the journey had been a nightmare. She was stranded in Greece when the train broke down, attacked by three men in a third-class carriage and had most of her money stolen. She still had her papers and her ticket for the ship from Athens and she finally got to England, although when she arrived she had no money and she couldn't speak the language. She was put into a hostel and Peter was born there. I had one letter from her telling me I had a son and that she was destitute. She begged me to follow her and help her, join her in England and marry her. I sent her money, said I would come later, and then the war began and the frontiers closed and it was eight years before I saw her again.'

She felt the old familiar pity that always enveloped her when she heard the sad stories of those abandoned, uprooted, displaced by the war. We had things so easy, we British, she thought. How difficult it is for us to comprehend the total destruction of peoples, families, stability. How difficult it is for me to understand the scars on someone like Peter. That is why it lasted eight years.

'Of course, when it was too late, when I saw what was happening, I knew I should have gone with her. I could have earned a living in England – many refugee musicians did. But at the time I thought it could not go on like that. I thought it was just a temporary madness that would eventually burn itself out. When it was too late I was filled with guilt. I did what I could – there were still many Jews in the opera, the theatre, the orchestra. And they were being betrayed. The old brotherhood of the theatre had collapsed. People in the *Staatsoper*, people I had thought were my friends, betrayed each other, betrayed me eventually. But we managed to help quite a few Jewish musicians get out, some into Hungary – it was safe there for Jews until 1944 – some down into Yugoslavia with the partisans; others – the ones who didn't

242

look Jewish – we fixed up with false papers and new identities. Everything I did was out of guilt – guilt for Marta and my son living alone and without protection in England.

'Then I was sent to Russia and I could help no more. I suppose I was lucky not to be arrested in view of what I had been doing. But most famous Viennese musicians were *not* sent to the Russian front in an infantry battalion. It was obviously my punishment. When I came back, the war was over, and when we all found out exactly what had happened, I was filled with an even greater guilt. I had no idea how to trace her – she couldn't still be at the hostel, but she wrote to me, at the *Staatsoper*. It was bombed of course, destroyed, but there were still quite a few of us who came back and by some miracle the letter got to me. She was a housekeeper, she said, housekeeper to a very old man who didn't pay her very much but who was prepared to accept the child. She'd had a lonely, miserable war, had made few friends, little money. She had just about managed to keep them going. She begged me to come and marry her, settle in England, provide a home for her and the child.

'It was almost impossible to travel across Europe at that time unless you were one of the conquering peoples. We were in disgrace of course, defeated, paired in guilt with Hitler's Germany, and with the four Allied Powers sitting straddled across our country. Nonetheless, I managed it somehow – the Red Cross, some old friends in the world of music who remembered me, one of the Jews I had helped to escape who had got to England and had established himself very creditably. They all helped and finally, by a miracle, I got to England, to somewhere called Hove, where Marta and Peter were waiting for me in a large, damp, cold house, very dark, very depressing.

'And there was a woman I didn't recognize, a hard-featured woman with a shrill voice, full of hatred and spleen for what I had done to her, for what we, the Austrians and the Germans, had done to her people. And the child looked at me in the same way, full of resentment and dislike. Only when she turned to the child did I see any resemblance to the old Marta; then there was just a slight softening, a tenderness, and if nothing else I was glad that at least she had someone who belonged to her, someone she could love.

'I gave her the choice – she could come back to Vienna, wartorn, desolate, occupied by the Russians and the Allies as it was. But with all that it was my own city and I knew that somehow I could support them there. The *Volksoper* had opened again in 1945, in May, and the Theater an der Wien in the October. I was working

243

already. Once conditions improved, once the Russians got out and things returned to normal, we could start to build a comfortable life. If she came back I would marry her. She said nothing would ever make her return to Austria after what they had done – and who could blame her for that? Only she went on about what they had done, the six million Jews, the concentration camps in Austria, Mauthausen, Ebensee, the whole horrifying litany of the dead, all this in front of the child and it was obvious he had heard it before, many times. He stood there staring at me, dislike and fear in his small thin face. He looked so much like my father I wanted to weep. So I said that, in that case, I would send her money, enough for her and the child. It would be difficult with the currency restrictions but I would find a way, providing she would let him come and stay with me every summer in Vienna. For that meeting had convinced me that the one thing I couldn't do was marry that sad, hating woman and live in a strange country away from everything I knew. Yes, I know, she had had to do it – that's what she said – "I had to do it, pregnant and penniless, I had to do it, so why can't you?" But I couldn't do it because suddenly I realized I didn't really like her. She was a different kind of woman from my mother, whom I had also disliked, but now I didn't like Marta either and the only way I was prepared to live with a woman I didn't like, and who hated me, was in my own city, my own country.

'So finally she agreed. I don't know whether she was relieved or not. Always, after that, she repeated that I had abandoned her twice, once in Vienna in 1938, and again in England in 1947, and of course she was right. But sometimes I think she was relieved that she didn't have to marry me and that the fault was mine.

'She married the old man eventually, the old man she worked for. I heard that when he got ill and helpless she threatened she would leave him unless he married her, so he did. I can't blame her for being hard. Between us, the war and I had made her like that, and she wanted everything for her son. So finally she got the big dark house in Hove, and the money the old man had left her, and as I prospered I sent her more and more. Every summer she would bring Peter to Vienna and turn straight round and go back again, and at the end of the summer I would take him back to Hove, and of course it was hopeless – hopeless, except for the opera. Only then, when I took him to the *Volksoper*, the Theater an der Wien, which had become the home of the *Staatsoper* while we were waiting for it to be rebuilt, only then did that boy of mine come to life and forget that I was the one who had murdered six million Jews and abandoned his mother penniless in a strange country.

'The summer when he was sixteen was the only good one we ever had. I put him into the *Konservatorium* – just for a summer course. It was wonderful at last, that summer of 1955. They were all about to leave us, the British, the Americans, the French, and above all the Russians. The Riding School came back, the *Staatsoper* had been rebuilt and was about to reopen – and can you think of any other nation that put the rebuilding of its State Opera House before anything else, and out of public collections too? The whole city was . . . like a party, like the old Vienna must have been before the First World War, and all at once I saw the magic of the city – the musical magic, you understand – take my son in its grasp. We didn't spend much time together that summer, for suddenly he had his own friends and spent the evenings the way all young people do, racing around the coffee houses, drinking a little too much, falling very slightly in love – a fellow student, who afterwards became rather a good violinist. For sixteen years he had been a Jewish refugee boy living in England. Suddenly his Viennese heritage took hold of him, not the Vienna of political madness and treacherous betrayal, but the other Vienna, the true Vienna, of Mozart and Mahler, Haydn and Strauss, all of them, the great tradition of the most musical city in the world.

'That year his mother came to collect him. He was old enough to travel on his own but she came anyway. She sat in my apartment and he wasn't there, and then suddenly he came bursting in with all his friends, his violin case slung over his shoulder – it was the fashion that summer among the students to tie a strap on and carry the case over the shoulder – shouting and laughing, being too noisy, too young, too happy. And Marta looked at him and started to cry, and he stopped laughing and remembered the six million Jews, and turned back into a cold young English boy, and then he looked at me and said he was never coming back to Vienna, to Austria, for the rest of his life.'

She wanted to weep for them all, those sad lives, destroyed by the war, by misunderstanding, youthful selfishness which would probably have resolved itself in some way if it hadn't been for the war. She wanted to weep for the man she loved – for the happy sixteen-year-old he had been, the tortured boy weighed down by the burden of six million Jews and a woman whose life had embittered her beyond hope.

'That was virtually the end of any real contact between us. I saw him in London from time to time over the years. We always met if we were working in the same cities, but it was never very easy, just a stiff formal meal together. He told me, quite early on, that he thought it would be best for both of us if our relationship was not acknowledged in public life. I did very little for him. I was as useless a father as I would have been a husband. The only thing I could and did do for him was to see he had the very best musical training, the best teachers, the best openings in the right theatres, the right cities. That is really all I have done for my son.'

Madge sat, feeling the weight of the world pulling her down, the hopelessness of the whole human condition enveloping her in sorrow.

'I see now why he is as he is,' she said at last. 'And I realize that I was wrong to leave him. I shall have to go back, on any terms at all. It won't be much of a life for us, but it will be better than nothing. And that's what we'll both have if I go away again – nothing.' She paused, then said slowly, 'I saw her once, you know. Marta, his mother.'

The old man gave a slight smile.

'She could have had a good life once he became famous. He wanted to buy her an apartment in London. He invited her to all his performances. She could have enjoyed his success, his money, his fame. Could have been, well, the mother of Peter Grun. But she refused everything and, just once, he took me to meet her. It was right at the beginning when, well, I suppose he was very "in love" with me then, and wanted to let me see just a little of his life.'

'And . . .'

'Just as you described – a dark, gloomy house in Hove. And her, just sitting there, determined to be unhappy, determined to make *him* unhappy. He never took me there again, and then she died.' She gave a small mirthless laugh. 'I suppose, in view of everything, it's amazing he ever fell in love with me at all. And that's why I'll go back – he's given me all he can, I suppose, and I'll just have to settle for that. And who knows, maybe, when we're both very old – all passion spent – when he's discovered that I'm not going to leave him, maybe then he'll consent to us attending a party together or even being seen eating a meal in a restaurant.'

'Maybe he'll even want to marry you,' the old man smiled, but she shook her head.

'That's the stuff of which operettas are made, Herr Direktor. Things like that only happen in Act Three.'

'But it was surely pure operetta that you came to work in Hochhauser – my son's girlfriend disguised as a prim stage designer – spying out the mystery of her lover's secret father. That was Act Two of the operetta, surely?'

'I didn't know you were his father when I took the job,' she said grimly. 'I decided I had to get right off the usual circuit, where we would meet all the time – you know how small our world is – so I took the Hochhauser job and when I told him . . . I had never seen him so angry, so raging and furious. I was terrified. I had wanted a space of time to get away from him . . . us, and suddenly I found I had inadvertently stepped right back into his past. I didn't want to get involved, not with you, not with him. I was . . . bruised. I didn't feel I could take any more.'

'So. That explains much about the sour Miss Grimsilk.'

She grinned and placed her hand over his. She had thought, all the time he'd been talking, that it would be bad for him, tiring and unsettling, but the voice had been gentle, rambling, almost as though he was wandering through a past that no longer had the power to upset him. He seemed quite calm and restful now.

'I shall go now. I must prepare the company for the distinguished audience that will fill the auditorium on Saturday evening.'

'Madge.' His old eyes were alight again, fixing her with a hopeful query. 'Madge, I want to come to that performance. I want to see my son conducting my company in my theatre.'

'You know that is impossible, dear Herr Busacher,' she said. 'You are ill. You must rest and be tranquil. There is no way the doctors would let you go to the theatre on Saturday.'

'But I want to come. I shall be quiet and not involve myself in anything. I just want to see Peter in my own theatre.'

'I shall come here afterwards and tell you every single thing that has happened.'

He sighed, stared at her hard, then closed his eyes.

'I think I shall sleep now,' he whispered, and relieved he hadn't persisted in his foolish dream, she crept out of the room.

'Please ask Willi to come and see me this evening,' she heard him say as she closed the door.

On the Friday and Saturday mornings Peter Grun worked Therese and Gesner almost to hysteria on the final rehearsals for *Der Zarewitsch*. Gesner, always lazy, and especially so on old productions, had never worked so hard in his life and it was only fear that made him toe the line when, with anyone else, he would just have refused to work at all. Grun had succeeded in totally demoralizing him and he was a very frightened man. For under the threat of Grun's total disregard for his worth as a performer in the Hochhauser Season lay a much greater threat. Grun had only to drop a casual hint, mention his record at Hochhauser over a drink in a theatre bar somewhere, and Gesner knew he would find it almost impossible to work again. He had heard, as had everyone else, of the illustrious audience coming down from Vienna and had decided that was his only hope. If he could pull out all the stops on Saturday night, someone might offer him work before Grun had the chance to put the word around that Gesner was 'a lot more trouble than he was worth'. So he sweated and sang properly right through the part, and took all the cold, scathing corrections to his performance that Grun administered with toneless disinterest.

Therese, curiously enough, found Grun's dispassionate autocracy very helpful. He did not attempt to enliven her performance, but he was ruthless in making her plot every step, every movement, every smile and turn of the head. He seemed to know that that was all she was capable of, a totally efficient, mechanical routine that wouldn't deviate one inch from the set of instructions he gave her. She suddenly felt safe again. All she had to do was stick to his minute instructions and sing. She could do that with the help of her tablet. She also, dimly, sensed Gesner's own particular panic and realized she had nothing to fear from him. He was too busy with his own problems to spare even a moment's hatred on her. She knew she'd get through it all right.

Grun finished with them on Saturday at one o'clock. They were exhausted, wrung out, and they just stared glumly at him when he said,

'That's the best I can do with you. I'll give you every assistance I can from the rostrum. If you get into difficulties leave it to me to get you out. Karl, your face is certainly improved but you will still need to make up the eye quite heavily if you wish to look passable.'

He waited for Gesner to say something but Gesner was a broken man.

'I suggest that now you both have a good lunch, then rest for the afternoon.'

They were too weary even to nod, and as he swung away, back up the gangway and out through the doors, they both ambled tiredly towards the wings. As they left the stage Therese was startled to hear Gesner address her.

'Do you think it will be all right?'

'What?'

'Tonight. Do you think it will go all right?'

If she hadn't been so tired, so uncaring anyway of anything except just getting through without collapsing, she might have been amused.

'Yes,' she said tersely, and walked away. Her thin veneer of self-control was incapable of sustaining a conversation with Gesner. She played opposite him by the simple device of blocking him out, convincing herself that he really was the Zarewitsch, Luxembourg, Count Tassilo.

Outside the theatre, Willi Zimmermann was waiting and a shudder of distaste – for herself – went through her. She nodded coolly, said, 'Good afternoon, Willi,' and prepared to walk past.

'Therese. Can I speak with you, please. Could we lunch together?'

'No thank you, Willi. I have to rest for this evening.'

'It is very important. If you won't eat with me, just give me a few moments, please. It is about the Direktor. He sent for me last night.'

It was the only thing that would have made her stop and listen to Willi. The reference to the Direktor.

'Is he all right?' she asked. 'I haven't been to see him. I was told he must not have too many visitors and I thought perhaps the sight of me might . . . might upset him. But is he all right?'

'Yes. He's fine. It was not a bad attack – I expect you heard – but of course he is supposed to rest and next week he is to have more tests. But . . .' He suddenly gave a huge puff and said, 'It would be so much easier to have this conversation sitting down and not in the street. Could we not go somewhere and have lunch?'

Oh hell, why not, she thought tiredly to herself. What does it matter? 'All right, Willi. I'll have a glass of wine or something. I've time for that.'

His face fell. 'I thought, something to eat. I haven't had my lunch yet and . . .'

'All right, Willi. But somewhere close.'

They went into the Old Vienna, the place where the company frequently ate their late but cheap suppers. It was a hot, crowded little place. All the tables outside were full and they had to sit in a corner close to the kitchen. There was no pretext at all of a gracious or romantic meal together. Willi ordered a stein of beer for himself and Therese, remembering with distaste the cheap and rather nasty wine they served, decided she would drink beer too.

'Now. What is it, about the Direktor?'

'Therese. He is insisting on coming to see the performance this evening.'

'He can't. He's a sick man. They won't permit it.'

'I've told him that. Madge has told him. The doctors have told him. It makes no difference. He says he is coming.'

'Oh dear!' A fresh wave of affection for the stubborn, kind, talented, autocratic old man swept over her, affection and sadness. He had been part of her former life, when she was young and happy, and he had been so kind to her here in Hochhauser, had done so much for her, and she had let him down. She was suddenly awash with sadness because she realized he probably wasn't going to be around for very much longer.

'Oh Willi! Why? Why is it so important? It's only a revival of an old production. Is it because of Peter Grun?'

Willi nodded. 'We none of us knew, did we? He never spoke of his past, of course, not his personal past, only his life in the theatre. I sometimes thought it strange. We were close friends. I think I was probably the closest friend he ever had, yet he never told me that his son was Peter Grun. He still hasn't told me anything, really – just that they have never been close. But when he said he wanted to see his son conducting this evening, his eyes were full of tears.'

'Isn't there anything we can do?'

Willi shook his head. 'Nothing. He's such a pig-headed old man! He has said he will discharge himself and if no-one will help him downstairs and into a taxi then he'll do it by himself, and if he drops dead on the floor it will be the fault of all his friends who have refused to help him.'

'What about the doctors?'

'They are furious. The cardiac professor said he washes his hands of him, said he wouldn't allow him back if he discharged himself. But the old man said, good, he wouldn't come back if they begged him. He worked himself up into such a furious state that finally the doctors have given in.'

'You mean they've agreed to let him come?'

'On certain conditions. They couldn't do anything else. The professor told me afterwards that he thought it would be better to let him go under hospital supervision than stay imprisoned in the ward or discharge himself the way he threatened.'

'What conditions?'

'He will be brought in an ambulance, with a nurse, in a wheelchair. And that is why I want to talk to you, Therese. He is very worried that when you see a man sitting in a wheelchair in the wings again, it might be a terrible shock for you.'

After the first stunned moment she began to laugh, quietly at first, then louder, more shrilly. She felt the control held so tightly over the last week begin to slip.

'Therese?'

She fought, closed her eyes, struggled, and won. She lifted her glass, took a large draught of beer and placed the glass back very, very carefully on the table top. With great care she stood it in the original ring of wetness. It took quite a little time to get it just right.

'Therese?'

'I think we are all quite, quite mad, Willi. Each and every one of us. I wonder just what will happen next.'

'I know what is going to happen next.'

'What?'

Willi took a huge breath, his face went white and he waved the approaching waiter away.

'I am going to ask you to marry me.'

She really didn't take it in and when she did, she didn't understand. She wasn't shocked, or surprised. She just didn't understand. She looked at him to see if he were joking but his frantic worried face convinced her that this was real.

'I'm sorry, Willi,' she said, bewildered. 'Just too much has happened to me lately. I can't really understand. I don't see why you're doing this.'

'Because I want you to marry me.'

It was like being on a giant Ferris wheel, going round and round: there was Gesner, now vicious, now humble, there was Busacher lying on the floor having a heart attack, there was Willi giving her a horrible pink and purple orchid, there was Friedrich – she shuddered – in a wheelchair, back to Gesner with a black eye, the great Sir Peter Grun sitting in a dirty office behind the Hochhauser stage, and there was Willi with a white, anxious face, his round little eyes fixed on her like a pleading spaniel.

The waiter, impatient, came up again with his pad.

'Go away, please,' said Willi. 'I'm not hungry. I don't want any lunch.' It was that more than anything that snapped her off the Ferris wheel, made her realize, startled, that Willi had asked her to marry him and that he meant it.

'Willi,' she said gently. 'It is very, very kind of you, but of course I can't.'

'Why not?' he said stubbornly.

'I . . . well. Think how unsuitable it would be.'

'I don't think it at all unsuitable.'

She was still trying to understand. Why had he done it? Was it pity? Did he feel sorry for her? She darted another quick glance at him and thought, no, it's not pity, thank God. I couldn't have borne that. It's not pity.

251

'Willi, if you marry again – and there is no reason at all why you shouldn't – it will be someone . . . someone special, and nice, someone who will manage your lovely farmhouse for you, be your partner on the opera committee, someone respected in Hochhauser, someone warm and gracious and charming whom everyone likes and respects.'

'That's you,' he said obstinately.

'Oh, Willi!' She suddenly felt annoyed. She had enough to bear without this. 'Willi, you've seen what's happened to me here in Hochhauser. You know everything about me now – no, not everything, but enough. I'm a mess, Willi, and no woman of my age has a right to be a mess. I've managed my life badly and I have no-one to blame but myself. Oh yes, a lot of people feel sorry for me, but I don't. Any other woman, a stronger woman, would have extricated herself from the mess years ago. I don't think I want to . . . involve anyone else in my life ever again, however nice they are.'

'I think you're wrong. You made one mistake when you were young, one mistake. You picked the wrong man, or maybe he picked the wrong woman, and you've let that colour the rest of your life.'

'Willi,' she interrupted firmly. 'Would you have done this if it weren't for last Saturday? Up on the mountain, in the rain . . . would you have asked me to marry you if you hadn't listened to me then?'

'No,' said Willi. 'I wanted to ask you to marry me, but I wouldn't have dared if it hadn't been for that.'

'Is it because you feel sorry for me?' The old spectre was back, the humiliating concept that he pitied her.

'No . . . you see, you don't understand. I know what I am, Therese, what everyone sees when they look at me, a funny, fat little man who eats and drinks too much, bounces about, gets on people's nerves, makes them laugh; that's what you see, isn't it?'

'No, Willi . . .'

'Oh yes. That's what you see, what everyone sees.' The colour had come back into his face but some of the joy, the animation had gone from it.

'Nobody ever really understands that funny, fat little men aren't funny and fat inside. All my life I wanted to be . . . romantic. Isn't that silly? Most men don't bother about that. Look at Georg, my son, he couldn't care less about being romantic; it embarrasses him even to think about it. But always I wished that someone would take me seriously, not laugh when I didn't mean them to, not be polite and well-mannered and amused when I gave them an oversized basket of flowers or the wrong-coloured orchid.'

She coloured up, suddenly stricken. 'Oh, Willi, I didn't . . .'

He placed his hand over hers on the table. 'That's all right, Therese. I wasn't criticizing. You were kind and gracious, as you always are. But I knew I had got it wrong again – that what was meant to be grand and romantic was funny and a mistake.'

She didn't take her hand away. His was warm and strangely comforting and she felt it would be unkind, abrupt, to withdraw her own.

'Gerda, my wife, she understood. She was the same. It never went wrong when I was with Gerda, but there was never any money for flowers or dinners in those days. But it didn't matter. We both felt the same. We must have looked a funny little couple together, I suppose. Once, when we took just half an hour off early one morning to walk up the mountain and watch the sunrise, we saw some climbers coming down from the hut and I heard them giggle at us. We were holding hands, you see. And Gerda hadn't taken her milking clothes off. I suppose we did look funny. I lost my hair very early, you know.'

She just didn't know what to say. There was nothing she could say.

'I fell in love with you years ago, when we went up to Vienna for that one week. A delayed honeymoon it was – the first time I could afford to give Gerda a holiday. And I fell in love with you when I saw you on the stage of the *Volksoper*. It was nothing to do with Gerda – Gerda was my life. You were a dream, a fantasy, the sort of creature who existed in that curious world where I was tall and handsome. It was nothing serious, you understand? It didn't interfere with anything at all – it was just a little starry dust on the top of my life.'

It was curious, for all around them was noise, people talking, eating, the smells of the kitchen wafting through and over them, and yet she felt they were cocooned in a silent world of their own, images lifting and falling from the past, making her understand things as he talked.

'When she died . . . I can't tell you what it was like. She was more to me than just a wife. She was the only one, the *only* one, who saw me as I was, as I wanted to be. You think, as you get older, it will all change, you won't care about these things any more, but of course you do, only it gets even more ridiculous because if funny, fat, bald little men are not romantic, then certainly funny, fat, *old* little men aren't either. And then you came to Hochhauser.'

'Ah yes,' she said. 'I came – the diva, the star of the *Volksoper*, the most divine singer you had ever heard.'

'Don't speak that way!' he said, suddenly angry. 'I hate it when you speak like that. You can only say that because you once *were* all those things. I never was. When I saw you, you brought that dream back into my life. It was wonderful, but of course I knew that someone like you would never take someone like me at all seriously. You were amused by me, yes, you thought I was kind, and I helped you once or twice, but singers like Aschmann, however tragic their lives, don't marry people like me.'

'Oh, Willi,' she said sadly. 'Anyone would be lucky to marry you. That's not the reason I can't.'

'Well,' he said bluntly, 'I never would have asked you if it hadn't been for last Saturday night, because suddenly I saw that although, yes, you were still a diva, the most beautiful thing I ever saw on the stage, you were also a woman, just a woman, like my Gerda, and you needed someone to look after you. You were hurt, and frail, and vulnerable and, I thought, I can't give her much, but I can give her that. I can look after her, make her secure so that she can go on being a diva.' He clenched his hand hard over hers. His grip was much stronger than she had imagined it would be.

'Of course you don't love me. How could you? But you like being with me, I know that. You're happy when you're with me. And sometimes I surprise you because I perceive things you don't expect me to see. And I'm not a singer, or a musician, but I am a devotee of the theatre, the opera, and that is the best possible role for the husband of a singer. Therese, I think you should marry me. I think you will be surprised at how happy you will be.' He suddenly raised her hand from the table, shook it slightly, then lifted it to his face and kissed her fingers.

She sat watching, overwhelmed by his kindness. She thought, swiftly and tiredly, of how lovely it would be to give in, let Willi carry her along with his boundless enthusiasm, his caring strength. How restful it would be never to go back to Vienna and start looking for work and a place to live, but just move up into Willi's farmhouse and have a home. And as swiftly as the thought came she put it aside.

'I'm sorry, Willi . . . it's not for any of the reasons you think – not because you are . . . who you are. It's me, you see. I haven't sunk so far, Willi, that I would go into a marriage when I have absolutely nothing to give, just taking everything from you, love, security, a home. I couldn't do that to you, Willi.'

'Nothing to give! What are you talking about? You are Aschmann . . . and you have nothing to give? Don't you realize that what I would love more than anything else in the world is to have Aschmann as my wife? Aschmann, the star, the voice, the most beautiful creature on the stage, and the wife of Willi Zimmermann, Burgermeister of Hochhauser! Therese . . . please don't do this to us! Don't you realize how rarely happiness is offered at our age? Do you think that either of us can throw it aside because of pride, or self-pity, yes . . .' he raised his hand admonishingly as she began to protest. 'Self-pity. You must not do this, Therese. You must just say, yes, Willi, I will marry you. Yes, I will come and live in your farmhouse and I will sing to the best of my ability and I will not allow anyone or anything to destroy my place on the stage. This time, with Willi beside me, I will succeed!'

He grasped her other hand as well and shook them both, quite hard. He was nearly shouting, oblivious of all the interested diners around them who had stopped talking and eating to listen and watch.

'Come now, Therese! Say yes. Say, Willi, I will marry you. That's all you have to do. And stop crying. I won't have you crying when I am proposing marriage to you!'

'I'm not crying.'

'Say yes, Therese. Say yes!'

'Yes, Willi!'

A small round of applause broke out from the tables around them. The waiter, standing poised like a pointer dog, leapt forward, on his tray a bottle of the nasty wine and two glasses.

'To celebrate, Herr Zimmermann. With the manager's compliments,' he said jovially. 'And may the clientele of the Old Vienna be the first to congratulate you!'

Willi beamed, graciously bowed his head, and reached for the menus.

'And now, some lunch,' he said expansively.

When he got back to the farmhouse he had achieved much. Lunch, a visit to Hochhauser's leading jeweller, where he had purchased Therese a modest, by his standards, ring of aquamarines and pearls, a visit to the hospital to acquaint his old friend with the wonderful news and also to check that all was set for the wheelchair visit, a bemused Therese deposited back at the Goldener Adler to rest – as much as she was able – before the evening performance, and now, he thought, for the most difficult part of all, to break the news to Georg.

His son was in the dairy, as he had known he would be. Georg had shrivelled into a piece of efficient machinery these days. He had to try and do something about it.

'Georg,' he said, not feeling, to his own surprise, any nervousness at all. He had braced himself for Georg's disapproval but somehow, in the face of everything else, it didn't seem to matter too much.

'Georg, I have some wonderful news. Wonderful for me, but not for you, I'm afraid. I don't think you are going to like it.'

Georg looked up, his face blanching slightly.

'Is it something to do with Suzi?'

'Suzi? No. Why should it be? It's about me, Georg. I'm going to marry again. Therese Aschmann has done me the honour of agreeing to be my wife.'

Georg stared dully at him for a moment, then said bitterly, 'That's all I need.'

If Willi knew a moment's sadness it was not for himself, but for his son.

'I had hoped, Georg,' he said softly, 'that you would share my good news with me, perhaps even be a little happy for me.'

Georg had the grace to blush. 'I'm sorry, Papa,' he said stiffly. 'Of course I'm happy for you.'

'I appreciate that at your age a stepmother could be a somewhat embarrassing feature of your life. But you'll be marrying yourself soon, and then you'll be wanting a home of your own, and I should have been left rattling around up here alone.'

'A home of my own?' Georg stared at him, bemused.

'Well, of course. You would hardly want to bring a young wife into our home, would you? That wouldn't be fair on her. I had always thought I would give you that piece of land up on the ridge so that you could build your own.'

'Not live here?' said Georg. 'I'd always thought . . .'

'Yes, Georg,' said his father kindly. 'I rather suspected that's what you thought. Just bring little Suzi over the ridge and dump her here to run things while you carried on with the business.'

Georg's handsome mouth firmed into a grim line. 'Suzi doesn't enter into it now,' he said.

'If you're thinking of Gesner, she hasn't spoken to him all week,' said Willi gently. 'She is obviously very unhappy, as unhappy as you appear to be.'

Georg stood staring out of the dairy window for a moment, and then he suddenly burst out, 'How could she do it! How could she do this to me?'

'Because she's human,' said his father mildly.

'After all we meant to do together – after all our plans.'

'What plans, Georg?'

'Combining the farms, building another dairy, expanding the business, taking on extra staff.'

'I never heard Suzi say she wanted any of those things, Georg. It always seemed to me, when you were younger, that she just wanted you.'

Georg flushed again and looked, Willi thought, rather like a sullen child.

'Well,' he mumbled. 'She certainly doesn't want me now.'

'Georg – if Suzi was, well, still Suzi, but she wasn't Gunther Hoflin's daughter and she lived, let us say, in the bakery down in Hochhauser. Yes, let us say that Suzi was the daughter of the Hochhauser baker, would you still want to marry her?'

He was distressed that Georg had to stop and think for a moment, but relieved when he finally said, 'Yes, of course.'

'Did you ever tell Suzi that?'

'There was no need.'

Willi sighed. 'Georg,' he said sadly. 'When your mother died I did the best I could. I fed you, clothed you, spent all my time with you, shared everything with you, the farm, the dairy, the theatre – although you never cared for that – but of course the one thing I couldn't do was make you understand about women. Only your mother could have done that. Do you remember, when you were small, how we would go down into Hochhauser on Christmas Eve and you would decide what gift to buy for your mama?'

'Of course I remember.'

'And do you remember the present she loved the most? The year you chose the perfect gift, even though it wasn't that expensive. Other years you had given her aprons, or shopping bags, but that one year you chose something she really loved.'

'The green scarf,' said Georg, smiling very slightly. 'It was made out of filmy stuff and it had little sparkly things sewn all over it. It was totally useless, but she loved it. She wore it to midnight Mass that night, and she even milked the cows in it next morning. She wore it all the time.'

'Remember that scarf, Georg. Remember the happiness you gave your mama with that scarf, even though it wasn't useful. And then try and think about Suzi, and remember when you last gave her a green scarf.' He patted his son on the shoulder and then left him. Georg was dour, practical, undemonstrative, but he was not unintelligent. Willi felt he had done the best he could, short of wooing Suzi himself.

When Therese arrived at the theatre that night the news had already got round. It was the kind of news the company needed, something pleasant happening to at least one of them in the middle of all the gloom and the threat of closure and the doubts about whether Herr Busacher would ever be well enough to come back and save the company. They clustered round Therese, hugging, kissing, full of delight that two such very nice people had managed, in middle age, to overcome the hurdles of courtship and reactivate the romantic dreams of youth. And Therese, still slightly bemused, standing there, accepting their good wishes, showing them her ring like a young typist in an office, began at last to realize that it was all true. She was to marry Willi Zimmermann. He wanted to marry her, and everyone said it was wonderful. Slowly she began to realize that indeed it was wonderful. She suspected that Willi would always be able to surprise her, that he never was, never had been, quite what she had thought. She remembered his comments about the orchid and blushed. She must never, ever underestimate Willi. He had a way of seeing straight through to the truth. But, however much he might surprise her, there were certain things about Willi that she did know, without hesitation, without doubt. He was loyal, totally trustworthy, and totally reliable. Like the uncles he would never let her down, never betray her. He might embarrass her sometimes, probably would, but he would never knowingly hurt her. In Willi the very human faults of malice and spite had been omitted.

And then, as she sat in her dressing room, staring bemused into the mirror, beginning to realize all the good things that would come from marrying Willi, a faint glimmer of elation began to grow in her heart. She remembered the . . . the *fun* that Willi brought to the life of the company. It wasn't just that he was steadfast and kind, solid in an emergency. The baskets of flowers when she had arrived in Hochhauser *had* been ridiculous, but what a way to start your comeback in a new operetta company! A huge basket and a little man covered in pollen that had made her laugh the moment she had arrived. And his party – corsages for everyone, inviting miserable little Suzi, unhappy Madge Grimsilk, all those boring people from the committee. Who else but Willi could have turned such an odd collection of people into a riotous evening? Even Madge Grimsilk passing out had been turned into an impressive finale, putting the seal on a wonderful party. She recalled how everyone cheered up when Willi came backstage, how people smiled when he walked into a restaurant, how he made Franz Busacher, that sad old cynic of the opera, laugh, and she realized that, indeed, life with Willi was never going to be drab or filled with despair. Willi and despair could not live in the same world.

The elation grew. She undressed, put on her wrapper, and began to prepare her make-up. And perhaps she did have something to give to Willi. Yes, he was stage-struck, always would be. And Willi's schoolboy dream of romance included living with a 'diva'. The thought of her as a diva was hilarious, but not to Willi. And she *had* been good, in her youth. She had been good. It would be immodest to pretend she hadn't. And damn it, she had been pretty good – for this sad little company anyway – in *Luxembourg* until Gesner had . . . done that. She knew she had been getting back into her old stride, she had felt it, had seen the way the hardened old lags of the orchestra looked at her afterwards, that considering, speculative look that meant she was someone to watch, to reckon with. And that was one thing she could give Willi – maybe she'd never get all her old shine back, but if what Willi wanted was a Hochhauser diva, that she could most certainly do for him.

She finished her make-up, climbed into the hired Circassian boy's outfit, the baggy satin trousers, the red boots, the white tunic. She pinned her hair flat, pulled on the wig and fur hat. It was a silly costume for a middle-aged woman, but she didn't really see it as she looked in the mirror.

There was a knock on the door and Willi, in black tie and dinner jacket, carrying an ice bucket with a bottle of champagne, entered the room.

'I know you don't really drink before a performance, but just a sip. I will drink the rest. It is your first performance as the future Frau Burgermeister of Hochhauser! And we must celebrate!'

'Oh, Willi! I feel as though I've been celebrating all day.'

'The Direktor is here. A nurse *and* a porter with him, and his chair tucked neatly into the wings out of the way. He can just see Peter on the rostrum.'

'I'll see him before I go on. I won't go out there now. There'll be too many around him.'

'Five minutes, Fräulein Aschmann.' From outside the door.

Willi undid the wrapping and wire from the champagne, popped the cork, and filled two glasses. He drank most of one glass, handed it to her, and picked up the other.

259

'To the most outstanding Sonja Hochhauser will ever see!'

Therese sipped, and smiled. And then Willi put down his glass, put his hand round her neck and pulled her face down to his. His mouth was as warm as his hand had been earlier in the day. She had kissed him before, at parties, to say thank you for flowers, on performance nights, but this time was different and if she was surprised she gave no sign. It was going to be all right.

'You look wonderful, Therese!'

She didn't know whether she did or not. But she felt wonderful.

The theatre was charged. Willi's loggia was full to bursting with the critics from Vienna. Odd seats in the front stalls had famous and recognizable faces in them, faces that Busacher knew well from the old days. He could see them before the lights went down, old colleagues, old rivals, old enemies. And his son, Peter Grun, was greater than any of them. Whatever they thought of his company, his singers, they would still have to concede that his son was greater than any of them.

The audience stilled, then applauded as Peter mounted the rostrum. He turned to them once, gave a small bow that verged on disdain, then turned back towards the orchestra. His eyes narrowed. Busacher had seen him do that before in performances. He was shutting out everything but the music. Then he raised his baton and, as the overture began, Busacher closed his eyes.

It had been worth it. He and Marta between them had nearly destroyed the boy, but what they hadn't done was destroy his talent, his music. If he had only done one good thing in his life, he had sired this prince of music.

'Please try not to get excited, Herr Busacher. Remember what the doctor said.' It was the nurse, a gentle hand on his shoulder, and Busacher pulled irritably away. His chorus were beginning now – offstage – and he could hear Luiza and Alfred pushing the rest along. It wasn't too bad. He had heard it worse.

Freddi and Rudi came on, only tiny parts in this, so it didn't matter too much what they did, but at least they were trying. Everyone would be trying this evening, with that illustrious Viennese audience out there. And now, here was Gesner.

Busacher leaned forward slightly, ignoring the nurse's hand that tried to hold him back. Gesner looked good, of course, in the old Mandrika costume, and he was doing all his usual things, striding and flexing and pulsing all over the stage. But he was doing something else as well. He was trying very hard with the voice. No easy sliding away, disguising lack of effort and discipline with lazy charm. He was working at the voice, measuring the tones correctly, using his breathing, sustaining where he should sustain, and using the wonderful control that he had when he could be bothered to use it. It was the audience, of course.

Busacher felt a touch on his arm, but it wasn't the nurse. Therese smiled down at him, mouthed a silent 'take care' and stepped on to the stage. Her costume was hideous and did nothing for her, but she moved wonderfully, like a girl, and a miracle had happened – bless you, Willi! – for it had all come back, the confidence, the stage presence, the charm and the magic that she had lost a week ago.

As he heard her sing he itched to leap down to the orchestra pit, seize the baton in his hand, and conduct her himself. This was *his* voice that he had restored and here he was sitting in a wheelchair unable to control it himself. Then he heard what Peter was doing – Peter had seen, heard it at once. Peter was making them play just for that voice. He was playing in exactly the way Busacher would have done.

At the end of the act they whisked him away into the office, just at the very moment when he wanted to point out that one of the violins was dragging a bit, and that the back of Alfred's tunic was hanging down. What was the matter with Wardrobe? They should have seen to that. The hired costumes were always falling to bits. But he had no chance to say anything and finally he decided it didn't matter. Nothing mattered too much. The music coming over his footlights was . . . exceptional.

Act Two was good – Therese out of that ridiculous costume and looking rather lovely in something Madge had made for her – but in Act Three the miracle happened, the miracle he had envisaged as just a remote possibility all those months ago when he had heard her in Vienna. The two voices, Aschmann, Gesner, joined and projected a sound of unsurpassed brilliance out into the theatre. Even the stupid nurse was silent, the stagehands were still. He closed his eyes and listened, and thought how you could never plan something like this. Such miracles happened at odd moments, at unexpected performances, but usually in the great opera houses of the world and with the great stars singing. They never happened in a place like Hochhauser.

At the end of the duet there was a moment's pause, then the applause and cheers. It wasn't just for the two great voices – it was for Peter, who had pulled them together, fused them into more than just two fine voices. The applause was for them, for Peter, for Hochhauser.

Somehow they finished the act – the ending of *Zarewitsch* was always something of an anti-climax, with Sonja left alone on the stage, but Therese was more than able to cope. She drooped tragically in a movement that was almost balletic, sang her last wistful note, and the curtain came down. He was suddenly very, very tired but he had to tell her what she had done.

She came off and stood in front of him.

'Therese . . .'

'I know, Herr Direktor. I felt it too. It was your son, and you, and everyone in Hochhauser, and Willi of course, dear Willi. And it was Gesner too, I suppose. I don't know whether we'll be able to do it again, but it did happen this time, didn't it?'

'It happened. It was worth every bit of my heart attack.'

She leaned over and kissed him. 'You must get well, dear Herr Direktor. We cannot manage without you.'

The storm of cheering from the audience was almost out of control. The new company manager pushed her back on stage.

Franz Busacher smiled, then turned to the nurse.

'I'm ready to go now. I'm tired. I've heard the best and so have you. You will never hear anything like that again in the whole of your life.'

On stage, flowers were handed up, three bouquets for Therese and, surprisingly, one for the little amateur dancer with the good legs. The Viennese critics had been quick to notice that some things about this incredible performance had been very un-balanced, and the dancer had been one of them. Suzi looked at the card on her flowers and frowned. 'You were very good. Georg.'

Peter Grun came onstage, took his bow with Gesner and Therese, and was about to retire when suddenly Willi popped up, stepped to the front of the stage, and raised his hands for silence.

'My friends – it has been an exceptional night in Hochhauser. A distinguished audience,' he gave a universal bow into the direction of the auditorium. 'A performance that we will, none of us, ever forget, and above all the presence of Sir Peter Grun, who has honoured Hochhauser's theatre with his direction and generous management.'

Another round of applause, but Willi raised his hand again.

'Our beloved Direktor is, you will be happy to learn, recovering from his illness, and finally, on this unsurpassed evening, I have an announcement of my own to make.'

Therese realized that this was going to be one of the occasions when Willi was about to embarrass her, but she had to get used to it, so she might as well begin now. She stretched a smile of

262

simpering delight across her face, told herself it wouldn't last long, and prepared to step forward.

'Tonight, our lovely leading lady, our divine Therese Aschmann, has consented to be my wife.'

Excited applause again. Therese accepted Willi's outstretched hand and swept forward once more, holding the simper, curtsying low, to the audience, to Willi. Her embarrassment was overlaid with uncharitable pleasure when she saw Gesner's face. No-one had thought to tell him the news backstage. Not surprising, as no-one was talking to him.

As she stepped back she whispered. 'Your mouth is open, Karl.'

'My friends! Thank you!' Willi stepped back. The curtain came down.

'I've arranged a party on stage,' he said. 'I telephoned Diemar's during the first interval. Bottles, glasses and food are outside. They're waiting to bring them in now.'

Who cared if Willi was embarrassing?

Peter stood with a glass of wine in his hand, an expression of distaste on his face. He hated these company parties, but it would have been churlish to leave when it was really a party for Willi and Therese. He eyed her speculatively over his glass. She wasn't quite ready yet, but would be very soon. He would direct her himself, next season. *Traviata* he thought, although that voice should really be concentrating on Mozart. But she would do Mozart in Vienna. He wanted to direct her away from Vienna – London, the Met, La Scala, if only he could cut through the interminable wrangles about productions that went on at La Scala. No, perhaps not La Scala. The audience and the critics could be savage there, depending on the quality of their pasta before the performances. He didn't think she'd ever be quite tough enough for La Scala. But he was going to do a lot with her, a great deal.

He saw Kramer, her agent, Zilinsky, Karl Michael, the scout from the *Staatsoper* and several of the critics converging on her and he sauntered over. He had no intention of allowing the management of this plum to slip away.

'Your plans for next season, Fräulein Aschmann? After Hochhauser, then what?'

'It is not decided,' Peter said coolly.

Zilinsky produced a card from his pocket. 'Perhaps you could telephone me on Monday, Fräulein. I would like to have some discussion with you and, of course, with your agent. Hans, perhaps we could lunch on Monday?'

263

'I'm engaged on Monday,' said Hans craftily. He, too, didn't plan to let his prize get away from him. 'We have to decide many things about Fräulein Aschmann's future, but this will be done in conference with Sir Peter Grun and Herr Busacher, when he is well enough.'

Therese stared at the faces around her, the flattering, cajoling, over-friendly faces. Through them she suddenly saw Willi, trying to smile but failing, looking anxious, a little frightened. Willi had no idea what the life of a diva was really like, nor the life of a diva's husband. She thought of what she might be offered and of how many years she might have before the voice cracked up: ten, fifteen if she was lucky. She thought of the farmhouse up on the mountainside, of Herr Busacher, of Luiza, and Freddi and Alfred, of poor Ingrid, who would never get a job anywhere else, and of the young ones, Rudi, Elisa, the terrified stage manager, Stefan with his ulcers won in the cause of the Hochhauser Season, and she suddenly realized what she was going to do.

'There's no question of what I shall be doing next season, gentlemen. I shall be back here in Hochhauser.' She had the satisfaction of seeing Willi's face relax, form itself into his usual cherubic smile.

Hans shook his head warningly at her, but she ignored him. 'I think you will agree that the Hochhauser company now has something rather special to offer. Of course, we still have many problems to resolve. Our grant needs to be increased, and I think it would be a good idea to invite guest singers from time to time. But I intend to stay here, with my husband and Herr Busacher, and build on the company's growing reputation. I believe Sir Peter also has the intention of directing here in the future. After all, this is his father's company and he is most interested in its development. Isn't that so, Sir Peter?'

Grun discovered, to his horror, that he had nodded. It was enough. With a stir of excitement they turned to him.

'You would prefer to work here than in Vienna?'

'What particular production were you thinking of for Hochhauser, Sir Peter?'

'Do you contemplate bringing in star singers from other countries?'

'Were you thinking of bringing some of your own already established productions to Hochhauser? Your famous *Eugene Onegin*, for example? Might we see that in Hochhauser at some time?'

Willi suddenly pushed into the circle and pulled Therese's arm through his.

'Although of course my wife will be based here, the Season is only a summer one. That may change later, but she may well wish to consider short engagements in Vienna or Salzburg.' He had suddenly thought how nice it would be for them to have little jaunts – not too long – to other cities, other opera houses.

Peter felt he had had enough. 'Excuse me,' he said. 'I have to leave now. I wish to call in at the hospital and see how my father is.' Amidst polite murmurs of good wishes and commiserations, he slid away. The last person he passed as he left the theatre was Gesner, glowering across at Therese and her band of admiring acolytes. Gesner pulled his arm as he tried to pass.

'Did they say anything about me?'

'Not a thing.'

'You bastard! You told them, didn't you? Told them not to employ me.'

Peter grinned. 'Didn't need to. You know how gossip spreads in this business – specially amongst the orchestras. Your reputation, everything you did, has already got around. And they know you're a spasmodic singer. You were good tonight, you were great tonight. But you only sing like that once every five years. Everyone knows that. Good night.'

Gesner felt himself beginning to tremble. He wasn't sure if it was with rage or panic. He suddenly realized that he must look ostracized, standing quite alone in the middle of a party. He saw Suzi on the other side of the stage and began to make his way over to her. He ought to be seen chatting to a pretty girl when it was this kind of festivity. He'd rather forgotten about her this week. Perhaps he ought to take her out to supper and back to the Franz Joseph. It might cheer him up a bit, be good for his morale. He was halfway over to her when, to his horror, he saw the young thug who had attacked him appear by her side with a half bottle of champagne in his hand. He turned quickly and gazed about the stage. Everyone who was anyone was clustering round Therese. Well, he supposed, that was what he had to do. If she was going to be Frau Burgermeister he had no option. She was obviously going to be the power behind the throne when it came to directing the theatre. He pulled a charming and ingratiating smile across his face and went over to try and make his peace as best he could. He really had been a little unwise over Therese this season, but how was he to know how it would all turn out? But if there was one thing he knew how to do it was charm a woman.

'Well, Therese my darling, we were pretty good tonight, weren't we? You and I. What a partnership! Just think of what we can do together in the future.'

'I'm thinking, Karl,' she said after a long and icy pause. He realized he had an awful lot of work to do, and he'd better start now.

Suzi stared up into the labouring face of her childhood sweetheart.

'Georg,' she said coolly. 'Thank you for the flowers.'

'I have a half bottle of champagne here, Suzi. I saw my father had only provided wine. I thought you might like a glass of champagne. There's just enough for you and me.'

'Thank you. That would be nice.' She stared pointedly at the half. He was really going to have to do better than that. He opened the bottle, very clumsily, spilling most of it on the stage floor. They stood side by side, sipping the remainder, and at that moment Georg suddenly saw Gesner pushing his way into Therese's circle. Georg smouldered.

'That man . . .' he began.

'It's none of your business.' There was an angry silence.

'You know my father is marrying the singer?'

'Of course I know. I'm delighted. Your papa is a darling and he's been lonely for years. I think it's wonderful that two old people like that are so happy.'

Another long pause.

'Suzi . . . could I talk to you . . . please. I have the van outside. I could drive you back home and we could talk.'

She was softened by the tone of his voice. It was suddenly the voice of the old Georg, the nice protective Georg who had looked after her for so many years.

'I don't want us to fight any more, Suzi. I . . . I don't have enough friends to antagonize the few I do have.' He laughed wryly and said, 'The few I do have? That's an exaggeration. I don't have any friends apart from you and your parents. You're right. I have no business to pry into your life. But I can't stand not seeing you, and when I do, we speak like strangers to one another. You may be right about us . . .' He paused and swallowed. 'Perhaps we've known each other too long and too well to be anything but friends. I must have been mad last week, coming into the theatre like that and knocking Gesner down. I think I *was* a little mad, but I've accepted it now, that I have no right to tell you what to do any more. You must make your own life. But still, I'd like to see you, talk to you if I can.'

She had to make a split-second decision, for, immature though she was, she realized their relationship was on the verge of change. He was doing his best, the flowers, the half bottle of champagne,

266

but the fire of jealousy had burnt itself out and though, as he said, he didn't want to lose her, their relationship was at that delicate point where passion and a love taken for granted over the years could gently seep away, leaving just an old affection. He needed her more than she needed him, but she suddenly realized that however awful he was – and he was – she did intend one day to marry him. But he had to change before she did that.

'I can't come home with you tonight, Georg,' she said, smiling warmly at him. 'I promised to go to supper with Ingrid and Elisa and Rudi. And tomorrow I am busy. But, if you like, we could have supper after the show on Monday. The Csarda is a very good restaurant, I'm told. I've never been there before. It would be fun to go with you.' It was also very expensive, and she knew Georg hated late suppers because of getting up early next morning for the milking. She wasn't going to do it to him too often, but he had to learn how to behave. To his credit he didn't even hesitate.

'All right,' he said. And then, 'Why are you busy tomorrow?' The fire of jealousy wasn't quite dead; she could fan it into passion again if she wanted to.

'I'm going with the others, up the mountain for the day. We see how far we can get – the week before last they said they got right up to the hut before they had to turn back. We take our lunch in packs. And everyone brings something special, a surprise, for lunch.'

'Who are the others?'

'Rudi, Edouard, Elisa, Ingrid, and sometimes Madge Grimsilk comes too. The Englishwoman.'

'I see,' he said bleakly.

'Why don't you come? I'll ask Rudi. Rudi!'

'No. Don't ask him. You know I don't get on well with other people. I'm not like my father.'

'Rudi! What a lovely party . . . look, it's all right if Georg comes on the climb tomorrow, isn't it?'

'Sure. We meet at the beginning of the track up behind the bicycle factory. We're starting earlier tomorrow; we want to get higher. Nine o'clock, and you have to bring a surprise to share for lunch.' He sauntered away before Georg had time to answer.

'Do come, Georg. I know you'd enjoy it.'

'No. You know I can't spare a whole day, Suzi. There's the cows, and the dairy, and the accounts. And the supplies still have to go down to the hotels.'

'Your father would help. And what about the cowman? He's

267

quite capable of making the deliveries if you fill the van up first. Milking would be over long before we set out.'

'No. I'll see you on Monday. I'll take you to the Csarda.'

'All right, Georg,' she said sadly. She felt sorry for him. He wasn't like his father. He didn't have any friends because he was such a solemn *old* young man. He didn't seem to know how to talk to people his own age. He had no sense of fun.

But at least he was taking her out to dinner. That was a start on the reclamation of Georg.

Peter left the theatre in a bad temper, and by the time he had checked to see his father was all right and had arrived back at the Franz Joseph he was in an even worse one. His final fury came when he discovered he had lost his room key. He never remembered to hand it in when he left the hotel, and now it wasn't in his pocket. He had to ask the night porter to find another one for him, and he went up in the lift wishing the whole of bloody Hochhauser at the bottom of an avalanche. He opened the door of his suite and saw a light shining through from the bedroom beyond.

'What . . . ?'

Madge was sitting up in bed, glasses perched on the end of her nose, reading Trollope. She always had read Trollope in bed. He was amazed at the surge of happiness that rose in him as he saw her there, then he damped it down. It didn't change anything. She knew the score. So did he.

'So. What are you trying to tell me, Madge? Or is this just one for old times' sake? And I suppose I didn't lose my key at all. You stole it from my jacket in the office?'

'Right. And it isn't one for old times' sake. I've given in. You didn't want me to go and I've decided . . . I'd sooner have the little you're prepared to give than nothing at all. I'm back, on your terms. Exactly as before. No commitments, no public pairings, just a few secret nights when we can manage it, telephone calls, and an occasional discreet holiday together.'

'Why?' he asked.

She knew that, while she must never, ever, reveal all that Busacher had told her of his past – Peter would recoil in horror at any hint of pity – she also had to tell him something of the truth.

'Because – sitting there watching your father in hospital, lonely, only a son who doesn't like him very much – I realized I didn't want you to end up like that. I'm hoping that when you're old and ill you might come around to being quite pleased if I'm there by your bed every day.'

He was stunned into silence.

'Are you trying to be funny again?' he said at last.

'No. I mean it. You don't want me to live with you, but I can't live without you, so I'll have to put up with whatever's on offer. I'll just hang around, Peter. I think you might be quite pleased one day.'

He stared at her disbelievingly.

'What did the old man say to you?' he asked finally.

'Not a lot. Well, yes, he told me how badly he had treated your mother.'

'He did. Appallingly. He was cruel and careless and totally selfish.'

'And he also told me a little of his own childhood – his mother abandoned *him* when he was five. His father had to bring him up alone and I gather it was fairly rough. Must have been – it was the twenties – famine and typhus and TB in Vienna then. Soup kitchens and children dying of starvation. One has read the whole story. But his father managed, apparently. That, I suppose, is why he never married, not your mother, nor anyone else. Didn't trust women, presumably. Funny how history repeats itself.'

'Why did he tell you that?' he asked slowly. 'He never told me any of that.'

'No, well, you and he hardly had a cosy chat kind of relationship, did you? Perhaps you should talk to him a bit about the past. His father sounded rather a good egg. You'd want to know about your forebears, wouldn't you?'

'But why did his mother – my grandmother – run off?'

'I don't know. I didn't ask. You'd better do that. All I can cope with is breaking the spell.'

'What spell? What are you talking about now?'

'The ongoing curse of the Busacher–Grun family. One lonely man abandoned by his wife, brings up another lonely man, who in turn abandons the mother of his son, who in turn, etc, etc. I plan to break the pattern. For one thing, this time there is no child to be discarded and scarred, and for another I plan to hang around, in spite of you. I won't let you be lonely. When you're eighty you'll be sitting in a restaurant on your own and you'll look across the other side of the room, and at another table I'll be sitting, eating my lonely dinner. And I'll look around very carefully to make sure no-one we know is present, then I'll wink at you and raise my glass. You won't be alone, you see. I won't let you.'

His dark eyes rested coldly on her face for a moment, fixed un-blinking, then to her horror she saw they were filling up with tears.

'Oh God, Madge,' he said. 'What am I going to do about you?'

'Absolutely nothing, old love,' she said. 'Except offer me *Manon* in New York. We'll see a bit of each other on the sly then, won't we?'

It was a glorious morning when they met at the start of the mountain track. Suzi, Ingrid, and Edouard were there first, and well after nine, Elisa and Rudi came hurrying up.

'Sorry we're late. But we've got some terrific news. We're all right for another season! And guess what – Grun is coming back to direct us, just one production: *Le Nozze di Figaro*. We're going up in the world!'

'It's just gossip,' said Ingrid disbelievingly. 'None of that would be decided yet. How would anyone know?'

'Madge Grimsilk told me this morning. She was coming down for coffee just as I was leaving – she's not coming, by the way – says she's too tired. But she spoke to Grun last night at the party – funny, I don't remember seeing her there. But anyway she was and she did. And he told her that he'd be prepared to mount just the one production, to help out. It'll put us on the map, of course. I expect we'll get our grant raised if Grun is coming.'

'Therese as the Countess, I suppose?'

'That's right. But no-one else decided on yet. Just Therese. He's picked it specially for her.'

'What about Gesner?'

'Nothing known. Doubtful, I'd have thought.'

There was warming and heartening silence while they went through the other parts in their minds.

'I wonder if I could manage Cherubino,' said Ingrid thoughtfully to herself. 'Perhaps if I asked Therese to speak to Grun . . . and perhaps she could help me work on it a bit before I auditioned . . .'

The eyes of Edouard, Rudi, and Elisa met over her head.

'Well, we'd better get on if we want to climb up past the hut,' said Rudi heartily. 'It's nearly half-past nine now. Guess your young man isn't coming after all, Suzi.'

'No.' She didn't know why she felt so disappointed. He'd told her he wasn't going to come.

'Up we go then. Over the tops!'

The sun was high and the lower meadows were full of wild iris and buttercups. Ahead and above them the first of the ridges stood out clear against the sky. A stream ran alongside the rocky track and a dragonfly hovered over the water. Rudi began to sing

Therese's entry music for *Countess Maritza*, and the others joined in, 'La, la, la, la, La, la, la, la, Diddle diddle de dum dum.'

Suzi began to cheer up. It was impossible to be glum on such a day. And the others were all so happy, knowing the Hochhauser Season was saved for the time being.

'I say,' said Rudi, who had pulled ahead and was standing on a small outcrop of rock. 'Here's that old Georg of yours coming up behind. We'd better hang on for a moment, though he's coming up fast. Fitter than we are.'

They stood waiting until Georg, uncomfortable, not knowing what to say, joined them on the track.

'Oh, Georg! I *am* glad you've come. The day will be just perfect now!'

He still looked awkward, but he smiled at her and, on impulse, she grabbed his hand and held it for a moment.

'And we've wonderful news, Georg. Sir Peter Grun is going to come back next year and stage *Figaro*. Madge Grimsilk told Rudi this morning.'

'Oh yes,' said Georg. 'I saw them as I was coming through the town. Do they go out together or something?'

'No. Why?'

'They were walking through the Maria Theresa gardens, and he had his arm round her. They both said good morning to me, so I thought it wasn't any great secret.'

'Well!'

'Do you mean he had his arm just hanging over her shoulder, sort of casually, or around her properly?'

'Oh, properly,' said Georg cheerfully. He had been terrified that he wouldn't know what to talk about to them. But it was all unexpectedly easy. 'You know – she sort of had her head bent slightly on his shoulder and his hand was on her bare arm.'

'Well! So that's how she knew about the new production. And I bet she'll be designing it too.'

Suzi held Georg's hand as long as the track allowed them to walk together. He fell silent again and she felt he needed every encouragement.

'I say, Georg,' said Rudi suddenly. 'Did you remember to bring something special for lunch, that we can all share?'

'Oh yes.'

'What did you bring?'

'A cheese,' said Georg modestly. 'One of my own.'

The window of the hospital room was open to the lovely morning

271

and he lay in bed, quite tranquil, quite calm. In his mind he had gone through the entire score of last night's *Zarewitsch* – not just the score but the way it had been played. That was something – to have seen his son conducting his own company. They didn't have much together – they never would have. It was too late for that, just as it was too late to undo the hurt to Marta or, in a much lesser way, the hurt to the other women he had thought he might marry and never had. He regretted his life a little now. His father had been the only one to wrench his heart. The thought of his father still had the power to hurt him, but he was gone and there was no-one, never had been, who either loved him, or whom he could love as much as that.

The blackbird outside the window gave his brilliant fluting call again. It reminded him of the opening bars of *Paganini*. There it was, the first four notes were exactly the same. *Paganini* – perhaps he should try that for next season. Therese as Anna Elisa? A possibility. He closed his eyes, and against the song of the blackbird, he began to cast *Paganini* and work out the budget for a new production.